Julia Ann Tevis, John Tevis

Sixty Years in a School-Room

An Autobiography of Mrs. Julia A. Tevis

Julia Ann Tevis, John Tevis

Sixty Years in a School-Room
An Autobiography of Mrs. Julia A. Tevis

ISBN/EAN: 9783337074395

Printed in Europe, USA, Canada, Australia, Japan

Cover: Foto ©Raphael Reischuk / pixelio.de

More available books at **www.hansebooks.com**

SIXTY YEARS IN A SCHOOL-ROOM:

An Autobiography

OF

MRS. JULIA A. TEVIS,

PRINCIPAL OF SCIENCE HILL FEMALE ACADEMY.

TO WHICH IS PREFIXED

An Autobiographical Sketch of Rev. John Tevis.

"Here I 'll raise mine Ebenezer,
Hither, by thy help, I 'm come;
And I hope, by thy good pleasure,
Safely to arrive at home."

CINCINNATI:
PRINTED AT THE WESTERN METHODIST BOOK CONCERN.
1878.

TO

Belle T. Speed,

MY ONLY AND WELL-BELOVED DAUGHTER,

This Work

IS AFFECTIONATELY DEDICATED.

PREFACE.

Two considerations have prompted the preparation of the following Autobiography: First, the
earnest and oft-repeated request of my dear husband that I should do so; second, the hope of
doing good, by furnishing information and encouragement to those who are engaged, or are about
to engage, in the responsible and laborious duties
of teaching, especially to those who have charge
of female boarding-schools. An experience of fifty
years in any pursuit can not fail to bring some
knowledge which a novice may find valuable. I
propose no dogmatic theories; but simply state
facts, and give my opinion as suggested by the
thread of my narrative. As to the value of the
information thus given, those will judge who take
the trouble to read what I have written.

Although accustomed to use the pen all my life,
this is my first attempt at authorship. I have
dressed my narrative, as I do my person, according to my own notions of good taste. I no more
affect a fine style than a fashionable dress. If my
language is intelligible I am satisfied. The period
is past when the flippant criticisms of vanity or the
idle remarks of ignorance could give me real pain.
I do not despise the opinions of the wise and

good, nor do I covet the applause of the frivolous or hypercritical.

My numerous pupils will doubtless recognize many scenes and circumstances here recorded. I have not intentionally written one word which could wound the feelings of the most sensitive. My heart glows with the warmest affection for them all, many of whom I have known and loved in other relations. Amid the weary toils and perplexities incident to the management of a large boarding - school I have had much to cheer and comfort me, and nothing more than the grateful affection of my pupils.

It seemed to me right and proper that the biography of my sainted husband should precede my own, not only because he has entered the better land before me, but because he was my leader in all things good and useful for thirty-seven years. The light of his pure and manly character shone like a lamp in my pathway, cheering with its bright and steady beam the darkest seasons of our pilgrimage. His foot-prints are still luminous, lighting me onward to our long-sought home in heaven. Our lives were one in common hopes and labors, in common joys and sorrows, bound together in the blessings of one home of love; and now the memorials of these lives, bound in one volume—he still leading the way—will go forth to the world.

JULIA A. TEVIS.

Science Hill, *March,* 1865.

CONTENTS.

Sketch of Rev. John Tevis.

Sixty Years in a School-Room.

MRS. JULIA A. TEVIS.

CHAPTER VII.

CHAPTER VIII.

CHAPTER IX.

CHAPTER X.

CHAPTER XI.

CHAPTER XII.

CHAPTER XIII.

CHAPTER XIV.

CHAPTER XV.

CHAPTER XVI.

CHAPTER XVII.

CHAPTER XVIII.

AUTOBIOGRAPHICAL SKETCH

OF

Rev. John Tevis,

OF THE KENTUCKY CONFERENCE.

"*But God forbid that I should glory, save in the cross of our Lord Jesus Christ.*"—Paul.

INTRODUCTION.

THE following Autobiography furnishes a brief, but characteristic, sketch of Mr. Tevis. His friends will see the same simple honesty, strong moral sense, and earnest piety, which marked his energetic life running through every paragraph. To him, "Life was earnest, life was real," and he lived and labored in accordance with his convictions. His creed was in his heart, and formed the basis of his character. Duty, in his vocabulary, was not a conventional term, used for the sake of euphony or embellishment, but a word of solemn signification, implying relations of obligation and responsibility to God and his fellow-men. It was his guide in all things. Theories and adventitious circumstances had little influence upon his decisions; and, when a question was once decided, action promptly followed. With an ardent and impulsive temperament, which many make an apology for impetuosity and irregularity, he maintained a consistency and uniformity of Christian conduct seldom seen in ordinary life. Over mind and heart, over reason and passion, his conscience ruled supreme. This I take to have been the prominent feature of his strongly marked character.

As a business man, but few surpassed him in those qualities essential to success in the pursuit or the use of wealth. Clear and far-seeing in his perceptions, he was never tempted to uncertain speculations, but confined his plans to the simple methods of legitimate increase. Strictly honest, to the value of a cent, he measured the commercial obligations of others by the same standard. He paid his debts with punctuality, and collected his dues from others with the same exactness.

His success in managing his extensive and complicated business affairs is the best proof of his qualifications in this respect.

Just and upright in all his business transactions, he was equally conscientious and discreet in his charities. The poor always found him a friend; not in word merely, giving good advice, and unwilling to give any thing more substantial, but a friend indeed, seeking them out, and relieving their necessities with a liberal, but provident, hand. Real want never appealed to him in vain; indolence and vice seldom deceived him. The blessings of the poor followed him to the grave, and the benedictions of the widow and orphan descend on his memory. He was, by common consent, the guardian of the poor in the village where he lived; and many a humble home mourned sincerely his death. Could the grateful tears of poverty avert the desolations of Winter, perpetual Spring would bloom round his tomb.

Mr. Tevis's religious character was strongly marked. His religion was not a sentiment, not a creed "fenced round with holy texts," but the life of his soul. He lived "by faith in the Son of God." This spiritual life was supported by constant intercourse with the mercy-seat. He loved the silent communion of the closet; and there, with his "Father in secret," daily "renewed his strength." The regular and prayerful reading and study of the Holy Scriptures was a daily habit. The devotional parts of the Scriptures were especially his delight. Here his spirit gathered strength for the conflicts and labors of life. "Prayer was his native air," his "vital breath." The family altar was not a mere "household ornament," but the shrine where, as priest of the family, he offered up morning and evening sacrifices. Like Abraham, he "commanded his children and his household after him;" and while he observed himself "the law of the Lord," he required all under his authority to do the same. Family worship, observance of the Sabbath, and attendance upon the public worship of the sanctuary were, in his view, matters of the first importance, not to be neglected for business, pleasure, or any other consideratton. Especially was his respect for the "Sabbath of the Lord" worthy of all praise. The servants knew it as a day of rest. Cooking was not allowed, except what was absolutely necessary. Feasting on Sunday, that vice of Christian households, was never known under his roof while he was master.

As a preacher, Mr. Tevis belonged to the old school. Thoroughly imbued with the spirit of Wesleyan Methodism, he was not only evangelical in his creed, but in his matter and manner as a preacher. He believed the Articles of Faith, as held by the Methodist Church, to be Scriptural; and he was prepared to defend them against all opposers; not by quotations from the Fathers, but by the Word of God. Yet, with all this, he was very catholic in his feelings, and fraternized heartily with all the orthodox denominations, and often filled their pulpits with acceptability. He loved all who love the Lord Jesus Christ. His personal ministry was greatly blessed. His imagination never led him astray from the simplicity of the Gospel. He was made presiding elder at a time when only the best preachers were appointed to that office.

He sleeps in Jesus. His grave is situated in one of the most lovely spots in Grove Hill Cemetery, near the beautiful and quiet village of Shelbyville, Ky.

W. G. E. C.

Science Hill, 1865.

REV. JOHN TEVIS:

An Autobiographical Sketch.

Chapter I.

I WAS born January 6, 1792, in Baltimore County, Maryland. My parents were descended from a reputable English ancestry, and were themselves regular and worthy communicants in the English Church, previous to the American Revolution. One of the earliest recollections of my life was family worship on Sabbath, and the regular catechetical instruction, not only of the white children, but also of all the younger servants in my father's family. It is to be regretted that family worship and systematic religious instruction of children and servants in the families of professed Christians should be so much neglected. By faithfully discharging these primary duties we fulfill the injunction to "train up our children in the nurture and admonition of the Lord," and may reasonably expect an early development of virtuous and pious principles in them.

My father, with several brothers of my mother, served in the Colonial army, in defense of their country. They were attached to what was known as the "Maryland line." One of my uncles died in the army at White Plains. There were many traditional incidents of the Revolution treasured in our family. Some of these possessed more than a mere personal interest, involving as they did historical facts connected with the leading events of the times. But they are gone, with the thousand unwritten stories of suffering and heroism; gone, with the actors, to the darkness and silence of the forgotten past.

My early education was limited to the elementary instruction imparted in a "common school" at that day. This would by no means compare with the improved system of common-school instruction of the present, but extended to little beyond the rudiments of a plain English education. It was sufficient, however, for ordinary purposes, and furnished an active and enterprising mind with the knowledge necessary to guide it in all the practical duties of life. Education can not create mind, or supply energy, but must be chiefly valued as an instrument for doing good. The degree requisite for this purpose will depend upon the general intelligence of the community, and the nature of the pursuit in which one is engaged. No person values a good education more than I do, or rejoices more in the improved state of our common schools.

My childhood and youth passed rapidly and pleasantly away, surrounded by the endearments of a virtuous and happy home. From a very early day, serious thoughts of my responsibilities as an immortal being deeply impressed my mind, and many earnest resolutions of amendment were formed. Under the influence of a sound moral training, and the restraints of a well-regulated household, I maintained the reputation of a moral young man; and this reputation was not undeserved. When about twenty-one years of age, my religious convictions became so strong as to render me at times very unhappy. I read the Holy Scriptures with care; also some of Dr. Scott's and Dr. Witherspoon's theological writings, but never embraced the peculiar views of these good men. I could not reconcile the narrowness of the Calvinistic creed with the liberal provisions of the Gospel. I turned away from the barren theological dogmas of the schools to the Word of God, and sought, by prayer and study of the Scriptures, to find the path of duty. I did not seek in vain; for He who has said, "If any man lack wisdom, let him ask of God, and it shall be given him," brought me to the "knowledge of the truth as it is in Christ Jesus."

I began, about this time, seriously to consider the duty of uniting myself with the Church. While thinking on the subject, and disposed perhaps to defer the step, an aged and esteemed friend urged me to immediate action. His counsel, seconded by my own convictions of duty, led me to join the Methodist Episcopal Church on Sabbath, May 9, 1813. I was not satisfied, at the time, that my sins had been forgiven; but I was sincerely seeking that blessing, and believed it to be my duty to identify myself with the people of God. I could not reasonably ask God to bless me while living in the neglect of a plain duty. It was a cross thus publicly to pledge myself to follow Christ in the communion of a people "every-where spoken against," and with whom my family had not united. I saw then, as clearly as I do now, perhaps, the great responsibilities assumed in this act; and I was not ignorant of my own weakness, and the consequent danger of "failing of the grace of God." But God, I trust, accepted the imperfect offering of myself thus made, and, in about four months after, made me rejoice in a sense of his pardoning mercy. This happy event took place while listening to a plain,

but forcible, sermon by Rev. Charles Holliday, from
Hebrews vi, 1: "Let us go on to perfection." As he
described the blessed change wrought by the Holy Ghost
in the heart of the penitent believer, he asserted that the
child of God may know it; as he repeated with peculiar
emphasis the declaration, "He knows it through grace,"
I felt

> "That which nothing earthly gives, or can destroy,
> The soul's calm sunshine, and the heartfelt joy."

I felt that God had, for Christ's sake, forgiven my sins—
had saved me. This was not a transient feeling, but an
abiding sense of the blessed Comforter's indwelling presence, which has cheered me through all the way of my
forty years' pilgrimage, and is now the solace of my
declining days.

According to the custom of Methodists in their social
meetings at that day, I was called upon to lead in prayer.
This was a severe trial to most young converts; but,
strengthened by the Holy Spirit and a fixed determination to do all my duty so far as I could, "the yoke was
easy, and the burden light." The family altar had long
been erected in my father's house, and I was now required
to assist in domestic worship. This, though at first
embarrassing, was a great blessing to me, and, I hope,
profitable to the family. I was thus early introduced
into the way in which it was God's will I should travel
the remainder of my life. The thought, however, of
becoming a minister did not seriously enter my mind for
the first year after my conversion. I did not choose it
as a profession; I entered it from a sense of duty.

In April, 1814, my religion was brought to the test
by a severe illness, which reduced me to the verge of the
grave. At one time my recovery was despaired of, and

I prepared to meet death; and such was my faith and hope in God that I ardently desired to depart and be with Christ. Death had lost its terrors, and the joys of heaven so entranced my heart that I had no wish to remain where I might prove unfaithful to the grace already given. I was mercifully restored to health again, and with it increased convictions of duty possessed my mind. I felt willing to do whatever God in his providence might appoint as my work. An opportunity to try the sincerity of this purpose was soon afforded. Without my knowledge, I was appointed to take a list of the taxable property in one of the districts of Shelby County.* This of course enlarged the circle of my acquaintance, and presented frequent opportunities to converse on the subject of religion, and pray with the families where I spent the nights while canvassing the district. I thank God he gave me grace to acknowledge him under these new and peculiar circumstances. I prayed in families where such a thing had perhaps never been seen before. My own soul was refreshed and strengthened, and I trust some good done to others. It was, as I now see, a providential preparation for the work in which I was about to engage.

About the time I finished my labor on the district as assessor, Rev. Wm. Adams appointed me leader of a class which met some four miles from Shelbyville. I entered upon the delicate duties of this responsible office with fear and much self-distrust; but found in this, as in all other instances of severe trial, strength and comfort imparted. I soon learned that to be happy I must strive to be useful.

---

* Mr. Tevis's family moved from Maryland to Kentucky, in 1808. They settled at first in Bullitt County, but subsequently removed to Shelby County, where he died.—W. G. E. C.

Near the close of this year the Shelbyville class, of
which I was a member, recommended me for license to
exhort. I accepted, with the belief that if it were God's
will to use me in this way he would make it known in
the humble attempt to do my duty. I asked the presiding elder what evidence I might expect as proof that I
was in the path of duty in this matter. He replied:
"Go forward cheerfully; accept every invitation to hold
meetings; and, if you are in the right path, your own
soul will be blessed and the cause of God advanced by
your labors." This I take to be wise counsel. One of
the first questions asked by Mr. Wesley of those who
professed to be called to preach was, "Have you fruits?"
This he explained by another question, "Are any converted under your preaching?" This is God's seal to his
own ministry. After receiving license as an exhorter, I
was strongly solicited to assist Rev. W. Adams on the
Salt River Circuit. But the time had not fully come for
me to enter upon this important work. My mind was
thus gradually being prepared to leave all for the cause
of Christ in the blessed ministry of the Gospel. Often,
in seasons of spiritual elevation, when my heart was filled
with a tender desire for the salvation of souls, I felt it
was clearly my duty to preach; but again, in seasons of
mental depression, a fear would interpose lest this should
all be only the heat of my own imagination, "sparks of
my own kindling." I, however, committed myself to the
"fiery and cloudy pillar;" that is, tried to follow the
indications of God's providence with a cheerful and submissive spirit. My time was spent in studying the Holy
Scriptures, prayer, and visiting for the purpose of religious conversation; seeking, by discharging present duties,
to prepare myself for whatever future labors God might

appoint me. My beloved spiritual adviser, Rev. W. Adams, urged me to commence immediately the itinerant ministry, by joining him on his circuit. His influence, supported by the growing convictions of my own mind, induced me to yield, so far as to consent to make the trial.

It now became necessary to consult my father, who had designed to make me the farmer of the family, my brothers all having engaged in other pursuits. I knew it would be a severe trial to him to see me enter upon the work of a Methodist traveling preacher; but I also knew that his circumstances rendered my presence and labor at home comparatively unimportant, and that he was too good a man to seriously oppose me in what I sincerely believed to be my duty. He thought some previous literary and theological training necessary before entering the ministry. This I did not possess, at least in the degree which he deemed requisite. My convictions, however, would not suffer me to give up the work in which my heart was now enlisted. My father reluctantly gave his consent, fearing, no doubt, as I did, the possibility of a failure.

CHAPTER II.

HAVING settled the question in my own mind, that I ought to give myself wholly to the work of an itinerant preacher, and having obtained the consent of my father, I now began to make preparation to join the preacher-in-charge on the Salt River Circuit. On the 10th day of March, 1815, all was ready, and the next day I was on the circuit. I remained but a few days on this work, when I was transferred to Shelby and Jefferson Circuits. Here the life of a traveling preacher began properly with me, and from this I date my itinerant career.

On leaving home, my father gave me his purse, from which I took three dollars. With this small sum, a good horse, saddle, saddle-bags, and a supply of clothing, a Bible, hymn-book, Discipline, Wesley's Notes, and the portraiture of St. Paul, as my entire "outfit," I began life. The Shelby and Jefferson Circuits had been united, and preaching at each appointment once in three weeks was changed to preaching every two weeks.

Revs. Thomas D. Porter and William M'Mahon had been the preachers on this work—both very popular with the people. They were excellent preachers—but few better. My first effort in this work was made under unfavorable circumstances. A large congregation had assembled to hear brother M'Mahon. I did the best I could, however. My youth and inexperience appealed strongly to the sympathies of the people, and, I doubt not, they bore the disappointment with as much patience as could be reasonably expected. I preached with much greater liberty a few weeks afterward to a small congregation at the same place. I spent the remainder of the year on this circuit, sometimes greatly comforted, and often much depressed in spirit; but, I can say, that from the beginning of my ministerial life to this present time my victories over self and circumstances have all been obtained through the grace of our Lord Jesus Christ.

The Conference met this year at Lebanon, Ohio. I was received on trial into the "traveling connection" at this session, and appointed to the Lexington (Kentucky) Circuit, with the Rev. Thomas D. Porter as preacher-in-charge. I received this, my first regular appointment, from that apostle of American Methodism, Bishop Asbury. But little apparent success attended our labors this year. God only knows what good was done.

I was comforted by an affectionate letter from my father during the year, stating, he no longer objected to my course, but expressed the hope that I would persevere and do much good. He offered me any pecuniary assistance I might need.

At the next session of the Conference, which was held in the city of Louisville, Kentucky, I was sent to the Salt Creek Circuit, Ohio. This was a large circuit lying east of the Scioto River, embracing Portsmouth, Piketon, New Richmond, and the Scioto Salt Works. There were some twenty appointments, which I visited every three weeks. The largest congregation on the circuit was at the old Scioto Salt Works, where were many worthy Christians, whom I hope to meet in a better world. Rev. David Young was my presiding elder. He took me to his quarterly-meeting in Chillicothe, and, to my surprise, put me up to preach at eleven o'clock on Sabbath.

Several preachers were present, some of them men of reputation—such as Beauchamp, Scott, Hinde, Dr. Tiffin, and others. Unexpected and strange as it was to be thus put forward, it pleased God to aid me, so that I have seldom preached with more comfort to myself or visible effect on the congregation than on this occasion.

While on this circuit I learned something of the hardships which the early settlers in the West had to endure. Many of them were poor families from Virginia, North Carolina, and Pennsylvania, with but little education or skill in the art of living. The forests were dense, and the labor necessary to open a farm was so great, that few did more than clear away a small "patch," on which they managed to raise a scanty subsistence. Among them were many sincere Christians, whose liberality in opening their houses for preaching, that their neighbors might hear the Gospel, was worthy of all praise.

About ninety persons were added to the Church this year, one or two of whom have since filled his mission as a minister of the Gospel. The year was altogether a pleasant and, I trust, profitable one. It was full enough of trial and full of mercy—many happy seasons which I shall never forget.

Having closed the year's labors, I visited my father and friends in Kentucky, and then attended the Annual Conference, which met in Zanesville, Ohio. Here I was ordained deacon by Bishop R. R. Roberts, and received into "full connection" as a traveling preacher. This year, 1817,* I was appointed to Zanesville Circuit, with

*This must refer to the end of 1817, when the Conference met in the Autumn or Winter, for, according to the law of the Church, he could not be ordained deacon until he had traveled two years. He joined on probation at the end of 1815.—W. G. E. C.

Rev. Samuel Glades as my assistant. Brother Glades was a deeply pious young man, of good mind and studious habits. His course was soon finished; he laid down the cross for a crown only a few years after this, when with me on the Zanesville Circuit.

This period was one of labor and trial. We toiled to cultivate an apparently barren soil. Our presiding elder was the good, the venerable Jacob Young, much beloved and honored in the Church. The infirmities of age, blindness, and feebleness are now rapidly carrying him to his last home. His sun, though shaded by a cloud, shines brightly, and promises a glorious setting.

The Annual Conference met for the year 1818 in Steubenville, Ohio. Here I saw, for the first time, that extraordinary man, Asa Shinn, and heard him preach an able sermon on the text, "If any man love not the Lord Jesus Christ," etc. He was a strong man in argument and apt in illustration, more impressive usually than reasoning with the multitude. He lived long enough, as he said to an old friend, to be "heartily tired of *reform*, both in Church and State." This was saying a good deal for one who had spent his life trying to "reform" what he could not improve. I have read few books with more pleasure than his "Plan of Salvation;" but his second work, on "The Divine Being," was a failure; he promised more than he performed. He was, in some respects, a great man.

I was sent this year to Columbus, one of the best circuits in the Conference. My colleague this year was Rev. Leroy Swormstedt, a man whom I loved and still love for his goodness. We labored harmoniously together, and under the divine blessing with much success, especially in the city of Columbus. Some sixty persons were added to the city society. In this place were some of God's most precious children. Here lived old brother M'Cormack, a pillar and an ornament to the Church; and Mother Rathbone, whose son we this year received into the Church, and who has been, for many years, a traveling preacher in the Kentucky Conference. On one occasion this excellent woman said to me: "I know not why my Heavenly Father continues my life, for I have lived as long as I desired; I have seen all my children brought into the Church." But she waited patiently for the salvation of God, and finally attained her crown. This circuit included the town of Delaware, at that time a small place. I think it probable that brother Swormstedt and myself were the first preachers who ever called the sinners of this place to repentance. I would like to visit it now to see what the Lord has done for it since our day there.

In 1819,* the Annual Conference met in Cincinnati, Ohio. Bishop George presided. This beloved shepherd was held in great veneration by the whole Church. He died at Staunton, Virginia, in 1828. I was ordained elder this year, and returned to Columbus Circuit, with a young man as my assistant. Rev. J. Collins was my presiding elder. He was a good man, a father in the Church, and one of my best friends. He was well qualified for the office, one of the most influential in the whole economy of Methodism. Wise in counsel, kind in manner, and energetic in action, he was always a favorite with the preachers under him. As a preacher he had but few superiors—not many equals.

---

*The date of the year 1818 is entirely omitted. He was ordained elder at this Conference in due course, having traveled four years.— W. G. E. C.

I was present at the General Conference of 1820, which met in the city of Baltimore, though not a delegate. I saw the working of the "radical" element, which resulted after the Pittsburg Conference, in 1828, in the separation of the "Methodist Protestant" from the Methodist Episcopal Church. At this General Conference it was determined to create a Kentucky Annual Conference out of parts of the Ohio and Tennessee Conferences. After attending the Ohio Conference at Chillicothe, I returned to Kentucky, intending to join this new Conference, I attended the session of the Tennessee Conference, which met shortly after my return, at Hopkinsville, Kentucky. Bishop Roberts, who was expected to preside, did not arrive, and Rev. Marcus Lindsay was elected chairman. I was solicited to take charge of the Holston District, in the Tennessee Conference. This was, by no means, according to my plans or wishes. I had been traveling but five years, and distrusted my qualifications for such a position, I earnestly asked to be excused if any other arrangement could be made. But Father Holliday came to me the second time to urge my compliance, which resulted in my saying, "I can go anywhere the Conference may please to send me." I had spent four years in the North-west; I was now sent to the South-east. But it is little matter to a Methodist preacher where the path of duty may lead him, comforted by the promise, "Lo I am with you alway, even to the end of the world."

CHAPTER III.

I WAS now about to undertake the responsibilities of a new office, among a strange people. I had no acquaintance with the country, preachers, or people; but every faithful minister has a better passport than a conference or bishop can give him, even "the Spirit of the Lord resting upon him." I was kindly received, and all endeavored to hold up my feeble hands and cheer me in my work. A gracious revival of religion prevailed throughout the district. Rev. Jesse Cunnyngham, father of Rev. W. G. E. Cunnyngham, now missionary to China, had evinced considerable tact and judgment in selecting preachers to fill the different circuits; for, after all that may be said and done, the presiding elders make most of the appointments. I had a corps of zealous young men who had given themselves to the work of the ministry. They read their Bibles, prayed much, and preached earnestly, and with great acceptability generally. Many souls were converted and brought into the Church through their instrumentality. I tried to retain some of them in the district as long as I was on it. I think, during the four years, there was a net increase of four thousand members within the bounds of the district. This would have been considered a large increase in any part of the country, but especially large for South-western Virginia, North Carolina, and East Tennessee. This glorious revival was instrumental in raising up many young men of gifts and grace for the ministry; and the Methodist

Church has continued to prosper in that country ever since, notwithstanding the "gates of hell" have raged against it. There was one young man of extraordinary gifts, who shall be nameless here. From a seat in the General Conference he found a seat in Congress. Thus, preferring the honor which cometh from man to the honor which cometh from God, he has lost both in the ruins of apostasy. Let young men remember that pride and vanity lead only to ruin. God is not mocked. Vengeance will sooner or later overtake the man who sells his commission as a minister for the empty honors or guilty gains of worldly ambition. Alas, poor man! He is now with Judas. But there were others, good and true men, who have proved faithful through the trials of thirty years. Rev. William Patton, of a Presbyterian family, began to preach, I think, in 1822. He labored long and faithfully in the Missouri Conference, but has gone to his glorious reward in heaven. George Horn, David Fleming, Josiah Rhoton, Creed Fulton, and Elbert F. Sevier were good and faithful men. Brothers Sevier and Fulton, the first from Washington County, East Tennessee, and the latter from Grayson County, Virginia, were very promising young men, and have fulfilled the promise. Creed Fulton, as agent for Emory and Henry College, did much for the Church and the cause of education in the Holston Conference. The establishment of this college was a most successful enterprise. It was very fortunate in its first president, Rev. Charles Collins, a man admirably qualified for the place and the times. Previous to the establishment of this college, South-western Virginia, East Tennessee, and Western North Carolina were peculiarly destituts of educational facilities. When I visited Emory and Henry College, in 1848, more than two hundred young men had gone forth from its halls to become teachers, etc.

Sanctified learning is the great instrument of social improvement; that is, a literature imbued with the pure morality of the Gospel not only elevates but refines society. Education which includes a knowledge of "the truth as it is in Jesus" furnishes the best safeguard against social and political anarchy.

Our most prosperous year on the Holston District was 1823. This year seventeen hundred members were added to the Church. Among the number was a young lady who was acting as preceptress to Miss Mary Smith, near Abingdon, Virginia, and to whom I was united in the bonds of matrimony on the 9th of March, 1824. In no case has the saying of the wise man, in Proverbs xxxi, 12, been more literally fulfilled: "She will do him good, and not evil, all the days of her life."

During the revival, this year, a gifted young man by the name of O. Ross, living in Jonesboro, was happily converted, and in the course of a few years became one of the most eloquent and popular preachers in the Kentucky Conference. He died young, but in the triumphs of the Christian faith.

Methodism has met with unreasonable opposition every-where. Bad men have hated and persecuted it, because it reproved the depraved customs and maxims of an ungodly world. Some good men have opposed it, because it differed from the theology and ecclesiastical economy of their own Churches. In the Holston District we were called upon to "contend earnestly for the faith once delivered to the saints," and I believe the truth "mightily prevailed."

At the session of the Tennessee Conference which

met at Huntsville, Alabama, in 1823, I was elected a delegate to the General Conference which was to be held in Baltimore, Maryland, May, 1824. "Radicalism," as it was called, had agitated the Church on the "Presiding Elder" question, and trouble was anticipated at this Conference. The storm, however, was not as furious as was expected. Bishops Soule and Hedding were elected at this session of the General Conference. I voted once for my old friend, Beauchamp; but, being satisfied that the peace of the Church would be promoted by the election of a Northern man, I gave my vote to E. Hedding, and I have seen no cause to regret it.

At this time I saw and heard the great and good Summerfield, both in the pulpit and on the missionary platform. His appearance was the most angel-like I ever saw. His preaching was "in power and demonstration of the Holy Ghost."

Having married in March of this year, and my four years on the Holston District at an end, I asked and received a transfer to the Kentucky Conference. I was stationed in the city of Louisville, Kentucky, where a spirit of discord had well-nigh ruined the early prospects of Methodism. A remnant had been left of humble, faithful ones, especially among the female part of the congregation. A change for the better was soon perceptible, but it was a hard year.

3

CHAPTER IV.

I HAVE now arrived at a period in my narration where an important event, the opening of Science Hill Female Academy, gave a new direction to my life and labors, and determined the local fortunes of my family. My dear wife, whom I found in Virginia (as Miss Julia A. Hieronymous), engaged in teaching, wished to continue an employment for which she was unusually well qualified. A good Protestant school was much needed. Roman Catholic schools had secured and, in some cases, nearly monopolized public patronage, because professing to be cheaper than the Protestant schools. Young ladies of Protestant families, educated in Romish institutions of learning, returned to their parents thoroughly imbued with Romanism. I believe the founding of Science Hill Academy was providential, and its long and prosperous career seems sufficient proof of this. It was opened in March, 1825, and has continued uninterruptedly to the present (1857), having now two hundred and thirty students. How often, in reviewing the last thirty-two years, I have felt the truth of the promise, "Seek first the kingdom of God, and his righteousness, and all these things shall be added unto you." We have enjoyed the pleasure of much temporal prosperity and domestic comforts. We have been honored as instruments of God in doing good, in diffusing useful knowledge, and in winning souls to Christ. To God be all the glory!

For the two Conference years of 1826 and 1827 I was

stationed at Shelbyville and Brick Chapel, spending much of my time in the school-room. I did not, however, neglect my pastoral work or reading and study preparatory to my pulpit labors. Previous to my connection with the school, but few persons lived more entirely free from worldly cares and anxieties. I gave myself to *one work*, and found that work *enough* for all my energies. Although teaching useful knowledge is a good work, and next to preaching the Gospel, yet I conscientiously think no man should, except under peculiar circumstances, connect any secular employment with his ministerial labors.

In 1827 the Annual Conference elected me a delegate to the General Conference, which met in the city of Pittsburg, Pennsylvania. "The Radicals" again made an effort to affect a change in our ecclesiastical economy, but failed. There were disaffected ministers; but few of the people really sympathized with the cry of "oppression" and "reform." At this session the Canada Methodists were authorized to form themselves into an independent Church. This separation has proved a blessing, while the Protestant Methodist has scarcely maintained a feeble existence.

The leading man at this session of the General Conference was the good and great Emory, afterwards Bishop Emory, of precious memory. When he rose to speak all gave attention, and some one said, "Emory not only gives the usual number of reasons for an opinion, but some eight or ten more." He seldom failed to carry his point. Radicalism received its death from the heavy blows of this giant.

For several years I received an appointment from the Annual Conference to Science Hill Female Academy, which was taken under the patronage of the Kentucky

Annual Conference. In 1832 I was again elected a delegate to the General Conference, which met in Philadelphia, Pennsylvania. At this Conference Revs. John Emory and James O. Andrew were elected to the episcopacy—men eminently qualified to fill that high and holy position in the Church of Christ.

One of the most important measures at this General Conference was the sending of our excellent brother Melville B. Cox to the benighted coast of Africa as a missionary. We saw "Ethiopia stretching out her hands to God;" it was with some fear that we attempted to respond to the call which all seemed plainly to hear. We had but little means, and we knew the expenses would be great. While these things were under discussion, brother Cox pleaded so earnestly, saying, "Here I am, send me," that we felt it must be God's will, and the question was settled. He left us to "go far hence to the Gentiles," "to preach the Gospel to the poor, to proclaim liberty to the captives, and the opening of the prison doors to those who were bound." He went forth weeping, bearing precious seed, which has brought forth fruit abundantly to the glory of God. "He fell at his post," "far from home and the friends of his youth;" but he fell with his armor on, and his face to the foe. How gloriously such men die! What a legacy of faith, love, and zeal they bequeath to the Church!

After having received regular appointments from the Ohio, Tennessee, and Kentucky Conferences, since the year 1815, my brethren, from the best of motives, and properly, as I believe, gave me a "superannuated relation" in the Kentucky Conference. This position, in a Methodist Conference, is not considered a degradation, but an honorable discharge from the *active* duties of the itinerancy, and may be employed with credit and great usefulness; and now, after a period spent in this relation, as long as that spent in actual itinerant labors, I can confidently affirm that I have strictly adhered to the first principles of Methodism in this matter. I have never lost my love for its doctrines and Discipline, or my faith in the efficiency of its ecclesiastical economy. Its itinerancy I believe to be better adapted than any other system of ministerial economy to "spread Scriptural holiness" throughout the world.

The "local" ministry of the Methodist Church has done much to establish Methodism in the Land. The "traveling" preachers were evangelists in their labors, and pastors properly in office, but, from the necessities of their work, unable to give much personal supervision to the details of the pastorate. They were therefore dependent upon the local preachers and class-leaders for the care of the Churches in their absence. The local preachers also "pioneered" the way into neighborhoods where the traveling preachers could not go, and many districts of country were supplied with Sunday preaching that would otherwise have been left without the Word of Life. While sustaining the superannuated relation, which is practically that of a local preacher, I have endeavored to improve my time and talents in the vineyard of the Lord as a minister; and now, when my day of labor is near its close, I can truly say that I have enjoyed much comfort in my ministrations. I should have preferred active ministerial relation to the Conference. It was in my heart to live and die in the itinerancy; but God willed it otherwise, and I am content, believing that all things have been ordered for the best.

March 10, 1858. The ninth and tenth days of this
month are anniversaries of the most memorable events in
my life. On the ninth day of March, 1824, which was
also the anniversary of my father's birth, I was united in
the bonds of holy matrimony with my dear wife, who
still lives, to enjoy life and cheer me with her love and
companionship. We have traveled, long and pleasantly,
the path of life together. Our way has been "ordered"
by the Lord. All our changes have been of his appointment, and we can truly say, "Goodness and mercy have
followed us all the days of our lives." God has bestowed
worldly goods upon us—given us friends and children;
for all which I sincerely thank him.

The 10th day of March, 1815, I left my father's house
to become a wandering messenger of mercy to my fellow-
men. For nine years I "gladly wandered to and fro,"
pitching my moving tent among strangers. I do not
regret the choice I made of a profession. I thank God
that he "thought me worthy, putting me into the ministry." I regret that my labors have not been tenfold
more abundant, but nothing painful disturbs the tranquillity of this review. One feeling pervades my whole
being: it is profound gratitude to God for all his manifold mercy to me and mine.

> "O, to grace how great a debtor
> Daily I 'm constrained to be!
> Let thy goodness, like a fetter,
> Bind my wandering heart to thee."

As the evening of life draws on, and the infirmities
of age press upon me, my thoughts turn more towards
the future—towards my eternal home. Age has brought
infirmities and decay upon my body, but no decay affects
my faith in God or hope in immortality. My spiritual

enjoyments were never greater than at this present time. "Thanks be to God, who giveth us the victory through our Lord Jesus Christ." "Unto him that loved us, and washed us from our sins in his own blood; to him be glory and dominion for ever and ever. Amen."

Obituary.

In 1857 Mr. Tevis suffered a slight stroke of paralysis, from which, however, he so far recovered after a few few months, as to be able to go about; and, in 1859, attended the session of the Kentucky Annual Conference. His feeble health alarmed his friends, and strongly admonished him that his end was drawing near. Still hope comforted his anxious family with the promise of returning health and strength; but the summons had been issued, and in August, 1860, the angel of death again smote him, prostrating mind and body. His power of articulation was limited to monosyllables, and that in an under tone. For several months previous to his release from sorrow and suffering, he was confined entirely to the bed. It is cause of thankfulness that, though helpless and speechless, he suffered but little pain. He slept sweetly every night, as an infant in its mother's arms. Thus peacefully and quietly the angels carried him down to the margin of the dark river, which he crossed on the 26th day of January, 1861, aged sixty-nine years and twenty days.

He received the holy communion on the Sabbath preceding his death, and at this Last Supper seemed to "eat and drink after a heavenly and spiritual manner." Thus died one of the best men in the land.

> "Servant of God, well done!
> Rest from thy loved employ;
> The battle fought, the victory won,
> Enter thy Master's joy."

W. G. E. C.

Sixty Years in a School-Room.

AUTOBIOGRAPHY

OF

MRS. JULIA A. TEVIS.

Autobiography

OF

MRS. JULIA A. TEVIS,

With Reminiscences of Sixty Years in a School-Room.

CHAPTER I.

I HAVE arrived at that period of life from which I can look back with a calm and grateful heart upon the various and shifting scenes through which I have passed; and I now undertake to record, for the gratification of my family and immediate friends, the recollections so clearly and deeply impressed upon my memory. I begin the review under a profound sense of God's goodness, which has rendered every trial, thus far encountered in the journey of life, subservient to my everlasting welfare. I can not doubt that the peace of mind which sustained me under the most sorrowful bereavements, and the sweet, calm sunshine that now warms and cheers my heart, are pledges of that perfect rest after which my longing soul aspires, and into which I hope to enter through the merits of my gracious Redeemer.

Guided by a conscientious fidelity to truth in every particular, a charitable regard for the opinions and feelings of all who may be in any way interested in what I say, and with a fervent prayer for divine assistance, I commence my narrative.

I was born December 5, 1799, in Clarke County, Kentucky. My grand parents, on both sides, were among the earliest emigrants from Virginia into this State. Their location in the vicinity of Boonesboro brought them into familiar intercourse and companionship with Daniel Boone; and my maternal grandfather, Ambrose Bush, with his four brothers, were among the most celebrated of the old "Indian fighters." Their numerous descendants were scattered over so large a portion of Clarke County as to give it the name of "Bush's Settlement." Thrifty and respectable farmers, they occupied a position in society both honorable and useful. The same may be said of my father's ancestors, who were Germans, as the name Hieronymous will suggest.

My paternal grandfather, with an elder brother, came to America before the Revolutionary War, and settled in the eastern part of Virginia. They were from Vienna, and thoroughly German in many respects; particularly in an obstinacy of character, which evinced itself in firmness of purpose and industrious habits. My grandmother was also of German descent, though born in America. The brother of my grandfather returned to Germany at the close of the Revolutionary War to get possession of their portion of their father's estate. He turned into money what he obtained in Germany, set sail for America, and, after many reverses, encountering storm and tempest during a long, disastrous voyage, reached home. But a change had come over his spirit; for, as the story goes, he spoke not a word to any one for fourteen years after his return. A few days before his death he exclaimed, as he fired a pistol from his window, "The devil's in fourteen." The reason why my queer old uncle should have thus retired within himself, no one could ever tell; but conjecture said, he had been crossed in his German love, or else had lost his chest of money in coming over the seas. The idea of crossing the ocean at that time, on a steamship, would have been as much ridiculed as the Irish gentleman's proposition to go hunting by the steam of his own tea-kettle.

My grandfather's perverseness was often exhibited in taking his saddle-bags on his shoulders when he went to town, and leading his horse; or taking off his shoes and stockings, and wading the Kentucky River when it was low, that his horse might not have the trouble of carrying him over. My father's name was Pendleton, and the name of one of his brothers, Benjamin; but my grandfather, disdaining even to make the effort to speak plain English,—though, it was said, he spoke well several European languages—would always call my father "Bendleton," and my uncle "Penny." One of his amiabilities was to walk over my tidy grandmother's nicely waxed floors with his muddy shoes, chuckling with delight at the discomfiture of the maid-servant, as she followed him with a floor-cloth by my grandmother's orders. He was very fond of hunting, frequently shouldering his shot-gun in the morning, and wandering for hours through the woods squirrel hunting, followed only by a little boy. When he saw a squirrel at which he intended to take aim, he invariably set his gun down while he took a pinch of snuff; meanwhile talking to the squirrel: "Joost you stay there till I takes mine binch of snuff, and den I prings you down, be sure, mit te teufel to ye." The squirrel did not wait, of course; and the fact is, he was never known to bring any game home with him, though he expended much powder and shot.

My grand-parents, on my mother's side, were as English as those on the other side were German. My

Grandmother Bush was a strictly pious Baptist; my grandmother Hieronymus, a Methodist of the old school, a real Wesleyan, thoroughly and decidedly religious. Alas, we seldom meet with such now! My soul longingly inquires for the old paths, that I may walk therein. I remember my grandmother Bush more distinctly, as much of my time between the ages of four and seven was spent with her. Like gleams of light come up now my joyous Saturday evenings and Sundays at the old homestead, and the many dear, merry, warm-hearted cousins, with whom I so often played "Mrs. Bush," or "Lady come to see"—the Bushes being so numerous that we had no idea but that they filled the world. Our world they did fill.

I can even now see, in the dim, shadowy distance, the tall, queenly form of my grandmother, simply attired in a dove-colored dress and plain white kerchief, with a cap faultless in shape, and of snowy whiteness, setting off the most benevolent of features. I can hear her quick step, and sweet voice calling, "Jennie, Julia, Esther, Polly!"—her four daughters; for when she wanted one she never failed to call them all over before she could get the right name. And from habitual quickness of thought, word, and action, she often made a laughable pell-mell of words. When she called for her black mare to be saddled—for every body rode on horseback in those days, there being nothing more than bridle-paths—it was, "Warrick, run up the black mare, bring down the backstairs, and put my saddle on it; quick, quick, for I must go to Sister Franky's right away." And how often have I ridden to the stone meeting-house behind her on that same black mare, and walked over and around the churchyard where now my beloved grand-parents lie buried, with many of their descendants!

Grandfather was often away from home, on the "war-path," for days and weeks at a time. During his absence my grandmother kept her little ones about her, and never failed to commend them to God in family prayer, night and morning. She was gifted with a fine voice, and I never heard her sing any thing but hymns. Often have I heard my mother relate thrilling stories about Indians, panthers, and wolves, that came stealthily around the solitary dwellings, their approach undiscovered, in consequence of the dense cane-brake, until their gleaming eyes, peering through the unchinked walls, aroused the family to a terrible consciousness of danger. But never did they seem able to molest that charmed circle within, guarded as it was by constant prayer. Indians would steal the horses, and fly; wild beasts found some other prey, and departed.

At the time that my grandfather, with his brothers and sister, came to Kentucky, many families traveled together for mutual safety and protection against the Indians, whose hunting-grounds extended to the border settlements of Virginia. On their way through the wilderness they encountered bears, buffaloes, wolves, wild-cats, and sometimes herds of deer. Thus they moved cautiously onward, in long lines, through a narrow bridle-path, so encumbered with brush and underwood as to impede their progress, and render it necessary that they should sometimes encamp for days, in order to rest their weary pack-horses and forage for themselves.

A space of country that can be passed over now in less than ten days, leisurely, was then a journey of many weeks, and sometimes months. I have heard interesting anecdotes related connected with the emigration of my grandfather's family through this wilderness. When they tarried, even for a day or a night, pickets were thrown out, and every pass was guarded vigilantly, lest haply some lurking foe might invade the camp. None dared to speak aloud, and generally the horses' feet were muffled, for fear of attracting attention. No camp-fires were lighted; and when night dropped her dark curtains around the weary travelers some rested or slept, while others gazed in death-like stillness upon the sparkling firmament, or listened to the music of streamlet and breeze, occasionally starting at the rustling of a leaf—any thing that broke the solemn silence striking terror to the heart.

Once, after having passed over many miles without interruption, the travelers grew careless, and scattered groups pursued their way without apprehension. One family, being considerably in advance, was entirely separated from the company. Several hours had elapsed without one of them being seen by those in the rear. Night came on; the stars shone in full glory, shedding a hazy light on a few of the nearer objects, but added to the dimness and uncertainty of every thing beyond. The profound silence was broken only by the restlessness of the tethered horses, or the low murmuring in dreams of the disturbed sleepers. So intense was the stillness that an imaginary noise more than once startled the guards into an apprehension of a night attack, deepening the ominous silence, and quickening the light step of the sentinel as he made his lonely round.

The report of a gun was heard, and then another, followed by the fierce war-whoop of the savage. Some of the young men, dashing rapidly onward, soon reached a spot where, in the gray light of the dawn, a scene of horror presented itself, not uncommon in those perilous times. A party of Indians had come upon the family stealthily, and, after a fierce struggle, had fled precipitately, with all the plunder they could carry. The light-footed, mysterious enemy had left the impress of his hand on the dead and dying, scattered in every direction. One young girl, about fourteen, had been scalped, and left for dead in a deep ravine. She had only swooned; and her brother, after the fray was over, seeing something in the dim distance that looked like an animal, creeping slowly towards them through the bushes, raised his gun to fire, when he saw a human hand uplifted in an imploring attitude. In a few minutes more he discovered it to be his sister, crawling on her hands and knees, her face completely covered by her matted hair. As he drew near she threw back her-hair, and, uttering the word "brother," fainted in his arms. She had been scalped, but not deeply wounded, and her only permanent loss was a portion of the skin of her head, rudely torn off by the firm grasp of an Indian. This young girl lived to reach Kentucky, grew up into womanhood, married, and became the mother of a number of sons and daughters,—a proof that scalping alone does not necessarily produce death.

One circumstance, often related to me, forcibly illustrates the keen instinct of the panther. My grandfather had been out on a hunt for many days. Weary eyes and anxious hearts were watching and waiting his return. It was midsummer, and the tall cane, with its gracefully waving leaves, excluded the view of every object not in the immediate vicinity of the lonely and scattered dwellings. About sunset, one lovely afternoon, my grandmother, with her faithful handmaiden, "Mourning," set out to fetch some water from the spring, which, though at no great distance from the house, was hidden from

4

sight. Always in mortal fear of ambushed Indians,
they were walking slowly along when startled by the
familiar sound of the lost hunter's cry of "hoo-hoo,"
which was suppressed at intervals, as if listening for a
response to assure him that he was in the neighborhood
of home and loved ones. My grandmother answered, as
she was wont to do, while her heart thrilled with the
joyful anticipation of meeting her returning husband.
"Hoo-hoo," in a loud voice, was again heard, and again
responded to—each time seeming nearer and more distinct; when, just as they emerged from the thicket, and
and caught a glimpse of the shelving rock that over-
arched the spring, they perceived something moving
among the bushes above. At first they supposed it to
be nothing more than a raccoon or an opossum, but it
proved to be a panther. This animal, when stimulated
by hunger, would assail whatever would provide him
with a banquet of blood. Lo! there he stood, on the
rock high above the spring, squatting on his hind-legs, in
the attitude of preparing to leap—his glaring eyeballs
fierce with expectation. His gray coat, extended claws,
fiery eyes, and the cry which he at that moment uttered,
rendered by its resemblance to the human voice peculiarly terrific, denoted him to be the most ferocious of his
detested kind. My grandmother, whose presence of
mind never forsook her, even under the most appalling
circumstances, retreated slowly, keeping her eyes steadily
fixed on the eyes of the monster, which seemed mo-
mentarily paralyzed by her gaze, until she and the negro
girl could turn by a sudden angle into the woods, when,
adding "wings to their speed," they soon reached the
house, and barred the door behind them.

I do not wish to give the impression that the name

of Bush is entitled to any patronymic distinction, or that any branch of the family claim nobility; nevertheless, they came from a pure and ancient stock, upon whose bright escutcheon no stain had ever rested. It had never been legally disgraced, and never forfeited its claims to respect and consideration. The family was originally English, as I have already stated, and the tradition among them is that the founder of the American branch, John Bush, came over among the first settlers of Jamestown, and was the friend and companion of Captain John Smith.

My great-grandfather, Philip Bush, possessed a large landed estate. His eight sons and four daughters were matrimonially connected with some of the most distinguished families in the "Old Dominion." My Grandfather Ambrose, the youngest child save one, married a Gholson—a family from whence originated statesmen and orators. My great-uncle, Billy Bush, came to Kentucky with Daniel Boone on his second trip. He was fortunate in securing the fairest portion of the land in Clarke County, by warrants and otherwise, extending from Winchester to Boonesborough. He gave away, or sold for a trifle, farm after farm to his friends and relatives, that they might be induced to settle near him. These seemed so well satisfied with the Goshen of their choice that even their descendants had no disposition to emigrate, nor, indeed, to enter the arena of public life. Thus they continued their pastoral and farming occupations, "lengthening their cords and strengthening their stakes;" marrying and intermarrying with the families in the vicinity, as well as among their own kindred, until the relationship can scarcely be traced to a vanishing point. There are the Quisenburys, the Vivians, the Elkins, the Gentrys, the Embrys, the Bushes, etc.—all uncles, aunts, or cousins; and at one time you might travel for miles without being out of the favored circle.

When I can first recollect it was a community of Baptists, and they all worshiped at the stone meeting-house on Howard's Creek. There is an interest attached to this old church that deserves mention. It is, probably, the first Baptist church built in Kentucky, and its foundations are laid deep and strong, though not large and wide. A community of Baptists, living on the Holston River, in Virginia, determined to emigrate to Kentucky in 1780. The ruling elder, Rev. Mr. Vinton, was their leader. They passed through much tribulation, and finally reached their destination, but had no permanent place of worship until the stone church referred to was erected, and called "Providence." The Rev. Robert Elkin was their pastor for forty-two years. Among the most prominent members for a long period were my grand-parents, who lived to see many of their descendants baptized into the same Church. I visited the neighborhood in 1824, and found attached to that congregation thirteen widow Bushes. During the past Summer, 1864, I had the privilege of entering within its hallowed walls, and hearing an excellent sermon from a Reformed Baptist minister. The Reformers preach on alternate Sundays with the old Baptists, and the two congregations worship together, generally without any disagreement.

The old church is in good condition. We reach it through a lovely blue-grass region, dotted with stately mansions, rendered attractive by green lawns and magnificent old sugar-trees, through whose foliage the sunlight, streaming down, covers the ground with enchanting figures of light and shade. The rugged hills surrounding the creek present a striking contrast to the green valleys where Summer sleeps upon beds of roses. Now and then a simple cottage is seen sparkling like a diamond in its granite cup; or on the top of some green and goodly hill a dwelling, white and fair, gleaming through depths of the richest verdure. In a lovely nook, nestled among the rock hills of the creek, stands the house of a dear old relative, with whose family I was privileged to spend a few hours during my recent visit—a golden link in the chain of reminiscences binding me to the past. What a tide of sweet memories swept over me as I listened and learned again the oft-repeated histories of my childhood's rosy hours; and stood once more in the graveyard, where, amid crumbling gravestones, rested the bodies of so many that I had known and loved in early life. What changes had passed over Kentucky since my grand-parents were deposited in that quiet resting-place! Their tombstones are hoary with age and crumbling into dust; but affection keeps the spot green with fresh memorials. Flowers bloom in loveliness around them. The sweetbrier sends forth its fragrance, and Summer roses are found there gushing with dewy sweetness.

Of my old Uncle Billy a word, and I am done with this subject, rendered somewhat tedious by the clinging fondness of my own recollections. This famous old Indian fighter, after having suffered, in common with the rest of the settlers, many privations, and having endured much, found himself with but a few hundred acres of that vast domain he had fought to defend. He had munificently given away much, and was, probably, bereft of some by defective titles. He spent his latter years in the visionary pursuit of silver mines, which he never found. Like the mirage in the desert they eluded his grasp—forever and forever vanishing as the spot was neared.

The glittering prize proved a "glorious cheat;" but it kept up its delusions, until "the silver chord was loosed and the golden bowl was broken," and the poor old man found a resting-place beneath Kentucky soil, with many other patriarchs of the infant State.

We look now to the soil where grazes the peaceful flock, when Summer shakes her sparkling wreath, and sheds her luster over the blooming landscape; to the fields, where wave the golden harvests; to the air above, where play the wings of the low-flighted swallow; and to the woods, where the passing wheels denote the course of men, and ask, Can this be so? Yes, over all these former hunting-grounds of a race fast fading away from this glorious country, once all their own, not a vestige is now to be seen.

How dreary, how sad our emotions, when we reflect on the multiplied hundreds of these poor, untaught children of the forest, hurried into the eternal world by their pale-faced brethren, who wrested from them all they loved, and usurped their hunting-grounds without once offering them the pipe of peace!

I recollect what an inexpressible feeling of awe crept over my childish spirit, as I listened to the veteran pioneers telling their exploits with the Indians, and recounting with peculiar zest their perils, their bloody struggles, their hair-breadth escapes, and their victories. The whites scarcely ever took prisoners; they considered it safer to dispatch them at once to another world. My heart-bubbling laughter was stilled, and my childish sports forgotten, as, listening, I crept closer to my grandmother's side. Once sole lords of a rich and almost boundless country, they have been crowded farther and farther from their sunny homes, farther from the noble rivers they so much loved, and the blue Atlantic, upon whose waves they thought many a good spirit dwelt. Some of them calmly submitted to their fate, and after the last struggle over the graves of their kindred—a spot ever venerated by the red man—departed never to return. Others fought long and desperately, choosing rather to die within sight of their homes.

The whole State of Kentucky was then a perfect jungle of beautiful luxuriance; and to the admiring eyes of the new settlers another Eden, with its green glories of cane-brake—which, in some places, grew twenty feet high—and forest, crystal streams and laughing skies; its luxuriant corn-fields and blue-grass woodland pastures. No wonder our good old preacher, with his own peculiar quaintness, when describing the beauties of heaven, called it "a fair Kentucky of a place." To the early settlers it appeared a fairy-land. Leaf-embowered streams, whose laughing waters danced over polished pebbles, that glittered in the sunlight like diamonds; hill and dale, mountain and glade, varied the scene to the charmed eye of the huntsman, as he wandered through the thick forests under a canopy of softest blue, while the lofty trees sang a pleasant melody at the bidding of the balmy, flower-laden breeze. No wonder that the tales of the past, which now in memory dwell, are full of mythical fancies, arising from those deep and beautiful solitudes, where—

> "All the boundless store of charms,
> Which Nature to her votary yields,
> The pomp of grove, and garniture of fields,"

fills the heart with emotions of love and gratitude to that great and good Being who created this earthly paradise, as if to reflect the glories of that world of light and love, where silvery vales and glittering streams, green fields, and budding flowers, "forever and forever rise." The land was beautiful in its native simplicity, and became more and more fascinating as discovery after discovery unveiled to the admiring eye of her settlers much concealed treasure. Her mountains contain unbounded mineral wealth. Her presiding genius, doubtless, sits enthroned in the mysterious depths of some jewel-lit cave. Her marble walls, rising in grandeur on the shores of the Kentucky and Dicks Rivers, are not less objects of curiosity than her Mammoth Cave, of world-wide celebrity. Variety of productions and mildness of climate appropriately render her the Italy of North America.

In the early part of the present century, the cotton fields in Clarke County yielded enough of the best quality of cotton to supply the wants of every family; and while tobacco was the staple of the State, rich harvests of wheat, extensive corn-fields, and every variety of cereal gladdened the happy farmer with the consciousness of a bountiful provision for his family. Sugar was made in abundance from the maple, whole groves of which were found in Kentucky before the utilitarian ax of the woodman laid them prostrate, to give place to the more useful blue grass. One of these groves, on my grandfather's place, contained a thousand trees, many of which are still standing. The sugar-making time in February, when the rich sap began to flow abundantly, was a glorious time, and long looked forward to with as much delight as Christmas. A regular encampment on the ground made a pleasant home for the two weeks devoted to this gypsy life. The children, including the little negroes—and there were swarms of them—to use their own words, "toted" sugar water in their tiny pails,

hour after hour, and were amply rewarded when the
sugar was in its transition state of waxy consistency
with as much as they could eat. My grandmother's
sugar-chest was every year filled with grained maple
sugar, whiter and purer than that made from the cane;
while a great quantity was put up in cakes for eating—
like candy; and as much molasses was reserved as would
abundantly supply the family until sugar-making time
came round again.

And now, while I write, I can see the camp-fires
lighted, the dusky figures passing and repassing, groups
of happy children laughing and shouting as they bring
in their contributions of crystal water for the steaming
boilers. I almost inhale the delicious breath of an atmosphere, redolent with a freshness and purity never known
in the crowded haunts of men. I have counted nearly
sixty years since those days of unmingled joyousness,
yet still the memory of that time is green, when I played
beneath the boughs of the lofty maple-tree, at whose
roots grew the fresh moss, clustered with tiny blue
flowers, or wandered through avenues of papaw bushes,
as I wended my way from my father's house to the dear
old grandfather's homestead.

CHAPTER II.

Being the second child and oldest daughter, I was sent to a country school at a very early age. I think I was but four years old on that bright and happy morning when my mother, after filling our little school-basket with a lunch to be eaten at play-time, sent my brother and me to school. The dew was yet upon the grass, and the birds were caroling their morning hymns as they fluttered among the branches of the trees which shaded our pathway. Ah, well do I remember that lovely morning. How joyously I tripped along, playing bo-peep with the sun as his golden beams glittered through a fretwork of green above my head, now and then stopping to gather wild flowers that seemed too beautiful to be left behind!

A little incident, though not amusing at the time, has afforded much merriment since. My brother, two years my senior, carried our basket, containing a square black bottle of milk, two or three nicely baked waffles, two fried eggs, slices of ham, two apple-turnovers, and buttered bread, rendered luscious by being thickly overspread with maple-sugar. We had scarcely gone half our way—the school-house was two miles distant from home—when it was proposed that we should rest awhile under the shade of a magnificent tree, and peep into the basket. The repast looked so inviting under the snowy covering that we were tempted to eat a portion of the good things; after which my brother, to whom the idea of school was not half so pleasing as to myself, begged me to go back and ask permission to stay from school that day. I agreed to it, and soon reached home and delivered my message; to which my mother replied by taking my hand, and, gathering a switch, she silently led me to the trysting-place where my brother awaited me; and after applying the rod freely, to quicken his indolent faculties, accompanied us to the log school-house, and handed us over to "the master," who seated me beside one of the larger pupils, bidding her teach "the little one" her A, B, C's from a board upon which they were pasted.

I recollect distinctly the house, and the school itself, which in its day was a model. A square room, with a fireplace large enough to hold nearly half a cord of wood; a puncheon floor; hard, rough, wooden benches, without backs; an opening in the wall, of an oblong form, opposite the door, for a window, with crevices enough in every direction to admit a free circulation of air! The furniture, consisting of a desk, at which the teacher was placed, or rather perched, far above all the miserable little urchins; a ferule, a rod, and a pile of copy-books, complete the picture.

At twelve, which was known by a mark on the door-sill—the primitive clock of our forefathers—the whole school was turned out for a two-hours' recreation and dinner. Such shouts of merriment! such ringing laughter! So much outgushing happiness, with an abundance of fun and frolic, unrestrained by hoops and heels, or the fear of soiling delicate costumes!

Our dinner eaten, how heartily we romped, bent young saplings for riding-horses, made swings of the surrounding grape-vines, and anon rested on the green sward under the wide-spreading beech-trees, until we were not sorry to hear the stentorian voice of the master calling out, "Bo-o-ks! bo-o-ks!" at the sound of which all ran eagerly to their seats, beginning to con over their A, B, C; to spell, A bit-sel-fa (A by itself, *a*), *b-e-l*, bel, Abel; *b-a*, ba, *k-e-r*, ker, baker; *c-i-d-e-r*, der, cider; while a class read aloud, "An old man found a rude boy," etc.; the teacher, meantime, passing around the room, rod in hand, encouraging all to "say out," which was done with a will, and without any apparent confusion, because each one minded his own business and not that of another; and it certainly taught the power of abstraction, if nothing else.

This day was an exponent of many others—days of unalloyed happiness, marked by rosy hours, the beauty of which still lingers. The cup from which we quaffed pure nectar, filtered through the clouds of heaven, contained no bitter dregs, and every beaded bubble sparkled with joy—evanescent, indeed, but singing as it vanished; and seeming now, in the moonlight of other days, as a lustrous pearl on the brow of life's young morning.

I do not remember how long I continued under the instruction of Mr. Pettichord, my Clarke County teacher, but I know that I soon learned to read; and reading has been a passion with me all my life, a source of so great enjoyment as to be appreciated and understood by those who have enjoyed in like degree the pleasure and profit to be derived therefrom. My excellent parents, being educated in the very best manner that the times and circumstances by which they were surrounded afforded, highly appreciated the advantages of a superior education, and determined to seek for their children opportunities that Kentucky did not afford; for which purpose they removed to Virginia when I was but seven years of age. Whilst my father was seeking a suitable location for a permanent residence—good schools being the principal object—we spent two years in Paris, a pretty little village at the foot of the Blue Ridge, in Loudon County; and there, amidst the sublimest scenery, of cloud-capped mountains, flowing streams, purified by percolation through granite rocks and snow-white pebbles; inhaling the pure mountain breeze, untainted by the miasma of richer soils and more favored climes,—our physical energies were rapidly developed, and constitutional strength fixed and settled, so as to tell for good upon my future health.

Nature here was beautiful in every season. The mountains, those grand and impressive waymarks of Deity, though stern and severe in character, presented a grandeur and magnificence of Winter scenery peculiar to to these snowy regions. Dark evergreen foliage dotted their sides; the brown leaves of the forest trees showed but sad remains of Summer's ornamental attire; yet the verdant moss and twining ivy still clung to the giant forms of the gnarled oak, and invested the less rugged structure of the tall and drooping elm and the more delicate aspen. And when the snow covered, with its spotless mantle, broad meadow, mountain gorge, and lovely vale, elegantly ornamenting the trees with incrustations on their stouter branches, festooning along the hedgerows, or hanging in full drapery where it drifted through them; and the moon shed her silver light on the mountain-side, turning each ledge and tree or ghostly stump into mysterious apparitions from the spirit-land,—the saddest, coldest dell became a cup of lustrous beauty, and there was presented the sublimest spectacle ever given to this lower world. Then came Spring, when primroses peeped from under withered leaves, whose

sheltering care was now repaid by decorations of pale
delicate petals; when the sweet crocus with the modest
snowdrop, like maidens in their gala-dresses dancing on
the green, and the rich clover, sprinkled the meadows
with their starry eyes. Summer, with all its bright glories, seemed really more beautiful in sweet Loudon County
than in any other spot I now remember. The blossoms
of Spring were replaced by the reddening and scarcely
less abundant berries, and every orchard was filled with
luscious fruits. What a memory scenes like these bequeath! How beautiful, through the vista of years,
now seems that moonlight track upon the waters of
my life!

Not the least in the happiness of those times were our
nuttings in Autumn, when a stroll was invited by the
rich, glowing tints that every-where burnished the land,
and the abundant harvest from the dwarf-hazel and chin-
capin bushes, with their brown treasures; the stately
chestnut, whose clustering burs were filled with delicious
nuts; and the majestic oak, dotted with acorns. All, all
was fruitfulness. The crimson branches of the red-bud
and the scarlet berries of the dog-rose showed that,
though Summer and the flowering season had passed
away, yet more substantial blessings had succeeded. We
crushed the dry leaves under our feet—we gathered the
sorrel from under the ledge of fallen trees; and this
sorrel, with its long pointed green leaves, yielded an
acidity far more agreeable than costly lemonades, as we
drank from the cool mountain spring. Wending our
way home, weary with a day's enjoyment, we watched
with pleasure the gossamer thread whose fine and wavy
lines were thrown across our pathway—frail and almost
viewless threads, that impede no more than do the shades

in which they lie almost unseen, or the lingering sun-beams in which they glisten.

I have often fancied, while recalling the beautiful sun-sets among the mountains of Virginia, that they must surpass those of Italy, so world-renowned. Often, in childish admiration, I have watched the declining sun, its fading light turning the dark rocks into masses of glowing metal, and the pine woods into a forest of spark-ling jewels, "limning and lipping" the trembling leaves of the forest with gold, and casting outlines on the back-ground of glowing fire; and whilst the glorious orb grad-ually disappeared below the horizon, rising vapors clus-tered around the mountain heights, crowning them with a revolving diadem; the bright blue sky deepened into purple; the pine-trees put on a drapery of black, as if to mourn the departing day; and in the dim twilight was heard the mountain torrents, chafing over their stony channels, without one glimpse of sunshine to light them on their way; while ever and anon a twinkling star was seen through the dense foliage like a gem on Night's dark curtain.

A few pleasing incidents connected with my sojourn at the foot of the Blue Ridge I will record.

When blooming Spring returned with her buds and blossoms, then came the dancing-school, which was held in the large upper room of a water-mill, cleared of its flour-bags and barrels for our use. Here we labored as hard all day on Saturday "to dance each other down" as we did during the week to keep the place of honor in our literary classes.

At the close of the first quarter in the dancing-school all the gentry in the neighborhood were invited to an exhibition, when each pupil was to display the acquirements of the term. The important morning arrived, I was dressed in a full robe of white muslin, which, being a little too long, was festooned with wild flowers and garden honeysuckles, until short enough to display my "clocked" stockings and sharp-toed shoes of red morocco. After having performed, for the twentieth time, my steps and pirouettes before a large, old-fashioned mirror in the dining-room, I started with my brother to the mill, on foot, having exchanged my white stockings and new slippers for walking-shoes. When within the immediate vicinity of the old mill I again donned my white stockings and dancing-slippers, smoothed my hair, and shook out the folds of my dress, the skirt of which had been pinned up by my careful mother to avoid contact with dust.

We were handed in by our attentive dancing-master, who was dressed in the full costume of the politest circles of the day,—neatly fitting small clothes, with silk stockings fastened at the knees, bows of ribbon and bright silver buckles—corresponding bows and buckles adorning his dancing-pumps. My brother made his bow, and I courtesied so low as almost to lose my equilibrium. After we had displayed our steps in classes, partners were selected for us, and we danced cotillions, Virginia reels, minuets, and shawl dances, to the intense delight of the ladies who were seated around the room like wall flowers, while the gentlemen stood about in groups.

At twelve we were collected on the green sward in the deeply-shaded woods, to share a rich repast of good things provided by the neighbors and patrons of the school; after which our dancing exercises were resumed and continued until evening, when all returned to their homes fully satisfied with the simple pleasures of the day.

No jealous thoughts, no heart burnings, no disappointed vanity marred our happiness or drove away "Nature's sweet restorer, balmy sleep," which came with night to close our weary eyelids, and catch reflected smiles from placid faces and rosy lips, while the stars that peeped quietly in at the windows lighted up dewy brows and healthy cheeks, unsullied by a tear.

Oh, how does the golden lamp of young life flood all its surroundings with light and beauty, leaving an illuminated page in memory's book, which no after cares can darken! Happy the young who may dwell in their own homes, filled with the domestic flowers of love and innocence, whence the voice of affection breathes on the ear, opening in the inner heart blossoms of piety and virtue, to which are duly apportioned the dew and the sunbeam!

I am not of those who are constantly bemoaning the "better times of the glorious old past;" and yet, I verily believe that the children of fifty years ago enjoyed life more, and were educated in a manner better suited to the development of their physical and mental energies, and to the fostering of that self-reliance so necessary for the life-struggle of mature age, than those of modern times. Our simple costume, unconfined by belt or girdle, and our bib-aprons, as distinctly separated the school girl from the young lady in society, as did the "*bulla* and *toga virilis*" separate childhood and manhood among the Romans.

With what pleasure, not unmingled with vanity, did I display my two school dresses for the Spring of 1812, both made of Virginia cotton cloth, home spun and home woven—one a white ground with pink stripes running lengthwise; the other, a blue plaid, which was the admi-

5

ration of all the unsophisticated girls in my class. And then our dresses cost, comparatively, so little. A simple frock, with a draw-string around the waist, three widths in the skirt, one of which was cut into gores, and a check apron was the height of our ambition. Though our dresses were not full and flowing, they were wide enough to admit of leaping, running, jumping, and climbing trees—a feat often performed by girls from eight to fifteen years of age. In Winter we faced the wind and braved the snow, and even sought the drifted banks, into which we literally waded without fear of cold or sickness—an evil almost unknown among the hardy little pine-knots of Virginia. Headaches were a myth, and indigestion never heard of. No colds or sore-throats; none of the various ailings which arise from lack of a little wholesome neglect. At playtime, in Winter, we built snow-houses, erected colossal statues, and bound their brows with icicles—rare jewels these when the sun shone on them! Coasting, sliding, snow-balling—oh, this was fun! The result, good constitutions, power to endure exposure, and exemption from asthma and consumption. People did not die then before their time came.

The little village of Paris, to which I have before alluded, afforded a good day-school, and many privileges in the way of a common education. The school-house stood in a beautiful grove that skirted the highway. There we learned to read, write, and cipher, and were thoroughly drilled in Dilworth's Spelling-book—the *vade mecum* of every country teacher—and were taught to "make our manners" without paying an "extra sixpence" a week. This excellent school-house was also occupied as the village church.

A favorite amusement with the children, at that time,

was swinging from the end of a grapevine torn from its
fastenings in the tree. A feat of this kind came near
costing me my life, when but nine years old. I was a
slender and delicate looking child, yet remarkably strong
and active, and could climb like a cat. By the aid of
one of my older companions I had gained firm footing
high up in a gnarled oak—easy enough to climb; but
venturing too far out upon one of its branches, and seizing with both hands a loosened grapevine, I attempted
to swing down gently, as I had often done before; but
the whole vine giving way too suddenly, I was precipi-
tated to the ground, from whence my frightened companions raised me in a senseless state. Happily no permanent injury resulted, as I fell upon the soft, green
sward, but it rendered me chary ever afterward about
cimbing trees. I rode on horseback when quite a child,
with the greatest ease and fearlessness—frequently mounting in my father's saddle, and riding round and round the
village, to my own infinite delight and the great amusement of the bystanders.

The old lady with whom we boarded during our first
year's residence in Paris deserves notice, as one of the
institutions of the place. Her house stood at the far-
thest end of a long street which commenced at the foot
of the mountain. She kept a genteel establishment called
a "tavern"—there were no hotels then. No liquors were
sold there. It was really a resting-place; and many a
way-worn traveler hailed with delight the entrance to that
old-fashioned brick building, whose signboard promised
"refreshment for man and beast." There was a coldness
and precision about the interior arrangements of this
dwelling that impressed every body painfully. The door-
steps, the window-sills, the sashes, the wash-boards, were

immaculately white, and kept so by the daily scrubbing of a withered-looking housemaid. The very knives, forks, and spoons were made thin by repeated rubbings. The best room was excruciatingly tidy. The heavy, high-backed chairs, mahogany tables; the well-waxed floor, in which you could almost see your face; the old fashioned family pictures suspended from the walls; and, indeed, all its appointments, were matters of great curiosity to me.

Madam R. was a little old woman between the ages of sixty and seventy, with sharp, attenuated features, long nose, and pointed chin; and when I first saw her she needed only a broomstick to make me think she was one of the witches described in my nursery tales. She wore slippers with long, slender heels, evidently to increase her height. I wondered how she could walk in them; yet she glided along noiselessly and gracefully, with her full skirts and ample train. A high-crowned cap, with a fine muslin kerchief folded over her bosom, a huge pair of silver-mounted spectacles, a heavy bunch of keys at her girdle, with scissors and pin-cushion dangling outside of her sober-colored gown, and a linen lawn apron, completed her attire. Her snuff-box and book lay always on her work-table; for she read novels and romances with as much zest as a love-sick girl—her Bible never, so far as I could see. This also made me afraid of her; for I had been told that *good* people always read the Bible.

I have since thought that the old lady must have been a nice mathematician. I have seen her divide a common-sized apple-pie into as many pieces as would serve eight or ten persons. She never thought of leaving any for the waiting children; and more than once I shed silent tears as I saw the last piece appropriated. She could "cut and come again" so skillfully from a round of spiced beef as not to exhaust it for two weeks, during which time it made its daily appearance at the table. Her tact was admirable; her economy wonderful!

A son and a daughter completed this family circle. The former was a mechanical sort of an old bachelor, who "moved, worked, and suffered"—a mere *attaché* of the establishment, to be ordered into service when needed. He was seldom seen, never heard; and from his unbroken silence it might be inferred that he had never learned to talk; the truth was, his lady mother and loquacious sister never gave him an opportunity. He must have kept up a "mighty thinking," however; for he showed all the ingenuity and shrewdness of a Yankee, in the many useful inventions and labor-saving machines resulting from a clear-sighted vision and a quick instinct of the profitable. In matters of trade and business Mr. Jerry was never at fault.

Miss Jane was tall and meagre; her visage sharp, swarthy, and unprepossessing, except for her keen gray eyes, that sparkled with intelligence. Strange that there should be any thing fascinating in an eye that belonged to so cold a heart! The sharpness of her tones, even in common conversation, repelled affection. Like her mother, she was so addicted to novel-reading that she lived in an ideal world. Mrs. Radcliffe's "piled-up horrors" and mysterious ramifications furnished the apartments of her brain, and shed a lurid light upon her soul. Her dress was characteristic of the tastes she had imbibed; and never did a faded woman upon the verge of fifty take more trouble to look like a heroine of romance. Girlish frocks tied around her thin form, flowing sashes, false curls peeping out from under a fantastic head-dress adorned with flowers or drooping feathers, failed to make her appear youthful. Nobody loved her; yet she was neither shunned nor ridiculed, because she was really polite to every body. She preferred the society of young persons, took part in their amusements, and delighted in bringing down her own thoughts to their comprehension. Her memory was filled with the most thrilling stories of hobgoblins and fairies, spiced with raw-heads-and-bloody-bones, distressed damsels, and brave knights.

I was an interested listener; and she tried to make me fond of her by coaxing and sweetmeats. By degrees I drew nearer, and still nearer, and would even sit on a low stool at her feet for hours, listening to her stories.

I must, however, do this woman the justice to say that to her I am partly indebted for my intense love of reading. Happy for me, at this period of pure fancy, before my brain was strong enough to bear severe reading, to have found one, burdened with the wealth of many beautiful things, who led me at will through all the Arcadian scenes of fiction, making the "Arabian Nights," "Fairy Tales," and "Robinson Crusoe" my text-books, instead of English Grammar and Mathematics. It only made me relish the more, as I grew older, and wayward fancy gave place to higher thoughts, veritable travels and biography. As my powers of retention grew stronger, History and Poetry stood ready to meet my intellectual wants. Thus, by degrees, was my world-wide curiosity in a measure sated, and deeper thought awakened, as I entered upon dryer and severer studies. The end, the use of things, must be seen before the means can be appreciated. It is better that reflection and fancy be germinated before than simultaneously with them; the attention will be less diverted.

CHAPTER III.

M Y father finally located his family in Winchester, at that time the most beautiful inland town in Virginia, eligibly situated at the entrance of what is termed the "rich valley" in Frederick County. It presented an inviting place of residence for many wealthy and distinguished families, whose hospitable mansions ornamented the suburbs, and whose hearts and homes welcomed "the coming guest," making that welcome so agreeable, that many—so the old story goes—lingered until they forgot they were not at home. Winchester and its lovely environs might well have been deemed an earthly paradise, which, had Mahomet looked upon from the mountain heights, as he did upon Damascus, he would have hesitated to enter, for fear the "Lotus Land" might make him forgetful of the Paradise above. So I think, at least, as I look upon it now through the golden haze of memory.

Here was an excellent Female Academy, under the superintendence of the Rev. Mr. Hill, a Presbyterian minister, eminent for piety, learning, and ability. He was assisted by the Rev. Mr. Streight, pastor of the Dutch Reformed Church. In this school I gained knowledge rapidly; learned the worth of time, and tried to improve it, by laying up a store of useful information, which proved a solid foundation for the superstructure to be raised upon it. For three consecutive years my first lesson in the morning was two columns in Walker's

Dictionary, giving the definitions and parts of speech. We spelled in large classes, and regularly turned each other down—the one who retained her place at the head of the class for the whole week, bearing off the prize-ticket on Friday afternoon; and, to this hour, though I consult other lexicographers, Walker is my standard.

Mr. Hill was one of those wise-hearted teachers, especially fitted for his important vocation. Rightly dividing the words of instruction and disciplinary admonition, he failed not to secure the love, as well as the respect and esteem, of his pupils. Strict, but not severe; uniformly kind, but not familiar; conscientious in the discharge of his duty, he succeeded admirably in training his pupils intellectually and religiously. From this "Academy" (bless the old-fashioned name!), which continued in successful operation for many years, went forth a number of interesting women to cheer the domestic hearthstone, to be useful in the world, and to shine like diamonds of the purest water in society. My reminiscences connected with this school have ever been a fruitful source of pleasure to myself and amusement to others; indeed, I never think of Winchester but a thrill of joy passes through my heart. "Like the music of other days, 'tis mournful, but pleasing to the soul."

Our school hours were from eight to twelve in the forenoon, and from two until four in the afternoon. During the Summer months many of us attended a sewing-school, taught from four until six o'clock P. M., by an old lady from Philadelphia, of "yellow fever memory." Nothing delighted her so much as the recapitulation of the horrors connected wiih that awful visitation upon her native city in 1793. Her memory was filled with incidents of people put in their coffins before

their breath was fairly gone; the dead, hurried by cart-
loads into pits dug to receive them; instances of resusci-
tion after burial; weeping mothers and dismayed children
flying from the homes where the husbands and fathers
had died; ghost-like figures, wrapped in cloaks, going
about the streets in search of shelter, invested already
with the floating pestilence. No wonder our samplers
and various kinds of needle-work dropped from our trembling hands, while, panic stricken, we were prompted to
run as if the terrible plague was already rushing upon us,
and could only be avoided by precipitate flight. Few of
her listeners but were slightly tinctured with superstition by these daily recitals; and many a poor, little, blue-
eyed, flaxen haired girl was rendered still more timid as
the shadows of evening lengthened. She would not have
dared, for the world, to wend her way homeward in the
dark without a companion somewhat bolder and stronger
than herself; indeed, none of us were disposed to tarry
by the way.

Friday afternoons and the whole day on Saturdays
we attended Monsieur Xaupe's dancing-school. This
accomplishment was carried on through all our academical
course. Dancing then was dancing, indeed! Characterized by graceful agility, it was exercise in the true sense
of the word, particularly if carried on in the open air;
no lackadaisical languishing on the one part, nor stiff,
awkward shuffling on the other. Graceful evolutions and
genteel cotillions, even among boys and girls, were carried on with the utmost attention to modest etiquette,
the personal attention of the gentlemen extending no
further than touching the tip ends of delicately gloved
hands. High heels and sweeping trains effectually forbid
elegant dancing nowadays. The custom among the boys

and girls of playing thimble at recess, or something that
required forfeits, I did not admire, and seldom joined in.
Once an awkward, red-headed boy, of about fifteen, was
required to redeem a pawn by coming stealthily and kissing me. I had withdrawn to a corner, and was deeply
engaged in reading. He was not quick enough. This
gave me an opportunity of slapping him violently in the
face with a book. He retired with a burning cheek from
the combat, but, forgetting the insult before evening,
attempted to walk home with me. I was sullenly silent
at first, but soon found an opportunity of pushing him
into a gutter. Thus ended my prospect for beaux. Child
as I was—only eleven—I heartily despised flirting among
boys and girls.

I have referred to the hardy habits of children fifty
years ago, and will give another incident, connected with
my school life at Winchester, showing with what impunity we reveled in the cold, and amid the ice and snow.

Near our school-house, in the suburbs of the town, and
just hidden from the dwelling of our teacher, was a large
pond, sufficiently ice-bound in the Winter to afford sliding for the girls, and good skating for the little boys who
timidly ventured there. One glorious noon a dozen or
more of us, after hurrying through our lunch, went down
to this pond, where we thought to have a merry time.
Two or three little blue-nosed urchins were made to give
up their skates to some of the girls, whilst others contented themselves with sliding; and we were scarcely
under way when one of our little romps fell flat on her
face, with her nose forced into a crack in the ice. Of
course, she tried to scream terribly; but her screams
were faint compared with the noise of those gathered to
her assistance. Some stumbled and fell; others tried in

vain to lift her up. After several unsuccessful efforts, however, we succeeded, and found her face scratched and nose
badly bruised. A few drops of blood so increased the
panic, and retarded the progress of matters, that we could
with difficulty get her to a boarding-house near by, and
take her stealthily up into one of the girls' rooms, before
the bell rang for school. The roll was called—"Mary
M'Kendlass." "Absent." "She was here this morning," said Mr. Hill; "what has become of her?" A
moment of silence, when one, bolder than the rest, said,
"She is sick; gone home." Mr. Hill looked incredu-
lous, but made no remark. I, for one, felt inexpressibly
relieved; for there was no mischief ever on hand that he
did not deem me one of the culprits. We sat all the
afternoon with cold, wet feet, not daring to approach the
large wood fire that blazed so cheerfully on the hearth,
for fear of attracting attention. Poor girls! A shadow
rested upon our merry faces that whole afternoon; not
that we dreaded sickness—it was a thing almost unknown
among us, although we spent nearly all our playtimes
out of doors, in defiance of the severest weather.

How wearily the hours dragged on until the time of
our dismissal. Several of us then went to take Mary
home, whom we found much refreshed by a long sleep.
We were delighted to think that our adventure was about
to terminate so happily. We walked gayly along with
Mary towards her home, when, lo! just as we were entering the back gate Mr. Hill appeared at the front door,
coming to inquire after his sick pupil. Our consternation
may well be imagined, but the scene was indescribable.
Mr. Hill's quizzical look was perfectly irresistible; and,
with a little encouragement from his laughing eye, we
confessed our fault, and, pleading guilty, begged for

mercy, which was granted, after amusing himself for some time at our expense; but we were debarred the privilege of another icy adventure that Winter.

Our excellent teacher was very successful in his reproofs; and though sometimes severe, he never failed to make us sensible of his affectionate regard and the real interest he felt in our welfare. We were happy children, full of life and sunshine, and he had no disposition to repress innocent fun and frolic. He knew there must be a safety-valve for the outgushing merriment of young hearts.

I have said that we were mischievous; but never malicious, I am sure. Once I was induced by a fun-loving girl to put sugar in the inkstands, being assured that it would meet the approbation of our solemn writing-master. We gazed with admiration at the black, shining words of our beautiful copies, as we left them open on the desk while we were reciting in an adjoining room. It was Summer, and the flies were so busy during our absence that when the master came around there was not a legible word to be seen. "Who did this? Speak, instantly!" No reply; but agitation and alarm were so visible upon my face that, placing his heavy hand upon my brow, he stretched open my eyes to a painful extent, while he threatened to box my ears. My ludicrous appearance and terrified looks seemed to cool his anger almost to the laughing point, except that he *never* laughed. Thus he left me with a positive threat of severe punishment should it ever occur again.

Children are not most effectually governed by too much fault-finding. Teachers and parents are slow to learn that there is a chord in every heart which vibrates more to the touch of kindness than to the rude shock of rough government. Serious faults should never be overlooked; and, to secure principles of right doing, a child should be taught that it is an accountable being. Morals are best inducted and principles most firmly fixed during the first ten years of a child's life.

Being so fully persuaded of the superiority of Mr. Hill's mode of instruction, and the benefits I derived from this excellent institution, I can not close this part of my subject without saying something of the long-debated question of making children write compositions. The younger pupils of this Academy were as much required to bring in weekly contributions of this kind as the older members of the school—something in the form of a letter or a familiar story—until they could write with ease, and sometimes express themselves with elegance.

My first effort was a letter blistered with tears, upon which more time had been spent than ever Cicero devoted to one of his finest orations. It was to be read aloud, and criticised before the whole school. Having an unaccountable dread of the slightest contraction of Mr. Hill's ample brow, I dared not look up as I tremblingly placed my epistle in his hand. It was folded in the most approved style, and addressed to a far-off friend. It commenced thus: I now sit down and take up my pen— "You sit down," interrupted my unmerciful critic. "Who do you think cares whether you sit or stand?"— and write to inform you—"Your friend reads your letter, why must you inform her that you give her the information?"—that I am well, and this comes hopping—"Astonishing! And so it is to go hopping? a most extraordinary epistle! I suppose it skips and jumps, too;" and so my censor continued through the whole page. My ears burned, my head ached, my eyes swam in tears, and my glowing cheeks were almost purple with confusion; but I bore it all, profited by the criticism, never tried to evade my weekly task, and have reaped a rich reward. No doubt my facility in letter writing is largely due to this initiatory ordeal, combined with my determined effort while a pupil of that good old-time academy.

Our text-books were few, but we obtained a thorough knowledge of them. I believe I could now, after the lapse of so many years, repeat the whole of Murray's Grammar from the beginning of Etymology to the end of Syntax, verbatim, after a slight review. Do not infer from this that memory alone was cultivated; on the contrary, much pains was taken to cultivate our thinking powers. I doubt much if the modern labor-saving books have not rendered education far more superficial. Self-culture and close thinking strengthen the mental powers—a slow growth of mind would make more useful men and women. The possession of knowledge is useless to the world, without the wisdom to apply it—hot-house plants often wither without bearing fruit. The young, in modern times, think too little and act too much; they are alarmingly busy and remarkably idle, and often good for nothing, unless controlled by stronger minds.

During *my* school-days we took lessons in *gymnastics* from *Nature*. To ride young saplings, to climb trees for cherries and wild grapes, was Nature's inductive method of teaching ease of manner and grace of motion; while with her delicate pencil she failed not to impart the glow of health and beauty. Can beauty exist where health is not?

We remained in Winchester more than three years. One bright page in my memory, during that time, is devoted to a visit to Bath or Berkley Springs, situated about forty miles north. This was a celebrated watering-place during the Revolutionary War, and the resort of many distinguished men since. Lord Fairfax had a Summer residence there, the ruins of which I have seen; and some of the outbuildings—the kitchen, for instance—were in good repair in 1857; and here, probably, he died of grief after Cornwallis's surrender, with Yorktown engraven on his heart. The house where Washington boarded while in Bath is still pointed out; and, though in ruins, held in reverence by the inhabitants.

The beautiful valley in which this little town is situated is overtopped by stately mountains, from which are poured a profusion of rivulets, keeping the grass fresh and green and fertilizing the soil. Thickly shaded groves, threaded with graveled walks and dotted with convenient resting-places; fountains of pure water, and every arrangement calculated to promote health and comfort, met the eye in every direction. Here are also found ample facilities for bathing. The dense vegetation, the ever-running stream of clear water that passes through the village, its banks fringed with trees, afford, perhaps, as perfect an idea of Arcadia as one is likely to meet with in this every day world. From the highest point of one of the mountains may be seen Maryland, Pennsylvania, Western Virginia, and, in the dim distance, the Blue Ridge and the peaks of Otter.

In the year 1811, a man by the name of Hughes, who had been imprisoned for debt in Richmond, Virginia, succeeded, by the aid of a shrewd and unscrupulous lawyer of that place, in publishing a pretended prophecy that a great part of the world would be destroyed by fire. This was to take place on a certain day in June. It will be understood, that the man had been so long in jail that the community had lost sight of or forgotten him. The pamphlet was secretly printed at the cost of the lawyer, who was to share the profits. Care was taken that it should not be circulated in the vicinity of Richmond, or where there would be any likelihood of the discovery of the fraud. It was disseminated throughout the most unsettled parts of Virginia, among the mountains, in the South and in the far West. One of these, like a stray waif, had fallen into the hands of some of our school girls. We read it with intense curiosity, and swallowed every word of it as truth. The news spread among us like wildfire; and, at each repetition, it became more and more exaggerated. We marvelled that it was not talked of in our families, and daily expected the communication through our teachers. Our eyes grew larger and more dreamy, and a settled thoughtfulness seemed to pervade the whole school.

But things went on as usual. Lessons were assigned and expected to be learned, our elders appeared as busily engaged in preparing to live as if no prophecy had been made. What strange apathy in all, save us school girls! We talked in retired groups, wept silent tears, and were, much to the surprise of our teachers, wonderfully docile. No romping or shouting or playing—the elastic step was gone, and we felt that—

> "Nothing so like a weary step
> Betrays a weary heart."

At last arrived the evening preceding the awful day. School was dismissed; yet we lingered around the old play-ground; the birds sang, the flowers bloomed, and the sweet evening breeze swept lovingly over us, oblivious of any coming change. Hard-hearted Mr. Hill turned his back upon us, and walked quietly into the

house, without bidding us good-by, as if nothing were to
happen. Mr. Streight looked colder, and was crosser
than usual, because our copies were badly written; I
wondered if he would look so should I meet him in
heaven. Intimate friends shook hands for the last time,
kissed one another with more than usual affection, and
turned back to bid yet another adieu, weeping as if their
hearts would break. I wandered listlessly to my own
home, and seated myself on the door-step to watch
the declining sun; it sank below the Western horizon,
clothed in purple and gold. I listened with a pleasing
melancholy to the twittering of the birds; watched the
domestic fowls as they retired to roost, and caught the
melody of the milkmaid's song mingled with the lowing
of the cattle in the distant meadows.

I lingered around my mother long after bedtime, and
kissing her with unusual fervency before retiring, went to
bed thinking I should pass a restless night; but Nature
would not be robbed of her dues. Troubled dreams of
darkened skies, muttering thunder, and flashing lightning
disturbed my rest. I awoke but once, to see the moonlight streaming in through the window, and slept again
until awakened for breakfast. A brighter day never
blessed the earth; it was a glorious vision of charming
Summer weather; and yet, with all this, when we met at
the opening school hour, we were afraid to enjoy our
own happy consciousness, and even while bent over our
books, one and another might occasionally be seen glancing at the window as if expecting something startling.
Thus hour after hour glided away, and not a cloud as
"big as a man's hand" was seen; and the closing of that
day brought with it the sweet assurance that our Heavenly Father is always "better to us than our fears."

6

How strange, knowing, as we do, but one thing certainly, that we must die—and of this we are warned from the beginning of Genesis to the end of Revelation—yet, the many make no preparation for it, and dream of long years to come, until startled by some pretended prophecy of sudden desolation; forgetting, meanwhile, the words of our Savior, who has emphatically declared, that "of the day and hour knoweth no man, no, not the angels of heaven, but my Father only."

Previous to the declaration of war in 1812 there was intense excitement throughout the whole country. The political animosity existing between the two parties, Federalists and Democrats, was bitter beyond expression; even the children caught fire in the general conflagration. Some were Democrats, the war party; others Federalists, "whose voice was still for peace." It was not an unusual thing to see the girls of our school in battle array on the green common, during intermission, fighting like furies; and though, like Pompey's patrician soldiers, carefully avoiding scratched faces and broken noses, many a handful of hair was borne off as a trophy, many a neatly made dress torn into tatters; while a system of boxing was practiced, that would have done honor to a Grecian gymnasium. The war party, of course, were generally victorious, as they were not only more numerous but fiercer, and more demonstrative, and would not *stay* whipped. Nothing was effected, however, in these *melees;* the battles ended when we were tired of fighting. But it is a positive fact, that our dishevelled hair and torn garments increased our good humor to the highest pitch of merriment.

Among my most vivid recollections of the opening of the war was seeing a splendid body of cavalry passing

through the streets of Winchester. It was a full regiment, handsomely equipped, bright new uniforms, a fine
band of music, with all the "pomp and circumstance of
glorious war." The spirited horses, and gallant bearing
of the officers, with their flashing swords and waving
plumes, rendered it an imposing sight.

The colonel was the cynosure of all eyes. Like Saul
among his brethren, he seemed literally head and shoulders above all the rest. The melancholy story of this
man invested him with peculiar interest, and he was a
welcome guest in every body's family. Shadows had
surrounded him from his childhood. None knew his
parentage, nor any of his family connections. Somebody
in Winchester had charge of him in early life; regular
and ample supplies of money were mysteriously sent
from time to time for his use. He was educated at West
Point, and joined the regular army before the war. He
was a noble-looking man; his keen gray eyes sparkling
with intellect, and his pale, thoughtful face surmounted
by an Olympian brow, upon which was stamped the sig-
net of true manhood. His taciturnity and absent-mind-
edness were so great at times as to render his sanity
doubtful. Poor fellow! There was no one in this wide
world upon whom he might bestow the wealth of his
affectionate heart. A mother's love and a father's care
were unknown to him; yet it was whispered—and he
knew it—that his mother lived, and that he was the only
lineal descendant of General Morgan, the "Old Wagoner"
of Revolutionary memory. He was killed in his first
battle, and few of his regiment ever returned to chase
away the shadows left upon the threshold by their departure. Such is war; God help us to appreciate the
blessings of peace!

How many hearts utter this prayer! and yet we glory in the prestige that surrounds a successful warrior. His garments may be rolled in blood, and his pathway strewn with mementos of human suffering; but no matter—he has achieved great victories. A thrill of horror may spread through sensitive hearts, mingled with agony, grief, and indignation at the devastations of war, the sufferings of age and innocence, and the violation of humanity, honor, and virtue; yet with the multitude all this is forgotten in the glory of illuminations and the intoxication of victory. War may be sometimes necessary; but, alas, how sad the necessity! How cruel the results, even though the object for which it is undertaken be a laudable one! The arts and sciences, and whatever might be expected to flourish from intellectual culture in times of peace, wither under the influence of war. Thus a Christian nation and an enlightened people should not only deprecate it as the greatest evil, but never undertake it except to show the world that the tree of liberty can only flourish in the genial atmosphere of freedom, the natural aliment of which is the general intelligence of the people. Knowledge is not merely the parent of liberty, but constitutes an element of its nature, and is as essential to its existence as the air is to animal life. Every philanthropic effort that is made, every peaceful act that is done for the regeneration of man, elevates him in the scale of improvement, and advances him to that state in which moral force shall triumph over the physical and animal.

Chapter IV.

WE removed to the District of Columbia in November, 1813, locating in Georgetown. Here I saw the first illumination I ever witnessed. The whole town, as well as Washington, was one blaze of light, in honor of General Harrison's victory over the British and Indians at the battle of the Thames, as well as the brilliant victory of Commodore Perry on Lake Erie, which just preceded it. Our little navy had crowned itself with laurels in its ocean fights, but Harrison's victory followed a succession of disasters by land. The death of Tecumseh in the battle of the Thames was also hailed with great joy by the nation, as it deeply depressed the Indians, who had become exceedingly fierce. Tecumseh was a host in himself; and had his lot been cast under favorable circumstances his powerful mind and heroic soul would have distinguished him, not only as a warrior, but as an orator and statesman.

The first Christmas spent in our new home was marked by a sad event, the remembrance of which a whole lifetime can not efface. Our new and handsome house was pleasantly situated in an eligible part of the town, and the last piece of furniture had been arranged in our parlor on Christmas Eve. We were rendered completely happy by having all the family at home. With what undisguised admiration we children ran from room to room, clapping our hands with joy as we examined the beautiful crimson curtains hanging in ample folds, and glowing

in the light of a bright wood fire burning on the hearth.
How resplendent the tall brass andirons looked! How
warm and soft the rich carpeting that covered the floor!
And then the large mantle-glass, reflecting the dancing
figures of happy children, who were extravagantly gay
with the joy of a new-found home, and with Christmas
just on the threshold! The brief past had no regrets to
fling across our minds.

> "Time flies fast, while laughing childhood throws
> Handfuls of roses at him as he goes."

We were up late, arranging Christmas presents for the
morrow, my busy, happy mother allowing me to aid her
in all her preparations. After all was completed, we retired to our comfortable beds and slept until aroused by
the awful cry of, Fire! fire! The prolonged echo thrilled
through every heart. It was just at the hour when silence
reigns supreme in the deserted streets. The watchman,
who commenced his rounds when "night and morning
meet," had called the hours of one, two, three, and retired
from our vicinity, when a servant-girl, dismissed the day
before for bad conduct, fired one of the out-buildings—
applying the torch in such a manner as to secure the
fulfillment of her purpose. The children were all above
stairs, my father and mother below, when the thrilling
cry was heard. They both rushed up-stairs, but were
lost in the dense smoke before they could reach our
sleeping apartment. Lurid flames, playing against the
windows, awakened me, and my terrific screams led them
at last to the spot, where they found us scrambling about
on the floor. I had pulled my little sisters out of bed,
and was seeking my own clothes. At last I succeeded
in getting on my dress wrong-side-outwards; but neither
shoes nor stockings could be found, nor any garments for

my little charge—both of whom, however, I thoughtfully covered with a blanket. Just at this moment my mother rushed towards us, took the two in her arms, and I followed, dragging another after me. How we got down-stairs I never knew. My next recollection was, standing on the cold pavement with my bare feet, among the rest of the family, who had all escaped.

By this time friends had gathered around us, and we were hurried over the frozen ground, and soon sheltered under a friendly roof about a square from our own. My father, as soon as he knew we were all safe, turned his attention to the stable, where there were several fine horses fastened in the stalls. There he was near losing his life in attempting to rescue, for the second time, a favorite horse, that had rushed again into the flames. He escaped, however, and the horse too; but he was so blackened by the smoke and scorched by the flame as almost to render his identity doubtful to those around him. His escape made us so thankful that we hardly thought of mourning over the loss of property. Much of the furniture was destroyed by the recklessness of those who tried to save it. Glass, china, and mirrors were indiscriminately pitched out of the window, and many things broken to pieces, as if the only care was to keep them out of the fire.

One thing connected with this fire would seem, in these days of steam power, very slow. Two lines were formed reaching to the river, from whence the water was brought, the weather being so cold that no water could be obtained from the pumps. Through one line the empty buckets were passed down, and returned through the other full of water. Police officers strode up and down the streets, compelling every looker-on to fall into the ranks. The house burned down; and the fact is, under the system pursued, I never knew one saved.

When the whole was over my father looked as calm as if nothing unusual had happened. The fiery ordeal had brought no shadow to his brow, because not one of his precious family was lost. "I have," said he, as he placed his hand upon his waistcoat pocket, "but one dollar and a half in cash; but I am rich in the possession of all my loved ones."

Energy, industry, and economy, with the blessing of God, soon restored to us the necessaries and comforts of life.

Happy in spite of external circumstances, my naturally buoyant disposition "gave care to the winds." My elastic temperament rebounded after the most intense pressure. I could not realize that there was any thing but beauty in the present and pleasure in the future.

My education was continued in Georgetown under the care of two excellent teachers, Mr. and Mrs. Simpson. A considerable portion of my time was devoted to music, drawing, and French, with various kinds of embroidery. The girls in this school wrought the most elaborate samplers with a variety of stitches, and bordered them with pinks, roses, and morning-glories, and sometimes, when the canvas was large enough, with the name and age of every member of the family. We did not buy French-worked collars then, but embroidered them for ourselves, and some of them were exquisite specimens of the finest needle-work; and the skirts of our white muslin dresses were wrought, frequently, half a yard in depth.

One interesting incident then, and pleasant to remember now, occurs to me. I was standing with a group of girls near a deep-toned piano, listening to some fine airs played by Mr. Simpson, when Miss Bowie, one of the grown pupils, stepped in with the "Star-spangled Banner" set to music. This was a charming advent to us, as we had heard of the piece, but had not before seen it. Every body's patriotism was at full tide then, as it was soon after the bombardment of Fort M'Henry and our successful repulse of the British at Baltimore. Mr. Simpson was an enthusiast in both music and patriotism; and the chords vibrated under his touch, sending forth peals of harmony that made the welkin ring. He seemed inspired to the very ends of his fingers. A dozen girls soon struck in with their choral voices, making the whole house resound with the music. A crowd of little boys collected around the front door and at the window, and a scene presented itself such as one might have expected among the French with their "Marseillaise."

How true it is that the fire of patriotism is often stirred into a flame, even from the ashes of despondency, by national airs! The "Star-spangled Banner" should be a consecrated song to every American heart, connected as it is with an event so thrilling in character—so marked among the honorable achievements of this nation, when the States of the Union stood up before the world, "distinct like the billow, but one like the sea"—when that bold, enterprising spirit that gave us a rank among the nations of the earth was abroad throughout the whole land. The powerful effect produced by this soul-stirring song was not owing to any particular merit in the composition, but to the recollection of something noble in the character of a young and heroic nation successfully struggling against the invasion of a mighty people for life, freedom, and domestic happiness.

The influence of association is strongly felt in giving

strength to patriotism, in the favorite national war-songs
of every country. Witness the success of Tyrtæus,
whom the Athenians, in derision, sent at the command
of the Oracle to Sparta during the second Messenian
war. He was a poor schoolmaster, of no reputation,
short, lame, and blind of one eye; but he possessed a
manly and elevated soul, and so inspired the Spartans by
his thrilling martial strains, that the Messenians were
reduced to subjection. For these services the Spartans
treated him with great respect, and granted him the
rights of citizenship. The war poems of Tyrtæus were
ever after held in great repute by the Ancients, who
placed him by the side of Homer as a heroic poet.

It was during my residence in Georgetown that the
fiercest conflicts of the war of 1812 occurred. An incident connected with this war impressed me deeply, and
gave me a terrific idea of mobs. Every well read person
is familiar with the history of the bloody drama enacted
in Baltimore, when the brave General Lingan was killed
by an infuriated mob, though he begged so piteously
that his life might be spared for the sake of his wife and
children. He besought them to remember how man-
fully he had fought for his country in the "old war;"
but his voice was scarcely heard amid the roar of those
wild beasts, who almost tore him to pieces. General
Lee (Light Horse Harry) and several other Revolutionary
patriots were so injured by the same mob that they died
soon after. They were opposed to the war.

Mrs. Lingan, with her family, was brought immediately by sympathizing friends to Georgetown. Never
shall I forget the appearance of that mourning widow.
Her tall, dignified form enveloped in sable garments; her
two daughters accompanying her, reminded me of Naomi

returning sorrowfully to her own people, to hide her bowed head and stricken heart among friends, who vied in kindness to the untimely bereaved.

This event, like many others, is rendered deeply interesting by a glimpse into the mysterious long time ago. The circumstances attending the Baltimore mob having been so lightly touched upon by historians, it will, doubtless, be interesting to my readers to have a more particular account of the matter from one who was living so near the scene of action. War was declared on the 18th of June, 1812. The immediate effect of this measure was a violent exasperation of parties. The friends of the Government applauded the act as spirited and patriotic—the opposition condemned it as unnecessary, unjustifiable, and impolitic. In the New England States, particularly, where the "Revolutionary War" found ardent and active supporters, a decided opposition was manifested. They conceded that abundant provocation had been given, but denied the expediency, as the nation was not sufficiently prepared for the conflict. But in many of our large cities the news was received with extravagant demonstrations of joy. In Baltimore, especially, the popular voice was strongly in favor of it, and the first announcement created the wildest excitement. Two great parties convulsed the country at that time. They were so evenly balanced that it was difficult to determine the preponderant element. The Democrats were powerful, but the Federalists were determined. Distinguished congressmen pleaded in favor of the war; and among them stood conspicuous the talented young Kentuckian, Henry Clay, pledging, to the utmost of its ability, the support of his own State to the President. Orators harangued the people, and their burning eloquence increased the fervor of their shouts for "Free Trade and Sailor's Rights." Oh, these were thrilling times! To warm the life blood and fan the fires of patriotism was the broad road to distinction. The Democrats were denounced as reckless demagogues by the opposition, who dreaded the rekindling of the fires of the Revolution, which had just been extinguished by the blood of multiplied thousands; but there was no staying the surging waves of the popular voice. The Democratic Republicans triumphed, and rejoiced in their signal success. Many noble patriots of unimpeachable integrity, and brave officers who had served their country well and faithfully, were conscientious Federalists. One of these was Alexander Hanson, who edited a paper in Baltimore called the *Federal Republican.* He ventured to indulge in some severe strictures on the conduct of the Government. The consequence was, his printing-office was destroyed by the populace, and he obliged to fly the city. Hanson was a bold man, and determined not to be put down; he therefore returned to Baltimore with a party of friends who had volunteered to aid him in forcibly defending his house. General Henry Lee, who happened to be in the city when the riots commenced, was a personal friend of the editor, and, with characteristic impetuosity, offered his services against the mob. They prepared for an attack by arming themselves and barricading the house. The enraged mob attacked the building with great fury, and even brought a cannon to bear in the assault. The besieged defended themselves coolly and successfully. The result was that two of the assailants were killed and a number wounded, which so exasperated the crowd that but for the arrival of the city military Hanson and his friends would, in all probability, have been torn to pieces. The magistrates came forward and interceded between the two parties—at first both were firm, but finally Hanson and his friends gave themselves up to the authorities, and were lodged in jail for safety. There was a temporary but a deceitful calm; the mob was not appeased, they thirsted for blood. During the night, while the "Argus" of the law slept, vainly supposing that a few timid guards would secure the safety of the prisoners, the storm gathered strength, and anon there came a distinct murmur on the night breeze. It soon increased to an audible sound, and "down with the traitors" was heard on every side. Frequent additions had swelled the numbers of the rioters, and they were heard sweeping through the streets of the city onward and still onward—no earthly power could check their mad career. They had been systematically organized by their leaders, and uniformed by having their coats turned wrong side out. The jail was broken open, and with waving torches and flashing weapons they sought their victims with fierce cries and bitter denunciations from cell to cell. A few of the unfortunate men broke through the crowd and escaped; the others were beaten and thrown down the steps of the prison into the street. The wounded would probably have all been killed had it not been for a humane physician who, turning his own coat wrong side out, mingled with the mob, and begged the bodies of those apparently dead for dissection. Mr. Hanson, upon whom every species of brutality had been practiced, lay helpless and as if dead upon the stone pavement. One ruffian waved a torchlight before his eyes and pierced his finger through and through with a penknife; yet by the mighty power of his will, the still conscious man showed no signs

of life.   Just at this period came the good Samaritan to
his rescue; who, positively asserting that he was dead,
dragged him aside, gave him a drink of brandy from a
flask in his pocket, and when sufficiently revived helped
him to turn his coat, and escaped with him.   It is a wonderful fact, and a decided proof of the indomitable obstinacy resulting from a conviction of duty that Mr. Hanson, after being driven from Baltimore by this fearful
tragedy, established his printing-press in Georgetown,
District of Columbia, and continued to publish his paper
during the whole war.

The revolution of '76 was a contest of doctrine.   It
resulted in the triumph of a principle—the sovereignty of
the people.   The permanence of this triumph was an
unworked problem, until the violent concussion of 1812
shook the newly-formed Government to its very center.
This shock only seemed to settle its foundation stones
more deeply and firmly, and taught the "sea-girt isle"
that we were not unworthy our noble ancestors, who
proudly felt themselves a part of

> "That happy race of men, that little world,
> That precious gem set in a silver sea."

Chapter V.

THE Winter of 1813 was protracted, and unusually severe. Terrible suffering resulted from impeded circulation in trade and commerce, and our newly-established Government, though firm, energetic, and untiring in its efforts to relieve the people, was yet too limited in its resources to do much more than provide for the army. From eighteen to twenty dollars was the price per cord for firewood. Coal was scarcely known as fuel in private families.

The country round about Washington and in the immediate vicinity of Georgetown was sterile to a proverb, and the market had been supplied from the more fertile counties in Virginia and Maryland; but now the river was frozen, and the roads almost impassable. Thus all classes suffered—but the poor especially. Pinched faces and tattered garments met the eye at every corner of the streets; and many a poor little half frozen child crept into our kitchen daily, begging for cold victuals and the privilege of getting one good warming during the twenty-four hours by the glow of a hospitable fire. How deeply are those sad scenes engraven on my ·memory, and it is not an exaggeration to say that these painful impressions and others connected with the horrors of that war have followed me through life; and I shudder, even now, as I think of them. For three years every breeze bore upon its wings the wail of the widow and the orphan, and the blood of thousands marked the footsteps of invasion; burning cities lighted armies to indiscriminate plunder, and told of the wide-spread desolation on the Atlantic shores.

My youngest brother, and the youngest child of my parents, was called William Henry Harrison, and lived to prove himself worthy the heroic name he bore. To this merry-hearted, laughter-loving brother we were all much attached, and amply did he repay our love and devotion. My mother's heart was bound up in the child; and when after the lapse of many years she became a widow, he was still more the idol of her affections. He finally went to Texas, and did good service in helping that State throw off the Mexican yoke. When its independence was fully established, being fond of adventure and reckless of his own life, he started again in pursuit of further excitement, and after leading for some years a roving life, suffering from exposure and sickness and reverse of fortune, he lost his life in attempting to swim across the River Brazos. My mother had passed away to her home in heaven before the news of his death reached us. It was well—she was saved one of the most sorrowful pangs a mother's heart can feel.

My oldest brother, Quin, who had the advantage of superior teachers, was well and thoroughly educated, and was said to be a classical scholar of no mean atainments. To him I was fondly attached—the playfellow of my early years, the friend and companion of my girlhood. We read together the legends of olden times, and lived in an enchanted world, rife with that pure, unmingled fiction which left no injury behind, but rather induced a love of reading. We laughed at the merry ride of "John Gilpin," and felt the strongest sympathy for the "Babes in the Wood," over whose fate we shed many tears; and we formed an attachment for the robin red-breast that so kindly covered the dead babies with leaves. O, how we reveled in a bright new story-book, which we both preferred to any other gift! We had a dear little corner in my mother's room, which, by the by, was always one of the largest on the ground floor—for "we were many," and she would have her children much about her; and when we were tired of reading we walked together through the flower-gardens, and over the green hills called Georgetown Heights. Beautiful, almost sublime, in every season, were these crowning glories of the pretty little city. There were goodly green meadows, spangled with starry eyes, making the loveliest play-grounds and the sweetest trysting-spots for the school-children.

It was a sad parting when my brother, young in years, entered the regular army. He was eighteen when a lieutenancy was offered him in the Twelfth Regiment, which was accepted, much to the regret of the whole family, and to my mother a life-long sorrow. He was her firstborn and the darling of her heart, and she had fondly hoped to see him established as a useful citizen in private life. His choice of the army left a shadow upon our household which was never entirely dissipated; for though he had no battles to fight, having commenced his career after the war closed, yet with all his tender sympathies, and warm, gushing affections for home, we know he could not be happy forever separated from his family. He was generous, ardent, and brave; soon formed many friendships, and rose rapidly to offices of honor and profit; but in less than three short years he died far away from home and friends, in Florida, where his regiment was stationed.

Many touching incidents of generous self-denial and

brotherly kindness, manifested to the soldiers under his command, are written in legible characters upon my heart and memory. Of all duties, the hardest is to forget a great sorrow. The very effort to forget teaches us to remember. It was as the friend and companion of this brother on one of his short visits home, in 1817, that I first saw General Sam. Houston. He was an officer in the same regiment—a young man of fine appearance, tall, erect, and well-proportioned, with agreeable manners. I remember him well, because my brother was much attached to him. Thirty-five years afterwards I met him in Lexington, attending the funeral obsequies of Henry Clay. Time had dealt lightly with him; he had not lost his soldierly bearing, and seemed yet in the vigor of manhood, though his hair and beard were frosted by the passing years.

In connection with General Houston I am reminded of Colonel Thornton Posey, who was intimately associated with my brother during his last visit to the home circle in Washington. This dear brother, not twenty years old, held the honorable position of first lieutenant in Colonel Posey's regiment. His youth and inexperience rendered him liable to many temptations "on the tented field," from which he was shielded by his noble colonel. The result was a sincere friendship, which, from its delicacy and beauty, its depth of devotion and unfailing tenderness, might be said to be like that of David and Jonathan. The effect upon each was like the brightening and softening radiance with which the pencil of Nature paints the West at sunset.

Colonel Posey had nobly distinguished himself in the war of 1812, and was retained in the peace establishment as a highly esteemed and trustworthy officer.

I first met him at a social party given at our own house to the officers of his regiment. He was the honored guest of the evening, and of course received much attention from the family. His appearance was prepossessing. A lofty forehead, finely cut features, a large, sensible mouth, flexible and expressive, but indicative of strong resolution, marked his individuality. His proud, pale face and dignified bearing fixed the attention of every observer. When drawn into conversation his noble brow seemed to expand, and thought sat visibly upon it, while a sweet, melancholy smile lit up his whole countenance, like that which gleams on the face of Nature when, after a stormy day, the sun bursts forth for a moment and then buries itself in the darkness of night. His conversation displayed an acute and cultivated intellect, and his engaging manners and delicate politeness as well fitted him for the courtly drawing-room as his soldierly bearing and bravery for the camp and battle-field. The feeling of interest awakened then deepened as our acquaintance ripened, and our admiration matured into esteem and respect. On the evening referred to, after he had passed through the usual polite observances of the occasion, he withdrew from the gay crowd promenading through the rooms, and remained in a recess apart, apparently occupied with his own deep thoughts, like one standing on the misty border-land which lies between this life and the world of shadows.

The sad circumstance that had cast a shadow on his pathway, and left an incurable wound in his heart, was explained to us afterwards, brightening his character in our estimation, and securing increased sympathy with him. He had been compelled in self-defense to take the life of a subordinate officer, who, having frequently

threatened and constantly sought an opportunity to kill
him, had at last assailed him when alone, and under circumstances which left him no alternative but to take his
life.   He was tried, and honorably acquitted—the world
justifying the act.   But, exquisitely organized as he was,
every pulse of his heart throbbing with benevolence, and
perhaps too sensitive and conscientious, he was over-
powered with the reflection of having destroyed a human
life, and his soul was filled with horror at the necessity
which forced him to the deed.   His admirable powers of
intellect and greatness of soul had elevated him among
his fellow-men, and on the battle-field he had won a name
above all hereditary titles—the bravest among the brave.
But this one sad event drew a dark cloud over all his
present and future.

Unfitted by his genius for the ordinary routine of
camp life in the peace establishment, he embraced the
first opportunity to battle again in the cause of freedom.
He joined General M'Gregor in an expedition against
Amelia Island, in South America.   His generous and
gallant soul would gladly have been instrumental in raising the banners of liberty over an enslaved land; but
when he found that a bold military expedition was about
to degenerate into a privateering enterprise, he threw up
his commission, and returned to the United States, where
he died of bilious fever, at Wilmington, North Carolina.
He went to his grave honored and lamented, and deserves
to be remembered by his country as long as the voice of
Liberty is heard in the land.

Oh, the days that are no more!

> " Each fainter trace that memory holds
>   So fondly of departed years,
>   In one broad glance the soul beholds,
>   And all that was at once appears."

Incidents fraught with cherished recollections, the rising forms of those I loved and admired in the irrecoverable long-ago, an unexpected meeting with a dear friend, the remembrance of a look even, come sometimes to me with a peculiar power, fresh as if it were but yesterday.

The treasures of memory are so much saved from the wreck of life, and once possessed they are ours forever. That which has happened becomes a part of our lives, and though for the time forgotten or overlooked, it yet rests there, in the storehouse of the mind, ready when the right chord is touched to start forth, mellowed, perhaps, though not weakened, by the lapse of time. Whatever may be our future, the memory of life's past joys is full of unspeakable comforts, and present griefs have often an added pang from such remembrances.

"Sorrow's crown of sorrow is remembering happier things."

Washington fifty years ago was a delightful retreat, full of bewildering loveliness. I loved to ramble over the grounds surrounding the magnificent old capitol and revel in its beauties—the beauty of lovely skies, luxuriant trees, rich herbage, and myriads of bright flowers. The hall windows of the quaint old building commanded an enchanting view of hill and plain, and at the end of an avenue of poplars a mile long could be seen the simple, noble mansion designed for the President of the United States—a fitting habitation for the executive of this great republic. In the distance, her feet laved in the gleaming waters of the Potomac, was the little city of Georgetown, her green hills crowned with groups of noble trees, some of them of ancient date, looking like the natural guardians of the charming country-seats scattered in the vicinity.

The Summer following the events just related was spent

by our family in sweet seclusion, which united a loving household more closely together. It was the last I ever spent here, and it is rife with some of the sweetest recollections and tenderest associations of this early home of my heart. The crowd of strangers, office-seekers, and resident ministers, with their gay retinues, had gone. After the adjournment of Congress the city was exceedingly dull to these pleasure-seekers. A strange atmosphere of repose pervaded the place. There was opportunity to enjoy life's leisure in its fullest sense.

My father had gone to the far West on business, and my two older brothers being away, I was left to the constant companionship of my mother, which I had been deprived of by my long absence at school. Even at this remote period my heart thrills at the recollection of this time—the quiet readings, the solemn Scripture teachings, which fell like the dews of heaven into my young heart, and I acknowledge with tearful thankfulness the sweet privilege then enjoyed.

The taking of Washington City in 1814 was marked by many interesting circumstances and unwritten incidents, affecting to the heart and worth remembering. August 24, 1814, was one of the sultriest of Summer days. The British, after a rapid march across the country, reached Bladensburg, eight miles from Washington, in the hottest part of the afternoon. A small number of hastily collected troops were prepared to meet the foe; yet, so exhausted were the way-worn British soldiers, that even these, few as they were, would have been sufficient to keep them out of Washington had there been any order or discipline. As it was, they were driven, fighting as they retreated, in great confusion to the capital. Their pursuers, however, were held at bay, for a short time, by the gallant General Winder, who, not being supported, was compelled to yield to the enemy, whose numbers more than quadrupled his own. The British commanders, flushed with success, drove the panic-stricken Americans before them, and entered the city amid the tumult and glitter of an army, with flying colors and beating drums. Dreading the mighty desolation which threatened them, the President and the Cabinet, with the principal citizens, fled precipitately through Georgetown and across the Potomac. Nothing was seen but people anxious to escape the dreaded catastrophe. Carriages, wagons, carts, vehicles of every description, crowded with women and children; servants hurrying in every direction, carrying away what goods and chattels they were able to bear; amid the wildest confusion of men on horseback and exhausted stragglers from the battle-field, made up a moving panorama for miles. It was a melancholy sight to behold, some wringing their hands and wailing, as if they were leaving behind all that made life valuable, and turning again and again to take a last glimpse of home; while others bitterly denounced their own selfish flight, forsaking friends who absolutely refused to leave.

The crowd swept on, wave after wave; but the most melancholy object among them was the President of the United States, whose delicate frame and feeble health might have rendered him an object of compassion, had he been an isolated man. Like poor David, when he fled from Jerusalem before his rebellious son, there were none to cry "God bless him." Yet Mr. Madison was worthy, for he had proved himself a patriot and an eminent statesman. The blame of this awful reverse rested upon the Secretary of War, whose name has been handed down to posterity shrouded in darkness. He might have prevented a deed equally disgraceful to England and to this country. He was either a traitor or totally unfit for his responsible office.

My father and mother tarried at home during this awful visitation, but all the rest of the family had been sent into the country some days previous. Every farmhouse was filled with supernumerary tenants, while many of the fugitives were sheltered in tents or haunted the skirts of the woods, eagerly detaining every passer-by with inquiries after the news. I was on a visit near Martinsburg, Virginia, enduring, for two weeks, the misery of the most exaggerated reports.

Mrs. Madison distinguished herself during these troubles by her admirable firmness and superior womanly tact. Nature had lavished upon her more of the materials of happiness and greatness than are usually found in women who sway the fashionable world. She sustained herself nobly, and from her own quiet elevation of character watched calmly the disastrous rout, and sank not, for one moment, into despondency. Mr. Madison might have been overborne by the triumph of his enemies, had *she* not by her own self-possession inspired him with an energy that enabled him to rise superior to his misfortunes. I do not believe the executive office has ever been filled by a worthier man or a better statesman since the days of Washington than James Madison; nor was there ever a presiding genius in the White House more beloved, admired, and respected than his elegant and graceful wife.

A few of the citizens of Washington remained in their own homes with a view of saving their property if possible. I heard a lady by the name of Coolidge relate an adventure, which I think worth recording. She had sent her whole family into the country and remained alone in her house, which was a large and handsome building at the entrance of Pennsylvania Avenue, and in the immediate vicinity of the President's mansion. She stood on her front door-step while the retreating army passed through with the redcoats close at their heels. She had prepared a tub of cool water, from which she gave a cup to each flying American soldier, and occasionally to a poor redcoat, whose exhaustion from fatigue and heat was pitiful to behold. About dark several British officers, apparently of high rank, halted before her door and asked for refreshments—demanding, imperatively, that a hot supper should be immediately prepared for them. She declined upon the plea that he had nothing in the house nor in the larder. They insisted, until at last she positively refused, adding, that if she had any thing to give it should be to her own people. Upon this a tall man, of majestic carriage and splendidly mounted, who, she afterwards learned, was General Ross, assured her that, by attending to their request, she would not only save her own house from being plundered or burnt, but those of her neighbors, if they would aid her in supplying what she could not furnish; besides which, she should be handsomely paid.

Supper was prepared, and she was invited to preside. The conversation was not only agreeable, but cheerful, almost to merriment among the guests. Before the meal was finished, however, General Ross turned suddenly to Mrs. Coolidge, and asked what was the opinion of the Americans in reference to Admiral Cockburn. The lady, quite at her ease through the politeness of the officers, replied, "What! the pirate Cockburn? Why, they regard him as a mere chicken stealer—a robber of hen

roosts. He has shown such an expertness in these feats
as would throw all the tricks of schoolboys and college
rogues in the shade. He certainly is a master forager,
and that is all he is fit for." She had scarce finished the
sentence when an officer on her right, striking the table
with his clenched fist, and springing to his feet, stepped
up to General Ross and whispered something in his ear;
upon which the General instantly arose, and introduced,
with the utmost formality, "Admiral Cockburn, of the
British Navy." Mrs. Coolidge was near fainting, expecting instant death for her temerity; but General Ross
quieted her fears, and requested the indignant Admiral
to withdraw his hand from the hilt of his sword, which,
in his anger, he had firmly grasped, saying, "We do not
war with ladies." The doughty Admiral, forgetting all
etiquette and gentility, swore in the frenzied excitement
of passion that he would finish his supper by the light
of the President's burning house; upon which he rushed
out with great precipitancy, and was soon seen striding
onward, torch in hand, to carry his threat into execution;
and he was actually the prime mover in the vandalism
that followed. It is said that he even stepped into the
dining-room, while the building was on fire, and drank a
glass of wine to the health of Mrs. Madison, whom he
familiarly styled "Queen Dolly."

General Ross was soon after killed at the battle of
Baltimore, and every body regretted that it had not been
Cockburn; the former possessing all the noble and generous qualities of a gentleman and a soldier, the latter
one of the meanest and most contemptible of mankind,
who, had he been reared in heathen Rome, might have
been a Nero.

The cannon foundry near Georgetown, which had

done so good service during the war, the British were
bent on destroying before they left the district. It belonged to a Mr. Foxall, a Wesleyan Methodist of the old
stamp. This excellent man had been living in Georgetown ever since the close of the Revolution; and was as
firm a patriot as though native born. A squad of soldiers was on the line of march toward the foundry
while the public buildings were burning. They had
reached the bridge thrown over the little creek which
separates Washington from Georgetown, when they were
called to a sudden halt by a tremendous explosion. Soon
after a courier came dashing up at full speed, warning
them not to cross the bridge; that the explosion just
heard was from Greenleaf's Point, a fort on the opposite
side of the Potomac from Washington, recently vacated
by the Americans. One hundred and fifty British soldiers had been blown up, their mangled remains flying
in every direction. The fact was, several barrels of powder had been thrown into a dry well by the garrison
before leaving, to keep it from falling into the hands of
the enemy. The detachment sent over to destroy the
fort were dying of thirst, and one of the men threw
a torch into the well to ascertain if it contained any
water—hence the catastrophe. The troops marching to
destroy the foundry were arrested in their course, for,
not knowing the real cause of the explosion, it was supposed there might be torpedoes placed under the bridge
for their destruction also; instead of proceeding, therefore, to their destined work, they returned to the city in
double quick time.

The alarm spread rapidly among the invaders, and
their whole army was immediately withdrawn, afraid
even to tarry during the night, although the poor,

exhausted soldiers were dropping by the way from fatigue and hunger.

Mr. Foxall's foundry was saved, and the good old veteran of the cross, true to his promise in prayer to God for the safety of his property and the lives of his workmen, forthwith built a church in Washington City, which is yet a standing monument of his faithfulness. This church is called the "Foundry," in commemoration of the event just related. If I mistake not, this was the first Methodist church erected in Washington. It was completely finished and furnished, even to the Bible and hymn-book, by Mr. Foxall alone:

> "A leaf of gold,
> Glowing in the warm book of gratitude."

Long after the close of the war, this pious old Wesleyan and his prim-looking wife—they had no children—might be seen walking side by side to this goodly church, where an excellent congregation still continues to worship.

On the night that witnessed the burning of the public buildings a fearful hurricane raged for some time with intense fury; roofs were blown off; shingles flew in every direction, like paper; chimneys fell, cottages were blown over, and there is no telling when the conflagration would have ended, had it not been for the drenching rain that followed. A few days after, some British ships visited Alexandria, and extorted an enormous ransom from the town, whence all our troops had been withdrawn. The whole surrounding country lay as much at their mercy as if entirely without inhabitants. For a few hours the red-coats paraded through the town, appropriating to themselves whatever they liked, notwithstanding the previous compact. This was not war, but devastation.

An incident occurred during this time illustrating the

courage and patriotism of a woman who kept a variety shop. A british officer, entering her store, asked:

"Have you a husband or sons? If so, where are they?"

"I have a husband and two sons, who are trying to defend their country at the risk of their lives; and I hope you may meet them yet."

"Indeed! and you have here an instrument of war?" striking a drum which lay on the counter.

"And here is another," she replied, taking a loaded pistol from a shelf; "and if you dare take another article in this shop you shall receive its contents."

Her hand was on the trigger. The officer involuntarily stepped back, saying:

"Put aside your weapon, madam. If your men had manifested as much firmness you might have been spared the devastation we have accomplished in your country."

It is well known that the battle of New Orleans was fought after peace was ratified by our Commissioners at Ghent, the news of which did not reach the United States until after the eighth of January. The universal joy felt throughout the whole country was scarcely less than that realized at the close of the Revolution.

General Jackson and his wife made their advent at Washington soon after, and created quite a sensation among the *elite* of that day. Mrs. Jackson, though uneducated, was an amiable Christian woman; and, while laughed at for her grammatical blunders, made herself loved for her kindness, and admired for her unsophisticated manners. The General, who even then bore the soubriquet of "Old Hickory," was cordially acknowledged as a noble, high-hearted man.

I had the pleasure of witnessing a theatrical entertainment, prepared in honor of these distinguished guests of the nation. Their entrance into the theater was announced by tremendous cheering. The General was tall, thin, and weather-beaten; but there was a Cassius-like firmness on his lip, and his brow was marked with the lines of thought and care. He was rather annoyed at being the observed of all observers, and oppressed by the attention that was paid him; while Mrs. Jackson, "fair, fat, and forty," with a good motherly look, seemed amused, and gazed with intense gratification at the display made in honor of him in whom her soul was centered. A flattering address by the marshal of the day covered the modest General with confusion, but elicited a few words of acknowledgment, which charmed by their unaffected simplicity.

Banners, transparencies, etc., passed in rapid procession across the stage, interluded with occasional cheering for the hero of New Orleans. The evening's entertainment concluded at last; and the idol upon whose altar all this incense was poured seemed as much delighted at escaping the adulation by which he was surrounded as a tired school-boy from a lengthened exhibition, and as if he would have said: "I am weary of this paradeful nonsense. I'd rather stand a siege, storm a battery, or charge a whole army, than encounter this again."

Chapter VI.

In 1815 I was placed under the charge of an English lady of deep piety and superior education. Her institution was in full view of the President's house—only a few squares from it. There were no regular streets at this time in this city of magnificent distances except Pennsylvania Avenue. They were laid out, it is true, but not built up. The school-house stood on a slight eminence near the Potomac, commanding a fine view of this noble river for a considerable distance. Unconfined by brick houses, we had a glorious breathing space, over which swept the sweet morning zephyrs, whispering through the foliage of magnificent trees; and the evening breeze from the Potomac fanned our glowing cheeks as we raced over the lawn, stretching almost to the water's edge, or sat on the doorstep watching the soft rosy clouds at day's decline.

Miss Taylor, our preceptress, was a dignified woman, eminently fitted for the charge of young girls; but she had a younger sister, who at times assumed an authority over us which caused much dissatisfaction. Miss Charlotte Taylor was loved and implicitly obeyed; Miss Julia, the sister, was feared, disliked, and often disobeyed, with a hearty good will.

Miss Taylor's father was an Englishman; his first wife died in England, leaving an only child, a daughter, who inherited a small property from her mother; and, being blessed with kind and wealthy relatives on the mother's side, the father thought it not amiss to leave her with them, and come over to America to improve his own fortune.

Here he married, and after some years was left a widower with three children—a daughter and two sons. A few more years, and the father died, leaving the children in a state of destitute orphanage. And now the excellent Miss Charlotte felt it a duty to forsake a luxurious English home, made pleasant by the dearest of relatives, and come over to America, to take charge of the three children, whom she loved and cared for as an elder sister should.

The two boys entered the United States service—one the navy, the other the army. Miss Charlotte and her sister came to Washington, at the instance of friends, to open a school, which was for some years the very best in the place, the pupils being instructed carefully in all the requisites of a liberal education. Miss Charlotte's thorough attainments in literature, her accomplishments, combined with elegant manners and superior tact in communicating knowledge, rendered her a model teacher.

I can not contemplate the devotion of this heroic woman to her brothers and sister without exclaiming, "A noble-hearted, high-souled action and unwavering purpose lead to righteousness." Such, in woman, far exceeds the proudest achievements of man. Weakness and shrinking delicacy, so characteristic of the sex, are not the groundwork of heroic feminine action. Man has shrunk and paled in the hour of peril, and drawn back from anticipated danger, when woman has borne the burden without a murmur and with silent resignation. Thus the weak have triumphed over the strong. Many an unwritten life, lustrous with the grandeur of woman's noble deeds, will be found among the records of heaven. Heroism may exist in all its strength in the most delicate constitution, and it attains its greatest power and glory in large and glowing hearts. Such a woman was Miss Taylor. She endured privations, labored day and night, made sacrifices of an extraordinary nature, and finally died,— most probably a martyr to her sisterly devotion.

The younger sister was one of the most unlovely of women. Fretful, proud, and impatient, with a temper at variance with every kindly feeling, and a mind perverted by vanity and selfishness. Fostered by the overweening indulgence of injudicious parents in early life, she was the torment of all around her, especially of her sister, whose good sense and amiability taught her that it was best to submit where she could not correct, and to leave open the safety-valve of passion, that there might not be an explosion.

Some of the most pleasant reminiscences of this school are connected with my excellent and lovely young friend, Eliza Lane, three years my junior, and yet my intimate companion. And now, as my thoughts slowly unravel themselves from that class of memories in which she is involved, I see her beautiful head appearing like a glorious vision, covered with a profusion of auburn hair parted in rippling waves from a clear and lofty forehead. I look into deep and truthful eyes, and upon her fair face, warmed with the flushes of a tender heart, and my mind wanders to those joyous, happy days when Time flew so rapidly that his glittering pinions reflected the golden flood of morning, the azure of noon, and the glory of sunset, seemingly, without an interval.

Indelibly impressed upon my mind are our rambles along the banks of the river, and our pleasant trysting-spots near a little rivulet, where violets grew in abundance under the shade of some dwarf magnolias, the lotus fragrance of whose milk white blossoms embalmed our bouquets, reminding us of those delicious climes we so loved to read and talk about. By the kindness of Miss Taylor, Eliza was permitted to spend many of her Saturday afternoons and half holidays with me in my own home, where she was very much loved. My father and mother took great delight in my "young David." She was a ray of sunshine wherever she went.

She returned to her father's, in Pennsylvania, before I left Washington: and from that time until 1824 I heard nothing of her. What was my astonishment and delight to find her in Shelbyville; thus strangely did we float together in life after a separation of years. She was permanently settled here in the midst of a widely extended circle of relatives and friends, and here again we renewed our loving and congenial intercourse.

But to resume my narrative. We were permitted, while at school, to enter occasionally into society, always under suitable protection; not as young ladies, but schoolgirls, to profit by what we saw and heard. My first and only public ball was the inauguration *fete* of President Monroe. Eliza and I, under the escort of my father, and with my aunt for a *chaperone*, were present at this august assembly. The impression made was that of an ostentatious display of wealth and splendor, little in accordance with the republican simplicity which should constitute the dignity of a nation so utterly rejecting high sounding titles and oriental magnificence. The barbaric splendor of gold and jewels, glittering and dazzling through this whole exhibition, made us almost imagine that we had been rubbing Aladdin's lamp. Visions of beauty flitted before our eyes, and fascinated our young hearts; clouds of lace and India muslin, in whose folds glittered the diamond and the ruby, danced up and down through this mysterious dream-land.

Mrs. Madison was there, in the meridian of life. She had been brought up a Quakeress, and never lost the simplicity of her early tastes, though she improved the style of her dress by chaste and appropriate ornaments. She wore that night a black velvet robe with an extensive train, a handsome turban of light material, with a snowy plume that rested on her shoulder. A delicate tiara of pearls adorned her brow, which, with earrings and bracelets, completed her costume. Her almost tiny husband appeared in a suit of plain black. He was grave and dignified, and was not the least of the evening's attractions.

The Spanish Minister, at that time, was remarkable as being the representative of the most contemptible Government of Europe. He was covered with stars and garters, gold lace and diamonds, looking for all the world, with his withered face, like a mummy done up in gold. His two daughters, fairer than Spanish girls usually are, with their lustrous black eyes and raven tresses, were real beauties. One of them, the Marchioness de Heredia, was married by proxy in Philadelphia, her husband being in Spain at the time. The father hastened the marriage that the Marquis, his son-in-law, might help bear the expenses of their establishment in Washington.

I was particularly impressed with the simplicity that marked the toilet of the young girls of the European aristocracy. Here England, France, Spain, Portugal,

Russia, and, indeed, every important country of Europe was represented. The graceful girl, with her sunny curls and face radiant with the reflections of an innocent heart; the noble and the gifted of early manhood, with the middle-aged and the old, were here mingled in one indiscriminate, republican mass. It was a gorgeous ball-room; lights flashed from brilliant chandeliers; silks rustled, plumes waved, and jewelled embroideries shone upon Genoa velvets. Courtly congratulations fell from every lip; not only to the President, whose star was in the ascendant, but to the one who was quietly retiring to private life, after having honorably fulfilled his mission as the executive of a great nation for eight years; and that, too, during one of the stormiest periods of this great republic. Wit sparkled, and the laughter of merry voices rang through the saloons, while dancing feet kept time to the tones of magic music; and yet I learned there one serious lesson, that sank deep into my heart—a glittering exterior is not always an exponent of nobility and refinement.

A lady was pointed out to me, dressed in crimson velvet embroidered in seed pearls half a yard in depth; a diamond necklace glittered on her painted throat; gems of priceless value adorned her fat fingers, and costly jewels encircled her wrists. "See," said one; "that woman wears the wealth of a kingdom about her uncomely form; she is the second wife of a Swedish nobleman, who married the rich widow of a soap-boiler, to mend his broken fortunes." His aristocratic daughters, at the other end of the room, dressed in pure white, wearing no costly ornaments, were models of grace and elegance. These Swedish maidens, their queenly heads adorned with a profusion of blonde curls, with eyes of the deepest blue sparkling with vivacity and intelligence, were beautiful; and all eyes followed them as they floated like snow-wreaths through the mazy dance.

The question occurred, Can wealth ensure respect or fix the mark of aristocracy? This *ci-devant* plebeian, though covered with jewels and bloated with pride, showed that her position in high life was accidental. True, she had unlocked the entrance to a baronial residence, and entered its lordly halls, but only to become more ridiculous, by assuming a position which she could not sustain. The true nobility of intelligence and moral worth needs not the aid of foreign ornament, it will find its level—Mount Olympus can not keep it down. From that hour I determined that I would seek the wealth of mind, and strive for that real worth which perisheth not.

> "Howe'er it be, it seems to me
> 'Tis only noble to be good."

Miss Taylor was sincerely pious, firm and uncompromising in her religious duties, and with her we all attended the ministry of the Rev. Mr. Hawley, an evangelical preacher of the deepest piety, and for more than forty years the pastor of a congregation that worshiped in the beautiful little Episcopal Church of St. John, near the President's house. We enjoyed the peculiar privilege of being well instructed in the sacred truths of the Bible, and regularly catechized at the close of each week in the doctrines of the Church.

That a person may be a member of the Church without possessing even the elementary knowledge of religion, or being at all imbued with its holy principles, was eminently proved by the contrast between these two sisters. Miss Julia was a regular communicant, and

admitted to all the privileges of Church membership that
her sister enjoyed, but hers was the *profession* without the
possession. Miss Charlotte's piety like

> "A beautiful rainbow,
>   All woven of light,
>   Had not in its tissue
>   One shadow of night;"

while her sister, though possesing a highly intellectual
and cultivated taste, clever, in the English acceptation of
the term, but not wise enough to forbear the exhibition
of her powers, was so entirely self-centered and decided,
so divested of all feeling for others, as to counteract her
loveliness of face and culture of mind. Had I been
a disciple of Pythagoras, I should have certainly believed
that she must have been a vicious cat transformed into
a woman. Her iron rule would have been intolerable,
had it not been for the outgushing tenderness of her sister, ever ready to grant even more than was asked.

Many things occur in a school-girl's life which serve
to relieve the monotony of its every-day routine. Saturday, the usual day for mischief, was always rife with
amusement. I was awakened one lovely morning, long
after sunrise, by the chattering of busy tongues.

"She must have her ears bored, and I can do it,"
said one, "just as well as the silversmith."

"Oh, no!" replied a pale, quiet little girl, who was
lying in a low bed, around which several were gathered;
"'twill hurt too bad."

"Pooh, nonsense, child! suppose it does hurt; you
must have your ears pierced; every body wears earrings."

"Well, but mamma did not tell me I must, and I
have got none."

"No matter," chimed in a laughing voice; "your

mamma will be glad when it is done; it will save her the trouble of doing it."

"Well, but Mary, let me ask Miss Taylor first."

"No you shan't, you little goose, for Miss Julia will be sure to refuse; so now be quiet, and I will lend you my nice little ear-bobs until you get a pair of your own."

The timid, half reluctant child at last consented, and expressed much delight when the operation was over and the rings put in, just in time for the breakfast-bell. I witnessed the operation, but declined assisting for fear of giving pain, though I have often regretted that I had not the moral courage to prevent it, as the consequences were so dreadful. The tender flesh being pierced with a brass pin, produced erysipelas, which terminated in St. Vitus's dance, and the poor girl was a sufferer the remainder of her life, at intervals.

How many disasters of the same kind have arisen from causes as slight! I took an item in my memory, and many years afterwards brought it into practical consideration, by punishing one of my own pupils, who would have performed the same operation upon a willing companion. There is not a more sensible truth than the one expressed in the childish verse—

"Satan finds some mischief still
For idle hands to do."

Children are always happier when usefully employed; and change of employment is sufficient recreation, and gives all the relaxation necessary during school hours. Their amusements, even, should tend to improvement mentally or physically. Not only in the study-room, but on the play-ground, may the Scripture truth be well applied, "Whatsoever thy hand findeth to do, do it with thy might." That sleepy, dawdling attitude, which girls are sometimes allowed to assume, is the result of dreamy indolence or stupidity. It affords neither healthful recreation nor profitable relaxation, but opens the door for the entrance of evil thoughts, and is really calculated to destroy correct principles.

The pure, unalloyed joys of early life should be mingled with those light and active pleasures, so peculiarly the evidence of health and good moral training. The dewy freshness of my own girlhood, ofttimes stealing upon my recollection, tempts me to wish I were young again—existence then was such a continual festival; but the thought is as evanescent as the shadow on the wall, and I am grateful that, as the world relaxes its grasp and enables my soul to plume her wings for a higher sphere, I strive

> "Nightly to pitch my moving tent
> A day's march nearer home."

Yet, I deem it a blessing to have been able to garner up the costly and countless treasures of those happy hours, and, as the day of life darkens upon me, these shine like stars amidst the gloom, to cheer and console with the sweet assurance that our Father in Heaven, who has dotted this desert world with so many beautiful oases, will never leave nor forsake those who love and trust him. God's love flows like a clear stream through a troublous world, washing away its impurities, removing the corruptions of the human heart, and softening life's perplexities.

Miss Taylor's school was broken up by the marriage of Miss Julia to an officer of the United States Army, who settled with his bride at Detroit. Miss Charlotte formed a part of their family for a while, and thence, a few years after, returned to her English home.

Chapter VII.

I REMAINED at home a few months under my mother's care, that I might become acquainted with some of those household duties, so practical and necessary in woman's life, and then entered the school of Mrs. Stone, an educated and highly accomplished English woman, of well-deserved reputation as a teacher. She had enjoyed peculiar advantages in her island home, and afterwards spent two years in Paris, where she acquired a thorough knowledge of the French language, which she spoke fluently.

Mrs. Stone was an amiable, benevolent woman, of easy, affable, and graceful manners. Her pupils were endeared to her by a thousand little delicate attentions and unexpected favors. Her residence on Pennsylvania Avenue occupied a position so very conspicuous upon this great thoroughfare as to oblige me to pass through the most thronged and busiest part of the city; thus my parents thought proper to board me in the institution. Three younger sisters were placed there also, but under my special charge; thus obviating the objection of sending them at so early an age from under the paternal roof. I found time, not only to attend to my own duties as a student, but to give them every requisite attention, and, besides, to aid them in preparing their own lessons. My daily recitations, four or five in number, were always well prepared, for I could not bear inferiority in my class, and, intensely anxious to excel in every thing

I undertook, I placed my standard above mediocrity.
Dancing lessons, during the Winter, were regularly given
by a master, who came once a week to the school.
French, Music, and Drawing were also considered indispensable. We took three lessons a week in Music—an
hour each; the same amount of time was devoted to
Drawing. We had a French governess, who chatted
French incessantly, and heard us conjugate French verbs;
while our Drawing-teacher, who was also a good French
scholar, corrected our translations. Mademoiselle did not
understand English well enough.

Thus we were kept fully occupied by our school
duties, in addition to which I not only made and kept in
order my own clothes, but those of my sisters while they
were with me. I remember to have had but one dress
made by a mantua-maker until after I was married; and
after leaving school generally made my mother's. I make
these statements for the benefit of the rising generation,
and to show girls that "where there's a will there's a
way," and "though Alps on Alps arise" before the ease-
loving and indolent, yet these impossibilities vanish before
persevering industry.

Mrs. Stone possessed much tact in communicating
what she knew, and was noted for her flashes of wit and
dazzling repartee. She spoke with great volubility, and
all her conversation with her pupils tended to their improvement. Universally kind, she was much beloved by
all who knew her. She had undoubtedly been handsome, and retained still much of the bloom of youth.

During the sitting of Congress the older girls were
taken by Mrs. Stone once a week to hear the celebrated
speakers, or listen to debates on interesting subjects.
There were "giants in those days," and among the most

conspicuous of the whole bright galaxy of intelligences that illuminated our legislative halls appeared Henry Clay, Speaker of the House of Representatives; John C. Calhoun, John Randolph, Sheffey, and others, who had been leaders of the war party, aspiring now to a place in the councils of the nation. Mr. Calhoun's features impressed me as being remarkably fine, and, though somewhat stern in repose, were yet capable of being molded to any meaning it was his will to express. He always commanded the attention of the House as a character of that lofty cast which seems to rise above the ordinary wants and weaknesses of humanity.

John Randolph was another of the great speakers who made a deep impression upon my mind. One of the queerest and most wiry-looking men I ever saw, he was unmistakably a great man. His genius had angels' wings, but fed on the bitterest extracts from Mount Hymettus. Always on the side of the minority, difficulty seemed to possess a charm for him, because affording an opportunity for displaying the energies of his soul. His voice was weak and squeaking—thin, and sometimes harsh; yet his eloquence was irresistible. He wielded his weapons of wit and ridicule with conclusive power.

An authentic anecdote is related of his having effectually laid upon the table a bill, introduced after the adoption of the Federal Constitution, to have the seats of each delegation wrought with some device descriptive of the staples of their several States. Mr. Randolph arose, after listening to a long debate on the subject, and suggested the more elegant and impressive arrangement of a marble statue for each State. "North Carolina, for instance," he said, pointing his long bony finger, and shaking it in the most significant manner; "let her fill a conspicuous niche, leaning against a persimmon-tree, with an opossum at her feet, and a sweet potato in her hand." It brought down the house—and the plan, too.

In the Congress of the United States, at that time, no man occupied a more enviable position than did our own Henry Clay.

Mr. Clay could, by the magic of his amazing will and his irresistible self-assertion, lift a great audience to dizzy heights of enthusiasm, and stir unwonted throbbings in the heart.

When in his magnificent moments men saw him agitate the Senate into fury, and then, as born to command, play with the whirlwind and direct the storm, they felt in their inmost souls that he had Nature's patent for his oratorical tyranny.

Possessing that liquid melody of tone so fascinating by its variety of inflection and its ever-changing naturalness, Henry Clay could hold his audience enchained for hours without wearying them, and in a great speech move on through the whole oratorical voyage as gracefully as a noble ship, whose snowy sails flutter and quiver in storm and breeze by turns, but always majestic and swan-like in its movements. Mr. Clay's gestures naturally aided his eloquence. His pantomime was the perfect painting of his thoughts, and each discriminating gesture told its own story.

A man who was somewhat deaf, and could not get near enough to Mr. Clay in one of his finest efforts, remarked, "I did not hear a word he said; but, bless me! did n't he make his motions?"

Mr. Clay was never declamatory, even in his most fervid moments. When wrought up to the highest pitch of enthusiasm, his modulations and intonations, diversified and distinct, were all subservient to that principle of melody so permanently stamped upon every thing he uttered,—even like the multitudinous laughter of the waves, mingling with the crashing breakers and sobbing billows, but all subordinate to and finally lost in the great ocean diapason, the majestic music of the sea.

Somewhat in the same way, and with the same un-broken velocity, spoke Wm. Pinckney, of Maryland, who among the contemporaries of Clay stood next in fame for eloquence.

Mr. Pinckney was a brilliant legal speaker, and held the office of Attorney-general of the United States under Mr. Madison when war was declared. He, as well as Mr. Clay, was an ardent advocate for the war. Mr. Pinckney was pre-eminent as a lawyer; his legal attainments were extensive and profound, and being enthusiastically devoted to his profession, he was ambitious of its triumphs. His oratory, though at times too declamatory and rhetorical, was rich, copious, and fluent in a high degree, adorned with the finest imagery, drawn from classic lore and a vivid fancy; the effect of which was increased by the manliness of his figure, a sonorous and flexible voice, and the animation and gracefulness of his delivery. By his application to the subject of elocution and the English language he had added to his natural facility and fluency a copiousness of elegant diction, which graced even his conversation, and imparted new strength and beauty to his forensic style.

In the first moments of his speech, it is said, he did not win, but rather repulsed; gathering headway, however, he gained more and more, till he took the helm of your mind, and led you hither and thither as the frenzy and the mood swept over him. Mr. Pinckney deservedly occupied a high position among the American orators of that memorable period, and yet he was not too proud to be vain.

I saw him in 1818, soon after his last return from Europe; and as his name had always been associated in my mind with something above the ordinary standard of men, I was not a little surprised to see him so magnificently dressed as seemingly to ignore that republican simplicity of which our great men boast so much. A splendid blue cloth cloak of ample dimensions, lined with rich crimson velvet, artistically draped his fine form and gave dignity to his appearance, conveying the impression that he had been accustomed to kingly courts rather than to democratic councils; yet there was nothing out of keeping with his position. There was a good taste, which reminded one of the beautiful tropes and metaphors abounding in his oratory—embellishing, not detracting.

When we observe the wonderfully complicated nature of man, the noble dominion of mind subject to his control, the vast achievements of his art and genius, and the intelligence which places him but little lower than the angels, what a mingled picture of light and shade does he present!

> "How poor, how rich, how abject, how august,
> How complicate, how wonderful is man!
> How passing wonder He who made him such!"

Often, when listening to the eloquence of these great legislators, I have thought, "How these patriots love their country!" Some did, I doubt not; but I have long since learned to distrust that ambitious political creed, openly avowed by many, of which *expediency* is the Alpha and Omega. Human interest will always mingle with human motives.

I saw Mr. Calhoun once in after-life. His ample brow was pale with anxious thought, deep lines of care were chiseled on his face; but there was still the lightning glance in his undimmed eye which told of the bold, intrepid spirit that had given him a lofty rank among the great men of his age.

While at Mrs. Stone's I was associated with many intelligent, interesting girls; but the one I best remember, and of whom I still have a sweet and touching recollection, was Laura Wirt, a daughter of the eminent Attorney-general. I never met with a girl of so universal talents—excelling in every accomplishment, and that without effort or pretense.

Miss Wirt was about seventeen years old, of very lovely person, delicate and fragile; her complexion pale, without any tincture of sallowness; abundant glossy hair, regular features, and eyes of rather a sad expression, but possessing an indescribable luster. Her manner was neither forward nor bashful; but affectionate, without familiarity, and quiet, without being dull. She possessed many qualities which rendered her an agreeable companion and an interesting classmate. I speak particularly of her, because I regarded her then, as I do now, a model pupil, as well as a model daughter. She neglected none of the privileges afforded her, but improved every opportunity to the greatest advantage, and though an extern she spent every leisure moment in the study-room, drawing, translating French or Latin, consulting maps or reading history, or in some way preparing herself for future usefulness.

Mr. Wirt had a large family of daughters, all younger than Laura, and the mother being in feeble health, the care of the children devolved principally on the eldest. I saw

Mrs. Wirt but once in her own home. She was reclining upon a sofa, giving the impression of extreme languor from ill health; her face as white, her features as passionless, as if carved in Parian marble. Yet she was said to be a woman of great strength of character, though sweet, patient, and amiable—enduring like a Christian the severe discipline of early disappointments, domestic bereavements, and constant ill health; and coming out like refined gold from her fiery trials.

Laura had an object of more than common interest in striving to secure knowledge. She intended that her acquirements and accomplishments should be put to a practical use. Her father's salary, as Attorney-general of the United States, was scarcely sufficient to support his family and give that prestige necessary to their position in society, and this excellent daughter accepted an appointment as clerk for her father, with a salary of a thousand dollars. The duties of this office she faithfully and satisfactorily performed, besides being much with her mother and sisters, and entering occasionally into the *beau monde*, where she commanded the homage and admiration due to real worth and superior elegance. A model pupil at school, a model daughter at home, a model woman in society, her hand was sought in marriage by some of the best and wisest men of the day; and she finally made a happy choice, but did not live many years after.

To die young is often the destiny of very superior, I might almost say of precocious, talents. We should regard long life as a blessing when God bestows it; yet we should not consider it less a privilege to die early if our Heavenly Father so wills it. And what matters it if no monumental stone be erected to such a memory! the fame imparted by the lofty marble is lost in the general wreck of matter, and those who would claim a tear and a memory must write their names on living hearts.

Mrs. Stone had some wayward pupils, who eschewed books and loved idleness. I have since had my own experience with such, and am prepared to exclaim, with sympathetic emotion, Woe betide the teacher who has to break in these vivacious specimens of humanity! They seem to set their minds at work to baffle every effort to reduce them to order. This arises, not from malice, but from want of early parental discipline. Often affectionate and placable, though impatient and passionate, yet I can truly say there is greater satisfaction in subduing one such sinner, and more joy felt, than over the ninety and nine who need no such correction. Kind, indulgent, and forgiving, Mrs. Stone was no disciplinarian; hence scenes of confusion frequently occurred among the boarding pupils never witnessed under the firm but gentle sway of Miss Taylor, whose dignified presence was alone sufficient to still the troubled waters. Miss Taylor often mingled with us out of school hours; Mrs. Stone seldom saw us except at recitations and meals, save by special request, though we were never left without the supervision of Mademoiselle or some under-governess, who was as little regarded as one of the girls would have been.

The habit before mentioned as fatal to good order, that of allowing girls to spend all their leisure time in their bedrooms, obtained here to a considerable extent. Six or eight would sometimes collect in one room for gossip, indulging in light, vain, and foolish, if not sinful, conversation. One may well imagine what scenes of riot and confusion were likely to occur among a number of idle young girls, divested of all restraint from their superiors. As long as the laughing and chattering in the several apartments during recreation hours was kept within such bounds as not to disturb Mrs. Stone, no notice was taken of the noise; and if ever the uproar attracted attention, then one or two of the younger children were brought forward as the delinquents by their older school-fellows, to suffer the reproof or punishment due, in general, to themselves. Feeling the responsibility devolving upon me in reference to my sisters, I spent my intervals of relaxation in the large and, for the time being, almost deserted school-room with them. We had no recreation grounds; not a blade of grass in the yard, which was crowded with out-buildings—thus compelling us to seek amusement within doors.

I am reminded in this place of a queer girl, one of my room-mates, whose peculiarities, though sometimes a source of much annoyance, often gave infinite diversion by her drollery. Born to be a trial of patience to all concerned with or about her—giddy, restless, mischievous, and unrestrained in spirits — continually getting into scrapes—often reproved, but never any better; her round, good-natured, merry face, and large, bright, laughing eyes, and eternally apologetic "Well, I won't do so again," usually made her peace with all. Once, striving to draw me from my quiet work in the school-room, she came screaming, at the top of her voice: "Oh, do come, Julia! they've got your beautiful quilt spread out on the floor, playing jacks; and some of them are sitting right in the middle of your bed, cutting papers all over it—and, such a mess!"

I followed her quietly up-stairs, and what a scene presented itself to my astonished vision! One girl was mounted on a chair before the looking-glass, half a dozen were seated on a handsome patchwork quilt, one of my mother's best—each girl having to furnish her own bed, bedding, towels, etc.—quantities of marbles were bouncing from the corners and center, while the girls were literally grabbing out the cotton wadding from my nice quilt, in which they had picked great holes. The little ones were rolling over the uncarpeted floor, and one was seated in the middle of a low bed with her shoes on, while another was unpacking her trunk; and Mary Wilson, the messenger, had left hers entirely emptied of its odds and ends. My presence quelled the storm in one sense, but raised a tempest in another. I was disposed to be fastidiously neat. I boxed the ears of one, shook two or three others, and contrived in a few minutes to push all the transgressors out at the door, at the same time locking it and putting the key in my pocket.

Such scenes were not uncommon. One bright moonlight night, being awakened out of a sound sleep by something falling heavily on the floor, I perceived a figure dressed in white bending intently over something in the middle of the room. Half unconsciously, with beating heart, I watched it gradually rise, until it seemed in the mellow moonlight to reach the very ceiling, and then sink slowly in one corner of the room. I expected it to vanish—it did not. Being now fully restored to consciousness, I arose softly, walked toward the object, and found it to be Mary Wilson, with a sheet wrapped around her, engaged in pairing her stockings and tying them together. "Asleep," thought I. "How terrible to have a sleepwalker in my room!" Just then she suddenly turned, and, seeing me, broke into a merry laugh, exclaiming:

"Well, you see, Julia, I've lost so many stockings that yesterday I had to wear one white and one gray one; and 't is so much trouble to keep the best foot foremost all the time that I thought, to-night, when the moon's lamp burned so beautifully, that I would take the opportunity to hunt up the odd ones and pair them."

"You silly girl! what will Mrs. Stone say to this night-prowling of yours? running the risk too, as you do, of scaring some of the children half to death?"

"She 'll never know it, unless you tell her," she replied; "and you, who are so full of energy, ought to commend me for mine. See; there lie three pairs and a dozen odd ones, with half a foot each—and so much daylight saved."

The clock struck two; she had been up since eleven.

"If you do not get in bed instantly, I 'll report you to-morrow," said I.

"I do n't believe you will," was the reply; "besides, I 'll be too busy all the morning to be punished; and in the evening we have to dance, and you will want me for a partner, with my clean stockings and red shoes."

Mary was incorrigible in many things, and delighted in nothing so much as in provoking and annoying her teachers. French and Spanish she could not, or would not, learn to pronounce; and while she rendered Mademoiselle frantic, was as cool as an iceberg herself. Monsieur Henri, who occasionally heard us read French, sometimes arose and finished his lesson by throwing the book at her head, because she persisted in pronouncing "*peut atre*" "patater;" and a "*joli garcon*" was a "jolly garkon."

Proper attention was given in this establishment to the externals of religion. Every body went to church twice on the Sabbath; it would have been ungenteel not to do so. I am not aware that any of our teachers ever manifested decided impressions of piety; and we were only saved from utter indifference on that subject by these formalities, through which we enjoyed the indirect influences of religion. I do not think there was an individual among the teachers or pupils who would not have thought it being "righteous overmuch" to do more than attend church regularly twice on the Sabbath.

CHAPTER VIII.

POLITICAL contests of great bitterness marked the period from 1815 to 1820. Hot disputes between Federalists and Democrats ended in a number of duels. One I distinctly recollect, as sending a thrill of horror throughout the land,—so sad in its results, and so strong a proof of the hatred engendered by political strife, sundering the ties of affection, and trailing in blood the banner of kindred love.

Colonel Armstead F. Mason and Colonel John M'Carty were first cousins—each the prominent man of his party. Mason, however, was held in high estimation, and respected by both parties; kind and forgiving, he tried to avoid a difficulty with M'Carty, who pursued him with a malignity almost without a parallel. Mason had thwarted his purposes—at least M'Carty fancied so; he had crossed his path at the bar of the courts, and circumvented his political designs.

The characters of the two men were as antagonistic as their politics. Mason, though a great statesman, was not an ambitious one; yet he hesitated not to stand in the breach, to stem the torrent of ungodly politicians, whose artful designs were ready to engulf our new-formed government. Mason was brave, high-minded, and full of noble impulses; M'Carty, stern, cold, and revengeful. Mason did every thing it was thought an honorable man could do to avoid a collision; but, alas! not all that a Christian should have done, or he had not fallen a victim

to that false code of honor which is a disgrace to the
civilized world, nor violated the law of God rather than
break through the cold conventionality of society. He
should not have forgotten his paramount obligations to
his lovely young wife, whose very existence seemed
bound up in his, and left his only child an orphan.

M'Carty gave provocation after provocation for a
quarrel. Mason was ready to explain, though he was
no coward; but his opponent was determined on a meeting, and refused all explanation. Thus the long evaded
crisis came. The vindictive M'Carty compelled him, at
last, to turn at bay—his hatred surrounded him like a
wall of fire. Among the modes of fighting proposed
by M'Carty was that each should sit upon a keg of
powder, near enough to apply the torch for the destruction of the other. Finally they fought with rifles
at Bladensburg—the Congressional duel ground—only a
few paces apart. Mason fell mortally wounded; M'Carty
fled before the last struggle was over, while the death
damp lay upon the noble brow of his murdered victim,
whose intellectual superiority he envied, and had blighted
in its bloom, leaving an example of one of the most
awful duels ever traced by ambition upon its bloody
pages. The survivor went forth with the mark of Cain
upon his brow, and with the awful denunciation ringing
in his ears, "Thy brother's blood crieth to me from
the ground."

Duelling—genius, virtue, freedom, and truth demand
its banishment from the world. That fearful tragedy has
never been forgotten—men cease not to remember it.
The torch of ambition, with its fitful glare, was extinguished in the blood of a relative. Thus was the light
of a happy home forever darkened. But yesterday the

freshness of young life, unwithered by the touch of time, rested upon husband and wife. The golden sun of the morning illuminated their household, and the incense of loving hearts floated through all its apartments; before night the affectionate father, the fond husband, the devoted patriot, closed his brilliant career in a bloody death, having reached only his thirty-second year.

Well do I remember the dusky twilight hour of that day; the raindrops fell upon the pavement, chilling the heart with their cold patter, as if in sympathy with the horrid deed of the day. My face was pressed closely against the window-pane watching the hasty footsteps of my father, who said, in a melancholy tone, as he entered the room, "It is all over," and called our attention to the rattling wheels of the carriage which bore away the reckless demagogue from the disastrous scene.

I listened eagerly to the rehearsal of all the circumstances, and shuddered as I wept for Mason's desolate family. Ah! thought I, the murderer may escape man's justice, but the eye of God he can not escape. Pale faces will look upon him from behind the dark curtain of the night with sad reproaches for the ruin of a wrecked household. He had wasted God's best gifts and separated himself from all that ennobles life, and had nothing to look forward to but a fearful judgment to come, the black shadow of remorse following him wherever he went. If the lot of a common murderer is terrible, what must be that of a wretch loaded with the accumulated guilt of a murdered family?

It was this same Colonel Mason who said of "Father Littlejohn," a man of deep, unaffected piety, combined with a cultivated intellect and industrial talent, "I have known the Rev. Mr. Littlejohn to finish a saddle, preside on the bench as a magistrate, preach a funeral sermon, baptize a child, and perform the marriage ceremony, all on the same day." After I commenced teaching in Shelbyville I became acquainted with this eminent apostle of Jesus Christ, when his snowy locks and bent form indicated great age; and from him learned the finale of the Mason and M'Carty duel.

Mrs. Mason, though heartbroken, tried to live on for the sake of her child. Supported by the consolations of religion, the heart may still throb on—on—on, when it has ceased to live for this world. She passed through joyless days and sorrowful nights, with her fair head bowed in meekness to the will of God, but often sighing, "Father, take home thy child;" and sweetly smiled when, at last, the summons came. The son lived to emulate his father's noble deeds, a comfort to his mother while she lived; but was killed in the early bloom of manhood, while fighting at the head of his regiment in the Mexican war.

Father Littlejohn, to whom I have just alluded, was a man of many sorrows, but, like St. Paul, he suffered willingly for the excellency of the knowledge of Christ Jesus our Lord; and like the same great apostle, all his trophies, all his spoils were hung upon the cross of Christ. The blessings of many years does not often crown a human brow without leaving thereon the impress of suffering. The good old man brought me his granddaughter to educate—a sweet, dove-eyed little girl, the sole blossom left upon the household tree. A kind tone of voice and a gentleness of manner were the characteristics of Catharine Littlejohn. She was like the delicious mignonette, lifting up its sweet blossoms laden with fragrance to be poured like incense upon the

heart of the dear old grandfather. Her looks, like the
cheerful smile of Spring, sent a glow of warmth upon
the Winter of his age. She was beautiful in her girlish
simplicity, quiet and dreamy when alone, gay and joyous
with her young companions, but sly and silent among
strangers, though there were no awkwardnesses that were
not as good as graces. She married young, died early,
and went home to join the family throng.

I can not close without a word more about Father
Littlejohn. His name must ever live in the annals of
early Methodism. He was accounted faithful among the
pioneers. "The Churches knew and loved and gave
him praise;"

> "For with untiring, apostolic zeal,
> He watered and refreshed them; his sacred
> Office was his joy—it seemed the well-spring
> Of his life—and all its sources gushing
> Forth in holy fervor, bore him onward,
> Fitting him for heaven."

The good man's labors cease, but memory retouches
the lines that marked its varied path—it has a thousand
tongues to hold companionship with such a guide.

Washington City was at that time more under the
influence of moral and religious principle than it has
ever been since. Every respectable family had a pew in
some church, and there was almost as much of that
Puritan feeling found in high places as was generally disseminated throughout New England. There was preaching at the Capitol every Sabbath, with a large and decent
congregation in attendance. Few loiterers were seen
on the public streets or at the tavern-doors; conventionality required a Sabbath stillness around every mansion.
This was, doubtless, owing to the unwearied faithfulness
of a few evangelical ministers, whose holy walk and godly

conversation almost worked miracles among the rich and the great; while they brought comfort and blessings to the lowly and humble.

Among these good men stood out, in bold relief, the pastor of St. Paul's Church, who for so many years "prophesied in Israel;" and the reformation affected by his labors among the gay, fashionable, thoughtless, and extravagant members of his congregation attested him to be, indeed, the messenger of God, by whom he was highly honored. There were others, as I have said, equally honored, but I knew him best, being a regular attendant upon his ministry. The memory of the just is blessed; and individuals, as well as nations, are exalted only in proportion to their righteousness. The names and the virtues of the holy men who have, from time to time, been appointed to enlighten and reclaim the world have shed a luster and diffused an influence upon mankind which shall expand and brighten to the end of time. Not so those who thrust themselves, uncalled, into the temple, and, Judas like, betray the Master whom they pretend to serve.

I shall never forget the sensation of disgust produced throughout the whole community of Washington by the levity of a celebrated preacher who, having for ten years officiated in one of the most prominent churches in B———, without spot or blemish upon his clerical character, was now *en route*, by a special call, to fill the presidential chair of a newly-founded university in the West. It was at the commencement of the gay season of 1818. The city was thronged with visitors and strangers. The Rev. Mr. H——— thought it not amiss to appear at a Saturday ·evening soiree at the French Minister's, and dance until the small hours of the Sabbath morning, captivating the *beau monde* with his easy, seductive elegance of manners, and then fulfill his appointment to preach in the Representative Hall at eleven o'clock. His congregation was large, but distinguished by the presence of many of the gay revellers of the evening before.

Is there not something fearfully wrong in what we call our highly civilized state of society, when it can tolerate such departure from principle? True, this man was brilliant, witty, elegant, accomplished, and gifted; but fearfully deficient in all the higher Christian virtues and nobler motives. He possessed that fire and energy, combined with novelty and elegance of ideas, and that loftiness of expression, which displayed an intellect at once refined and gigantic. The institution in the West, over which he presided for a few years, suffered from his bad example; and so pernicious was his influence, that, like the deadly shade of the Upas, it withered, if it did not destroy, every virtue that came within its circle. Finally, after a few meteoric flashes, the brilliant star of his unfulfilled genius sank into a rayless night.

The name of Madame la Comtesse de Neuville, wife of the resident French Minister, is embalmed with some of the most pleasant recollections of my later school days. She was the intimate friend of Mrs. Stone, with whom she had been associated in Paris at school. When Madame de Neuville came to Washington she seemed eager to renew their friendship upon the old terms of intimacy, notwithstanding the different spheres in which they moved. Monsieur and Madame de Neuville, although exponents of the highest European nobility, possessed much of that republican simplicity of which we Americans boast so much and show so little. In our aspirations, as a people, after wealth and position, we seem to ignore the very spirit of our institutions and the equality proclaimed in our Declaration of Independence, where no patent of nobility is granted, and none recognized, except that to which is appended the great seal of moral and intellectual superiority.

At the door of one of the plainest brick buildings on Pennsylvania Avenue, Madame de Neuville's splendid carriage was frequently seen standing, being sent to convey Mrs. Stone to a dining or an evening party. Everybody delighted to accept her invitations, and attend her gay balls and magnificent dinner parties; and we school-girls felt as much flattered by the attention paid our beloved teacher as if it had been ourselves. The fact was, we all loved Madame de Neuville for her plain, unostentatious manners, and what we deemed her condescension in noticing us. She had no children in her own house, no merry voices and pattering feet to greet her at home; hence she took particular pleasure in the pupils of her friend, and delighted in bringing down her own thoughts and feelings to their comprehension. Her love for the young and her interest in their society kept her happy.

We were the frequent recipients of her favors—flowers, delicious fruits, assorted French candies, etc., etc.— all very welcome and charming to schoolgirls. The greatest delight of the older girls was to see Mrs. Stone dressed for one of Madame's gay parties, and admire her petite figure, covered with rich laces and jewels; then await her return and listen to her descriptions of all she had seen in the gay world. Madame de Neuville possessed that true nobility of spirit which evinces itself in a cheerful and general politeness; that amenity and want of pretension so fascinating in high life. Her ordinary language was the purest and most graceful French; but she spoke English with ease and with considerable accuracy for a foreigner.

Monsieur de Neuville we seldom saw, except in their daily walks, in which he invariably carried an umbrella and she a shawl, no matter what the condition of the weather.   Their splendid equipage, with footmen and outriders, was often seen rolling through the streets, containing no one but a secretary, Charge d'Affaires, or, perhaps, my lady's maid on a shopping excursion; while the minister and his wife were taking long walks over the commons or on the banks of the river.   They had a tall, handsome footman, who looked so elegant in his gold-laced livery, that mysterious stories were whispered about among the ladies of his being a nobleman in disguise, and the poor fellow was persecuted with billets-doux and constant espionage, to escape which he finally abandoned his position and took refuge in his own country.

Chapter IX.

I HAVE said, that I was fond of reading, but what I read previous to the age of seventeen had not been well digested; it was rather a species of cramming, which a maturer judgment taught me to reject, and I now began to discriminate between healthy literature and the hot-bed productions with which the press teemed then as now: yet I did not eschew all fiction, and often, when reading an interesting novel, to which daylight could not be devoted, the moon lent her friendly aid.

My imprudence in thus straining my eyes, though it did not render me very nearsighted, prevented my being able to see things distinctly at a great distance common to good eyes. 'Tis a dangerous experiment to read by moonlight. My naturally strong gray eyes suffered less injury than weaker ones might have sustained.

I had traveled much into the dangerous realms of fancy, and frequently went beyond my depth; but not altogether without advantage. From the character of the innumerable heroines presented to my mind I formed an ideal of excellence; and many grains of wheat gathered from bushels of chaff were carefully stored in the treasure-heuse of memory.

As I advanced in years and stepped upon the threshold of womanhood, my mirror plainly told me that, though comely and symmetrical, I was not to depend upon my "face for my fortune;" or, in other words, I could never expect to be a "belle" on account of my beauty. I decided, therefore, that my attractions must be of the mind.

I read history, travels, biography, and general literature; learned much of the known world through the eyes of others; acquired a knowledge of Scotland and England through the writings of the "Great Unknown," which I read as they were issued from the press. It was a banquet of sweet things to my intellectual taste, never cloying. As far as I can judge, I retained the good without any of the evil. Certainly the reading of Scott's historical novels tended to purify my taste for fiction, and turned my attention more immediately to history.

At this critical period I began to acquire a taste for solid reading and useful information. A new world was open to me. I did not, however, lay down any plan for mental improvement, but tried to store my mind with the most useful knowledge. I have found reason, again and again, to be thankful that my thoughts were turned at this period into a channel which saved me from the desire of entering too early into society, and checked a career that might have been marked with the merest frivolities—resulting from a naturally gay disposition and exuberant spirits.

I spent one of my Summer vacations in Mrs. Stone's house, that I might profit by the instruction and conversation of our French governess, who alone, of all the teachers, remained during the holidays. We walked, talked, and read together; and as Mademoiselle was my sole companion, and spoke English too imperfectly to make it a pleasure to converse with her in that language, I was compelled to use the French, though she was as anxious to learn English as I was to learn her language. Her blunders were my principal source of amusement.

We were one morning very much interrupted by the noise of a crying child, who was neglected by its mother, the cook. "Ecoutez," cried Mademoiselle; "'t is villanous; dis woman no care if the leetle child die; she be bad more than the cow—when the leetle cow cry the mére no forget to mind him." She once said to me, "The English grammaire is noble, magnifique for every ting but de conversatione; me no never pronounce de langage, but me have learned toute la grammaire by hell." I started with astonishment. She looked amazed, saw that she had committed some terrible blunder, but knew not how to explain; finally, after many ineffectual attempts, I found she meant, "by heart." The want of analogy in the English language renders its pronunciation the most difficult in the world to foreigners.

During the vacation alluded to I wrote and translated a great deal, which was of infinite use to me, in after life, as a teacher. A part of my time was spent in sketching, drawing, and painting—making only an occasional visit home. Mademoiselle stayed but a few months with us; and then returned to La Belle France, disgusted with the rudeness of American girls and with the English language.

Miss Hallet, a tall, dignified woman from one of the Spanish islands, took her place. She spoke English, French, and Spanish with equal fluency; and though cold and reserved in her manners, I was determined to make myself agreeable to her, in consideration of the superior advantages I might derive from her conversation. I rendered myself useful by assisting with the little girls' lessons, and in various ways aiding her in her mental labors. She became genial, yet retained her Spanish stateliness to the very ends of her fingers and toes. "I like to live in America," she said; "but I fear I shall never become accustomed to the rapid evolutions of so fast a people." She told me that she landed in New York on the Sabbath, while the bells were ringing for morning service, and imagined, from their rapid walking, that the people were hastening to a fire. With her I learned to talk French, which she preferred to her native language, the Spanish.

I have had frequent occasions, during a long career as a teacher, to rejoice that such facilities for the thorough acquisition of the language were thrown within my reach, and that I was wise enough sedulously to avail myself of them. I confess to an ambitious desire of becoming more than a mere atom floating in the sunbeam of prosperity. I coveted a distinct individuality, yet it is my deliberate opinion that I also loved learning for its own sake.

Many things occurred during my residence in Mrs. Stone's institution which might amuse and interest the present generation of pupils, but probably would not tend to their improvement. I remained with her until I entered my nineteenth year, at which time I left the precincts of the school-room as a pupil, and returned to my dearly loved home. My studies were not, however, abandoned; some hours were daily devoted to reading, some to household duties; and I continued to receive tri-weekly lessons in French and music from excellent masters who came to the house. I practiced much on the piano (and, by the by, copied nearly all the music I used), but performed with more taste than execution.

Ballad singing was much in vogue—the sweet Irish melodies and the touching songs of Burns, with occasional marches, waltzes, etc., seemed to please the taste of every body. We invariably played and sang the air.

We did not play an accompaniment and sing the air at the same time; but when we did sing we pronounced the words distinctly, and felt the sentiment expressed. We never inflicted tedious pieces upon our auditors—no matter how brilliant they were considered in our text-books, by which we acquired a knowledge of fingering and facility of execution. "Auld Lang Syne," "Roy's Wife," "Bonnie Doon," "Washington's March," and the "Cottage Rondo," were sung and played *con amore*.

I enjoyed my stay at home—sweet home—in the midst of those loved ones, so much the more because hitherto I had been but a visitor there.

To greet my father's cheerful face every morning—to rise sometimes before daylight, that I might accompany him to market (and we often went two miles for that purpose), where we saw the busy world in miniature—to spend a portion of each day with my dear, kind mother, trying in the mean time to help her bear the burden of her domestic cares, which were not a few, was a real joy to my heart; the very memory of which is like music to my soul, touching a chord connected with the fondest recollections of former years. Other memories bring but the shadows of things long since fled.

The first Winter I spent at home was crowded with so many incidents that it seemed extended over a longer time than usual. My father's residence was near the Capitol; and several members of Congress, with their families, boarded with us, forming what was familiarly called "a mess," the family constituting a part of it. This afforded me an opportunity of becoming well acquainted with some of the most distinguished statesmen of the day; among whom were Henry Clay, Judge Poindexter, Dr. Floyd, Mr. Calhoun, and others. One of my most agreeable friends was an old gentleman—General Stevens, of Revolutionary memory—who had taken part in the destruction of the tea in Boston Harbor, and to whom I was ever a willing listener. When he spoke of the Revolution, he kindled a fire of patriotism in my heart that made me almost wish I had lived in those stirring times.

I had another old friend who often discussed the politics of the day with us, while I read to him the newspapers and journals. This was General R. J. Meigs, who had long been a Government Agent among the Indians. He had many stories to tell of those wild sons of the forest, whose wrongs and injuries bore heavily upon his heart; and while he spoke of the injustice of the whites towards them, and the sad extremities to which they were driven, he taught me to love, to pity and to forgive them. His son, the Postmaster-general, was a warm friend of my father, and kindly aided me afterwards in procuring an eligible situation as a teacher by his letter of recommendation.

My gentleman friends at this time were all old men, who appeared to take pleasure in answering my curious questions. I learned much of my country, its Constitution and political affairs, from the discussions that were frequently carried on at the dinner table, to which I was ever an eager and interested listener; and yet, I can not say that I did not listen occasionally to the animated discussions of my lady friends upon the color of a ribbon, the cut of a dress, or the fashion of a bonnet.

One of the most interesting members of our family at this time was the young and lovely wife of an eminent Senator, who had distinguished himself as a judge, a governor, and as a legislator in the halls of Congress; and who was equally notorious for his separation from his first wife, who was still living; and for having killed his friend and benefactor in a duel. This second wife, of whom I speak, was a girl of scarce seventeen Summers, when he wooed and married her. Strange, indeed, that those who loved her most should have been willing to crush the bud of real affection in her heart, and sacrifice her to the glitter of wealth and pride of station!

I never can forget the first evening she came to our house—so fair, so beautiful. Her large blue eyes, shaded by deeply-fringed lashes, when raised to the face of the speaker, resembled the blue and cloudless heavens, lit with the cold and distant glory of the stars; and there beamed a softened light which penetrated the soul of the beholder. The dew was yet upon the blossom of her life, when found by this man of the world nestled away among the roses and woodbines of a widowed mother's humble cottage in Louisiana. Young and lovely, the damask of a happy girlhood still lingered on her cheek; her face was radiant as if an angel had left a kiss upon her brow. She had loved and was beloved by one every way worthy of so bright a jewel. He was poor (it was thus she told me), and they were to have been married as soon as he could get into some business by which he could maintain herself and mother comfortably. Entirely devoted to each other, the future presented to them a paradise on earth. They would gladly have spent life together in the humblest home—but, alas! like the serpent among the flowers of Eden, the destroyer came, and so changed the scene, that never did bud or blossom bloom again in the garden of their young hearts.

The timid girl, though long resisting the ambitious pleadings of her relatives—for her heart had no part or lot in the matter—and touched by the tender emotions of filial love, which prompted her to place her mother in an affluent home, yielded in an evil hour, dashed the cup of happiness from her lips, and stepped into a state of existence which rendered her life a burden, shutting out the purple mountains of hope forever from her view. She married; but her silken robes and glittering jewels covered an aching heart, and blanched the roses on her cheek; and if, indeed, angels camped around her, they had folded their wings in dismay and pity. The most careless hearts would have wept could they have penetrated the tragedy of that life.

Her bridal trip was to Washington, and her first entrance into society was in the fashionable world of the capital of this great nation. As the wife of a wealthy United States Senator she had the privilege, if such it might be considered, of being surrounded by splendor, and enjoying all that could be enjoyed in high life. I distinctly remember her appearance when dressed for a levee at the President's. She was enveloped in snowy folds of the finest India muslin; jewels glittered amid her wavy brown hair, and shone with peculiar beauty upon her finely molded neck and arms. She looked the very personification of youthful loveliness, as she lifted her timid eyes to the face of her haughty husband, filled with an expression of exaltation mingled with awe, melting into that trustful submission which marks woman's sacrificial devotion; and yet there were plainly seen, flitting across her face, varied emotions which told of an internal struggle to crowd back some passionate recollections that would not be still beneath all this paradeful splendor.

Her husband was proud of her beauty, and well he might be; but he only looked upon her as reflecting the glory of his own ambition. Poor young thing! she

sought my companionship and sympathy, for she was
very near my own age, and nothing soothed her more
than to pour into my willing ear the tale her sorrowful
disappointment. So fleeting had been her early dream
of love and happiness, that even then she recalled it only
as a glimpse of heaven given in a dream, and shuddered
when the "angel of memory rolled away the stone of
apathy," and bade her dead dreams arise.

Night after night she was left to weep alone in her
solitary chamber, while he, who had promised to love and
cherish her, spent the waning hours at the card-table or
at wine-suppers. She would sometimes send for me to
come and sit a few hours with her. I learned to pity and
love her, and never forget the lesson taught by her sad
history. When we "choose our own ways" instead of
seeking God's direction, we fall into sadness and sorrow,
which nothing earthly can remove, and are utterly crushed
beneath the tread of time.

The finale of this sad story is woven into the history
of many a life. The Winter over, she returned to her
home, now a stately mansion half hidden among magnolia
blossoms; but neither the fragrance of their lily cups,
nor the glancing wings of the mocking-bird through the
vine-covered bowers at evening, could bring comfort
to her weary heart. A few short, bitter years, slowly
marked by weary days and sleepless nights—the entreaties of her soul going up all the while to the source of
mercy and power, hopeless, save in the goodness of God,
she lingered on, until at last, through infinite mercy, her
disembodied spirit was carried to the throne of light.
She passed away, and soon another wife trod those lofty
walls—a proud, haughty woman, who completely managed the decrepit and prematurely old man, who had

killed with cold neglect the lamb he had cruelly taken from the fold of love. The victim had been adorned, and fell a sacrifice upon the altar of ambition.

The vivid impressions made upon my mind during this period resulted from the ever-varying and exciting scenes amid which I lived. Our new formed republic had not yet reached a dignified maturity. The people were intoxicated with the liberty they enjoyed. The great men of the Revolution, whose stern Puritanism had contributed to rear the beautiful temple of liberty upon a respectable foundation, did not live long enough to secure its durability; and the noble warriors, whose blood had cemented the bond of union between the States, were sleeping their last sleep beneath the soil so dearly purchased.

The fluctuating waves of a revolutionary war had scarcely subsided when the tocsin was again sounded, and liberty struggled for three years more to gain the ascendancy. This accomplished, the people were enjoying it, not in quiet gladness throughout the land; but, true to their Saxon origin, the genius of which is strong and rapid, were pursuing, with an unaccountable activity, avocations in business or pleasure. Strangers, like the locusts of Egypt, were flocking to our shores; and Washington, during the Winter, was filled with a multitude of office-seekers and foreigners, who were lookers-on, to see how this experiment of republicanism would work throughout so large an extent of country. But, alas! the disease of our race seems to be stupidity; and the propensity of the human mind is to forget that no superstructure can stand, unless founded upon religion and virtue.

Our Congress, which ought to have been a model of

wisdom, did not, even in its youthful vigor, always show the dignity expected in the councils of a great nation. Statesmen of prestige, and of the highest ability, plunged into an excess of dissipation that would have disgraced heathendom. Some of our Senators, it is true, were grave and reverend, and among our Representatives were found men of great integrity and supereminent virtue; but even to the eye of the uninitiated many of our legislators were utterly unfit to be intrusted with the important duties that devolved upon them. How often I have felt shocked to hear of the recklessness exhibited by men high in power, and in whose hands were placed the dearest rights of the people, suggesting the thought, "If such things are done in the green tree, what may be expected in the dry!"

At a dining party, upon one occasion. I heard a white-haired old man say to his neighbor: "I am a Senator from North Carolina, and when I left home I sold corn at twelve and a half cents a bushel to procure money for my contingent expenses whilst in Washington; and last night I was fleeced of every dollar at the gambling-table by the two honorable gentlemen who sit opposite me." It was said loud enough, and probably was intended, to be heard by his *vis-a-vis;* whereupon Mr. C., without the slightest change of color, arose, and in his blandest manner asked the old gentleman to take a glass of wine with him, as oblivious of the past and a pledge of future friendship. The gray-haired Senator took the offered wine, and, with his face composed to an expression much resembling that of a chief mourner at a funeral, replied, "I may forgive, but never forget." The two gentlemen replied by a hearty laugh, echoed by fair women and grave men. Novice as I then was in every thing that related to political affairs, I felt troubled for our newly formed government. The idea of men legislating for millions of people, after spending the live-long night at the gambling-table, besotted with wine and strong drink—one shudders to think of it!

James Monroe, the fifth President of the United States, I had the pleasure of seeing often. A plain, unostentatious, honest man, diligent in business, he worked hard to secure the highest interest of his country, though not then known to be the great statesman which time has since proved him. Mrs. Monroe was a perfect contrast to Mrs. Madison. The latter was a woman of superior elegance, devoted to society, and yet possessed of a clear head and an accurate judgment. She was said to be not only the better but the wiser half of Mr. Madison; and while she could play with a lap-dog or grace a dining party, or be the cynosure of all eyes in a ball-room, she could preside in council, write out state documents, and give the finishing touch to the President's Message.

Mrs. Monroe's domestic habits unfitted her for the eternal round of receptions required in her position, and she very soon retired with disgust from the artificial surroundings of her station, abolished the weekly levees, and scarcely appeared, even on "New-Year's Day," to receive the greetings of the people. Yet she was admired; for, like Cornelia, she placed most value upon the jewels of her own household. A married daughter took her place in society, and gloried in the prestige of the Presidential Mansion.

CHAPTER X.

A MID the scenes of my early girlhood, so many interesting incidents crowd upon my memory that it is
difficult to make a selection.   Every spot in and around
Washington and Georgetown is connected with some
pleasant association, some tender recollection.   Our family circle was unbroken, save in the absence of my elder
brother.   I loved my mother tenderly, and almost worshiped my father; was happy in the very necessity devolving upon me as the elder sister of paying much attention to the younger children.   Blessed arrangement of a
kind Providence, that affection and solicitude are increased
and deepened by the helplessness of those who are dependent upon us!   Dear little brothers and sisters! every
sigh that rent their hearts made my own quiver with
pain; so every joy I shared with them was rendered
doubly dear. Even now my heart swells with emotion
when I think of our wanderings in search of wild flowers
on the borders of the little stream which then so sweetly
murmured over its pebbly bottom at the foot of Capitol
Hill, and of our moonlight walks in the midsummer,
watching the pleasure boats as they floated gently down
the river with gay streamers and snowy sails, and I can
almost hear the sound of the flute falling upon the entranced ear.

There was a little island sleeping on the bosom of the
Potomac—an emerald of surpassing loveliness in Spring,
and of glowing beauty in Summer.   It attracted many

visitors, who were welcome through the kindness of the benevolent owner—a Mr. Mason, who, like Alcinous, made every visitor an honored guest. One of his daughters was a schoolmate of mine at Miss Taylor's, and I must confess I sometimes envied her the possession of such a home, and often, while wandering through the intricate mazes of that luxuriant spot, felt sorry that she could not enjoy it as I did. Alas, poor girl! she was an invalid, a subject for sympathy; and I, possessing exuberant health, should have been very unwilling to exchange places with her.

How truly may it be said that this is a world of compensation! Mine was comparatively an humble home, but I had good health and an active mind; Miss Mason's was one of luxurious surroundings, which she could not enjoy with her weak and frail body. I knew of the elegancies of that earthly paradise, but nothing more, save that pale disease flitted occasionally through the family mansion and somber clouds hid the bright sunbeams from the buds and blossoms of Hope; and that finally this lovely island was sold to a stranger from a far-off country, who "was not of us," and then the young people from Washington and Georgetown sought another spot for their picnics and holidays.

One may be pardoned for dwelling so long upon the scenes of early life, the impressions are so vivid. The flowers we knew in childhood do indeed fade; their petals may perish, but the fragrance is with us still. The heart keeps every joy of former years that is worth preserving, and the flitting visions of happiness known in this world shall grow into paramount bliss in heaven.

The current of my life flowed smoothly until I entered my twentieth year,—then came a tide of misfortunes which well nigh sank our family into despair. Poverty, sudden and unexpected, came by one of those not un-common catastrophes expressed in these bitter words, "Taken for security debts." My father was a generous man, liberal to profusion, and had never learned to man-age dollars and cents economically. He could not say "nay" to a friend who wished to borrow. In an evil hour he indorsed to a large amount for one who proved a traitor to the best of friends. The integrity of my truly excellent father forbade his taking any advantage by that evasion so often practiced under such circumstances, and which amounts to downright swindling. He placed all his property at the disposal of the creditors, not re-serving even the smallest amount of personal property.

There was no hiding away of silver spoons or valuable plate,—even my paintings were sold at auction; but what grieved me most was the loss of my piano—one of supe-rior tone and quality, knocked off under the hammer for thirty-five dollars. Then came the pinchings of close economy, which, notwithstanding the industry of my mother and the untiring energy of my father, failed to place us in comfortable circumstances again; and it was found so exceedingly difficult to live in Washington that my father resolved to seek a home in St. Louis, where he had friends and relatives who were willing to aid him in procuring some lucrative business.

Before he left I had sought and obtained a situation as a teacher in the interior of Virginia. In this I was aided by the influence of some kind friends in high places, who, being persuaded of my fitness for the posi-tion, soon procured me ample patronage. But, alas! the place selected for my new home was at the distance of three hundred miles, which I was to travel by stage in the dreary month of December, and over the worst of roads, three weeks being the time required to accomplish it.

I was placed under the care of a respectable old gentleman who lived at Wytheville, whither I was going to try my fortune as a school-ma'am. The afternoon upon which I left my home can never be effaced from my memory. Ours was a silent meal, as we surrounded for the last time the family board together. My tears flowed fast, and every mouthful of food that I attempted to swallow seemed as if it would choke me. Though my own heart was breaking, I tried to smile, that my dearly loved father and mother might the better bear my departure. The scene that followed that meal is indescribable. I left the house clinging to my father's arm, without daring to look behind me; and he handed me into the stage-coach after one more convulsive pressure in his arms. I closed my eyes for a moment in agony,—and when I opened them again he was gone. I never saw him more. I can not now, after the lapse of nearly fifty years, dwell upon this without anguish—'t is never to be forgotten "while life or being" lasts.

We tarried, my old gray-headed friend and I, the first night in Alexandria. Externally it was a dreary night— the wind blew, and the cold raindrops pattered on the pavement, as we drove up to the gloomy-looking old tavern where the stage stopped. Our supper was cheerless—mine was untasted. Retiring early to my solitary chamber, a flood of tears relieved my overcharged heart, and with tolerable composure I began to make arrangements for a night's rest. The wind was whistling through the long, wide passages of the old tavern, rattling the broken shutters, and roaring in the empty closets, of which there were two in the chamber I occupied; and

then, to cap the climax, my door had no fastening. I
placed the table against it, and upon the table a chair,
and, surmounting all, my little old hair trunk (for who
ever heard of a Saratoga trunk in those days?), so that,
if any one should attempt to enter, the noise of the falling furniture might awaken me. Useless precaution! I
slept none; and the gray dawning light found me still
treating my pillow to a tear-bath, and resolving, in the
agony of my soul, that I would abandon my journey,
and return home.

A bright morning sun, however, dispelled much of
the gloom that surrounded me; and better thoughts,
with happier anticipations, enabled me to go forward in
the path of duty. I had always a very strong confidence
in an overruling Providence, and it seems to me now that,
even when a child, my faith in the goodness and mercy
of God formed a part of my very being. I began to
pray at so early an age that I can scarcely date the
period; and I then lifted up my heart as sincerely in
prayer to God, believing as firmly in his existence and in
his parental love as I have done ever since, though my
expanded mind and maturer judgment, with the constant
experience of his loving-kindness, have rendered me more
deeply sensible of my own unworthiness of the multiplied
mercies that I have enjoyed.

After leaving Alexandria we had a disagreeable journey of several days over roads almost impassable, with
frequent joltings over corduroy bridges, before we reached
Richmond. Here we rested for a day, as we had yet a
journey of nearly two weeks before us; and here I had
the good fortune to make the acquaintance of a citizen
of Wytheville, Granville Henderson, Esq., a member of
the Virginia Legislature, then in session. Mr. Hen-

derson was a man of excellent abilities, sound judgment, and a warm heart. He showed me much kindness, and manifested great interest in my welfare; giving a cheering account of my future prospects, insisting, at the same time, that I should make his house one of my homes, especially during his absence, as his wife was alone with the exception of a little daughter, who would be one of my pupils. "Mrs. Henderson," he added, "was anticipating my arrival with great pleasure, as were other prospective patrons of the school."

I visited both houses of the Legislature, composed of very respectable and dignified looking men, who appeared to transact business with quiet decorum and great dispatch; the members showed more respect and politeness towards each other than is usually seen in legislative halls.

The principal object of interest in Richmond was the Monumental Church, founded on the very spot where the theater was burned. This melancholy and startling event marked the close of the year 1811. During the representation of a popular tragedy, "The Bleeding Nun," the stage scenery caught fire from the lamps. It was at first thought to be a slight affair, as the fire was promptly arrested, and supposed to be entirely extinguished; but, in less than five minutes after, the exciting cry of fire! fire! was heard from behind the scenes, and the actors came rushing across the stage in the greatest confusion; some on fire, others striving to pull down the burning curtains. The terrific scene that followed was beyond description. There was but one mode of egress from the theater, and the flames were spreading with unexampled rapidity; the passage was so crowded in a few minutes that many were trampled to death; some sprang from the upper windows, and others tried to escape across the stage, though it was enveloped in flames. Seventy-two persons lost their lives in the conflagration; among them the Governor of Virginia. The inhabitants, while the flood-gates of grief were open in their hearts, and sorrow a living object before them, planned this church as a memorial of the dead buried under the ruins of the old theater. They poured out their money like water. Art, taste, and genius lent their aid, and the work went on rapidly for a while; but more and more slowly, as the awful scene faded from their memory, and the building in 1819 was yet unfinished, though another theater had been erected in another part of the city, as if to show how narrowly joy may be partitioned off from sorrow; how the merry-hearted and the broken-hearted may be unconsciously pillowed in proximity; and how the world jogs on in its daily routine indifferent to the feelings of either.

What a picture of the instability of human character—the evanescence of human feeling. The church, however, is now finished with a monument in front—the pale, cold, beautiful marble pointing heavenward in commemoration of the event.

A gentleman of undoubted veracity, and not in the least tinctured with superstition, collected and published some remarkable dreams and mysterious forebodings of coming events connected with this awful catastrophe, one of which still lingers in my memory. A young officer had procured tickets for himself and his betrothed, an interesting girl of great worth and beauty, whom he had persuaded to attend the theater with him on that fatal night. She was opposed to such amusements, but promised to accompany him for this once, as he was to leave the next morning to join his regiment. Calling for her at the appointed hour, he found her in tears. "Why, Mary, what is the matter? why are you not ready? You surely do not intend to disappoint me. Come, we have not a moment to spare." She shook her head sadly, as she raised her tearful eyes to meet the reproachful look of her lover. "It is of no use, Edward, I can not, I dare not go." "What! can you have the heart to refuse me this little request, when I leave you to-morrow—it may be forever? I know you are a Christian, Mary, but I did not think you so sanctimonious as to condemn this innocent recreation; but," he added, betraying considerable nervousness at seeing no smile in her half-averted eyes, and receiving no response from her trembling lips, "tell me the cause of this sudden change." She replied, with some hesitation, "I dreamed last night we were in the theater, and deeply interested in the performances, when the cry of fire was heard, and the whole house was enveloped in flames. Amid the alarm and confusion that followed we were attempting to force our way down stairs, and were crushed to death by the advancing crowd." "All this is sheer nonsense," said Edward. "Dreams go by contraries. You can not possibly be so superstitious as to make this a pretext for staying at home." An unwonted pallor spread over the face of the young girl, and she shuddered as if striving to suppress the intensity of her feelings. Overcome by the pressing entreaties of her lover, and dreading the ridicule of her gay friends, she reluctantly consented to go; but her fears were not dispelled. Edward and Mary went, but never more returned. Her dream was literally verified; they were actually trampled to death in the gallery, and their remains could only be distinguished

among the heaps of crushed and mangled bodies by
his silver-hilted dagger and the inscription on her engagement ring.

Many premonitions and warnings by dreams and otherwise were recorded in that book.   Perhaps great calami-
ties have some mysterious power given them to send
forward a dim presentiment of their advancing footsteps,
impressing the mind with the idea that in to-day already
walks to-morrow.

At the end of three weeks we arrived at Wytheville,
just in time to be at the marriage of the oldest daughter of my good old friend and traveling companion,
Mr. Oury.   The stage drove up early in the forenoon to
his door, where we were met by the whole family, and
received with that warm cordiality which belongs to Virginia and to Virginians.   We were ushered into a comfortable room, and I felt that we were surrounded by
warm hearts; every body talked, and nobody listened.
Scarce two hours had elapsed after my arrival, when Mrs.
Smith, Mrs. Henderson, her daughter, and other ladies
came, in the friendliest manner, to welcome me to Wytheville, and each one begged that I should make her house
my home.

If time were always counted by incidents, how much
longer would some days be than others!   That day would
have made a week of ordinary life.

On leaving Washington for Wythe, a letter was handed
to me by General Daniel Parker, recommending me to
the "most favorable consideration of those whose acquaintance" I might "wish to cultivate."   Shortly after
my arrival at my new home I was gratified to know that
the kindness of my friends at Washington was yet fol-

lowing me, as the subjoined letter from Dr. John Floyd,
then a member of Congress, will show:

WASHINGTON, *January* 20, 1820.

MISS JULIA,—I spent the evening a day or two ago with your
father and mother. They informed me you had gone to Wythe C.
H., at the instance of General Smyth and Mrs. Oury, and wished
me to write to you and inclose a letter to some of my friends in
that part of the country. This I do with great cheerfulness; at the
same time I am persuaded that the friendship of Mrs. Oury and
General Smyth make it almost unnecessary. Your family are quite
well.   With respect, your obedient servant,

JOHN FLOYD.

CHAPTER XI.

WYTHEVILLE was noted for a total indifference to religion. There was not a church or any place of worship in the town. The only preacher in the vicinity was of the Dutch Reformed Church. His example was of the worst kind—carousing, drinking, cockfighting, and playing cards during the week, with an occasional sermon on the Sabbath to a sleepy, ungodly congregation, that seemed to know as little about the truths of the Gospel, as if our Savior had never made his advent into the world. Strange to tell, however, there was much refinement among the better class; for this we do not generally expect where there are no godly ministers and no churches. Politeness, kindness, and true Virginia hospitality reigned pre-eminently.

My first introduction into their midst was at the wedding before mentioned. The company was collected before six o'clock. The ceremony, which took place about seven, was novel and, to me, very interesting. The minister took his station with his back to the fireplace; the bride and bridegroom walked in first, each having an attendant holding a lighted candle, as if to give the company full opportunity for seeing them distinctly. The minister began the service, and every one rose. The windows, being open, were soon filled with the black faces and woolly heads of the servants, who had collected to see "young missus" married. The ceremony was long, followed by a tedious lecture, at the close of which was the usual amount of kissing, which occupied nearly an hour. We were then ushered into the ball-room, the bride and bridegroom occupying the first place in a "Virginia reel." The "new school-teacher," who had previously received an introduction to nearly every body present, was taken out and placed third in the set.

I was passionately fond of dancing, but would have preferred being a spectator on that evening had I not been afraid of giving offense. Some amusing mistakes were made in the various attempts to speak correctly the unpronounceable name of "Hieronymus." My first partner asked the pleasure of dancing in the reel with "Miss Roundabuss;" the next, a lad about seventeen, very pompously called me "Miss Hippopotamus." Afterwards came a young disciple of Æsculapius, who had recently put up his Galen's-head in the town, and whose family I knew in Winchester. He thought he had the name precisely when he called me "Heterogeneous;" others called me "Hatrogenous;" but all agreed that it was far easier to call me "Miss Julia Ann," and this was almost universally adopted.

At twelve o'clock my principal lady patroness, Mrs. Smyth, who had claimed me from the first as her guest and boarder, carried me off to her own quiet home, not a hundred yards distant. The dancing continued all night, and many of the guests were invited to breakfast the next morning at Mr. Oury's hospitable house; and the gay young folks who had not succeeded in "tiring each other down" the night before continued their dancing until noon.

My first night at Mrs. Smyth's was spent sleeplessly, but with feelings of the deepest gratitude to God that I had found so much kindness among strangers. True, I

had left a home to which in all probability I was never
to return,—never again to meet in the home circle father,
mother, brothers, and sisters. I was now to stand alone,
and must necessarily rely upon myself. The broad highways of the world were now before me, and I must
emancipate myself from all customary indulgence, take
my place among the thronging multitude, and commence
life's struggle in earnest.

Oh, how my solitary spirit yearned to see once more
those whom I had left behind! No more sweet girl
friendships, no more pleasant walks and drives along the
banks of the lovely Potomac—a name that even now
touches the tenderest chord in my heart, and stirs up
the life-blood in my old veins! A long and weary
way, the difficulties of which I shuddered to think of,
separated me from those I had loved and cherished from
the first dawn of life. Oh, how much anguish is often
crowded into our hearts, battling with bitter memories!
But in the midst of all this darkness the trembling star
of Hope still faintly shone, and ere the rosy light of
morning came my soul felt stronger, and with the natural
elasticity of a cheerful disposition I commenced immediately to prepare for my new vocation. I soon learned
that the life of a faithful teacher must be one of toil and
unremitting care. All my fairy visions of romance faded
into stern reality as my responsibility for others increased.

And now came to my aid those early lessons of piety,
so deeply impressed upon my mind, not only by home
influences, but by the privileges enjoyed under the ministry of the Rev. Mr. Hawley. I was a regular attendant, having been baptized and confirmed there, though
not a communicant, and consequently not recognized as
a member of the Church.

But to return to my school. I rented a large upper room in a house contiguous to General Smyth's. The kindness of my patrons relieved me from all trouble and expense as regarded desks, benches, etc. My school-room was neatly fitted up for the accommodation of thirty or forty pupils. All the little misses in the village attended—some grown girls—and a few little boys. A few of the girls were larger and considerably taller than the teacher. One, I remember, stood over six feet in her shoes, and had seen but sixteen Summers. This, however, was an exception.

The first day, with all its petty vexations, passed off smoothly, though I retired at night with an aching heart, burdened with a painful interest for my pupils. I was rather doubtful whether, with my inexperience and want of tact, our association would be for weal or woe. I began again the next morning with renewed vigor, class-ing and arranging my pupils so as to give me as little trouble as possible; and then commenced my course of instruction with the elementary principles. By the end of the first week I had learned an important lesson myself, which can not be too deeply impressed upon a teacher's mind. A person who has not the patience to communi-cate knowledge, drop by drop, should never undertake the instruction of ignorant children, since it is impossible to pour into their minds by copious streams. The heart, too, must be deeply interested in the work, or there will be no success. That teacher, who feels no conviction of the importance of the cause, and no solicitude about the issue, should give up the office.

And now, like a beam of light across the shadows of the past, comes the memory of my much-loved pupil, friend, and companion, Frances Smyth, who, though only fourteen years of age, rendered herself both useful and agreeable to me. A certain expression of frankness about her won my heart immediately. So natural and without disguise was her character, and so winning the simplicity of her manners, due to her child-like innocence and sweet feminine timidity, that she soon became the sunshine of my daily existence, helping to dispel the clouds that sometimes gathered around my heart. There was something noble in the lineaments of her fair face, brilliantly lighted up at times, and corresponding with her graceful figure. Eyes "bright and blue as the Summer sky," and a mouth trembling with half-smiles, arising from the very buoyancy of inward gladness; a complexion enriched by the sweetest and most delicate bloom, allied to a tone of cheerfulness; and her every motion so light and free that a poet might have supposed her some "Hebe or fair young daughter of the dawn." She was my constant and efficient aid in carrying out every arrangement; yet she was gentle, confiding, and one of the most obedient of my pupils.

My first serious difficulty was with a little girl about ten years of age, the youngest child of a large family, who had been badly spoiled at home. She was noisy, indolent, and impatient under restraint. Continually teasing and annoying others, this little nettle-top went on from bad to worse, until endurance was no longer a virtue. I was anxious to keep her in school, as I had five from the same family, and it was quite to my interest to get along pleasantly with her. But it could not be. One afternoon her resistance to my authority reached its climax; so I quietly removed her from the school-room to an adjoining apartment and gave her the well-merited punishment with my slipper, the first she had ever had in her life. Her screams were terrific. There was an awful silence in the school room, and you might have heard a pin drop, as I led her back, and, placing her bonnet on her head, ordered her to go home and never return. I then quietly resumed my seat, and the lessons proceeded as usual until the hour of dismissal.

I remained alone until nearly night, weeping, praying, and struggling to conquer what I thought my own ungovernable temper. I began to think that teaching was not my vocation. I understand it all now. I was well pleased so far as the dictatorial part was concerned. In the control I had hitherto exercised over my sisters while at school, I had never been contradicted; and, notwithstanding the constantly recurring petty trials in early life, I had not learned how to be calm and unmoved when my will was opposed. Every possible pains had been taken to secure for me the best education. I had been the idol of my father's heart, and the object of my mother's tenderest solicitude; but, while the love of knowledge was carefully instilled into my mind, I had failed to learn that modest diffidence in reference to my attainments, which presents an effectual barrier to disagreeable parade and pedantry. Every thing I did at home was excellent, and no opportunity was lost to parade my attainments to friends and visitors. The shock I sustained in being obliged to devote my talents to the dull routine of a school-room, instead of making a display in society, was terrible; but a sense of duty to God and to my parents sustained me. I knew I could teach, and I determined I would not be an inferior teacher. But let me here remark that young persons should cultivate a humility with regard to themselves, which is the life and soul of youthful exertion.

After this contest with my little pupil, I retired to my room with a violent headache, deeply humbled, but perfectly determined to sustain my dignity at all hazards. The first voice that I heard in the morning uttered this expression with deep feeling: "She will drive away all her pupils; people will not submit to such correction." "I hope not," was the gentle reply, "and I'm sure she had better commence in the right way, and let them know what is due from the pupil to the teacher." This I heard as I descended the stairs which opened into the breakfast-room. General Smyth was there, looking cold and reserved. Frances ventured one kind glance from her sunny blue eyes, but Nancy, her younger sister, sat trembling, with her face flushed to an unusual redness, and my sweet little Nannie Henderson, the granddaughter, a child six years of age, seemed fluttered and amazed at my presence. Mrs. Smyth bade me good morning with her usual cordiality. No one spoke during the breakfast except by way of courtesy.

I went immediately after this silent meal to my school-room. It was early, but most of the girls were already assembled, some conversing in an undertone, others studying diligently. I spoke pleasantly to them, and gave kindly answers to the few timid questions asked about their lessons, though my heart was oppressed in reference to the possibility of my losing five pupils instead of one. I would not, however, have taken a step backward if I had lost my whole school. But, lo! I had scarcely finished calling the roll, when in walked my refractory pupil, followed by the other four. The little girl walked rather irresolutely to my desk and placed a note in my hand. She stood with downcast eyes while I read it. The contents were somewhat in this style: "Please receive my penitent little girl again, with the positive assurance that every thing shall be done to prevent future trouble; and we will aid you in subduing and punishing any disobedience on her part. We are satisfied that you will do every thing in your power to promote her highest interest, and are willing to leave the matter in your hands."

The struggle was over. She remained with me as long as I was in Wytheville, first an obedient, afterward an affectionate pupil. I loved her the more because she profited so well by my correction. Indeed, the whole family continued among my best and fastest friends, and I had the pleasure of meeting some of them after a lapse of many years.

Indolence may be sometimes excited into action when it can not be driven; and often a vice, though it may not be forcibly and immediately eradicated, may be starved and withered in the shadow of an opposite virtue, by a skillful and assiduous cultivator; but impertinence and resistance to legitimate authority, and, in fact, every species of disobedience in a school, must be promptly subdued.

Previous to my leaving Washington, my kind preceptress, Mrs. Stone, gave me, with the following letter, a great deal of instruction which I practically applied in teaching:

CITY OF WASHINGTON, *January* 2, 1820.

Although an entire stranger at Wythe Court House, the interest I take in the future of my friend, Miss Hieronymus, is such that I can not help giving my testimony of her full capability to the instruction of young ladies. During the three years of my intimacy with Miss Hieronymus, part of which time she was a resident in my family, her conduct in every respect has been such as to inspire the affection and esteem of all around her, and nothing reconciles me to the painful necessity of her going so great a distance from us, but the certainty that her talents are such as to make her useful to others and gain friends wherever she is known. Miss Hieronymus has had the advantage of being educated by an English lady who kept a large boarding-school in Washington, and having always paid the greatest attention to her studies and the instruction of those about her, she will now be rewarded for all her exertions by being useful both to others and herself.   ANNA MARIA STONE.

Mrs. Stone also gave me a number of patterns for drawing and painting, and a quantity of white velvet on which to paint in water-colors; trimmings for ball-dresses, belts, capes, aprons, and reticules were painted on this material. Red roses blushed in gay confusion among blue morning-glories and modest violets, half-hidden by a verdant covering of green leaves. I had attained great skill in the use of the pencil, and copied flowers from nature so correctly as rarely to need an India rubber. A few specimens of this ornamental painting, carried by my pupils to their homes, gained me quite a large drawing-class, which increased considerably the profits of the school.

There were two or three pianos in the village, and a demand for music lessons soon came. I had been teaching the two Miss Symths from the commencement. They both learned rapidly; but the younger was a prodigy. She could play upwards of fifty tunes before she could reach an octave with her tiny fingers. Music seemed to dwell in her soul, and the sound of a musical instrument thrilled through her whole frame like electricity, and what was most astonishing she learned pieces with more facility by note than by ear. She never wearied practicing, and flew to the piano at playtime, rather than dance on the green with her young companions. When I left Wytheville she was only ten years old, and then played correctly nearly one hundred pieces—simple, to be sure, but it was wonderful.

As I had no piano and was unable to purchase one, I could take but few music scholars, being obliged to go to the homes of my pupils to give lessons, between school hours. The first lesson I gave was at noon, a very lazy hour I must admit, and as I entered the parlor I found my pupil sitting in a large rocking-chair at the piano, swaying herself backward and forward, playing, and singing at the top of her voice. She had a fine ear for music, and had taken a few lessons from a lady in town, but played all her pieces by heart, never having learned her notes.

"Good morning, Miss Julia Ann," said she, as I entered. "Take a seat, here 's your chair."

"What!" said I, with astonishment, "do you intend to sit in that chair while taking your lesson?"

"Why, yes; it is mighty comfortable and high enough, see!"

With that she commenced running up and down the scales until I was perfectly astonished at her facility.

"Stop," said I, "rise from that chair, and take the piano stool."

"Oh, no, do n't, Miss Julia Ann; I shall be so tired sitting bolt upright."

"You will oblige me by taking the piano-stool."

"Well, Miss Julia Ann, and are you going to stand the whole hour?"

"Yes."

And I stood sullenly the full sixty minutes, pointing to the notes and instructing her. It was the custom then to give three lessons a week, an hour each, for the small sum of sixteen dollars per session. My pupil did not attempt the rocking-chair again at a lesson, though, I doubt not, she often practiced in that way. I afterward learned to love this young girl for her amiability and proficiency.

The fact is, I did not then realize the honorable position that a faithful teacher holds in society, and was yet mourning over my disappointed expectations. I had hoped to be a lady of literary leisure. A few years taught me more wisdom, and I learned to be sincerely thankful to my Heavenly Father that he chose for me a better and a more useful path in life than that of living for myself alone, floating down the stream of time with no higher aspiration than that of mingling with the "great and little vulgar" of this world. I wonder now that I ever should have desired it. I had no taste for fine dressing and did not enjoy fashionable life; would always have preferred a quiet country home to the amusements and frivolities of a city; and yet, had I chosen my own ways I should have been a mere item in this great world, nothing more.

I soon found it impracticable to attend to my school, give lessons in Drawing and French, and do justice to my few music scholars, so I concluded early in the Spring to send for my sister to aid me. She was a fine performer on the piano and well qualified to teach both English and French. In the meantime I toiled on, and the more I had to do the more my energy increased. None of the labor-saving inventions patent now in every school were then known, not even the convenience of ruled letter-paper. Having no time during the day for extra duties, I was obliged to take the copy-books of the whole school at night to my room, which were first ruled and then the copies set. The teacher, if she did her duty, was as much a drudge out of school as in it. I was often obliged to sit up till twelve o'clock at night, copying music, of which there was not a printed sheet in the village, preparing sketches for my drawing class, or examining text-books. I never would teach a lesson that I did not thoroughly understand. A fatal mistake, made by some young teachers, is that of attempting to teach through the medium of a book, what they do not understand themselves. This excites the contempt of their pupils. Children are scrutinizing observers. Providence has made them so, for they must learn every thing, at first, by imitation.

The houses of Wytheville were built in close proximity; this promoted a kindly intercourse, that rendered the whole village almost like one extended household. The persons with whom I resided were pre-eminently aristocratic by wealth, position, and intelligence; but they assumed none of the airs of that self-styled class. Families, whose nobility is patent, no matter how great their rank or riches, are not afraid of coming in contact with the humbler classes of society, if their virtues entitle them to sympathy and respect.

Health and poverty, so said General Smyth, characterized Wytheville; but I found its more definite characteristics to be genuine kindness and unostentatious hospitality. I never knew any suffering poor among the inhabitants. They dwelt in their own tenements, were cheerfully industrious, and lived plentifully—some luxuriously. The abundance of pure air and fresh water in these healthful regions was a constantly recurring joy. The whole country was rife with rosy cheeks, nimble feet, brawny shoulders—athletic men and beautiful women.

No wonder the inhabitants of mountainous districts become strongly attached to their homes, where mountain, valley, forest, living streams, and deep rivers please the eye and fill the heart with enthusiasm. New River, so remarkable for the variety of its flowing outlines, its bewildering mazes, and cloud suffused precipices, looking down gloomily on the quiet valley beneath, where flows the laughing, sparkling waters in which is mirrored as blue a sky as ever shown upon the eye of beauty, formed one of the attractions in the vicinity of Wytheville. A beautiful narrow glen, opening into a broad valley richly wooded, presented the agreeable prospect of substantial, well-built houses, surrounded by forest trees, extensive orchards, and cultivated fields. I can not forget my first visit to the house of a friend who lived in the midst of this panorama of loveliness. Words are inadequate to convey an idea of the sublimity and grandeur of the scene. A painter could give but a faint picture, for no canvass could reproduce the light and color that played around this charming region in Summer; no skill could catch the changing hues of purple, green, and gold that bannered the horizon at sunset; nor the glories of the morning sun, when just appearing above the misty mountains, whose base afforded a fantastic and fitting channel for the gleaming river; sometimes hid beneath shelving rocks, now rushing forth in a rapid torrent, and then flowing by many a quiet homestead. Upon its banks were found the oak, the ash, the walnut, the maple, and the chestnut. Sheltered among the branches of these trees a myriad of singing birds poured forth their sweetest notes, the whole Summer long, making the air vocal and the spirit glad. In the dim distance were seen stately firs clinging to the rugged sides of the precipitous cliffs, all pointing upwards and seeming to have no common interest with the earth; but like the rocks amid which they grow, they remain ever stern, dark, and still. The celebrated "Hawk's Nest" is found on one of the highest and almost perpendicular precipices of New River; an Alpine eyrie fitted for birds of prey, and from which one might expect to see the circling flight of the American eagle.

I found a kind and generous friend in Captain John Matthews, Clerk of the Court, who, having no daughter, sent his little son, Thornton Posey, about eight years of age, to school. This child became peculiarly dear to me. His sparkling eyes and always animated countenance showed every emotion of the generous, loving child, as evening after evening he came to my desk to demand the bundle of quill pens to carry to his father, who mended them at night and sent them back in the morning. I had never learned to make or mend a pen, and steel substitutes were then unknown. This saved me much time and trouble, and the kindness of Mr. Matthews is written on my heart, not as with a pen, but as with the point of a diamond, never to be effaced. This is only one instance among the many kindnesses received from him and his excellent wife.

Chapter XII.

I HAVE spoken of my routine of school duties as being so various, that the question may be asked, How my time was divided, so as to give each duty proper attention? I used the monitorial system to some extent, which gave me an hour in the morning and one in the afternoon to attend to my French and Drawing; but in the same large room where the whole school was seated; thus I had an opportunity of overlooking the appointed monitress, who heard the recitations of the younger children, and taught the a, b, abs, as successfully as I could have done it myself. The last half hour in the forenoon of each day was devoted to writing; my music lessons were given at noon and at night.

I still retain a clear recollection of many interesting circumstances connected with my early teaching, and relevant to the object of this work. Some of my pupils were very lovely girls, and gave promise of future usefulness in life; others possessed a brilliancy of mind that enabled them to improve rapidly, and were a constant source of delight to me. They come up now like beams of light through the opening clouds of the past; and among these heart-shadows, so strangely dear, are visions that will not depart,—sweet memories that will never die.

One among my Wytheville pupils forms a beautiful picture. Classical features, a well-formed head, crowned with hair dark as the raven's wing, a high, pale forehead, large, dreamy eyes, imparting an air of melancholy, might have characterized her as a Jewish maiden, had it not been for the beautiful clearness of her complexion. Her obliging disposition and lady-like manners rendered her agreeable to her school-mates and attractive to her friends. I have often looked at her as she bent quietly over her books during study hours, and thought her exceedingly beautiful, more like a dream of poetry than a visible reality, and I mentally repeated :

> " Earth hath angels, though their forms are molded
> But of such clay as fashions all below ;
> Though harps are wanting, and bright pinions folded,
> We know them by the love-light on their brow."

This young lady was the daughter of a queer old Irish gentleman, who had amassed a fortune by industry and economy, and, having the good sense to know when he had enough, retired to a beautiful farm with his family, that he might enjoy it. He was a widower— three interesting daughters, and an only son, the pride of his father's heart and the idol of his sisters, formed the domestic circle. But the son upon whom so many hopes had been built was doomed to an early death by consumption. His leaf had already begun to wither on the tree of life ere he reached the age of twenty. He had genius, and would have distinguished himself as an author had he lived,—what he accomplished before he died left its impress.

Oh, how many beautiful hopes and anticipations were buried in his early grave! But it was a blessing to know that the good seed of eternal life had already budded, blossomed, and brought forth fruit in his heart; and in his dark, lustrous eyes dwelt a holy light that spoke of better things than the earthly honors and distinctions so coveted among men.

"The fadeless flowers of intellect shall bloom
When youth, with all its pride, reposes
Deep in the tomb."

The earthly immortality of the mind is a type of the immortality of the soul.

I had often been invited to visit the family; but long declined their invitations, simply because I had no suitable visiting dress, and I knew the Miss F.'s entertained a good deal of company. Finally, by Mrs. Smyth's advice, I determined to prepare myself for a little recreation in the country, and accept some of the many invitations given me. After much consultation, it was decided that I should purchase a black India satin. Five yards was a full dress-pattern, and would cost only a little upwards of six dollars. This, made to fit neatly, but without any extra trimming, was relieved by a rich collar of thread-lace and full cuffs of the same—some of the remains of my Washington finery—and gave me quite a stylish appearance.

Why did I purchase a black dress? In the first place, black silks or satins were fashionable; and Mrs. Smyth thought I looked so well in my old rusty black silk that a new one would not only promote good looks, but economy. I wore no ornaments save a handsome pin that fastened my collar. I always had the impression that good taste required no decorations except those that were, or appeared to be, useful. Finger-rings and ear-rings I never wore, even in my gayest days; so that if I had any living grace it was not destroyed by ornament.

One bright Friday afternoon I gratified myself, and doubtless gave much pleasure to my sweet young pupil,

Sophie, by going home with her, to spend a day or two. This home was a beautiful one, in the midst of a picturesque country; and all its surroundings exhibited so much taste that I could but be convinced that the father possessed a genuine love of the beautiful, though he was an unlettered man. He met us at the gate. "Welcome ye are, see, madam"—his peculiar manner of expressing himself. "Come in, see; you 're right, see, Sophie, to bring the school-ma'am home with you. Here, Esther, come see the school-teacher. Glad we are, see, madam, to have you with us." Being a widower, Miss Esther, the eldest daughter, presided over the household affairs. Every thing bespoke energy, industry, neatness, and at the same time that entire comfort to be found in many a Virginia home.

On Saturday we had a regular dining; some of the neighbors were invited, who paid me marked attention, as if they felt that I had conferred a favor by coming among them.

Just before dinner was announced, my blunt but kind old host took his seat by me, placed his hand upon my satin sleeve, and, shaking his head ominously, said:

"Fine ye are, see, madam; too poor ye are to spend so much in dress."

I was startled for a moment, the blood rushed to my face, my eyes swam in tears at this apparent rudeness; but after a moment's reflection I felt the truth of his remark,—I *was* dressed with apparent extravagance for a person in my condition. Satin and rich laces, with an immense comb of real shell—as was then fashionable— did seem inconsistent; but looking up into the old man's face, which shone with good humor and real interest, I laughingly replied: "Oh, no, you would not think so if

I should tell you how economically all these have been preserved, and how little they cost me; and this is the only handsome dress I have in the world."

"Well, well, right ye are, see, madam," and he pressed my hand kindly; "so, so let it be."

His daughter was taking French lessons from me, and his next question was:

"French woman ye are, see, eh?   From Paris?"

"No, sir, I am a native of the United States, but I speak French fluently."

An incident occurred at the dinner-table which will illustrate what an incessant talker I was.   After the first course was removed, a servant passed around with a large tray filled with sweetmeats, preserves of various kinds, rich creams, etc.   It was handed to me first, but instead of helping myself, as was expected, and suffering her to pass on, I placed one dish after another on the table around my plate talking all the time with great volubility to my neighbor, yet wondering why the servant did not place the things upon the table herself.   I had scarce finished my arrangement, when she replaced them all upon the tray and passed on, leaving me minus every thing.   I looked up and found there was a general titter going around the table at my expense, by which I discovered my blunder.   Not the least confused, however, I joined in the laugh, which relieved the embarrassment, and, at the same time, made them feel kindly in spite of my awkwardness.

The following Monday, after my visit above described, I returned to the school-room and attended to my duties with more than usual energy.   The girls were good and industrious, and I think I discovered that day in some, who had seemed particularly dull before, the kindlings of capacity, perhaps because I was rested and consequently more patient. How true it is, that the smallest flame has its moments of brightness; and there is a period in the life of every child that may be turned to its own advantage, enabling it to perform something good if not great. Experience has taught me that many of the severest trials, and constantly recurring vexations of daily life, arise from our own want of preparation to struggle against them. Petty annoyances are the true touchstones by which the glittering gold of our philosophy is put to the test; the most boasted philosophy, when submitted to this test, is often found to sink into a common metal.

About this time I became acquainted with the widowed mother of one of my pupils by the name of Crockett, a charming old lady, whose reminiscences of the war of Independence were full of interest for me. She showed me a dress of the olden time containing, to my astonishment, twelve or fourteen widths of rich brocaded silk, embroidered with large bunches of pinks and roses, all wrought with the needle; the skirt was so stiff that it would almost stand alone. It was worn open in front and had a train more than two yards in length, such being the fashion in the middle of the last century. Her father had paid twenty pounds sterling and a horse for the dress-pattern before the war. My tall pupil was the old lady's daughter. I paid many visits to this hospitable family, as they resided near town.

So soon as the school was properly organized, I began to feel anxious that my pupils should spend the Sabbath in a religious manner—the Sabbath, "sweet bridal of the earth and skies"—that I had been accustomed to spend in church-going and in the quiet observance of religious duties. I have before mentioned that there was no place of worship in the town, no preaching except an occasional sermon from an itinerant preacher who held forth in the Court House; and none but the boldest of this class of preachers would venture to remain an hour after service for fear of some mischievous tricks being played upon him.

I witnessed none of this irreverence, however, during my stay there. Whenever an appointment was made for preaching, I collected as many of my pupils as I could, and marched them two by two to the Court House, where we were honored with reserved seats inside the "bar." After service, I took them all back to my school-room, tried to enforce upon them the truths they had heard, lectured them, if necessary, and then sent them home.

I remember only once attending preaching during the week. The Rev. Mr. Lorraine, with whose friends I afterward became well acquainted, and whose writings, particularly his articles in the *Western Christian Advocate*, I have since read with pleasure and profit, preached one Wednesday night in a deserted school-room. It was a contracted space for the large congregation, and many chairs, great and small, were crowded in between the rude benches. His discourse was eloquent. He presented the benefits of religion so forcibly to his auditors that they actually began to talk of building a church, which, however, was not done whilst I remained there.

My whole school was present at this meeting. I took special care always to make my pupils kneel down during prayer, though but few others did so. That memorable night a mischievous girl who knelt opposite another on the same chair tied the strings of the sunbonnet of her *vis-a-vis* to the chair back, and when the poor child, who had been too devout during prayer to notice her companion, attempted to rise, the chair, with a sudden rebound, was thrown over her head, and nearly knocked a lady down. The culprit continued kneeling, afraid to raise her head for fear of detection. I understood the whole affair in an instant, and my mortification was extreme; but you may be sure the delinquent was not permitted to pass unnoticed the next day.

I know not how it is, but I have always been under the impression that sublime mountain scenery inspired devotion; and the stillness that pervaded this wicked little place on Sunday, with the entire absence of the weekly din of mechanics, confirmed me in this opinion. There certainly were the faintly reflected beams of Christianity shining in all its surroundings, and seemed only to need an "angel to trouble the waters of the pool" to cleanse and heal the waiting people. I earnestly prayed that I might do my part in bringing in the children.

Being well acquainted with the morning and evening service of the Episcopal Church, I adopted the plan of having all the girls meet at my school-room every Sabbath morning for religious instruction. First I read the morning service, and then offering up an extemporaneous prayer, dismissed them. I strove at these meetings to make the girls feel that they were "treading on holy ground," trying to drive away the world with all its cares during this consecrated hour. My own heart enjoyed it.

The worth of the Sabbath and its sweet associations can hardly be estimated until we find ourselves deprived of that dove-like peace which settles over the soul while discharging its hallowed duties. Time and eternity here meet for a few fleeting hours. "From earth to heaven a scale sublime rests on either sphere." A distinguished orator has said, "You might as well put out the sun and think to light the world with tapers; destroy the attraction of gravity and think to wield the universe by human power as to extinguish the moral illumination of the Sabbath and break this glorious main-spring of the government of God." When the Sabbath is conscientiously kept it arrests the stream of worldly thoughts, interests, and affections, soothes the heat and hurry of existence, and throws off the burden of week-day responsibilities, brings rest to the weary soul and renewed vigor to the body, and, best of all, gives us a special opportunity to make ourselves acquainted with the being, perfections, and laws of God.

CHAPTER XIII.

IN March my sister came. She was young, but intelligent and well educated, and in every respect fitted to render me assistance. Spring had made its advent, but the weather was still cold when she arrived. Only a few trees had as yet ventured to put forth their scarce unfolded leaves, and the prolonged and melancholy sweeping of the wind proclaimed the continued reign of Winter. Emily was soon domesticated in a most excellent family, that of Mr. Richard Mathews, where she was rendered as happy as she could be under the circumstances.

We spent our days together in the school-room, with an occasional interval devoted to talking of home and the dear ones there. Oh, blessed memory of those twilight hours, when, the school and all its cares forgotten, we transported ourselves to the dear love-nest of "Home, Sweet Home!"

Emily was as remarkable for industry and energy as I was for perseverance and hopefulness. She was often at the school-room at an early hour, and had kindled a fire upon the hearth, which spread a rich and cheerful glow around as if to welcome my appearance. I have known her to wade through the snow to perform this duty before sunrise, and then go back to her breakfast and return in time for the opening of school. Her devotion to me was equal to that of a child to a parent; we had scarce ever been separated in our lives. As her chirography was remarkably beautiful, she entirely relieved me in the writing department and copied nearly all the music we used. She brought from Washington several large bound books of her own copied music.

Our first examination, held in June, was almost as new to myself as to my pupils; for since my school-days in Winchester, it had never been customary to have examinations in any school that I attended; but it seemed to be the demand of the people here. I very well know that the desire proceeded principally from the wish to have the children brought forward in *exhibition*, rather than *examination*. A public examination is never a true test of what a child knows, although it does have a good effect in making the children more diligent with the view of having their knowledge brought out publicly. Reviews are certainly very improving, and many of the exercises on such occasions tend to develop ease and grace of manner, and, while they do not take away the modest diffidence so lovely in a female, they give a degree of self-confidence which is generally effectual in banishing awkwardness.

I may as well say here, once for all, that I believe far more ease and elegance are acquired through the medium of poetical recitations, dialogues, and compositions than in the dancing-school. Many of these beautiful little dramatic scenes containing the purest morality and into which girls enter with infinite delight, forgetting themselves while personating others, I have successfully proved to be the best medium of promoting that gracefulness which is universally supposed to be attained only by dancing. The idea was first suggested by a desire to avoid the dull routine of an examination in a foreign language, such as reading, translating, and conjugating verbs, for a long time the only method of exhibiting the progress of a French class. A dialogue, though not one word may be understood, is an agreeable pantomime, always fascinating and at the same time showing the facility with which girls can chatter in French.

My selections were from Berquin's "Children's Friend," and from the beautiful little dramas of Madame de Genlis, written expressly for her pupils and published under the title of "Théâtre d' Education." Hers was a domestic school, and there is nothing purer than the morality taught in the family circles of France. I used also the school dramas of Madame Campan, composed for her school of young girls connected with the most distinguished families of France. These were designed for exhibition before their own household and a few select friends; thus they were models of propriety. I had also the examples before me of Madame de Maintenon's success in promoting ease of manner and elegance of address, while the heart's best affections were cultivated by the rehearsal of those model little dramas, composed by Racine at her request, expressly for the use of her protègees in the Seminary of St. Cyr, which she founded in connection with the convent of that name, and where, under her special supervision, nothing impure was ever permitted to enter.

This examination closed my first half-year, and, of course, the material was somewhat raw; but with the assistance of my sister and some of the older and more intelligent pupils, matters were so arranged as to give entire satisfaction to the community and infinite delight to my patrons. Owing to our success, the fame of which was spread abroad through the country, our next term opened with increased numbers, and the school became much more profitable.

I enjoyed the intervening vacation with a zest I never felt before. It was as the mellow moonshine to the path of the weary pilgrim. I took long walks, sat under shady trees, read interesting books, with my affectionate sister ever by my side. Frances Smyth was generally with us, gathering wild flowers, for she had already begun to take great interest in Botany. As the Summer advanced we gathered fruits and berries, which were very abundant. We wandered through the woods and up the mountain pathways and often tarried to watch the golden sunset, steeping in splendor each wood and dell, and flooding the Western sky with glory. How sweet the recollection now, and how almost impossible to realize the lapse of years—years full of joy and sorrow.

At the close of one of those beautiful days, having retired to my room quite early, and while preparing for a night of balmy sleep, a servant girl knocked at my door and handed me a letter with a large black seal. My dear little Frances, who was my room-mate, and whose soul was full of sympathy for me, caught a glance of the seal, and, turning pale from apprehension, threw herself into the nearest chair, and covered her face with her hands. 'Twas long before my trembling fingers succeeded in breaking the seal, and some minutes before I dared read the whole contents of that letter, the commencement of which ran thus: "My dear young friend,—I am so well aware of the deep affection you bear your family, that I can scarcely believe but you are making some arrangement to bring your widowed mother and the dear little orphans that are left to your present home." For some moments I was unable to read further; the word "orphan" sounded like a death knell to my heart, which seemed only to be saved from breaking by deep sobs and groans, while my poor little Frances wrung her hands in utter despair at being unable to comfort me. After the lapse of an hour or two, I had read and re-read the contents of this sad letter in which was stated, not the whole, but the partial suffering of my mother and the children since the loss of my father, who had died some weeks before at New Madrid, Arkansas, having secured through the agency of Colonel Briarly, his warmly attached friend, an Indian Agency in that State, which would have been the home of his family had he lived. The letter concluded by saying, "I will see that your friends do not suffer while they remain here, and will aid you in getting them off." How kind, how considerate. True friendship shines out in bold relief in times of adversity, and "dies not in the storm."

The remainder of the night my mind was occupied and somewhat soothed in planning for their removal; and I felt the truth of the expression, that active misery is more easily borne than self-indulgent sorrows. Our Heavenly Father has mercifully ordained that in thinking and doing for others we are measurably delivered from that weight of grief which worketh death. The sharp arrows of affliction, which would otherwise rankle in the heart and drink up its life-blood, rendering us unfit for earth and heaven, may be withdrawn by deeds of mercy and duty.

Anxious and troubled as I was about my mother and her helpless little family, the night seemed interminably long. Day came at last, and, after consultation with my friends, I obtained, through their kindness, money enough to accomplish my purpose. This was borrowed, for all my own earnings had been previously used in the purchase of a piano. My plan, immediately put into execution, left me nothing to do the remainder of the day but to read, think, and pray. How I blessed God, that he had given me a mother who had early taught me to carry my sorrows to a throne of grace; and now that he had taken my earthly father, I prayed that I might have a double share of his love. Yet, with all this, my mind would revert with inexpressible anguish to the departed one. Oh, if he had but been spared to return home to die in the arms of those he loved so tenderly, and his last loving looks and words been left as mementos in the bosoms of those who loved him.

My affliction was increased by the pangs of remorse; his last affectionate letter had been to thank me for a small sum of money I had sent home, and to entreat me to write to him immediately, or he might not probably hear from me again, as he was about to leave home. I had neglected writing until it was too late; this, with many other little omissions, that I would not have remembered had he lived, kept open the flood-gates of sorrow, and added to the poignancy of grief, and rendered me almost frantic under the dreadful stroke. A few weeks elapsed, and I had the comfort of being reunited with those I best loved on earth. My affection for them was increased tenfold. Ah! 'tis death that teaches heavy lessons, and hard to bear; yet it is often by such means that our great Creator brings out the exhaustless treasures of those heaven-descended virtues which prepare us for usefulness, and kindle anew the flames of undying love—at the same time, making the fire burn brighter on the domestic hearth-stone for those that are left.

The memory of the delicate attentions bestowed upon my mother and the family by the little community of Wythe are beyond the oblivious touch of time. Pleasant,

13

too, the memorials of God's mercy to me at that period.
If we were accustomed to rear an altar wherever we receive a mercy, how many of these memorials would be
presented in the retrospection of our lives: and the review
of the past would create confidence for the future.   I secured a pleasant boarding-house for my mother until I
could make arrangements for housekeeping, which was
very soon done.   The house we procured was large
enough to accommodate six or eight boarders, which
added considerably to our income, and increased the reputation of the school.   My mother's prudent economy and
good management enabled us to live very comfortably.
The children were all at school, while my mother had
them under her own moral and religious training.

Time wore on, and we were becoming so well recon-
ciled to our situation that we regarded Wytheville as our
permanent home.   We had two young ladies from North
Carolina placed under our care, the elder of whom was
a devotedly pious Methodist; and was, as I afterwards
understood, then engaged to a Methodist preacher, whom
she would marry on her return home at the close of the
year.   She was one of my best students; and while sitting quietly at her desk one morning poring over her
books, a knock was heard at the school-room door, which
opened into the street.   A servant entered with a note for
Miss Dickson.   It contained the request that she would
go to the tavern immediately to meet the Rev. Mr. K.,
who was just from her home with letters, etc.   I desired
the servant to inform the gentleman that if he wished to
see Miss D. he must call upon her, for she could not go
to the tavern.   Scarce half an hour elapsed when the
door of the school-room again opened—but without a
knock this time—and in walked the Rev. Mr. K.   With-

out taking the slightest notice of anybody in the room except Miss D., he advanced and took a seat at her desk without invitation, crowding out her companion sitting on the other side. The poor girl was in such a dreadful state of confusion, that I carefully avoided adding to her distress by making any remark. In the meantime it was difficult, by the sternest looks I could assume, to prevent the whole school from bursting into laughter. The gentleman sullenly kept his hat down over his brow, and even had the temerity to lay his arm on the back of her chair, while he talked incessantly in an undertone—she making no reply whatever. When he had finished, he arose and walked out as abruptly as he had entered. He paid dearly for his indiscretion. They were never married, and I feel assured it was partly on this account. A delicate, sensitive woman is not apt to forgive one who so offends against good taste and propriety as to expose her carelessly to the ridicule of others. This man haughtily assumed the right to control and direct before he had the power; and she had the good sense to anticipate tyranny, if not oppression.

Nothing occurred for some months worth relating. My school was full; I had many interesting pupils from the neighboring counties and some from North Carolina. Our labors were increased in proportion, yet so low were the prices for teaching, that we were not able to do more than live comfortably and keep out of debt. We were grateful to God that we enjoyed the blessing of being together, bound by stronger ties in consequence of the necessity of mutually aiding each other.

One morning in the following Spring I received a letter from General Smyth, enclosing a proposition from Captain Frank Smith, of Abingdon, offering me a very advantageous situation in his family as governess to his only child, offering a salary equal to the present income from the school, stating, at the same time, that a comfortable residence could be procured for my mother and her family only half a mile from his house. "Now," said General Smyth, "having complied with the request of my friend, I can not advise you to go, because I know you are doing well here, and may do better. We hope to build up an institution in this place through your instrumentality, which shall bear your name. Receive, therefore, the assurance that I speak the sentiments of the community when I say we should prefer your remaining; but we feel too deep an interest in your welfare to assume the responsibility of asking you to decline this favorable opportunity of securing a pleasant home, with less care for yourself and an ample support for your mother and her children."

I felt exceedingly grateful to Gen. Smyth for this kindness; I knew that he was interested in having me remain, because his two daughters and granddaughter were making rapid progress under my care, and I knew too, that he was sincere in all that he had said; besides, I had become very much attached to every one in and around Wytheville. It had been a pleasant home to me, my toils and cares had been lightened by the smiles of affection. Even now, when I think of the wealth of love that was bestowed upon me by those persons who had scarce known me two years, and the loving kindness of some of my pupils, my heart beats faster and my pulse quickens with the rush of fond memories. Every hill, every stream, and almost every tree had become endeared to me by association. My first impulse was to stay. I might make new friends, but none that would be dearer.

At the close of the day I consulted my mother upon the subject. She was decidedly opposed to the change. "We are comfortable now," said she, "and I am satisfied we can not do better. A rolling stone gathers no moss." I retired that night with a fixed determination to decline Captain Smith's generous offer; but before the close of the next day, after much deliberation, we came to a different conclusion and determined to make our arrangements at the close of the session for a permanent settlement in Abingdon. This was not done, however, without many regrets on my part.

CHAPTER XIV.

MY journey from Wytheville to Abingdon was sad enough. I had parted for an indefinite period, perhaps forever, from many whose friendship and affection would cling to my heart through all my future career, and yet, those were with me, to whom I was bound by the strongest ties of love, I had the promise of a visit, at no distant period, from my beloved Frances, should she not be sent away to school. This somewhat relieved my overburdened heart, for of all the dear ones I left behind, none were so dear as she. Her remembered acts of kindness and love forced upon me the conviction, that we never value what we possess in the same degree as we value what we lose.

We left Wytheville in the early dawn of a most beautiful Summer morning. It was a journey of only sixty miles to Abingdon, but it would take two days to accomplish it. We wended our way slowly over a broken mountain road which had never been graded—a macadamized turnpike was unknown. We traveled in an old-fashioned nine seated stage coach, drawn by four horses changed at long intervals. We lunched and rested at mid-day beneath the spreading trees, whose interwoven branches made network of the dark blue light of day. Water from a gushing stream, the depth of whose source defied the heat of Summer, quenched our thirst, while we inhaled the fragrance of rock-hung flowers, the sweet brier and the health-inspiring pine.

On the evening of the second day we reached our destination. With that natural repugnance to meeting strange faces and mingling with strange people, who neither knew nor cared for us, we were not sorry to enter the town after the "downy hand of rest" had sealed the eyes of most of the inhabitants. Stopping at a tavern kept by a Mrs. Soule, we were soon made to feel comfortable and quite at home by this agreeable woman and her pleasant family of daughters. Before sleeping a night in that house we felt sure of finding the same friendly hoshospitality in Abingdon as in Wytheville. A more intimate acquaintance proved the social intercourse to be charming,

My mother soon procured a dwelling, comfortable and sufficiently spacious to admit of one large room being fitted up for my sister's prospective day-school. This was in a short time filled with young girls, among whom were half a dozen music scholars. Mrs. Smith, from the "Meadows," the name of Captain Smith's place, came as soon as she knew of my arrival to take me to her home. This home was but a short walk from my mother's, yet I had the convenience of a carriage to go and come as I pleased. My kind and excellent patrons manifested so much interest in those I loved best in the world, that my heart was completely won. My dear mother had a great passion for gardening, was particularly fond of the cultivation of flowers, and had here ample space to indulge herself in the sweetness and beauty of the fairy creations she cherished.

I can scarcely find language to convey a correct idea of the beautiful surroundings of my new home, "The Meadows." I arose early the first morning after my arrival to wander about the grounds; yet not too early to find the milkmaids abroad, and other servants engaged in their proper occupations. The sweetest influences of nature shed a peculiar loveliness over this beautiful domain. A profusion of wild flowers sprang up amid the grassy meadows; the dew glittered on the lawn, and the murmurs of a nameless music made vocal the sweeping branches of the grand old trees in the neighboring woods. The beauty of the place at this quiet morning hour stole like a charm over my senses. I stood by a gushing spring whose pellucid waters flowed in a wide stream of sufficient depth to reflect the sky in masses of crimson shadows, "a liquid mirror, imaging all the woven boughs above, and each depending leaf," murmuring gently onward with its wealth of sunshine to disperse its translucent waters through the green meadows. I felt actually oppressed with delight as I viewed this enchanting scene. Every breath I drew was a deep inspiration of rapture. I inhaled with it the odor of roses and sweet Summer flowers, and my heart swelled with gratitude as I exclaimed, "The lines have fallen to me in pleasant places."

I met Mrs. Smith in the door-way as I returned, with her little Mary, who had been introduced to me the evening before, but was too timid to allow me to progress far toward acquaintance. Now she welcomed me with a pleasant smile, and her large eyes seemed full of emotion, as her mother said, "Mary is prepared to love you, and I trust she will be a good girl; but, if she should be naughty, do not fail to report it or correct her as you think proper." As I afterward found, Mrs. Smith had pursued a very judicious course with this child. Being an only child, she was surrounded by influences well calculated to spoil her had it not been for the firm and steady hand of her mother, who regarded her as her most precious jewel.

Mary was but nine years old, with a sweet, chubby little face and bright, sparkling eyes; truly one of the most lovable children I ever knew.

Captain Smith was a man of prepossessing appearance and agreeable manners, an open, good-humored countenance, with merry eyes, full of fun and frolic. He was devoted to his wife, and her influence over him was unbounded; but the silken cords by which she led him were not visible to the common eye. He was naturally disposed to be economical, but she rendered him munificent. Their unvarying kindness to numerous friends and relatives made their house a Mecca to the hearts of all who had once enjoyed its hospitality. Captain Smith and his wife contributed much to the happiness of the whole community in which they lived.

A few weeks of experience taught me that my little Mary needed the emulation of companionship; for, though confined but a few hours during the day to her books and music, I found that it required a great effort to keep up that interest necessary to rapid improvement. No sooner was the suggestion made to her parents than they invited three little cousins, near Mary's age, to come and enjoy, with her, the benefits of regular instruction. Very soon we had Mary Campbell, Rachel Morgan, and Elizabeth Trigg domiciled in the family, and members of my school. I had four scholars, no more; and the privileges the little cousins enjoyed cost them nothing. Captain Smith paid me a liberal salary for his own daughter, and I did not desire to have it increased. My school-room was sufficiently secluded to prevent interruption, and many were the peaceful hours I there enjoyed, reading some interesting book, while my "little nest of singing birds" were preparing their lessons.

From the window of my own cheerful room, where I sat after school, I could see the town in the distance, and near by was the sunny nook in which was planted the flower-garden, whose faint, soul-dissolving odor diffused itself through the whole room in Summer. Fairy-like were the beautiful shadows that fell from the pensile branches of the weeping willows, and changeful the golden light that shimmered through the delicate aspen leaves. Grapevines flung their leafy garlands from branch to branch, and grapes were hanging in green clusters, giving promise of an abundant harvest of this luscious fruit in due season. Cattle were collected in groups under the friendly shade-trees, which dotted the green meadow land; and the white sheep were grazing on the distant hills. The green carpeted lawn, gently sloping toward the road, was studded with knots of delicate blossoms, minute but beautiful. On the left was an orchard of apple and peach trees, whose branches were bending to the earth with delicious fruit; on the right the lawn with its rich sweep of grass, so vividly green. How pleasant to sit here and listen to the ever-moving air as it whispered from tree to tree. The balmy breeze, freshening as the sun declined, brought the rich perfume of pinks, roses and lilies, while the flitting shadows of evening and the mysterious silence that hovered over all stole into the heart with an unseen power, hushed its passionate throbbings and gave rise to pure and beautiful thoughts, steeping the soul in visions of bliss caught from the quiet skies above.

Who could gaze upon such a scene without looking through "nature up to nature's God," and mentally exclaiming, "My Father made them all!" These were scenes never to be forgotten. All those influences, so tranquilizing to the heart, so quieting to the temper, made me feel sensibly that the providence of God had brought me to this lovely place, where I might enjoy a home-life calculated to train me for heaven; for,

> "Hearts grow holier as they trace
> The beauty of the world below."

I received, always, the most respectful attention, not only from the family, but from their friends, relations, and visitors. Mrs. Smith had the good sense to appreciate the position of her daughter's teacher, as a model from whom she must receive moral and intellectual training. My authority was never interfered with, and Mary never lost an hour from her school-duties without my consent.

We had frequent conferences in reference to my little school. I found in this excellent woman a true and sensible friend; I might almost say an elder sister, whose companionship was perfectly delightful to me.

About this time I became acquainted with that excellent but eccentric old lady, Mrs. Russell, through the medium of General Frank Preston's family. Mrs. Russell's first husband was Colonel Campbell, the hero of "King's Mountain." Mrs. Preston was the only child of this marriage, and the heiress to a portion of the Salt Works, in Western Virginia, which were for a long time the source of immense revenue to the family. Mrs. Smith inherited the largest portion from her first husband, Mr. William King, whose memory is still cherished throughout that country as one of the best and most benevolent of men. He came from Ireland a poor boy without a penny, one of the many instances of a man rising to wealth, honor, and distinction by virtue and industry alone. Mr. King was a man of unsullied reputation, and it might well be said of him, "An honest man's the noblest work of God."

Mrs. Russell was in every way an extraordinary woman. The sister of Patrick Henry, she possessed some of his characteristics. Her second husband, General Russell, was quite as distinguished as the first for worth and bravery. Both she and General Russell were faithful members of the Methodist Church. They were converted in the good old-fashioned way, when nobody objected to shouting, if it came from an overflowing heart filled with the love of God. The old General walked worthy of his vocation until he was taken home to a better world, leaving his excellent widow a true type of Wesleyan Methodism. "Madam Russell," as she was generally called, was a "mother in Israel;" and the Methodist preachers in those days esteemed her next to Bishop Asbury. She lived for a while in Abingdon, but as the gay society of that place, particularly among her own relatives, was uncongenial to her, she withdrew to a retired spot near the "Camp-ground," in the vicinity of the sulphur springs. At this place a wooden house had been erected under her special superintendence, and according to her own ideas of consistency. Here she lived like the good old Moravian, Count Zinzendorf, who wrote over the portals of his mansion:

> "As guests, we only here remain,
> And hence the house is slight and plain
> (*Therefore turn to the stronghold, ye prisoners of hope*).
> We have a better land above,
> And there we find our warmest love."

There were two rooms below, large and spacious—the one first entered being her common sitting-room. A door from this opened into one much larger, which contained a pulpit and seats for a moderate-sized congregation. When a preacher visited her she said: "Brother, how long will you tarry? There's the pulpit; shall I send out and call together a congregation?" No visitors came to see her, and remained an hour, without being asked to pray. If they declined she prayed herself, mentioning every person for whom she prayed by name.

She dressed in the style of '76—full skirts, with an over-garment, long, flowing, open in front, and confined at the waist by a girdle, and made of a material called Bath coating. In this girdle were tucked two or three pocket-handkerchiefs. The sleeves of her dress came just below the elbows—the lower part of the arm being covered with long, half-handed gloves. She wore a kerchief of linen lawn, white as snow, and sometimes an apron of the same material; and on her head a very plain cap, above which was usually placed a broad-brimmed hat given her by Bishop Asbury in days long gone by, and worn by the old lady with probably the same feeling that Elisha wore Elijah's mantle. She was erect as in the meridian of life, though she must have been seventy years old when I first saw her. A magnificent-looking woman, "she walked every inch a queen," reminding me of one of the old-fashioned pictures of Vandyke. She never shook the hand of a poor Methodist preacher in parting without leaving in it a liberal donation; she knew the Gospel was free, but she also knew that "the laborer was worthy of his hire."

The celebrated Wm. C. Preston, of South Carolina, her eldest grandson, loved her with a devotion highly commendable to himself and agreeable to his grandmother. In his yearly visits to his native home his carriage was found first at the door of her humble dwelling.

He gave evidence on his dying bed that his grandmoth-er's religion had been his guiding star, and his love for her shone as brightly in the evening as in the morning and meridian of his life. I knew Wm. C. Preston well. He was distinguished as a man of cultivated intellect, sound judgment, and warm affections. As an orator, I do not think he ever had his superior in the United States, though he sought not the world-wide celebrity he might have attained. He was heard to say, while Pres-ident of Columbia College, in South Carolina: "I believe teaching is my vocation; and I would that I had spent my whole life in striving, like Socrates, to educate the young; for I have proved the difficulty of instructing those more advanced in life."

An anecdote related to me by Mrs. Russell illustrates the estimation in which Patrick Henry was held through-out his native State. When she first came to South-western Virginia she attended a camp-meeting when, her relationship to Patrick Henry being whispered about, such was the crowd that immediately pressed around her, to get a glimpse of one so distinguished, that she was only rescued from being crushed by the surrounding mul-titude by mounting upon a stump, where she was com-pelled to turn round and round, amidst the uproarious demonstrations of an enthusiastic people, who cried out, "Hurrah for Patrick Henry!" with an occasional shout for Colonel Campbell.

CHAPTER XV.

IT is the generally received opinion that an only child, and particularly an only daughter, must be petted, spoiled, and to a certain extent made disagreeable; if so, Mary Smith was an exception to the rule. Her mother's judicious treatment effectually prevented that selfishness often found among children nursed in the luxurious lap of indolence.

Mrs. Smith was decidedly a religious woman, and early impressed upon little Mary's mind that she had a Father in heaven, whom she should love and obey; while she taught her that there was an evil spirit "going about like a roaring lion, seeking whom he might devour."

Mary was sitting one morning at the breakfast-table when only four years old, and Charlotte, her maid, who was quite a character, stood at the back of her chair, asking what she would have. The child burst into tears, and cried bitterly.

"What's the matter, Mary?' said her mother.

Almost suffocated with sobs, she replied, "I want some batter-cakes."

"No, no, Mary," said Mrs. Smith; "think again. You know you can have batter-cakes; Charlotte will help you"—which was no sooner said than done.

Mary continued to cry bitterly.

"Look at me, Mary; wipe your eyes, and tell me the truth."

The child obeyed, and said, timidly: "Mother, I wanted cheese; but the devil whispered to me, and said, 'Ask for batter-cakes.'"

After breakfast Mary went with her mother to a retired place, where much conversation ensued, the result of which may be imagined.

Mary was taught to do every thing for herself that she could—to dress and undress herself, even when she was a tiny child, while Charlotte watched the process. If at any time she needed a whipping her mother gave it to her conscientiously, and spared her not for her pitiful cries of, "O mother, will you whip your *only* child, your *only daughter!*"

Thus did this excellent mother go on sowing the good seed, the fruits of which she was blessed in realizing, and doubtless carried the memory with her to a better world.

I have said that Mary was but nine years old when placed under my care; yet she was better instructed than children of her age generally, and though a playful child, of exuberant spirits, she was thoughtful, sensitive, and rather mature for her age. Her father allowed her at that time a monthly stipend, to use as she pleased, and I do not remember a single instance of her spending one dime merely for a selfish gratification, though I have many reminiscences of her benevolent tendencies.

She was sitting, one evening, sadly resting her head upon her hand, apparently in deep thought. It was about the middle of a very cold month; her mother was sewing—I was reading. Captain Smith entered, and Mary sprang to her feet.

"O father," said she, "my monthly allowance is all gone, and Charlotte says there is a poor woman with little ragged babies, living about a mile from here, who has no warm blankets to cover them, no warm shoes and stockings to run in the snow."

"What will be done, Mary?" said her father. "I do not like to advance money to a little girl who gets rid of it so rapidly."

"Father, lend me five dollars, and I will try not to want any more next month. Charlotte says I can get a pair of warm blankets for that."

The money was given; she went with her charitable Methodist maid, bought the blankets herself, appropriated them, and the happy little girl kept her word, asking for no money the next month. The woman to whom Mary gave the blankets came frequently the next Summer to bring marketing, which Mrs. Smith always bought, though their extensive farm supplied them with every thing they wanted.

Captain Smith, though a lawyer by profession, was a practical farmer. Thriving orchards, rich pastures, fertile meadows, and productive grounds, attested the constant supervision of the master, as well as the industry of those under his authority. All around bespoke thrift and comfort—every thing was well-conditioned, even to the lowest menial on the place. Mrs. Smith, though in feeble health, and accustomed to all the luxuries that wealth could procure, did not make these an excuse for indolence or self-indulgence. She looked well to the ways of her own household, giving to each a portion in due season; and, with a heart open as "melting day" to the sweet influences of charity, she stretched out her hands to the needy. Truly "the crown of the wise is their riches."

The poor woman alluded to was a humble Christian, of well-known piety, contented and industrious, with a large family, which she found it difficult to support; but her faith grew stronger as poverty grew sterner. Upon one occasion, after Mrs. Smith had paid her, she stopped on the front steps, put down her basket, and, looking up at the lordly mansion, exclaimed, "Well, I would like to go all through this house once." "You shall do so," said Captain Smith, who was present. "Come, I will go with you." She followed him, stepping, as daintily as she could, over the well-waxed passage, and up the grand stair-way, entered into every apartment, and, after giving each a hasty glance, returned and said, as she took up her empty basket, "This is a beautiful house, Captain Smith; such a one as I never saw before and never care to see again; but I would not have it if you would give it to me, even if it were filled with gold, for I should lose my own soul by forgetting God in the splendor that surrounded me. I would rather sing, 'No foot of land do I possess,' and feel, in truth, I am a pilgrim in the wilderness of this world, with the hope of heaven in my heart. My Bible tells me that the road to eternal happiness is not paved with gold." It was a little sermon, not intended as such, however, but it reached the heart of the proud man who thought but little of his soul's welfare, and left, for a few moments, a shadow upon his brow.

The even tenor of my life during the first year of my residence at "The Meadows" leaves the memory of but few things worth relating. My dear mother and her little family were comfortable; my sister's school was profitable and pleasant. I visited them regularly once a week, sometimes oftener, and I remember no pleasure more exquisite, during my whole life, than that I experienced at the end of each quarter, as I placed my little linen bag of silver dollars in my mother's lap, and heard, from her own precious lips, expressions of maternal love and tenderness. I can almost feel now her hand upon my head as I knelt at her feet with beating heart and throbbing brow, and I thought then, as I do now, what an inestimable privilege to be enabled, even in part, to pay back the immense debt of gratitude one owes to a parent, and especially to a mother. The wealth of maternal love, who can estimate?

Just here it is quite proper for me to say to the rising generation of girls who never "have time" to accomplish any thing, as they affirm, striving with things impossible, and seeing nothing but the receding wings of flying opportunities, that, at this time, I not only attended to my regular duties as a teacher, but continued to make the dresses of my mother and sisters as well as my own. To be sure, new dresses came few and far between, and it was easier to sew up three widths than nine or ten. I have often cut out a dress at early dawn and worn it at the tea-table, aided by no sewing machines or other fingers than my own.

I saw a great deal of company necessarily, and though I never suffered my school-hours to be interrupted, yet my toilet was always made in such a manner as to be prepared to meet incidental guests in this hospitable mansion daily, and I am sure that my whole wardrobe did not cost me more than twenty dollars a year at that time. Mrs. Smith always dressed elegantly; never conspicuously or expensively. This gave her the opportunity of showing kindness to others, and I was not forgotten among the many recipients of her generous favors. A handsome dress occasionally, a pair of gloves or some muslin for collarettes, filled up beautifully the deficiencies in my scanty wardrobe, and rendered me presentable at all the dinner-parties. These occurred very often at

"The Meadows," but at country hours, so that all the guests might depart in peace before dark; and as they seldom gave evening parties in this wisely-governed house, our nights were

> "As tranquil and still
> As the mist slumbering on the hill."

One dining now looms up before me. My little girls were taking dancing lessons from a queer little man by the name of Fry, whose school they attended every Saturday. This "*maître de dance*," though he could teach the five positions and cut the "pigeon-wing" to perfection, was, by no means, fitted to impart grace of motion, ease and elegance of manners to his pupils; nevertheless he tried, and was particularly unsuccessful in teaching them to courtesy *a la mode*. At this dinner party, which consisted of the *elite* of the neighborhood, among whom were the Prestons, Johnsons, etc., critics in style and etiquette, Mrs. Smith and I were particularly anxious that the girls should appear well when introduced into the drawing-room before dinner. They were directed, therefore, to make their best courtesies on entering. Elizabeth Trigg, the youngest, and least likely to be abashed, came first; the others following in regular routine. She rested on her left foot, poised her right toe in front for an instant, and then wheeling half-round, presenting her back to the company, courtesied so low as almost to lose her equilibrium. Poor little Mary Campbell followed in quick succession without raising her eyes from the floor, her sweet little person reminding me of a dove unfurling its silver wings for flight. Then came Rachel Morgan, but before her evolutions were quite finished, and just as Mary was advancing Captain Smith exclaimed, to the extreme mortification of the girl, "Fry,

Fry, Fry, hold on; no more of it." My confusion was so great that it almost blinded me, while my poor little pupils tucked themselves as much out of sight as possible. We were all soon relieved, however, by the genial, laughter-loving General Preston, who walked up and brought the little girls out of their hiding places, commending them for trying to imitate so practically their dancing-master, whose business it was to teach them to make their manners.

One might suppose that it would be exceedingly difficult to give sufficient variety to the studies and pursuits of only four children without sometimes producing weariness and disgusting them with the school-room, but their exercises were rendered sufficiently interesting and agreeable by much oral instruction. They had text-books, of course, but were never required to commit to memory any thing that was not first thoroughly understood, and many were the fragrant flowers of affection culled during those school-hours.

We had daily exercises in music, French, and drawing, but experience had taught me that the elementary branches of spelling, reading, and arithmetic should be thoroughly learned at an early age, for these are the *arts* by which the sciences are to be acquired. We can no more expect a thorough education without them than we can hope to erect a palace without a foundation. Our language deserves the highest degree of attention; and to expect children to become acquainted with the principles simply by hearing others talk, is ridiculous and absurd. A child may learn to spell correctly before its powers of thought are well developed. In spelling, children should be made to enunciate and pronounce each syllable distinctly; and spelling-books and dictionaries will not complete the course. Words, sentences, and even whole pages should be dictated to them; the words spelled incorrectly, underlined by the teacher, and the pupil made to correct them.

I once had a pupil nineteen years old who had taught two years before being placed under my instruction. She read well and talked well, and had much general information, and yet could not write two lines without spelling incorrectly. It took her three hours to write a letter of three pages, with the dictionary before her, to which she constantly referred; and, after all that, the letter could not pass the ordeal of a single glance from a practiced eye without the detection of many egregious mistakes. This was the result of her having learned to read before she could spell.

I formed, about this time, an intimate friendship with Mrs. Henderson, a widowed niece of Mrs. Smith's first husband, one of the most genial, pleasant women I ever knew. She possessed that charming candor so fascinating when connected with elegant manners and defined taste; and though in the meridian of life, and twice a widow, she had not lost her sympathy with the young. Extreme goodness of heart, united to a glowing imagination, brought a large circle of friends and acquaintances under her mystic influence. My heart was completely won by the pleasure she seemed to take in my society. I often visited her home in Abingdon, then the centre of attraction for nearly all the agreeable young people in the village. Her family consisted of herself and two young cousins, John and Rachel Mitchell. Mrs. Henderson had four sons at school, but they seldom came home for any length of time. Her pleasant little parlor was the favored spot of many joyous reunions.

Rachel Mitchell, scarce seventeen years of age, was a rare example of genuine enthusiasm in every thing good; but this enthusiasm was under the control of sound judgment and discretion. Her face was peculiarly expressive of cheerfulness and benevolence; calm, modest, so full of sweetness, and, above all, of ingenuousness and truth, that, upon the first look, you felt that you could take that countenance on trust, there were no misgivings about it. Her brother John was a merry, laughter-loving soul, who sought to render others as cheerful and joyous as himself.

The social whist-table was frequently introduced; for whist, nothing more, was as common an amusement then, in the first circles, as dancing. Card-playing was indulged in to a great extent, even by Church members. I recollect the trouble the Rev. Mr. Hawley had in Washington, when striving to banish this evil from among his communicants. One lady, a leader of the *ton*, was willing to give up public assemblies, decline attending the theater, but cards she could not forego. "No," said she, "I would rather be excluded from the communion-table. I do believe, if I were dying, the shuffling of a pack of cards would revive me."

I would not have my readers understand that I look back upon these things with approbation; I only wish to show the state of society at that time. The morally refined, who would have shuddered with horror at the bare idea of a coarse expression or the introduction of any thing low and common into their charmed circle, would wear away the hours of the night, even until three in the morning, playing whist with a few select friends. I think now, with the deepest mortification of my frequent participation in this evil; and yet, I thought I was a Christian.

Alas! how difficult it is to know one's self. I never neglected duty at any time for pleasure or recreation, and this was a salve to my conscience. Having fulfilled the labors of the day, I felt at perfect liberty to waste precious hours in this sinful amusement at night. We never played for money; but how great a delusion to suppose that any thing upon which we dare not ask the blessing of God is innocent. No one that has ever indulged in this evil practice, but knows how fascinating it becomes; and dancing, except for young children, and in the open air on the green, is not less dangerous and delusive. The votaries of the ball-room become so passionately fond of it as to make it almost the business of life. I thank my Heavenly Father that I never did become so much infatuated with either as to forget the responsibility I was under to others; nor do I ever remember retiring to rest, no matter how late, or how much fatigued, without offering up an earnest prayer for God's blessing and forgiveness. I read the Scriptures with interest, and prayed fervently to be enlightened on divine subjects.

I never saw a card-table nor attended a dancing party in Captain Smith's house. Mrs. Smith was not a member of any Church when I first knew her. She preferred the Methodist Church to any other; but, as this denomination had no house of worship, and the society was "little and unknown," she united with the Presbyterians—the only denomination that had a church and pastor.

The Rev. Mr. Bovell was a pious and excellent man, but by no means a popular preacher. His utterance was slow and indistinct, and many of his congregation not decidedly pious felt so much the drowsy influence of his monotonous voice, as to make it an excuse for staying at home on the Sabbath.

During a protracted meeting held in this church I became acquainted with the Rev. Mr. Gallagher, from Tennessee, and a Mr. Glenn, a preacher from the same neighborhood. Mr. Gallagher was a perfect Boanerges; no one could go to sleep under his preaching. He was one of the most eloquent pulpit orators of that day, and as remarkable for his indolent habits out of the pulpit as for his energy in it. He said he preferred riding on horseback to walking, but a coach to either; but it was far the most agreeable to sit quietly in his arm-chair, surrounded by his books and papers.

Mr. Gallagher possessed fine literary taste and a highly cultivated mind. I respected and admired him, not only because of his exalted Christian character, but because he loved and spoke so kindly of my oldest brother Quinn, who had once been his pupil. No one ever accused him of neglecting his high and holy calling as a minister of the Gospel, but he was proverbially improvident in worldly affairs. He received from his parishioners, who almost idolized him, an ample salary, but somehow he always got through it before the end of the year. Upon one occasion he invited a friend home to dine with him, without consulting his wife, who whispered to him after the cloth was laid, "We've nothing but potatoes for dinner." "Bring them in," said he, cheerfully; and soon the table, covered with a snowy cloth, was garnished with a large dish of smoking Irish potatoes, and the usual condiments—salt and butter. "Come along, Glenn," said Mr. Gallagher, "come and eat, 'tis as good as we deserve—better than our Lord and Master had." I will not vouch for the authenticity of this, but knowing his character so well, it certainly bears the impress of probability.

CHAPTER XVI.

How we love to linger over the most trivial records of the heart. The recollection of every thing connected with my stay at "The Meadows," and the pleasant associations there formed, quicken even now my pulsations, and bring the light of other days to my faded eyes. How beautiful does this brief episode appear!

My pupils improved satisfactorily, and my patrons were well pleased. We had an examination, at the close of the year, in our own little school-room. A very select audience, composed of the home family and a few invited friends, manifested the deepest interest in all that was going on. 'T was *recherche* in the highest degree. We had a French dialogue, in which the four little girls chattered and gesticulated so charmingly *a la Francaise*, that General Preston insisted he understood it quite as well as if it had been English. They were complimented upon their graceful manners, having entirely given up their courtesies *a la Fry*. They passed a good examination upon the elementary branches; their drawings were pronounced neat and pretty, their music agreeable; and they were flattered and praised until every thing to them was *couleur de rose* for that day.

And now came an interval of entire relaxation during the hot weeks of July. About this time I discovered that, though not nearsighted, I could not see things distinctly at a great distance. It may seem strange that I had not known it before; it was simply because I was not obliged to hold my book close to my eyes like a very nearsighted person. My strong gray eyes could not absorb the usual amount of light without pain, and I could see better in the morning and evening twilight than at noon.

Late in the afternoon of a July day I was walking with some friends through a lovely green meadow. Suddenly we were all startled by an exclamation, calling our attention to some object in the deep blue heavens above, which all pronounced to be a kite sailing majestically through the atmosphere; sometimes a mere speck, and then floating nearer to view sporting, as it seemed, with the light clouds, its long and graceful tail resembling that of a comet. I listened to their remarks, and vainly looked in the direction to which they all pointed; nought could I discover but the piled-up clouds, bannered in the golden rays of the setting sun.

"Don't you see it now?" said Captain Smith, after a long explanation; "it is the largest and most beautiful kite I ever saw, and floats so majestically. Look, look!"

"I can not see it," said I, sorrowfully.

"You can, if you will; it is downright affectation. Why do you squint so? You keep your eyes half shut; no wonder you can't see."

"The light hurts them," I replied; "I have not the eyes of an eagle."

"Well, they look as strong and as gray as an eagle's, anyhow."

I felt somewhat troubled at first by the discovery that beautiful visions in the distance were not for me; but I was gratified to know that, blessed with the power of seeing clearly what was going on around me, I should not, while star gazing, stumble over gems and pearls that might be strewn in my pathway.

I found, at last, that I could not distinguish a man from a donkey, at a distance at which others could recognize an acquaintance; could not read the signs across the street, and often made laughable blunders by mistaking one person for another. Yet, I thought I did not need spectacles, and was not pedantic enough to don them as a coat of arms. I never wore them until many years afterward, when I found myself putting my hand into a plate of butter for a plate of cheese. I am now an old woman, and put aside my spectacles when I wish to read or write, and can do the finest needlework without them—have never changed the number of the glasses I wore forty years ago. I might not have found it necessary to wear glasses had not my vocation as a teacher required a minute examination into the far-off corners of a large school-room, that I might ascertain what the girls were doing so diligently when they were doing nothing.

Days and weeks passed swiftly by. August, 1822, came, and my young friend, Rachel Mitchell, was to be married to Mr. Litchfield, a resident of Abingdon. Rachel was but eighteen, yet she had not taken this matter in hand unadvisedly; it was the result of time, reflection, and the approbation of her friends. Happy as a Spring bird, surrounded by an atmosphere of pure affection, she naturally felt timid about changing her relations in life. I loved her devotedly, and was pleased and satisfied with her choice.

Mr. Litchfield was dignified, and possessed as much ease of manner as a sensible man need have or a rational woman desire. The heart generally chooses wisely when left to follow its natural impulses; and that it was so in this case, has been proved by a long life of wedded happiness. I was bridesmaid, and watched with interest the timid, but perfect confidence manifested by my young friend in the object of her choice. I could but note the sober change of manner which told how she dreaded to step from young and irresponsible girlhood into a position new and untried. A serious thoughtfulness, a subdued tone of voice, marked the coming matron; yet there was no doubt, no mistrust as to the future. A select company of friends was present to witness the ceremony. The bride, to my eye, was the very ideal of innocence and loveliness; the bridegroom, a model of dignified manhood, whom it seemed natural to respect, esteem, and love. More than forty years have since elapsed—noble sons and lovely daughters have grown up, like olive plants, around their table, and I have had the pleasure of educating two of her daughters, whose useful lives will prove a crown of rejoicing in eternity. Two of her brother's daughters have also been sent from Abingdon to the far West to be educated under my care.

Not many months passed after Rachel's marriage and removal to her own home, when Mrs. Henderson began to feel that it was not "good to be alone," and decided to accept the offered hand of Mr. Branch, a gentleman who, though her junior in years, was not younger in heart and feeling. Mrs. Henderson was in the full freshness of blooming womanhood when she took unto herself a third husband. I was a second time selected as bridesmaid in that family. The marriage was to be strictly private, and, for once, Madam Rumor failed to get an inkling of the approaching wedding.

The day before the morning upon which the marriage

was to take place, one of Mrs. Smith's grand dinner-parties came off, at which Mrs. Henderson declined appearing, though Mrs. Smith seemed scarcely willing or able to do without her. She finally consented to come, provided Captain Smith would make no allusion to her intended marriage. He faithfully promised every thing required of him. The company assembled; Mrs. Henderson was, as usual, the life of the party—gay, witty, and good-humored. The brilliancy of her conversation attracted more than usual attention; yet I could see an occasional shadow flit across her face as she cast furtively toward Captain Smith a deprecating and uneasy glance when she caught his eye. Dinner was nearly over; the dessert and wines were on the table, when we were all electrified by Captain Smith's calling out to Mrs. Henderson: "Well, Rachel, do you intend to surprise your friends by changing your name to-morrow morning? Do you all know that she is to be married?"

"Why, Captain Smith, how can you?"

Her blushing face and almost audibly beating heart would have betrayed her had not the attention of every one been attracted by the Captain's merry laugh, and the blank expression of Mrs. Smith's face.

"There, now, I told you nobody would believe it,—neither do I."

Mrs. Henderson was relieved, and joined in the general laugh. Every body looked upon it as a ruse of Captain Smith to produce a little excitement and resuscitate the flagging conversation; and there was as much astonishment the next morning, at the announcement of the marriage of Mr. Branch to Mrs. Henderson, as if it had never been mentioned.

How strangely some apparently unimportant incidents

fix themselves upon the mind and heart,—intended, it sometimes seems, to foreshadow coming events! The first time I ever heard the hymn, "He dies, the friend of sinners dies," was during a little excursion with Mr. and Mrs. Branch, immediately after their marriage. Mr. Branch was on his way to Richmond, and parted with us at a retired country place. We were sitting just where he left us, in a little vine-covered porch. Her heart was doubtless sad, and mine sympathetic, when she commenced singing that sweet hymn, and her charming voice sounded like the music of heaven lingering on the ear; and as she uttered, "Lo! Salem's daughters weep around," I could not restrain my tears. Visions of the blessed Savior, who had suffered so much for me, and whose burden of grief had weighed so little on my ungrateful heart, rose up before me in condemnation, and I felt like Jacob when he vowed a vow, saying, "If God will be with me, and keep me in the way that I go, then shall the Lord be my God." I had thought all along that I was striving to be a Christian; but I felt now an aching void, which could not be filled without a deeper knowledge of divine things—a something I had not yet known.

Soon after this I was invited to act as bridesmaid for Mrs. Nancy Trigg, a widowed sister-in-law of Mrs. Smith, whom I had learned to love and appreciate during my residence in Wytheville. The wedding was to take place during the Christmas holidays, and was to be followed by grand festivities, in which, according to the fashion of the day, dancing was to be the chief feature. I found that the gayeties in which I should be involved would dissipate my serious feelings. I hesitated, tried to beg off; pleaded Mrs. Smith's anxiety to have me remain and attend the quarterly-meeting, and her desire that I should become acquainted with some pious friends who were to be her guests. My mother, though she did not positively object, looked sad at the idea of my being exposed at this inclement season. She also wished me to attend the meeting in prospect; yet with her ever quiet and self-denying manner, indulgently said, "Go, if you think best." It was the first time we had been parted since our reunion in Wythe. I afterward realized that it was not best to choose pleasure instead of duty. Strange that the visible but transient things of time should have more influence over the human heart than the unseen but eternal realities of a future world!

We started for Wythe long before daylight. It was clear and cold, and the moonlight lay like a blessing upon the sleeping inhabitants, of whom I would gladly have been one; for I was not quite satisfied with the choice I had made. The wind whistled mournfully through the ice-clad branches of the trees, which stood like grim sentinels on the outskirts of the town. With these dreary surroundings, we had the prospect of a two days' journey over the roughest of roads; but we were made of sterner stuff than to dread cold or personal inconvenience. My own courage was strengthened by the desire of looking once more upon the faces of familiar friends. We traveled all day, through a violent snow-storm, over frozen ground and ice-bound torrents, stopping only twice to change horses, ere we reached the old stone tavern where we were to tarry for the night. It was near ten o'clock, the family were all in bed; one little tallow candle burned in the window, casting a feeble light upon the pathway that led to the door standing wide open for the expected stage passengers.

The cheerlessness of the room we entered was made visible by the flickering rays of a few expiring embers. In the middle of the apartment was a square table, upon which was heaped in pewter dishes, cold beef, fat pork, cabbage, potatoes, with a large dish of cucumber pickles. A brown jug of milk and a show of tea-cups and saucers intimated arrangements for tea or coffee. My head ached so violently that I turned from the supper-table with disgust, and stepped into an adjoining room in search of fire and some place upon which to rest my weary limbs. I threw myself upon what I supposed to be an empty bed, and in so doing awakened squalling children. Rising hastily, and turning toward another, I saw the vision of a red flannel night-cap popping from under the bed-clothes, which so frightened me that I flew to the other side of the room, and sunk despairingly into an old arm-chair, where I remained until my companions had supped, after which we were shown up-stairs into a cold room. The feather-bed, which I immediately appropriated, was made up like a grave, and surmounted by two little pillows, either of which I might have put into my pocket, and both of which I lost somewhere in the recesses of the bed during the night.

My companions were soon asleep; but I suffered too intensely to lose consciousness until about an hour before we were called up to resume our journey, my mind actively engaged all the while in repentant thoughts and ardent wishes that I had not thus tempted danger; cold and sickness rendered me any thing but a pleasant *compagnon de voyage.* The second day was as uncomfortable as the first. My languor and headache continued until we reached our destination, where we were ushered into the warm and cozy parlor of Mrs. Trigg. There we found bright faces awaiting us, and were received with overflowing joy and cordial greetings.

Mrs. Smythe was there, and claimed me for her guest, saying, "This is kind in you to come so great a distance to see your old friends. You must stay with me; for I have much to ask and to tell, which can not all be thought of at once." A night of sound sleep in my old room made me quite myself again; and, rising early, I took my station at the window, to look out upon old familiar objects. The snow-storm was over, and left no trace in the calm, blue sky; but the snow lay like a white robe of unsullied purity upon the roof-tops, and almost untrodden upon the streets. The wintery clouds were alternately gathering and breaking as they whirled around the "keen, sky-cleaving mountain," whose icy spires of sun-like radiance announced the coming day.

Whoever has not seen Winter in its reposing beauty among the mountains of this country knows nothing of its pictorial wealth,—silent images of eternity, awfully magnificent, yet thrillingly beautiful,—

> "Palaces where Nature thrones
> Sublimity in icy halls."

I watched the rising sun as it turned the snow and sleet into myriads of sparkling gems, and the ice-clad trees whose nodding tops were thickly hung with diamonds, and,

> "Nature breathed from every part
> The rapture of her mighty heart."

My soul was filled with emotions of gratitude to God, who had made this world so beautiful in all its changing seasons. An involuntary prayer of thanksgiving arose from my lips to the great Giver of all good. How natural the tendency to adore him in all that is good and beautiful.

The forenoon was agreeably occupied. Friends were to be met from every direction. My old pupils clustered so fondly around me that I felt quite at home. No birds singing in the sunshine ever made sweeter music to my heart than their young voices; and, though they all talked at once, there was perfect harmony. A thousand things were to be said of what had taken place since we parted; many plans were proposed and amusements projected before they could think of letting me go back to Abingdon.

The afternoon was spent in preparing for the wedding party that night. The eventful hour arrived. All the young men of the village, a crowd of fair girls, blushing at the thought of their own loveliness, and a goodly number of blooming matrons, accompanied by their self-satisfied spouses, circled through the brilliantly lighted apartments. Amid the crowd none looked more attractive than the bride, none happier than the bridegroom. An expression of generous feeling and open sincerity in his countenance invited confidence and respect. Her gentle, down-cast eyes and fresh complexion made her look quite youthful as, receiving the congratulations of friends, she "blushed in crimson touched with pale." No one could have regarded the scene without a pervading sentiment of pleasure at thus witnessing the perfection of social happiness combined with the prospect of domestic felicity in store for the newly-married pair.

The ceremony being over, dancing commenced immediately, and was kept up till beyond the midnight hour. I was a mere looker-on; for, though I had been passionately fond of dancing, my heart was not in it now. The room, as if some fairy palace lighted up, the gay company and splendid supper, all failed to interest me. My thoughts reverted to the last time I had danced in this very room. Eighteen months had elapsed and I was here again, but with what different feelings. I shuddered at the bare idea of ever again participating in an amusement so light and trifling. I had withdrawn to rather an obscure corner, with some married ladies, when a gentleman acquaintance, on the wrong side of forty, with whom I had often danced, came and asked my hand for the next cotillion. I declined.

"What," said he, with surprise, "have you given up dancing? I have not seen you on the floor this evening."

"Yes," I replied, "I never expect to dance again."

"Nor will I, for to-night," he said, "if I may be allowed to join this company."

After conversing with us for a while, he suddenly turned around and looked upon the gay and giddy throng passing and repassing.

"How supremely ridiculous," he exclaimed, "those men and women appear. I never saw it in this light before. I shall follow your example, my friend."

A few intervening days and I was on my way back to Abingdon. Having left all my gay companions behind, and there being no one in the stage-coach whom I knew, I had full time for reflection. Painful sensations oppressed me. How my hopes and plans and wishes had altered since I first went to reside in Wythe. I had left behind me that delightful period of youth when hope walks by our side, and with her delicate pencil touches every thing with the hues of heaven. With me this period had been an unusually bright one. It was now like a dream that I had ever looked forward to substantial happiness in this world, where, as Petrarch says, "Nothing lasts but tears."

I began to realize the fact that "he builds too low who builds beneath the skies."

My nature was essentially unfitted for fashionable society. I went into it because it was easier to go than to refuse the kindness that forced on me those uncongenial amusements. I had often prayed to be saved from temptation without, perhaps, forming any resolution to resist it. From early childhood I had desired to be a Christian. Could I expect that God would do all this for me when I had never even formed a determination to *resist* evil? Did I really desire to serve God? *To serve God*, what a thought! Now, for the first time, I realized its import. If I do serve God I can not serve the world. What is it to serve the world, and what will be its reward? Is it to follow its fashions, to love its spirit of levity and vanity, to seek its pleasures, and forgetting God, be the ungrateful recipient of all his mercies? The reward will only be "the pleasures of sin for a season," and then the future, the dark, unending future.

CHAPTER XVII.

I REACHED my mother's home late at night; a shadow had fallen upon that hearthstone during my absence. The dear sister, who had been my companion from childhood, had been ill, and was still so great a sufferer that we feared her health was permanently impaired. This had prevented their enjoying the Christmas holidays and increased my regret at being absent.

Mrs. Smith had much to tell me about the quarterly meeting, and the interesting religious persons with whom she had become acquainted. The presiding elder had tarried with them during the meeting.

"I wished for you often," said she, "and I am not sorry to hear that you had a rough journey, and that you suffered inconvenience from your trip."

"This will teach you," she added, pleasantly, "to obey God rather than man."

All things conspired to deepen conviction in my naturally susceptible heart and to increase thoughtfulness. The subject of my soul's eternal interest was constantly before me, and I can never be sufficiently thankful to my Heavenly Father that the circumstances by which I was then surrounded were favorable to the growth of piety. Inclined to be romantic, had I not been compelled to steady exertion, my love of novelty might have fascinated and drawn me from the line of duty. I have thanked God a thousand times that I was not permitted to choose my own way, and that I was compelled to lead an active life.

I have never seen the time when I had "nothing to do." Had it been otherwise, I might now be compelled to look back upon the wreck of former years, affections wasted, pleasures fled, and hopes numbered with the dead.

My sister gave up her school on account of her feeble health, and spent much time with me at "The Meadows." The kindness of Mrs. Smith, at this time, increased my affection for her tenfold. I never think of the virtues of this excellent woman without a swelling heart and tearful eyes. The very atmosphere around her breathed peace and tenderness. Summer days pass, earth's blossoms fade, but love, founded on esteem and gratitude, can never die.

The first Methodist church in Abingdon was erected in the Spring of 1823, a comfortable frame building, spacious enough, as it then appeared, but which seemed shrunken almost to insignificance when I saw it after an absence of more than twenty years. Previously to my attending the meetings in Abingdon, I had not been inside a Methodist church more than two or three times in my life. Divine service was regularly held here by the traveling preachers of the circuit, the society not being rich enough to support a stationed preacher. The membership increased rapidly. Prayer-meetings, class-meetings, and *band*-meetings were formed and regularly kept up. These Mrs. Smith and I frequently attended, though she was a Presbyterian.

By special invitation the traveling Methodist preachers often spent their "rest-days" at "The Meadows;" a rest indeed. One of the younger preachers, a modest and very pious man, well known for his faithful devotion to the cause of Christ, was urged to come and spend a few days in the "prophet's room." He declined the invita-

tion, because of his threadbare clothes. The knees of
his pantaloons bore evident marks of frequent prostra-
tions before the throne of grace. His humility and
diffidence were touching and beautiful—"he should like
to go, but could not; no, he would tarry with an humble
brother by the wayside." This humble brother, Wini-
fred, was as famous for his hospitality and his love of the
Christian Church, particularly the Methodist, as were the
primitive disciples. A complete new suit soon found its
way privately into the young brother's saddle-bags; he
came, and mutual pleasure was felt. No wonder that the
blessing of God rested upon such a household!

We were sitting one evening conversing upon the
subject of the great revival that had occurred in the
Methodist Church during the last two years, and the
changed aspect of things, when Mrs. Smith, after praising enthusiastically the new presiding elder from Kentucky, who had been a guest in their house during the
Christmas meeting, and who seemed to have inspired her
with a degree of reverence that left her scarcely any
thing else to talk of, exclaimed—

"I wish you could see him and hear him pray."

"How does he look?" I asked.

"Tall, dignified, fine looking, but by no means handsome; yet there is so much character, so much real
worth expressed in his face, that you would never remark
his prominent nose and wide mouth, except as indicative
of intellect."

"But he must look odd in one of those *Methodist
coats?*"

"No, he does not; every thing he wears is becoming;
it could not be otherwise, with a man upon whose brow
is written the simplicity of a Christian."

"Well, I hope I shall have an opportunity of seeing this paragon of yours, but I warn you, I almost feel prejudiced against him, when I remember the Scripture declaration, 'Wo unto those of whom *all* men speak well.'"

"I do not know that everybody does speak well of him—I am sure that sinners must feel exceedingly uncomfortable under his searching sermons. I am told that quite a number thought the first sermon he preached at the Court-house powerfully severe, unveiling as he did the iniquity of the age with firm hand, and making them see themselves as God sees them."

We were interrupted by the entrance of Captain Smith, just from town, who exclaimed—

"Polly, have another roll of blankets put on Tevis's bed; he will be here to-night after preaching."

"Indeed! I am truly glad; we were just speaking of him, and I am gratified at so soon having an opportunity of introducing him to our young friend. This is his rest week; he will spend it with us, I hope."

I was conscious of a desire to see the man whose wonder-working energy and pious efforts had been crowned with almost unexampled success throughout the district over which he had for two years presided.

The history of these two years has been so often spoken of, connected, as it was, with many co-workers whose biographies have been published, as to make it unnecessary for me to enlarge upon the subject. It does present a scene of benevolent exertions, telling upon the destiny of thousands; exhibiting in a strong light an earnest devotion to God and a love for precious souls by the humble, earnest, pious, and faithful Methodist preachers of that day—the results displaying the power and goodness of that merciful and gracious Redeemer, of whom they were the honored instruments. Those early itinerant preachers, inspired with zeal, and clothed with the armor of righteousness, sought not their own but the glory of God. They were, doubtless, raised up by an all-wise and gracious Providence, in pity for those wandering sheep scattered over the wilds of the far West, as well as for a more settled and prosperous people, who had strangely slighted the copious overflowings of divine love. Such preachers of the Gospel came as instructors, and shed a reproving light upon the corruptions of a time-serving world, bearing the high credentials of messengers from heaven; and as examples of prayer and faith transmitted to the Church, not for admiration only, but for encouragement and invitation. Such only can arouse sinners from their stupor and bring them into the fold of Christ. Such honest embassadors of the Savior are blessings to the world.

The guest came, and I was introduced to him, feeling a disposition to criticise his appearance and scrutinize closely his manners and conversation. There was nothing, however, to criticize but his dish-shaped coat and straight collar. I dared to think these pretentious; but a second glance at the quiet face, radiant with peace, hope, and faith, resulting, doubtless, from an inward and spiritual grace—a confidence which seemed to be that of reposing strength,. changed my opinion—for in those dark grey eyes slumbered a world of energy. His voice was clear and distinct; his movements calm, but always prompt, decisive, and rapid; directed, at the same time, with discretion. During his rest week in this part of the Holston District, which embraced a circuit of nine hundred miles, he found a welcome retreat at "The

Meadows," where he might be refreshed after the toils of traveling over bad roads and mountain passes. His room, in a quiet part of the hospitable mansion, afforded a secluded sanctuary for private devotion; while, in his friendship and society his worthy entertainers felt themselves recompensed for all their kind offices and concern on his behalf, and that the prayers and presence of God's ministers brought ample blessings to the household.

The week passed away, and the wayfaring man of God had gone; but not so the remembrance of his fervent prayers and pious conversation. Mrs. Smith had often expressed her fears that living out of the Church, as she did, was not in keeping with her duty to herself and her family, though she had always been a strict attendant on the services of the Presbyterian Church, in which she had been brought up. She had lived in the world without partaking much of its spirit, and now she was almost persuaded to become a Methodist. Her husband opposed it steadily, but not violently. The law of rigid simplicity, which reigned at this time so pre-eminently among the Methodists, was not according to his taste; and he feared the influence of religion in earnest, and that a change in his household arrangements, superinduced by these rigid people who were turning the world upside down, might cast a shadow over his daughter's entrance into the gay world, and throw her too much out of its dress-circle. Thus he ridiculed the precision of its members and their particular exclusiveness, which did in reality make a dividing line between them and other religious sects, as well as the outer world.

I do not intend to affirm that Mrs. Smith's sense of duty was at all affected by the ridiculous light in which Captain Smith placed straight coats, broad-brimmed hats, plain bonnets, and Quaker simplicity—not at all. She was decidedly pious, without any subserviency to worldly creeds; but she finally decided to join the Presbyterians, whose right-heartedness before God none ever questioned, and between whom and the Methodists of Abingdon there was a constant interchange of friendly Christian courtesies. It is a well-known fact that, in proportion as divine grace abounds in any Church, so does that charity which is but another name for God's love abound in the heart. Mrs. Smith lived and died a worthy member of the Church she had chosen, with sympathies widening and deepening for all other denominations. She is now a bright jewel in the Redeemer's crown, at whose feet she worshiped while a pilgrim on earth.

CHAPTER XVIII.

EARLY in the Summer my mother, having received pressing invitations from her friends in Kentucky to visit them, resolved to break up housekeeping and return with her little family to the home of her youth, leaving to the future whether she would settle permanently in Kentucky. Her youngest brother lived at the old homestead, and many of her nearest relatives in the immediate vicinity; indeed, her family connections, as well as those of my father, were so numerous that she thought it would be delightful to spend a year or more in visiting, while I remained to finish my engagement at Captain Smith's. As there was no expectation of her ever returning to Abingdon she turned all her effects into money, and soon after left in a comfortable private conveyance, journeying by the old Wilderness road. My heart was soon gladdened by the reception of a letter announcing their safe arrival among friends and relatives, who gave them a warm welcome.

Meantime my little school held on the even tenor of its way. My loving, industrious pupils improved so rapidly as to make me feel that I was doing and receiving good; and these would have been halcyon days, indeed, if I had been perfectly satisfied with myself. I felt an intense yearning after something that would satisfy the earnest longing of my soul for higher attainments in a Christian life. Clouds of heaviness, and sometimes of darkness, rested upon me. I was assured, and I do not deem it presumptuous to express it, that my Heavenly Father had led me onward by his gracious providence up to the present time, and I could but hope he was preparing me for future and more extensive usefulness—I knew not when, how, or where. I read the Bible much, and prayed often; and cheerfully relinquished those frivolous amusements into which I had been drawn, more by circumstances than taste—never having been fully satisfied that they were in keeping with the wants of an intellectual nature; yet I still continued to attend cotillion parties, and occasionally a "practicing ball" with my pupils, who were never permitted to go to these places, although a part of the regular routine of a dancing-school, unless I would accompany them.

My previous experience in a religious course had been too formal; and now Reason began to detect the sophistry of the world's promises, and experience, to reveal the bitterness of its delusions. Wealth, honor, and pleasure appeared as visionary phantoms; and I asked myself, with a beating heart, "Are all the forms of beauty here presented, the songs of melody, or the streams of pleasure which tend to lure us from the narrow path that leads to a better life, suitable desires for a creature who is to die to-morrow?" A long life continually rises up in prospect, but every day's experience proves the fallacy of depending upon that for a preparation to die. I thought so, at least; and I felt that a crisis had come when I must choose between the life of an earnest Christian and a compromise with the world. A prophetic light seemed to be shed upon my inward vision, and with the eye of Faith I sought the anchor of Hope and the influence of the Spirit; praying that the world might be unmasked, and its vanities fully exposed, that I might detect the poison concealed in the chalice presented by the pleasures of earth.   Life would still remain a blessing, and heaven still be attainable.

A protracted-meeting was to be held in Abingdon, and I determined to avail myself of its privileges.   The whole family attended Church on Saturday, and proposed being present at the eleven o'clock service on the Sabbath, but I wished to be at the early morning love-feast as well.   The walk to town was short; but as the weather was exceedingly hot, and the road dusty, I requested to have the carriage to convey me thither at early hour.

"No, no," said Captain Smith, "you must not go before eleven,—it will be too much of a good thing this long, warm day."

I made no reply; but his opposition only made me more determined, and in less than twenty minutes I was walking slowly through the orchard on my way to town. A few minutes more elapsed, and the carriage had overtaken me; it was ready before I left.

"Captain Smith has sent the carriage, ma'am—please get in; he thought you wa'n't in earnest about going in so early," said the polite coachman, as he sprang from his seat and threw open the door.

"No, go back," I replied; "I find it pleasant enough to walk."

The perplexed coachman was saved further remonstrance by my walking hastily onward; and I soon reached the house of my friend, Mrs. Branch, who had become as much interested in the Methodists as I was.

Mrs. Branch accompanied me to the church, which was filled to its utmost capacity by people whose anxious, serious, and interested looks betrayed the state of their minds.   Curiosity, no doubt, had attracted some, as such a meeting was a novelty in the community. The gallery was crowded with sable faces, peering inquisitively around. The first hymn was sung with spirit and feeling, and was followed by a prayer unusually impressive and comprehensive. There were many from other Churches present. All knelt with the deepest reverence, and after a short address from the presiding minister the bread and water were handed round, of which all partook in token of Christian fellowship.

That love-feast made a deep impression upon my heart, every avenue of which seemed open to the reception of divine truth. The sweet songs of Zion, the outgushing effusions of some happy in the love of God, the soul's burning incense mingling with the deep, hushed sobbings of penitent hearts, and occasionally a well-connected and touching narrative, which fell from the lips of one who had experienced the efficacy and power of divine grace, all enhanced the interest of the scene. On the one side was heard the soothing voice of comfort and encouragement, joined to the impetuous spirit's cry, and on the other,

> " Words low spoken seemed to bear
> The pleadings of an earnest prayer."

Intervals of what appeared celestial music played upon the harp-strings of a regenerated spirit vibrated sweetly upon the listening ear, making the melody of heaven in the soul; and when the whole congregation sang together the praises of redeeming love, I felt as if listening to the music of seraphic choirs, and could almost hear the rustling of angels' wings. The question arose, what can the world offer that will compare with the divine peace that softly flows like a pure stream over life's burning desert, gladdening those who put their trust in God? My decision was made, then and there, to be a Christian without compromise; and as my soul whispered the words, "I am resolved what to do," my restless and anxious spirit was quieted, and I thanked God for having made me acquainted with a people who regarded religion as an earnest matter. I knew their doctrines to be the same as those of the Church in which I had been baptized. Now I felt an aspiration for a zealous consecration to God, that I might no longer live under the miserable delusion that it was possible to serve God and the world at the same time. I wanted that religion which kindles upon the heart's altar a living faith in Jesus Christ, our Redeemer.

An interval of an hour, during which many kept their seats from fear of being crowded out, and then came the eleven o'clock preaching. Silence reigned throughout the assembly as the solemn-browed minister arose and gave out a well-known hymn, which the whole congregation sang with "the spirit and the understanding." The words were distinctly pronounced without interrupting the melody; a short, but earnest prayer, a few preliminary remarks after the second hymn, and the preacher opened upon the sublime subject of the atonement, portraying the unsatisfying nature of all that the world calls good and great. Never did the mutability and the insufficiency of all earthly things to satisfy the demands of the soul appear to me so plainly exhibited. Never did the world and its allurements, considered as a source of human happiness, appear so unavailing. He proved to a demonstration that a consciousness of present acceptance with God was more valuable than crowns, kingdoms, thrones, and dominions; and more to be desired than all the boasted honors and privileges of this sin-banished world. These were nothing, yea, less than nothing, compared with the vital importance of a conscience purified by the blood of the covenant. The bliss of piety on earth, with its triumphs in a dying hour, were never presented to a listening audience in purer strains of persuasive eloquence. The great and precious promises of the Gospel came forth with unction from the preacher's lips to the hearts of his hearers; indeed, with holy fire fresh from the altar above. The streaming tears and ascending shouts of the vast assemblage testified that it was a season of refreshing from the presence of the Lord; a flood of glory seemed poured in upon the congregation from the open gates of light. Sinners were awakened, and believers built up, comforted, strengthened, and established in their most holy faith. It was a time of the outpouring of the Spirit never to be forgotten, and the fruits of which will, doubtless, be seen in eternity.

A few weeks after this tickets were issued for a grand ball to be given on the Fourth of July. The wave of religious excitement, that had passed over the town and vicinity, had drifted many from their worldly moorings, and fastened them firmly to the "Rock of Ages;" but the community, in general, were settled down to their usual routine of every-day life, and there seemed to be an intense interest felt by the lovers of amusement in the coming celebration. Everybody felt bound to attend the Fourth of July ball, as it was a national festivity. The young went to dance, and the old to look on. Mrs. Smith never attended any place of the kind, and I was expected to go with my young pupils. Here was a temptation hard to resist. Was it not my duty, under the circumstances, to go with them, even if I declined participating? Would it be kind to deprive the girls of a privilege which they did not often enjoy? Would it not offend some whose good will I desired to retain? I tried to make it a subject of fervent prayer, and the struggle was soon over. I positively refused to attend the ball, or to give my countenance to it in any way. Some of my friends, whose opinion I valued, thought I was "straining at a gnat," even if I did not "swallow a camel;" but I was spared the hardest trial, for neither Mary Smith nor any of her companions complained at my decision; and, to my surprise, seemed glad to be relieved of the trouble. Thus we often find the path of duty made easy as well as plain for us, when we choose the right and ask God's blessing upon it.

One of my warmest friends, whom I admired and loved devotedly, commended and encouraged me by her example. Mrs. Joseph Trigg, "Cousin or Aunt Betty," as she was familiarly called, to whom all the young people of the country around were particularly attached, in consequence of the interest she took in them, being an ardent promoter of, and participator in, their social gatherings, was a woman of deep feeling, energetic and life-giving in whatever sphere she moved. Her enjoyment of society was intense, and rarely did a shadow darken her brow or dispel her unfailing good humor.

Aunt Betty had now become a Methodist, combining the characteristics of Martha and Mary, and was as prominent a member of this straitest of all sects, as she had been a leader in the fashionable world. She worked now as energetically in striving to promote the cause and kingdom of the Savior, as she had formerly labored, to use her own expression, "to establish the kingdom of Satan."

A quarterly-meeting was to be held in her neighborhood, eighteen or twenty miles from Abingdon, on the Saturday and Sunday preceding the Fourth of July. It was arranged between us that I should attend; but how? I would not ask for the carriage, because I knew that Captain Smith was opposed to the whole matter. I had no company; it was finally agreed that Mrs. Trigg's old and faithful servant, Solomon, should be sent for me on Friday, and I could not have had a more trusty escort. We started early Saturday morning for the grove where the meeting was in progress, and where I was to meet Mrs. Trigg.

Solomon had a fund of religious anecdotes with which he entertained me on the way. He had long been a devoted Methodist, loved the cause and loved the preachers, none of whom ever tarried a night at his master's hospitable house without their shoes being blacked and their horses well cared for by him. He it was that held the bridle when the preacher left in the morning, and bade him "God-speed" on the way. He told me he had been a great sinner, and cared not how hard he had to work if he might but attend a horse race or a cock fight on Sunday; but it had pleased God to bring him among the Methodists in Western Virginia, and since he had heard them preach he had turned "right round and put his hand to the Gospel plow, and had been trying, ever since, to make a straight furrow toward the Kingdom." He had not been without his temptations to turn back, and his particular thorn in the flesh was his brother Jupiter, whom he wanted to go with him to the heavenly Canaan. But Jupiter was a hard case, and resisted all Solomon's efforts—loved his old ways and would not be persuaded to be a Christian, and, said Solomon, "de fact is, ma'r'm, I b'leve my brudder

Jupiter done sold hisself to Satan, and I can 't somehow see why 't is dat ole Solomon can be happy in spite of all dis; but I knows I loves him, and will keep on lovin' him and pray for him to be kept out of de pit, and trust my God for de rest."

Solomon was a proverb among his own people for honesty and industry, and his shining black face was a welcome sight to them, though he often interfered with their sinful amusements, and ceased not to labor for their good. The white people welcomed him into their churches, his real piety being well known to all. He would shout in the Presbyterian Church, if he was happy, with as much energy as if he had been among the Methodists, and yet he never shouted without "blessing God that he had ever seen the Methodists." Upon one occasion he was so happy, and shouted so vociferously, that a quiet gentleman at his elbow said, "Stop awhile, old man, or your religion will all run out;" to which he replied, "Bress God, full 'um up again."

A few hours brought us to a large, old-fashioned barn, whose ample enclosure held a modest congregation of simple-hearted people, assembled there for the purpose of holding a love-feast before the morning service. The bowery trees afforded a delightful shade for a large number of persons who waited for the hour of preaching. My friend was ready to receive me, and led me to a reserved seat among the professors of religion. I expected only to be an observer, as upon a former occasion, of what was passing before me. Again my soul was thrilled and vibrated in sympathy with the many speakers who arose, in quick succession, to tell of God's dealings with them, until, no longer able to control my feelings, I arose and asked an interest in the prayers of the people of God, stating in a few words, which were listened to in the deepest silence, my own convictions and determinations. This novel proceeding excited great interest in my behalf, which was increased when I asked permission to meet them the next day at the communion-table, that I might there pledge myself in solemn covenant to Jesus, my Redeemer, by partaking of the sacred emblems of the eucharistic feast. Assuming a determined attitude to resist any temptation to look back, I would join the Church at the circuit preacher's next appointment in Abingdon; I would then ask to have "the doors opened" for my especial benefit, that I might take the step openly among my friends and under no excitement. The ministers present held a consultation on the subject, and my request was granted. We had two sermons that day, and the crimson hues of sunset yielded to the silvery tranquillity of moon and stars before we reached Mrs. Trigg's dwelling, a few miles from the preaching-place.

The next morning, Sabbath, I anticipated the sun in rising that I might read, pray, and meditate upon the solemn covenant I was that day to make; and oh how earnestly I prayed that I might not eat and drink to my own condemnation. I caught a glance of myself in the old-fashioned mirror, just before I descended to the breakfast-room, and was startled at the incongruity of my dress for the occasion. My large double collarette of book-muslin seemed more conspicuous than ever before; my hair, dressed *a la mode*, with curls on the face, would contrast strangely with the Quaker-dressed people, with whom I was to be associated. So I exchanged the collarette for a simple muslin kerchief, folded over the bosom, and combed my hair smooth behind my ears; not that I thought this a matter of vital importance so far as

I was concerned, but I feared many would regard it as unsuitable to my profession; and, like St. Paul, I was willing to conform even to the prejudices of good people. I had no jewelry to dispense with; I never did admire, and scarce ever wore it,—not even a finger-ring.

That day was an eventful one in my life, and the place where I worshiped was a waymark on my journey, a bethel to my soul. I returned to my every-day duties with fresh energy, and was occupied, during the next two weeks, at intervals, with the help of Mrs. Smith, in re-modeling my fashionable wardrobe, removing flounces, making plain substitutes for my standing collarettes, re-ducing my straw bonnet to moderate dimensions, and taking off all the trimming except a plain ribbon.

My gay young friend, John Mitchell, would call every day or two to see how I was getting along, as he said, "in making myself as much like old Mother Russell as possible." Should he go to town and get me some Bath-coating, that I might have a long train like hers? had I a suitable girdle for my numerous pocket handkerchiefs? or wouldn't Aunt Smith make me some half-handed gloves? Captain Smith "hoped I would not require Mary to dress as I did, by conforming to this demure costume." Mrs. Smith laughed; I bore it with great equanimity of temper, and thus conquered by not being annoyed.

During the two weeks of probation, my intention of joining the Church was much talked of, and I verily believe the congregation was increased on that day by the curiosity of many who still doubted, I know not why, unless it was that to be a Methodist required so many sacrifices. This denomination insisted upon a marked distinction between the world and the Church.

There was to be no compromise, and I had lived so long in the fashionable world that those who formed their opinions without reflection judged of me by the standard of their own experience. But my decision was made with due deliberation, and I determined to follow the narrow path of a pilgrim to the better land.

The appointed Sabbath came. I walked slowly through the orchard, the nearest way to town. It was a charming morning. Summer was arrayed in her brightest tints. The blue sky above was cloudless and purely beautiful; and, to me, the air was never so balmy, the trees so green, or the song of the birds so sweet. The dew sparkled in the fragrant flower-cups, and I rejoiced in the assurance that all these lovely objects were the exponents of God's wisdom, tokens of his benevolence, and the perfect image of his greatness.

When I entered the church I took my seat near the altar, in company with Mrs. Smith, my thoughtful young pupils, and my two good friends, Mrs. Branch and Mrs. Betty Trigg. The pulpit was filled by the Rev. Josiah Rhoton, the young man of threadbare memory. I heard but little of the sermon, though I tried to listen. It was said to be eloquent, but I was too much absorbed with my own thoughts and the importance of the step I was about to take, which I hoped and believed would bring me within the inner circle of God's providence. The sermon over, the preacher walked down from the pulpit and asked, "Are there any who wish to join the Church? If so, let them come forward while the congregation are singing the first hymn." I arose and stepped inside the altar before the first two lines were finished. I was alone; no one followed my example. The hymn finished, the congregation seemed to sit in breathless silence, while my name was announced, and the usual preliminaries were gone through. I was admitted into full member-ship, according to my own desire, after which I was com-pletely surrounded by Christian friends, who wept and rejoiced over me as a new-found sister. Some would have thought this too severe an ordeal and would have sought a different mode of admission into the Church. I argued otherwise, and was strengthened in the performance of what I conceived an imperative duty by God's blessing in the very act. He who knows all hearts, knows that I did not intend to make an ostentatious display, but, at the same time, I was not willing to sit in "Nicodemus's corner," desiring rather to make an open renunciation if haply my example might do good to others.

My introduction into Methodist society made me ac-quainted with many excellent people whose simple man-ners and unaffected piety showed plainly the source whence it was derived. The religion of the Bible was worn as an every-day garment, and not kept for a showy Sunday suit. Conscience never permitted them to neg-lect real duties for the performance of imaginary ones. Among them, I learned that the essential worship of a true Christian consists in the daily discharge of temporal obligations, beautifully interwoven with daily spiritual worship before a throne of Grace, not forsaking the as-sembling together at proper times and places, as well as public worship on the Sabbath. The Ganaways, the Winifreds, and others in and about Abingdon, were true types of that Methodism, once termed by a Scotch divine "Christianity in earnest." They seemed to live always in sight of heaven.

I was still privileged to hold sweet counsel with my excellent and tried friends of former companionship, who were now also striving to walk worthy of their high vocation—my amiable and sympathizing Mrs. B., my warm hearted, though undemonstrative, Mrs. L., whose sunny good nature seemed to crystallize into a cheerful serenity that sparkled beneath the darkest skies; but, above all, I loved to talk with Aunt Betty, and we often reverted, with wonder, to the superficial feelings upon which we had hitherto lived, without knowing the depths of our own hearts. Together we attended all those places "where prayer was wont to be made," and felt as if just beginning to learn the true object and mystery of life.

Thus the "velvet-footed" days flew noiselessly by. The rainbow of promise was before me, and a holy light seemed dawning on my vision; yet I was without any bright manifestation of a Savior's pardoning love, for which I was taught to pray and confidently expect. I was unwavering, however, in the determination that I would never stop short of any possible attainment in the glorious pathway to eternal life. Pride and vain self-confidence had long been my besetting sins, and I continued to strive against them by constant prayer and watchfulness. Alas! how difficult the task after the deceitfulness of sin has taken such deep root in the soul! Yet, I did find a degree of peace so soon as resolution was enthroned as the guide of my soul, and I was enabled, in all sincerity, to disrobe myself of that pharisaical religion which had given me nothing but a heartless experience of the folly of those spasmodic efforts to do good and be good, without some settled principle. I prayed constantly for faith and a persevering adoption of the spirit of Christ.

Chapter XIX.

Summer waned and Autumn came. In September, 1823, the annual camp-meeting was held near the Sulphur Springs, in Smyth County, Virginia. A beautiful grove of grand old trees in a lovely mountain gorge marked the spot that had, for this especial purpose, been generously donated to the Methodists for the term of a hundred years by Colonel Thompson, the son-in-law of old Mother Russell. Mother Russell's unobtrusive dwelling was in the immediate vicinity, and she not only attended constantly this means of grace herself, but her house was the temporary home of many who came from a distance. The camp-meetings held on this spot were widely diffusive of good, and were really necessary in a country so sparsely settled as was this part of Western Virginia at that time. It was not uncommon to find persons attending from Tennessee and North Carolina.

We reached the camp-ground late in the afternoon of a brilliant Autumn day; while yet flakes of sunshine, sifting through the pendant branches, fell like tremulous, gleaming gems upon the heads of the assembled congregation. Near by, but hidden under the foliage of the water willow, whose branches hung over the clear stream, was a spring widening into smooth, deep water—a miniature lake, throwing back the sunshine like a mirror, and keeping all its secret depths unlighted; then con-

tracting into a narrow stream it ran, glittering like a
silver thread, through the valley beneath. Beyond it
rose a magnificent mountain, skirted with woods and,
even to the very summit, dotted with farms and dwellings rendered quite distinct on a clear day. Nearer, and
upon one side of the green and goodly valley where the
tents were pitched, was a less elevated mountain, covered
with every shade of green foliage, interspersed with flowering shrubs; among which predominated the luxuriant
and richly-tinted "laurel," with its deep green leaves so
refreshing to the eye. The declining sun touched everything with a soft and tender light, and the few fleecy
clouds, visible in the fathomless blue air, seemed like
white doves of peace, floating with wings outspread
in benediction over the assembled multitude of God's
people, who had come up into the wilderness, apart from
the dust and heat and hurry of existence, that they
might hold sweet communion with each other, and bow
with united hearts before their great Creator, here to
worship him under the overarching skies in a "temple
not made with hands."

A winding pathway up the mountain side, quite concealed from the passers-by, led to a spot high up, where,
under the spreading oak and chestnut, prayer was offered
up during the intervals of public preaching for earnest
seekers of religion. Pious and experienced women, who
were ever laboring for the good of souls, and who felt
that a cup of cold water given to famished lips in the
spirit of the Gospel is a pearl of great price in the sight
of Him who has pronounced it "more blessed to give
than to receive," were accustomed to pray there with and
for the female penitents and seekers of religion. All
along its steep ascent were quiet nooks and shady dells,

where no prying eye or careless footstep would be likely to intrude.

I had come to the meeting by the special invitation of Aunt Betty, whose hospitality I was to share, and whose large heart and ample provision made it a pleasant resting-place for many of her friends. Her tent—or, rather, cottage—was erected by her kind husband, with great attention to comfort and convenience, having an upper story containing small sleeping apartments, while the lower story was appropriated to prayer-meetings and the reception of transient visitors. The bountiful table was spread under the shade of the trees, near the little temporary kitchen where old Solomon presided as chief. To his heart's delight, he found ample time not only to wait on the preachers, whom he almost worshiped, but also to attend prayer-meetings among his colored brethren, and occasionally fill their preaching-stand as an exhorter; besides, he never neglected the preaching hour among the whites. It was pleasant to see his shining black face, softened by a magnificent fleece of white wool, with dilated eyes and half-open mouth, as he sat at a modest distance during the service, drinking in large draughts from the same pure fountain of mercy as his white brethren; and it was exciting to hear his deep, suppressed, "Amen, massa! bress God!"—the tears flowing fast as he occasionally exclaimed, "Free salvation, glory to my Massa in heaven!"

My first night at the encampment was full of beauty. At each of the four corners of the camp-ground was left the stump of a large tree, four or five feet high, the tops of which were rendered fire-proof by a layer of brick and mortar, and upon these blazed burning pine knots, lighting up all the surroundings with their tall flames.

Among the dark, green foliage glittered the flickering
lights of numerous lamps attached to trees; beautiful
white vapors floated in the star-lit sky, now resting an
instant, then glancing onward, hiding the face of the full
moon like a snowy veil cast over the jeweled brow of a
queen. Green trees, grassy meadows, wild flowers, and
mountain scenery always seem to raise me above the
earth and its cares,—thus I may be pardoned for what
might seem an unnecessary fullness of description of the
singular and beautiful scene; and there are connected
with this meeting incidents so vividly daguerreotyped
upon my heart that even now Memory, with her magic
power, lights them up as beautifully as at first.

In the stand were reverend, good-looking men, whose
very appearance inspired confidence. The trumpet was
sounded, and long lines of people were seen wending
their way to roughly constructed seats, made for the
occasion. I never saw more perfect order, more attention to politeness and decorum, in any assemblage of
people. The hymn was announced,—all sang together;
in those days singing was worship,—the beginning, as it
were, of prayer. The assembled multitude rose up to
sing, and, after repeating the last two lines of the hymn,
fell upon their knees, to continue that act of devotion in
prayer; and there was a power in it, felt by all. When
we arose again a well-known melody poured forth from
the hearts of the whole congregation, full of freedom, of
simplicity, of feeling, and of energetic sentiment. It was
as the wings of seraphim, upon which the assembled multitude were borne heavenward, thus elevating preachers
and hearers in the introductory, so that the whole subsequent service showed its effect. Never did truer music
gush from the human heart; and a more efficacious

means for inspiring the minds of the hearers with the
love of religion could hardly be conceived than when its
sublime sentiments are clothed in sweet musical harmony
that captivates the senses, and touches the soul through
the medium of the ear and the heart.   Many of the old
tunes, habitual in the worship of those days, seem instinctive to the devotional feelings of our people.   If our
congregations had not then the artistic appreciation in
the execution of music which belongs to the present day,
they had, at least, more of that heart-gushing piety which
flows in sweet music from the exhaustless fountain of
true religion; and their choice tunes showed a higher
musical taste than now prevails among us.   Charles
Wesley's hymns, so full of glowing piety, would kindle
a heavenly flame in the hearts of any assembly sincerely
desirous of praising and worshiping God.   We ridicule
many of the old tunes, as well as the poetry to which
they were sung, as not fit for a genteel congregation.
The reproach is just to some extent, but not so fully as
is supposed; for there was a period when these melodies
were used almost exclusively with Charles Wesley's noble
strains.   The fact is, the primitive Methodists were more
exempt from doggerel follies than we are.   Methodist
singing, at church and at home, once had a charm of its
own, almost as much as Quaker apparel had a fashion of
its own,—and every body liked it, because it made melody in every heart.

Our surroundings were favorable to devotion.   We
were too remote from cities and towns to be annoyed by
the curious and the idle.   Even those who came to observe
and to be observed remained to pray.   Public services
never continued later than ten o'clock P. M.,—at that
hour all were expected to seek repose; yet in some of the

tents the voice of prayer and praise was heard at a much later hour, and, at intervals, the prolonged shouts of happy souls.

The sound of the trumpet at early dawn awakened all slumberers for morning prayer; after which a frugal meal—nothing hot but tea or coffee—was prepared, and then an interval of two or three hours spent in private devotion before the eleven o'clock preaching. We dined at precisely one o'clock, giving an opportunity for the serious and penitent to withdraw again for private prayer. Religious exercises, thus conducted, even the most censorious and fastidious must acknowledge to be productive of great good, and was the very thing most needed in a thinly settled country, where the visits of a minister were only occasional, and preaching-places were few and far between. Here rich streams of Gospel grace caused all hearts to overflow with love to God; and the hallowed music of many voices mingled with the songs of the redeemed in heaven.

Returning one evening with some friends from our mountain retreat, we were attracted by a crowd standing before the open door of a large tent. Agreeably to the simple customs of the place, we entered without ceremony, and saw a young woman lying on a couch, in a state of total insensibility. The pallor of her face and her closed eyelids, the coldness of her marble brow, and the icy touch of her folded hands, would have indicated death; but the heart gently fluttered like a caged bird, and the very spirit of tranquillity hovered over that sweet face. She had been in this state for several hours, and some were apprehensive that the soul was about to leave its clayey tenement forever; but before midnight the color gradually returned to her face, and, as the vital spark was rekindling, she opened her eyes and softly whispered,—

> "This sweet calm within my breast
> Is the best pledge of heavenly rest;"

and the quiet eyelids closed again, as if seeking that deeper rest. I know this to be true; but have no comments to make upon it, except that this young person was well known, and loved and respected, as a model of unpretending piety. She worshiped God with inward zeal and served him in every action, and never afterwards referred to this trance as any thing remarkable, but frequently spoke of the melody and love with which her soul was filled. Had she heard unutterable things, and seen visions that were ineffable?

I tried to improve every privilege afforded me at this meeting, but from day to day, without any bright evidence of my acceptance with God. I knew full well that a change had been wrought in my heart, that the things I formerly delighted in no longer captivated my senses; but I knew also that I was not truly converted, and I began to doubt—not the truth of the doctrine of sudden conversions, but that I was ever to expect to be changed in the twinkling of an eye, as was St. Paul. I would not be discouraged, however; having put my hand to the plow and turned my face Zionward, I determined, by the help of God, never to look back. I would wait patiently with the perfect assurance that my Heavenly Father would never have implanted desires that could not be fulfilled.

On the afternoon of a day that had been filled with intensely interesting scenes, I went with a few pious friends up into the mountain to pray. "Aunt Betty Trigg" was among the number, her soul full of love and prayer. We knelt beneath the wide-spreading branches of an oak whose leaves had been repeatedly agitated by the breath of fervent prayer, resolved to wrestle like Jacob until the blessing was obtained. All prayed; but one voice was heard to swell above the rest, and then came the hallowed silence of humble saints absorbed in prayer for me, whilst I felt the full force of that beautiful expression, "I can but perish if I go, I am resolved to try." It was a season of holy influences. I can not tell—I never could; but this much I know, I felt willing to yield all to the will of God, and place my hopes of happiness for time and eternity at the foot of the cross; and then came a "joy and peace in believing" that words could not express, and I sat like Mary at the feet of Jesus and wept, with that sweet song in my mouth:

"In such a frame as this,
I 'd sit and sing my soul away,
To everlasting bliss."

From this time the meeting was full of enjoyment. I could now raise my voice to swell the chorus of redeeming love. I felt that I was a creature of mercy, called by the word of God to seek my everlasting peace in the covenant of redemption.

The events connected with this precious week spent among the godly tents of Jacob and the tabernacles of Israel are so full of interest to me that I must be pardoned for prolixity. The time of parting came, and I left many behind whom I might not meet again this side of heaven. All, all must part on earth, yet there will be a meeting hereafter in those gardens beside the waters of life, a glorious and eternal meeting for all who die in the triumphs of the Gospel.

When at home and in the school-room again, I found

my dear little girls looking curiously at me, as if desirous of knowing what would come of all this. I afterward understood that some of them had resolved to test the change and try the strength of my religion. They well knew that a hasty and impatient temper was my besetting sin, and that I never could tolerate idleness and want of order. An inkstand was overturned; silence was interrupted during study hours by suppressed tittering or low whispers, loud enough, however, to catch my attention, with various other indications of insubordination; and to cap the climax, badly recited lessons continued for several days.

I stood the test tolerably well for I was on my guard and prayed for help, yet I failed not to punish and firmly held the reins of government without any scolding. Finally they gave over, and came with faltering voices and tearful eyes to ask pardon, which they would have done upon their bended knees if permitted. After this we had a pleasant time enough, and the dear little penitents began to hold class-meetings and love-feasts and almost daily prayer-meetings among themselves. This was done with sincerity and in the full tide of new and joyful emotion, hence, no one interrupted them. These reunions were finally given up, because, at their last meeting in the meadow under the shady trees, while one of the girls was praying and the others weeping with intense feeling, some thoughtless boys, perched in the branches of the trees, were amusing themselves at the expense of the girls, pretending to weep, one, to-day known as Parson Brownlow, wiping his eyes with a brickbat and another with a shingle. The noise they made attracted the attention of the girls. Deeply incensed and greatly shocked, they fled precipitately into the house, and determined never again to place themselves under circumstances where holy things could be ridiculed, yet they did not carelessly cast aside those sweet influences of Christianity, still continuing to sing hymns, holding class-meetings occasionally in their own room and praying together frequently.

Who shall say that these young girls, brought up under the happy influences of the Gospel, and so readily responding to the Savior's call, "Daughter, give me thy heart," were not the objects of God's peculiar care? What a charming spectacle was this family of docile and dutiful children, increasing in knowledge and virtue as they grew in stature.

Years passed; these sister-spirits attained to womanhood; their souls being constantly watered by the dew of Lebanon, were kept ever fresh and green. Each lovely and beloved, exerted, in her own sphere, a pure, elevated, and holy influence, beautifully exemplifying the effect of early training. Three, having nobly fulfilled the work assigned them on earth, have gone to their eternal reward. One yet lives to bless the world by her example as a wife, mother, and friend, the fragrance of a loving household, and the light of the circle in which she moves.

Those who thus begin life's pilgrimage find that religion becomes more and more pleasant every day. It is like ascending a mountain, where the prospect, hour after hour, expands and becomes more glorious; like watching the dawn growing brighter and brighter, until hill and vale, lake and forest, are bathed in a blaze of effulgence. Our divine religion is the soul's native air, its portion, its celestial home, the coronet of youth and the crown of old age.

CHAPTER XX.

I HAD expected to remain at "The Meadows" until Mary's education should be completed, and this was ardently desired by all concerned; but the period was rapidly approaching which was to make an important change in my future. In the latter part of September, Mr. Tevis tarried a few days at Captain Smith's, on his way to his Kentucky home, where he was accustomed to spend a week at the close of each conference year. Having had frequent opportunities of learning the true elevation of soul which characterized this self-sacrificing, noble-minded Christian, and contrasting the true value and lofty worth of the things of God and eternity with the vanities and follies of the world, it was very natural that I should esteem and honor one so thoroughly a missionary of the cross, one in whom goodness seemed personified. His prayer for the family, on the morning of his departure, was more than usually fervent, and characterized by a simple and lofty eloquence that kindled a devotional spirit in every heart; and when he bade us farewell, a glow of holy feeling beamed on his face, as if it were to be his last meeting with us on earth. Almost involuntarily, I walked to the window to watch his receding form as he passed rapidly down the lawn through the gate-way and mounted his horse and quickly disappeared. I was conscious then of a deeper interest in Mrs. Smith's model preacher than I was willing to acknowledge even to myself.

Scarce two weeks had elapsed when I received a pastoral letter from him, post-marked Knoxville, Tennessee, requesting a reply at Shelbyville, Kentucky. Not a single expression in his letter evinced a deeper interest in me than he might have felt and expressed for others of his numerous charge. I readily accepted the opportunity of corresponding with one whose pious advice might aid me in my onward efforts through the new and almost untried path before me. A truly religious friendship, imbued with the spirit of the Gospel, is one of the greatest of earthly blessings. My reply found him at his father's home, near Shelbyville. Our correspondence was continued without the slightest allusion to the prospect of a more intimate relationship, though we both afterward acknowledged to an occasional glimpse, somewhat vague, it is true, of a more united interest thereafter for time and for eternity.

The usual Christmas quarterly-meeting brought him back to Abingdon, but he tarried in town with a brother Wills. On New Year's Eve a long letter, written closely and with great care, was handed me. This contained a plain, matter-of-fact proposal of marriage, but sufficiently tender for a dignified minister of the Gospel. He requested my earnest and prayerful consideration of the matter, previous to a personal interview, which he desired might take place on the morrow. Early on the first day of January we quietly talked the whole subject over, as we sat in Mrs. Smith's dining-room, one on each side of the fire-place. We were not young enough for romance, he being thirty-two years of age and I twenty-four; and we were both too serious for affectation or trifling. Thus, after settling some difficulties which appeared to me insuperable, relating to a continued provision for the comfort and support of my mother and family, all of which were obviated, as soon as presented, by this liberal-minded Christian, who cheerfully promised to aid me in all that I might be required to do for them, an engagement was agreed upon. We felt assured that the blessing of God would follow a union so entered into; and that, bound together by the most sacred of earthly ties, we might toil and weep and pray and rejoice together in this fallen world and meet as friends in the Celestial Paradise, where there are greetings such as only angelic hearts can know.

Captain Smith, though thoroughly vexed at the derangement of his own plans, entered heartily into ours. He could not forbear exclaiming, however, "Well, I'll never invite another Methodist preacher into my house unless he be ugly, old, and disagreeable." The day of our marriage was fixed for Tuesday, March 9, 1824, in honor of the birth-day of my future father-in-law. During the interim our regular duties were not interrupted. The presiding elder did not ride a mile less, nor did he omit the preaching of a single sermon. My books and pupils occupied my attention as completely as ever, though at intervals I plied diligently the swift, shining needle, for I was still my own mantua-maker.

For the benefit of my lady readers, and especially to satisfy the curiosity of my pupils, I will merely advert to my trousseau. My wedding-dress was an India muslin robe, made in the prevailing style, only three widths in the skirt, and severely plain in every respect; no chaplet of orange flowers gleaming with pearls; no rich laces, no ornaments of any kind, not even a bridal veil. I did expect to take a trip, but I should need neither a traveling dress nor a large trunk. A pair of common saddle-bags would carry all I wanted. The only expensive dress that I had was a black Canton crape robe, purchased at what I considered at the time to be an enormous price, twelve dollars.

The eventful day at last arrived. It was cloudy and drizzling, cold and cheerless, with only occasional glimpses of sunshine. Mr. Tevis spent the day in his own room, having donned his wedding-suit when he first arose, to the complete astonishment of those who met him at the breakfast-table. I have said that the day was unpleasant; leaden clouds hung low on the misty horizon; but no gloomy doubts pressed upon my mind. Late in the afternoon the clouds in the West broke away, and the sun, sinking into night, threw his parting beams upon the earth.

No cards of invitation had been issued, but some twenty or thirty of our mutual friends were made acquainted with the day and the hour. Thus, soon after early candle-light, the wedding-guests came dropping in until the parlor was comfortably filled. The ceremony, performed by the Rev. W. P. Kendrick, was long and impressive; and as we knelt down in solemn prayer, offered up at the close, the whole company knelt with us. Then came the usual congratulations, warm greetings, and the social interchange of sentiment and feeling. A sumptuous and costly banquet followed, where brilliant repartee and well-timed compliment lost nothing from the exhilarating influence of happy hearts. No pains had been spared to render the evening agreeable, and the effort was not only fully appreciated, but eminently successful. Even Mr. Tevis, always serious as eternity, and whom I had never known to laugh, was compelled to smile frequently at the sallies of our ever-mirthful friend,

Captain Smith, who was, on that memorable evening, as gleeful as a school-boy.

It was impossible to be untouched by the sympathetic kindness of the warm-hearted Virginians whom I had known but a few years; not a solitary relation among them, and yet there were friends that might be called mothers, sisters, and brothers.

O Virginia, name ever dear to my heart, there is music in the sound. Why are those events in my past history, connected with Virginia pictures, so freshly and beautifully before my eyes while others have been swept into oblivion? It was there beside the gushing mountain rill, in childhood's happy hours, I gathered sweet forget-me-nots and pressed them between the leaves of affection. There, in riper years I tasted the joys of pure Christian friendship, and was the recipient of that warm hospitality so peculiar to the "Old Dominion." It was there, too, that I fully adopted Joshua's resolution and registered my determination to "serve the Lord all the days of my life."

We spent one quiet day at "The Meadows," and started early the following morning upon our wedding-trip to Greenfield, expecting to receive the congratulations of a few pious friends, and to attend a quarterly-meeting then in progress. It was a delightful Spring morning, unusually mild for the season. The scenery was magnificent, touched by the light of two happy hearts. As we rode on, sometimes in silence, I felt an inexpressible peace in the comfortable assurance that we were directed by Providence in the step we had taken. Why was it that, when driven to the necessity of teaching for a support, I had found a home in the Western corner of Virginia instead of among my own people, who knew my qualifications and could have aided me in building up a reputation? Why was it that my husband, after having traveled several years in Ohio and Kentucky as an acceptable preacher, should have been transferred to the Western District without having asked or desired it, commencing his career as Presiding Elder of the Holston District the same year that I began my school at Wytheville? And why did we two, total strangers, meet in Abingdon under circumstances so favorable to the development of a personal interest in each other, which ended in an agreement to walk life's pilgrimage together? Surely Providence would smile upon a companionship of sympathetic souls actuated by the noblest motives and purest principles.

I have often wondered that people talk so much of wedding paraphernalia, magnificent establishments, and a grand position in the world, as the things most desirable in married lfe, as if the only object in view was to live at ease; and now I felt fully convinced of the folly of such anticipations and desires, and, from my inmost soul, indorsed what I had often said before, that I would rather be the wife of a faithful, devoted missionary of the cross, poor though he might be in this world's goods,—yea, the wife of even a Methodist itinerant, darn his stockings, patch his elbows, and brush his threadbare coat,—than be clothed in purple and fine linen, and fare sumptuously every day, if I might only be an humble instrument in aiding him to promote the highest interests of mankind. I was happier then, far happier, riding on my saddle-bags, than if I had been rolling in a coach with footmen and outriders. I neither wished nor expected a life of inglorious ease; on the contrary, I was charmed with the prospect of being a colaborer in Christ's vineyard with one who had adopted as his motto, "Earnestness is life."

Neither of us had any sympathy with that tranquillity never ruffled by a storm nor dimmed by a passing cloud. We both felt that life under such circumstances would become insipid, the spirit of action droop, and the slightest annoyances and molestations become real misfortunes. We must have something to do, as a means of stimulating the slumbering energies of human nature. How admirable is earnestness in the pursuit of noble objects, when guided by the wisdom that prompts the heart to fervent prayer and the hand to deeds of self-denying goodness! Firmness with intelligence, dignity in principle, sincerity in faith, and buoyancy in hope,—these are the true springs of action.

We talked of our future plans; I promising never to interrupt his itinerant course, while it was agreed that I should continue my vocation as a teacher, by locating in the beautiful village of Shelbyville, within two miles of the home of his aged parents. All these plans were carried out. I do not think he ever preached a sermon less, and, thank God! there was never any impediment in his having, as St. Paul would say, "a wife to lead about." We were happy then in arranging these plans; happier, under God's blessing, in being able to carry them out. How fully we realized the sweet promise, "Seek first the kingdom of God, and all these things shall be added unto you," will be seen in the course of my biography.

. On Monday we returned to our usual vocations—he to his district appointments, and I to my school-room. "The Meadows" was now, by cordial invitation, a home for both of us; yet Mr. Tevis could be there only at long intervals, as his district, comprising nine hundred square miles, required not only celerity of movement, but constant work. A presiding elder in those days preached usually one and sometimes two sermons every day, besides attending quarterly-meetings; whereas now the districts are so much smaller that the presiding elder is only required to attend his quarterly-meetings, and seldom has an appointment during the week, giving him an opportunity of resting ten or twelve days at a time.

Chapter XXI.

In May Mr. Tevis left for Baltimore, being a delegate to the General Conference which met there in 1824. This was very agreeable to him, as, in addition to the pleasure of meeting brethren from all parts of the United States and delegates from the British Wesleyan Methodists, it afforded him an opportunity of seeing two of his brothers, who resided there.

My school duties prevented my accompanying him; but we arranged to meet on his return at Wytheville, where he, as well as myself, had many warm friends. I was to go as far as Wythe with Mrs. Smith and family, who were to leave home about that time for their usual Summer trip.

The rapidly revolving weeks soon brought the wished-for period, and we started on our journey; but we met with a woful disappointment by a breakdown a few miles from home, making it necessary to return for a new conveyance, less elegant, but more substantial. This detained us two days. Meantime Mr. Tevis, who was punctuality itself, reached Wythe, and, not finding me there, was obliged, after waiting one day, to go back forty miles, to attend an appointment, without seeing me. When this was told to old Mother Russell, who, by the by, always insisted that he might have served God better in single blessedness, she clappped her hands and shouted aloud, exclaiming that she knew her elder loved the Church better than he did his wife.

Two days later I reached Wytheville, and had to wait patiently until my husband should be released from his Church duties. I knew he would be prompt in coming to me. Early Monday morning I was awakened by the sweet, musical voice of a dear little four-year-old girl of Captain Mathews, who came running into my room, clapping her hands and crying out, "Get up, lady, get up, quick; man down stairs want to see you." I hastened down, and, sure enough, found Mr. Tevis, who had driven nearly all night, after the meeting was concluded, that he might breakfast with me. Not then, nor ever, did he neglect the smallest duty for pleasure, and yet he was as fervent in affection as ardent in zeal.

After a few days spent in social intercourse, and in the enjoyment of that sanctified Christian friendship which will beam more brightly and glow more warmly in heaven, we returned to "The Meadows," where we had been so pressingly urged "to be at home" during the absence of the family. The good "lady of the manor" had not only said, "Occupy till I come," but had made ample arrangements for our comfort and convenience before she left, placing every thing at our disposal.

Our return was hailed by the servants with unmingled delight. Scarcely had the sound of the wheels that whirled us over the graveled walk reached their ears, when they came with their glowing welcomes, crowding the doorway and hovering around the carriage. Old Aggy, one of the privileged characters of the establishment, such as are frequently found in Southern families, noted for their devotion to "massa" and "missus," had every thing in perfect order for our reception. Aggy was reverenced and respected by the colored folks, and trusted by the white ones. Ever faithful and true to the family, more than usual honor had been heaped upon her. Filling the place of an under-housekeeper, she carried an enormous bunch of keys at her girdle, which usually announced her appearance by their jingling. Aggy was one of the persons who scorned the fashion of narrow skirts and sober colors. Her gay red calicoes were full and ample; and as a matter of curiosity, whenever the shuffling of her slippers was heard, every eye was turned towards her shining, good-humored, black face, surmounted by a red Madras handkerchief. Shoes she had renounced because of a severe fall "once upon a time," caused by the slipping of her high heels upon the waxed floor. Coming into the dining-room one day, she fell prostrate, to the infinite amusement of the company. "Save the wine!" exclaimed one of the guests; and she did save it, holding up the bottles to the extent of her two polished ebony arms. Arising, and retreating rapidly, she had another fall before she vanished.

Aggy's husband, familiarly termed "Old Billy," was a perfect specimen of conjugal devotion; but considered it a positive duty "to dress her," as he called it, occasionally, at the risk of being himself re-dressed. Billy, who was one of the ugliest and sternest and blackest of his race, being a sort of major-domo over the darkies in general, kept up a strict regimen in his own family. One morning, during the absence of Mr. and Mrs. Smith, the most awful screams were heard from Billy's cottage, mingled with the sound of the lash. Mrs. Smith's brother ran in haste to the scene of action, and found him whipping his wife severely. "Stop! stop, you barbarous old wretch, quit that instantly!" Aggy ceasing her cries and turned fiercely around, said, "Go 'long 'way from here, Massa Joe; Billy shall whip me whenever he pleas' to." "Be it so," said the young man, and left the affectionate couple to settle it themselves.

We had now a beautiful gig, light, but strong, and well fitted for journeying over rough roads, and a strong gentle horse, the gift of our excellent brother Benjamin Tevis, of Baltimore, who had long before acknowledged his brotherly affection for me by frequent letters, and in the more tangible form of beautiful and valuable presents, the exponents of his life-long kindness and generosity to us.

As Mr. Tevis was seldom at home, I should have felt lonely during the absence of the family, but for the kindness of my Abingdon friends, who kept up a cordial intercourse by frequent interchange of visits; besides, I was much occupied in striving to fit myself for a more extended sphere of usefulness as a teacher. Looking upon the bright side of every thing, the dew-drops of hope, reflecting the sunlight of happiness, formed a glit-. tering bow of promise that spanned the gulf between the present and the future. The discipline of my life had been salutary; the foundation had been laid deep and firm by the hand of necessity, not choice, and thus I was gradually prepared by Providence to perform a work that my heart, strong, proud, and self-commanding, would gladly have rejected. I had marked out a different course of action from that of the toilsome thorny path of a teacher, the anticipated confinement and drudgery of which was not at all to my taste. But misfortune and sorrow came to tear aside the thin delusions of my own conceit, and I have learned the glorious truth, that "labor is the grand pedestal of God's blessings upon earth." There are few blessings in life unalloyed, few trials unmixed. The good we sometimes ardently desire has an unseen evil which will rise to cloud it in the very moment of possession, and the evil we deprecate produces some happy effect which does not always cease when its immediate cause is withdrawn. If Ephraim-like we cling to our idols we perish with them; but if we cease to strive against the dealings of Providence, crooked paths will be made straight. God's time and will are beautiful, and through the darkest clouds of judgment gleams of mercy often come.

Early one Summer morning I was taking a drive with Mrs. Branch to the house of a friend, where we were to spend the day and night. We were wending our way slowly that we might enjoy the delightful scenery, and as I felt that this was probably the last time I should ever pass along this beautifully shaded road, I was silently enjoying the sights and sounds of nature. Suddenly the sound of wheels attracted our attention. In a few moments we met a stranger of gentlemanly appearance, driving a weary-looking horse as if he had traveled far. A genteel servant on horseback followed the master's gig. The gentleman passed slowly, acknowledging our appearance by a polite touch of his hat. We turned involuntarily to look after the passing stranger, and found him also looking back at us. Who could it be traveling this out-of-the-way road? "He resembles your husband," said Mrs. Branch; "I wonder if he can be a relation?" We discussed the matter no further, but on our return the next day we found the stranger to be my brother-in-law, Mr. Joshua Tevis, on his return to Baltimore, from Kentucky. He came through the wilderness road that he might make the acquaintance, as he afterwards told us, of his brother John's wife. He rendered himself very agreeable by a cordial recognition of our relationship.

18

My brother being anxious to see Mother Russell, of whose eccentricities he had heard so much, I readily consented to accompany him to her house. That we might have an hour to spend with this good old lady, and afterwards dine with a relative at the Sulphur Springs, we breakfasted at early dawn, and were on our way in time to greet the rising sun. We enjoyed greatly this *reveille* of nature, and pitied the indolent sleepers who lost the opportunity of drinking in these pure libations of the morning. A brisk drive of a few hours brought us to the humble dwelling of Mother Russell. Her door stood wide open; no liveried footman announced her visitors, though she belonged to one of the wealthiest families of the land. We were met upon the threshold by her cordial welcome, and, after the introduction of my brother-in-law, she exclaimed, "What! another brother Tevis? How kind to come eighteen miles just to see a plain old woman!" This was heartfelt, and blended with the most refined and polite cordiality. There was a dignity and gravity that would have graced any drawing-room—forbidding alike criticism and familiarity.

Brother Joshua was charmed, and the conversation flowed smoothly onward, touching upon various interesting topics. Patrick Henry was thoroughly discussed, and then she talked of Colonel Campbell, General Russell, and other distinguished revolutionists, of whom she gave many interesting anecdotes unknown to us before; thence, by an easy transition, she introduced the theme of religion, and from other denominations proceeded to speak of the Methodists. "They are a distinct people, brother; disrobing themselves of all worldly honors, they seek no popular favor, no splendid vestments of purple interwoven with gold, no distinction save that of being the true worshipers of God. How noble is simplicity, brother—simplicity of dress as well as manners." My brother tried to conceal his linen cambric ruffles, and quietly folded his vest over a diamond breast-pin which sparkled in the sunlight. "Formerly," she continued, "the Methodists were few and scattered, but now they have become a great people, and just as far as the human foot has trod the soil *there's* the Methodist."

An hour had passed; she arose from her seat, and, solemnly raising her hands, asked my terrified brother to lead in prayer. I declined for him, and the old lady prayed herself, mentioning his name first, praying that he might have more courage in the performance of his duty, and that his mouth might be filled with prayer and thanksgiving. Her voice was strong, her prayer solemn and impressive, notwithstanding her peculiar manner of mentioning, by name, each person for whom she prayed; and we arose from our knees full of reverence for this remarkable woman. I am sure Joshua never forgot that visit of an hour spent within the holy atmosphere of this aged Christian's home. After a few more days of pleasant intercourse he left us for his home in Baltimore.

Finally, came the last camp-meeting of the district, and, as we were to leave for Kentucky immediately after, it was a season of great interest to me. I did not remain on the camp-ground, but was hospitably entertained at the house of an old Baptist friend, Father Newland, a most remarkable man, who deserves more than a passing notice. He was upwards of ninety, but vigorous and active, enjoying a green old age. Both his wife and himself reminded me of the primitive Christians. Exhibiting the true spirit of the Gospel, they were not forgetful of entertaining strangers, and had a prophet's room ever ready for the itinerant messengers of grace, of whatever denomination.

At early dawn, after my first night's rest under his roof, I was awakened by the stentorian voice of the old patriarch, "O folks, come to prayers! You John, Dick, Harry, Lucy, Dinah—come, all come!" Hastily dressing and coming down into the family room, I found the assembled household, and among them many dusky figures, whose ebony faces evinced the deepest interest, as, with bowed heads, they listened to their master's instruction. With distended eyes and reverential wonder they heard his comments upon the lesson read from the Book of Life. What an example for those more elevated in the scale of intelligence.

The charity of this Christian master for his slaves resembled the sun bathing in floods of glory, not only the nearest worlds but irradiating light and heat to the remotest planet of its system. He read a portion of the twelfth chapter of St. Luke, and dwelt particularly upon the parable of the rich man, whose grounds brought forth plentifully. His occasional parenthetical comments ran thus: "Pull down his barns, indeed! Why didn't he feed God's poor with the surplus?—wrong, all wrong! bad man, didn't deserve to be rich! 'Soul, take thine ease.' Fool! talking to his soul like it was a dog or cat! Take thine ease! Yes, listen, folks: 'This night thy soul shall be required of thee,'—oh, terrible! and where did it take its ease? why, in hell-fire, to be sure." And then he exhorted all to be faithful servants of God's bounty, and closed the service by offering up a short, but fervent prayer, master and servant kneeling before heaven's eternal King. Then commenced the business of the day, everything moving on pleasantly. No jarring string interrupted the harmony of this good old patriarch's family. After these pious morning exercises every worldly duty seemed sanctified.

Camp-meeting was usually the time selected by all the mothers of the country around to have their children baptized, making the occasion as public as possible; and many thought they could give no greater evidence of devotion to the Church, nor evince greater respect and esteem for their presiding minister than to give their boys his name. I was told recently, by a friend, that my husband, while traveling the Holston District, baptized not less than twenty at one camp-meeting that were named for himself—a severe test, I am sure, of his modest humility, and no matter for boasting, for I never heard him speak of it.

The closing scenes of this meeting, the last we attended in Virginia, away off from the busy haunts of men, amid the wild and rugged scenery of Wythe County, can never be forgotten. Many of the old Christians seemed to tread upon the very threshold of heaven, their souls holding meet communion with God, while many hearts overflowed with rapture unexpressed, save in the thrilling hymn and the bursting eloquence of sobs and tears. The aged forest bowed its lofty head in reverence and waved its trembling arms on high as if to join in the general praise to the great Creator. How deep the well-spring of eternal love! Oh, that we might drink more of these pure waters while on earth! I had often heard of that sanctified love, which lifts the soul so far above this world as to give it a glimpse of the green vales and still waters of that celestial paradise promised to the children of God. I doubted it before, I believed it then.

Chapter XXII.

THE green glories of Summer were fast fading into the sober hues of Autumn when the absent family returned to "The Meadows," and the time of our departure drew near. I longed to go to my Kentucky home, but dreaded leaving my Virginia friends. I visited again and again each familiar nook and glen—hallowed spots where I had so often enjoyed a book or indulged in those pleasing dreams that creep imperceptibly into the heart and hold the imagination entranced in delightful, irresistible delusions, full of rapture, variety, and beauty. My footsteps lingered beside the spring-brook—the sweetest that "ever sang the sunny hours away;" I wandered through the quiet garden, among those brilliant Autumn flowers whose rich colors I had often admired on the very verge of Winter, and inhaled for the last time the aromatic breath of many fragrant herbs which I had found here and nowhere else. My eyes rested, for the last time, upon the misty ridge in the blue distance, up whose rugged sides I should never climb again to gather the blooming laurel and the wild honeysuckle that looked so lovely in the dancing sunbeams, and upon whose brow the daylight loved to linger.

I knew not, up to the hour of parting, how much it would cost me to sever the ties that bound me to my Abingdon friends. I particularly regretted that Mary's unfinished education must be completed by another, who,

I feared, would neither understand her capacity nor love her as I did. Young as she was, she was capable of the strongest attachments. I had been her almost constant companion for three years, and had never noticed more than a passing shadow cloud her brow; but now that she anticipated a separation for years, and perhaps for life, from one whom she had learned to love with a confiding affection, she was dissolved in tears and felt a sorrow hitherto unknown.

My mind frequently reverts to Mary and her little cousins, coming up to my idea of happy childhood. Their voices were the very echo of joyous thoughts. No darkness pervaded the household that was not dissipated by the sweet smiles and merry voices of these lovely children.

My heart was fully satisfied with the lot I had chosen, and perfectly stayed upon "that best earthly friend whom God had given me," but my cup of happiness was dashed with a taste of bitterness that belongs to this probationary state; and, so sorrowful was I at being separated from those whose kindness was now like a living picture before me, that for the time I could not rejoice in the brightness of my future prospects.

Days, months, and years have rolled on, new scenes and new situations have occupied my busy mind; but the associations, thoughts, and experiences, "linked by a hidden chain" to this period of my life, and "lulled in the countless chambers of the brain," can never be obliterated. "Awake but one, and, lo! what myriads arise!" A moving panorama of intense interest passes in review. Precious forms, that have long rested in the deep shadows of the grave, start into life before me pale, purified, passionless as the angels of heaven, faces beaming with love and eyes kindling with spiritual beauty, hallowed presences inciting me to holier thoughts and more fervent aspirations after heaven and immortality.

Some of my happiest school-vacations were spent among my friends and relatives in Eastern Virginia, and some of the most sorrowful as well as happiest hours of my life were spent in the south-western part of the State Thus the name to me, like that of the beloved and "beautiful City" to the Jews, is not a mere lifeless abstraction of the head, but a sacred and delightful image engraven on the heart. 'Tis the soul that gives tenacity to the memory as well as activity to the understanding; and hence it is that Virginia rises before me so distinctly the morning star of memory.

I spent no tiresome days packing and repacking. Our limited wardrobe, though sufficient for neatness and comfort, was easily stored away in a small trunk which just fitted behind the gig, while one still more tiny served me as a foot-stool. The gig-box comfortably accommodated our few books; thus we had quite enough baggage for our mountain journey.

A few friends accompanied us the first day's journey, tarrying all night at Mr. Campbell's, there to bid us a second farewell the next morning.

We looked forward to a journey of three hundred miles, but "we dreaded no lion in the way." The light of God's countenance was upon us. The first day, however, was passed in subdued sadness, mingled with the deepest gratitude, little interrupted by conversation. Memory reviewed the past, and hope was busy weaving golden threads into the web of our future lives. We were traveling onward amidst sublime scenery. Mountains clothed with trees whose gorgeous and many-tinted foliage rustled in the Autumn wind. Deep ravines, silvery streams, chestnut trees loaded with their rich fruit just ready for gathering, flinging their shadowy arms far out across our pathway, with occasional sprinklings of wild flowers by the road-side, the stimulating fragrance of pennyroyal and mountain-balm, all seemed combined to steep our senses in pleasant thoughtfulness. Occasionally we read while passing slowly over a rocky road, and as we traveled on an average only thirty miles a day, we had time to enjoy, to the fullest extent, the beauties and glories by which we were surrounded. Our brave horse bore himself admirably, not appearing wayworn, because he was well cared for by his master, who never sought his own rest until his horse was properly provided for.

The wilderness through which we passed was sparsely settled, yet Mr. Tevis had so often traveled through it that he had friends at every stopping-place, making it unnecessary for us to travel by night. One very sultry day we stopped for dinner at a little wayside tavern, apparently lost among the mountains, there being no neighbors within many miles. I passed immediately into an inner room for a nap and left Mr. Tevis reading in the vine-covered porch, at one end of which was the bar-room, the rendezvous of all straggling guests.

I was soon aroused from my light slumbers by a rough voice uttering the most blasphemous oaths in conversation with his fellows; and then I heard my husband speak. Listening in breathless silence to his pointed reproof and solemn admonitions to this profane swearer, my heart sank within me for fear of a difficulty in this lonely place. The ruffian, however, made no reply; he seemed dumb with astonishment. My terror may well be imagined, when, called to dinner, I saw a great, rough-looking man, a perfect Anak, with a shock of fiery red hair, and eyes as fierce as burning volcanoes, come in and seat himself just opposite me. He ate but little; and, though with trembling anxiety, I showed him more than ordinary politeness. He answered in monosyllables, and was continually glancing from under his shaggy brows at Mr. Tevis, who maintained the greatest composure without bestowing on him a word or a look. As we arose from the table I could have screamed in an agony of fear, had I dared, as I saw him take hold of my husband's arm, saying, "Will you walk a piece with me, stranger?" "Certainly, sir," was the reply. They were gone more than twenty minutes—it seemed an hour to me—when I saw them returning, apparently in friendly conversation.

Our carriage was at the door, and, as we stepped into it, the man, standing at our horse's head, said, as he gave us a parting wave of his hand, "God bless you, sir, and madam; I wish you a safe journey; I shall never forget."

I learned, to my astonishment, that he not only felt the admonition so solemnly given, but took occasion to satisfy his conscience by telling Mr. Tevis that he had a pious, widowed mother, from whom he had been separated many years, who had taught him in early life to read the Bible and reverence his Creator. These instructions had long slumbered in waveless silence, but the words, that day "spoken in season," had stirred the very depths. of his soul and brought back the sweet memories of his early childhood, and he said, "God being his helper, he would not only strive to profit by the advice given, but become a praying man and a Bible-reader."

That same day, winding up the mountain road, we met, at a most inconvenient place for passing, a wagon and team driven by as surly-looking a fellow as ever cracked a whip. He bawled out, prefacing what he had to say with a vulgar oath, "Get out of the way with that 'ar consarn of your'n; my leader's not goin' to pass it! Get out of the way or I'll pitch you to the bottom of never," casting his eyes, as he spoke, down a precipice which seemed almost fathomless. My heart beat audibly as I seized Mr. Tevis's arm and earnestly begged him not to reply. The ruffian evidently expected a difficulty, for he stopped and rolled up his sleeves; but we both bowed politely as our vehicle was turned aside. The man was astonished, evidently touched, for he muttered, as he returned our salutation, "Well, now, you see, I didn't mean to be cross, but hang me if my horses ain't scared now at that queer thing you're ridin' in; see how my leader throws back his ears!" His wolfishness was literally broken down, showing that silence as well as a soft answer turneth away wrath. He actually turned his head to look after and warn us of a bad place in the road, wishing us a pleasant journey. I doubted not some good seed was sown in his heart; thus the golden opportunity was not lost.

We traveled several days through some of the wildest scenery, and some of the most unfrequented portions of our whole country, rarely seeing a plowed field or a cultivated spot; but hill and dale, mountain and valley, with an occasional dwelling surrounded by trees dressed in the gay and bright livery of Autumn. Our hearts, swelling with admiration, acknowledged the beneficence of the Creator of this world, so full of grace, elegance, and sublimity.

That same night darkness curtained the hills before we reached the place where we expected to tarry, and we were fain to check up our weary horse before a very uncomfortable looking dwelling. Numerous white-headed urchins met us at the threshold looking as wild as little Arabs. One girl about ten years old was lugging a great baby on her hip, as she hopped along after me with wondering eyes, trying to carry some of my luggage into the only room below, where we found a good looking old man sitting by a bright fire, the most cheerful thing to be seen. He called out to the girl "to take that 'ar baby," which was fretting and screaming at a tremendous rate, "to its mammy." "She won't take it, she's got to git something for the strangers to eat, and she'll whip me if I go back." A few broken chairs, a family bed, and a deal table constituted the furniture of this parlor, dining-room, chamber and hall; not even a Yankee clock ticked behind the door.

Supper was soon announced, and I sat down with a good appetite to rye coffee, stewed rabbit and biscuit, but alas! it was soon cut short by finding a dirty yarn string in the first biscuit I opened. Not wishing to interrupt Mr. Tevis' supper, I turned silently away from the table, only to find the mischievous little imps in my work basket. Spools, silk, tape, etc., were tumbled out pell-mell on the floor, one spool being entirely denuded of its thread. "Look 'ere, 'oman," cried a little five-year-old, "what a nice whirl-i-gig this yere is!" The mother soon flew to my assistance, shook and boxed them all around, flinging one into a corner and another on the bed, leaving me to gather up as best I could my goods and chattels.

At my request she took a candle and showed me up a rickety stairway into our sleeping apartments, so near the broken roof that the stars peeped through without let or hinderance. A dirty patch-work quilt covered the bed, under which were two *blue yarn sheets.* What was to be done? I could not even touch the bed until I had spread a clean pocket handkerchief for my face, and improvised a pair of sheets from some clean clothes in my trunk. And this was a regular stopping place for travelers! "Entertainment for man and beast!" The morning sun found the wayworn travelers on their way to seek a breakfast ten miles ahead, with some Methodist friends well known for their hospitality and excellent fare.

The day that closed our journey through the wilderness and marked our entrance into the settlements of Kentucky is memorable. Late in the afternoon we reached a solitary mansion standing in the midst of green fields, and in the center of a large yard filled with forest trees. The soft shadows of approaching night were investing everything with a mysterious thoughtfulness. The house stood about half a mile from a deep mountain gorge, through which we did not like to pass after nightfall, and as there was no other house within ten miles, we proposed to spend the night here. Our request was refused upon the plea that there was no room for us. The yard was full of people as a wedding was to take place that evening, and we two poor solitary wayfarers with our little gig and horse could not stay; "it was moonlight, we need not fear," they said, "and we could be better accommodated at the next stopping place." In vain we entreated, urging the weariness of our horse and his unfitness to tread the rocky road before him. One of the bystanders whispered, with a knowing wink at Mr. Tevis, that there was to be a dance; the broad brim and straight coat would be in the way. The rights of hospitality to strangers could not be exercised at this place at the expense of pleasure. My heart sank within me at

the prospect of passing several hours *en route* through
that lonely ravine; but my husband, in whose piety and
prayers I firmly believed, and my never failing faith in
God's protecting providence, quieted my fears as onward
we went.

Already the drowsy tinkling bell was heard, as the
sheep-boy whistling leisurely followed his flock to the
fold, admonishing us to hasten. The last rays of the
setting sun had vanished, the rocks, and dells, and secluded places began to darken in the glow of twilight;
but in a short time the beams of a full moon, reflected
from the gigantic cliffs and distant tree tops, silvered
every object they touched, mellowing, softening, spiritu-
alizing the realities around us into airy creations. The
winds were asleep and the moonlight glanced and shimmered through the trees that clothed the steep sides of
the mountain up to the topmost battlements.

The road was over the bed of a shallow stream which
passed all the way through the gorge, seeming to issue
from some exhaustless source, the ripple growing louder
as the stillness of the night increased. The horse's hoofs
struck against the pebbly bottom of the mountain stream,
the valley rang with the echo, and we caught the faint
return made by the more distant hills. The softness and
beauty of this moonlight night, combined with the mysterious wildness of the scenery, made glorious revelations to
our devotional hearts; yes, sweet and solemn revelations
through light and shade, with prophetic intimations of
the still brighter glories that lie beyond, reminding me
now of those beautiful lines:

> "Man is a pilgrim, spirit clothed in flesh,
>   And tented in the wilderness of time;
> His native place is near the eternal throne,
>   And his Creator, God."

The works of God never appear so exquisitely beautiful as amidst silence and solitude.

About the hour of ten, as we slowly issued from the deep valley, a light greeted our eyes from the window of a modest dwelling, which we afterward learned was kept burning there all night for the benefit of travelers emerging from this dark gorge. The noise of our carriage-wheels wakened the kind host even before we knocked. A good supper, a comfortable bed, and then a dreamless sleep until awakened in the morning by the industrious family, rendered us oblivious of yesterday's troubles. We were called to breakfast soon after daylight, and before sunrise were again on our way.

Mr. Tevis prayed with our hospitable entertainers before leaving. This he never failed to do night and morning wherever we stayed, among friends or strangers. It was, indeed, the general custom of the early Methodist preachers to ask this privilege if not invited. Mr. Tevis never spent an hour on a visit without praying with the family if circumstances permitted; and yet he was neither officious nor presumptuous. Noted for that true politeness that springs from the heart, he never deviated from the strictest sense of propriety with regard to others; hence his reproofs, in or out of season, did not give offense.

Neither the pen of a ready writer nor the brush of an Italian painter could give even a faint idea of that September morning. The glorious orb of day announced his coming by gradually gilding the Eastern sky and touching the dark green foliage of the wilderness with his rays of light, gently drawing aside the curtain of the night, that his beams might fall slowly and softly upon the face of the sleeping earth, till her eyelids opened and she went forth again to her labor until the evening. We seemed on the verge of a new world—a world of light and glory. We inhaled new life from the dewy freshness of the balmy atmosphere as we sped rapidly along into the thickly-settled portions of the State. White clouds and great woodlands and purple crests of far-off hills floated into the golden atmosphere of the enchanting scene. The voluptuous earth, brimming with ecstasy, poured out songs and odors, leaves like fluttering wings flashed light, and blades of grass grew tremulous with joy. Tranquilizing and gentle emotions, stealing on us unawares, filled our souls with peace, pleasant harbingers of days to come.

Chapter XXIII.

OUR first night, spent among Kentucky relatives, was in the large old family mansion of Mrs. Robert Tevis, near Richmond, Madison County. I was struck with the beauty of the widely-extended lawn in front of the house, shaded with splendid old forest trees flinging their shadows far out upon the soft sward; the branches lifted and fell with a fanning motion to the evening breeze; and, here and there, a bird was singing her farewell to the sun as we passed over the stile.

I have often wondered why people in the West either select a building spot where there are no trees, or else cut down the natural growth and plant stunted evergreens all about their dwellings. The grounds around this place presented a beautiful contrast, reminding one of some old baronial residence, so frequently described in English books. The beauty of departed Summer still shone on garden and meadow, draping in gorgeous splendor the whole landscape. The woodland pastures of blue grass were green enough to be refreshing to the eye, while the adjacent forest was one mingled mass of orange, brown, and crimson; and the coral berry of the mountain ash gleamed brightly among the fading leaves.

Mrs. Tevis was a true type of widowhood. Her soft brown eyes were filled with tears as she embraced me; and her sweet, quiet face, seen beneath her modest cap, I often call to remembrance. From all that I saw and afterwards heard, she possessed an angelic spirit. The

19

light of a heavenly hope beamed in her eye—a hope brought from her closet. She made God her salvation, and to her was the promise, "With joy shalt thou draw water out of the wells of salvation." She had suffered much from bereavements, and her soul was doubtless purified "as by fire." And of what avail is affliction if it does not soften and purify the heart? Why are those called blessed that mourn, if it is not that they learn the bitter lesson that grief alone can teach?

Our friends would gladly have detained us several days. Finding we could not tarry now, they urged us to return at some convenient season. Our hearts said, Yes, but circumstances never rendered it practicable. In after years, however, the bond of friendly relationship was renewed and strengthened by my having many of her grandchildren in my school.

With a bounding heart and excited imagination, I continued my journey the next day. Before another sunset I should see all I held most dear on earth, together. We did not stop to dine. Thus, early in the afternoon, we entered the woodlands of my uncle's farm. My eyes wandered continually in search of some familiar spot of my child-life. A sudden turn in the road brought into view the round-topped sugar-tree, "whose brow in lofty grandeur rose," crowned with a magnificent dome of emerald leaves, tinged with the rich hues of Autumn; here and there a ray of sunshine strayed through some crevice in the thick foliage, casting a golden light upon the dark green moss beneath.

I hailed the old patriarch with delight, sacredly associated in memory with my childhood's home, a guiding star in former days to the wandering hunter. It rose far above the heads of its forest brethren, and was the compass by which land navigators steered their course through the tangled cane-brake and the dreary wilderness, and it still stands—1864—the cynosure of all the surrounding settlement. I gazed on it with tearful eyes, and thought how, as a merry-hearted child, I had played around its base; and an involuntary pang darted through my heart as I remembered the many loving faces I should now miss from my father-land.

Most of the old landmarks had been swept away; the pawpaw bushes were gone; the double line of cherry-trees that formed an avenue from grandfather's to my Uncle Gholson's white cottage on the hill, under which I had so often stood holding up my little check apron to receive the clustering cherries thrown down by brothers and cousins, were no longer there. A slight shower in the forenoon had filled the woods with fragrance, and the pattering raindrops, occasionally falling from the over-hanging branches, sparkled like diamonds on the tufted grass by the wayside. Chirping birds hopped blithely among the trees, as if loath to leave their Summer home, while they could enjoy the sweet breeze that wooed them with kisses as it slightly ruffled their glossy feathers.

A wizard spell is thrown around the spot where child-hood played. Olden visions, "faintly sweet," passed before me, and dreamy reveries invested my soul with a mysterious joy. There was the same old stile to be crossed before we could enter the yard, even then covered with a living green as soft and rich as in midsummer. There was the quaint old brick house, the first of the kind ever built in Kentucky, with its projecting gables, and its ample door standing wide open to welcome the coming guest; and soon there came a rush of children across the yard, and I was almost smothered with kisses by the dear little ones that looked shyly at the tall stranger standing beside me. I reached the doorstep, and was encircled in my mother's arms, her tears falling like raindrops as she folded me again and again to her heart. In the old family room many were waiting, who greeted us with the greatest cordiality, making our advent joyous indeed.

The next day, the news being spread throughout the neighborhood, a numerous delegation of uncles, aunts, and cousins came to welcome and invite us to partake of their hospitality. The family tree, transplanted from Virginia to Kentucky soil, had lost neither beauty nor glory. Its branches were widespread and flourishing, and from its roots had sprung a thousand ramifications, whence arose many a "roof-tree," affording shelter and protection to wayworn travelers and homeless wanderers.

Kentucky, garden - spot of the earth, where blooming beauty scatters flowers through the valley and clothes the hills with verdure,—how I loved thee then, dear native soil! how I rejoiced in thy smiles after an absence of twenty years! And how deeply, fervently, I love thee now, after a residence of fifty years among thy people, and in one of thy most favored spots! I have looked with heartfelt gratitude upon thy broad fields of golden maize, traversed with pride and pleasure thy far-famed blue - grass regions, gazed upon thy stupendous river cliffs, and wandered through the mysterious soundings of thy Mammoth Cave, with one whose affectionate heart ever vibrated in unison with my own.

My eyes wandered around the best room in search of some familiar objects. The same old clock stood in the corner, ticking its "ever, forever," as regularly as of old; and, near by, the little square table, with its deep drawer, in which my grandmother kept the cakes, baked every Saturday afternoon for the children that generally came with their parents to dine on Sunday. The wide-open fireplace brought to mind the "yule log," Christmas fires, and Winter cotton picking. I could almost see the little woolly-headed cotton-gins of olden times, each with a fleecy heap of cotton before him from which to separate the seed, and sundry little grandchildren plying their nimble fingers in the same manner, grandmother superintending the whole,—the click of her knitting-needles, meantime, as uninterrupted as the ticking of the clock. Our tasks done, cakes, nuts, etc., were distributed, and then followed a game of romps, which my grandfather enjoyed as much as the children! and he could laugh as loud and long as any of us.

I recalled old Uncle Billy Bush, of Indian memory, who lived near by and frequently formed one of the merry group, chasing us about the room with his cane. How we all loved to see his ruddy face, so full of intelligence and good humor, a lurking jest ever in his eye, and and a smile about the corner of his mouth, with a voice loud enough to hail a ship at sea without the aid of a speaking-trumpet! It was wonderfully rich, too, harmonizing admirably with his blunt, jovial face; and this warm, rosy scene generally closed with an exciting Indian story, in which Daniel Boone figured as well as himself.

During our stay here we spent one charming day with "Aunt Franky Billy," the widow of this old uncle, so called to distinguish her from another Aunt Franky, and noted for her good housewifery, as well as her boundless hospitality. Simple-hearted, right-minded, and pious, she was loved by all who knew her. So free from selfishness, so liberal, so every thing a nice old lady ought to be,—what a pleasure it was to see her still presiding at her own table, abundantly spread with all that could minister to the most delicate taste, or satisfy the most craving hunger. Indeed, her children sometimes expressed a fear that she would cram some poor wayfaring traveler to death with her good things.

Upon this occasion she received me with a heart full of love, and testified her honest affection for "Cousin July Ann's" husband by proffering, with modest politeness, the various dishes and savory viands of her bountiful table—all the time apologizing for the meager fare, and thinking nothing good enough for us. We would gladly have remained for weeks with our kind relations, but could only spend a few days; and of the thirteen widow Bushes in the immediate neighborhood we visited only two.

Before leaving, it was definitely arranged that my mother should come to Shelbyville in the Spring, purchase a comfortable house, and make it her permanent residence. Here, too, we expected to locate our school. We left early Monday morning, and were now to travel through the celebrated "blue-grass region," represented as ever "bathed in golden dawns or purple sunsets dying on the horizon—the great blue canopy of heaven drooping over all like a dream." This, too, was the land illustrated by a thousand scenes as picturesque as they were significant; where, in solitary and rudely constructed forts, that strange, old, rude, poetical, colonial life had gone on. Brave men had struggled, breast to breast, and contended fearfully with the wild beasts that roamed in multiplied thousands over the land. Through a lovely grove we entered the main road leading to Lexington. The air was soft, balmy, genial, the sky of that delicate azure which gives relief to the rich beauty of the earth, glowing all around with the ripe, mellow tints of September—the finest combination of trees and shrubs, the rarest effects of form and foliage, bewildering the eye with recesses apparently interminable. A subtle fragrance, developed by the night dews, floated in the air; the lulling music of the branches, swayed by the gentle breath of morning with all these hallowed influences, reminded us, by association, of life's perpetual changes—types of our restless world; while the heavens above, so holy and tranquil, spoke to the heart of that rest prepared for the faithful, where no changes like those of earth ever come.

Our horse, too, appeared to feel the beauty of the scenery, for he walked slowly along the highway, snuffing the fragrance of the sweet-scented meadow land, over which roamed flocks and herds—an Arcadian scene of great beauty. Every step of the road I was contrasting the past with the present. Instead of the bounding deer, the dark forest and the rudely-built log house, white dwellings gleamed through clustering shade trees. The approach to Lexington was through a leafy labyrinth leading imperceptibly to a slight elevation, from whence we had the first view of the town, with its mass of roofs and chimneys peeping through the trees. There were no magnificent dwellings, and there was no architectural display in churches; but brick houses, low-roofed cottages, with here and there a mansion of more hospitable dimensions. The town was surrounded by woodlands, interspersed with bright green meadows, edging off on every side into fields, orchards, and farms; and in the distance were shadowy hills, indicating the vicinity of the Kentucky River.

And this was Lexington, the aristocratic town of the

West, of which I had heard so much! The early chroni-
clers state that it stands on the site of an ancient city of
great extent and magnificence. Tradition says there
once existed a catacomb, formed in the limestone rock,
fifteen feet below the surface of the earth, discovered by
the early settlers, whose curiosity was excited by the
appearance of the stones which covered the entrance to a
cavern. Removing these stones they entered the mouth
of a cave, apparently deep, gloomy, and terrific. They
were deterred by their apprehensions from attempting a
full exploration, but found, at no great distance from the
entrance, niches occupied by mummies preserved by the
art of embalming, in as perfect a state as any found in
Egypt. The descent to this cave was gradual; and, by
calculation, after proceeding as far into it as they dared,
it was supposed to be large enough to contain three
thousand bodies; and who knows, says the historian, but
they were embalmed by the same race of men that built
the pyramids? If not, how shall the mystery be solved?
The North American Indians were never known to
construct catacombs for their dead, or to be acquainted
with the art of embalming. The custom is purely
Egyptian, and was practiced in the earliest ages of their
national existence. The whites who discovered these
mummies, indignant at the outrages committed by the
Indians, and supposing this cave to be a burial place for
their dead, dragged out the bodies, tore off the bandages,
and made a general bonfire of these antiquities—perhaps
the oldest in the world.

Progress in refinement is necessarily connected with
the prosperity of a civilized country, and we might naturally have expected to find some specimens of the arts
and sciences, exhibited in splendidly decorated edifices,

borrowed from the classic taste of Greece, in this town of
Lexington, which was certainly not built yesterday, in
keeping with Dickens's view of every town he saw in the
United States. The first inhabitants had the good sense
to see that nothing artificial could improve in form or
beauty the sublime works of the Creator, which in de-
sign, color, light, and shade, form perfect pictures in the
human eye. They erected plain, comfortable dwellings,
in the vicinity of which were profusely scattered the
beech, the spotted sycamore, the stately poplar, and the
graceful elm, whose outer branches drooped with garland-
like richness; and the locust was so abundant as to form,
at intervals, a mimic forest.

The Lexington of 1824, with its enchanting scenes
of pastoral beauty left a picture on my memory that
remains fresh after the lapse of fifty years. I have visited it at different seasons since, and, though divested of
its wild luxuriance of natural scenery, it was still, with
its surroundings, the Eden of Kentucky. In the Spring,
a paradise of loveliness; in the Summer, rich in its abundance and glorious in its regal robes; in the Autumn,
when the dim haze of the departing year hung like a
pall over its magnificent woodlands; and, in the Winter,
when the Summer birds had left their withered homes
and gone to seek a sunnier clime, when the rich flowers
had perished, and the blossoms of the valley had found a
grave upon the scentless soil that gave them birth,
sublimity still clung to it like a garment.

The principal street, teeming with foot passengers and
carriages, showed that the life-blood of a busy population
throbbed healthily and steadily. Kind looks met us in
every direction, and the music of cheerful voices fell
pleasantly upon the ear. As we did not intend to tarry

in town, we drove on till we reached a modest looking
house of entertainment in the suburbs, where we stopped
for refreshment and to rest our horse for an hour or two.
In the vine-covered porch sat the landlord, almost as
large as a prize ox, and as jovial looking as Falstaff himself. We were ushered into a pleasant sitting-room,
whence I soon retreated into an adjoining apartment in
search of my usual nap before dinner. As the door
opened into the room occupied by Mr. Tevis and the
landlord, I was kept awake by the following dialogue.
Mine host began,—

"Been traveling long, sir?"

"Several days," was the reply.

"Got far to go yet?"

"Not very"—a long silence.

"Stranger in these parts, sir?"

"Not altogether."

"The lady with you a relation?"

"Yes, sir;" another silence, my husband meanwhile
reading diligently.

"Ahem! that lady's your cousin, I suppose?"

No reply.

"Well, sir, won't you take a drink of prime old
Cognac?" and suiting the action to the invitation he rose
and took a bottle from the closet. "I allers takes a
drink afore dinner, and I never charges travelers for a
drink or so, specially as I drinks with them," then he
laughed loudly.

"Thank you," said Mr. Tevis, "I never drink spirits
of any kind."

"What! not before dinner? Well, I does." He
turned up the bottle and drank from it long and largely.
"Well, sir, as I was a-sayin', that lady's your cousin, I

'spose; but she favors you mightily, and may be she's your sister."

No answer.

(Desperately). "I say, mister, is she your sister, or your cousin, or your aunt?"

"Neither, sir."

"Well, if I may be so bold, what is your name, and who is she?"

"My name is Tevis, and the lady is my wife," which laconic reply stopped further questioning.

Dinner was announced; and as I met the old brandy-bottle with his red-hot nose face to face, I could scarcely refrain from laughing outright. We were introduced to a tidy little body sitting at the head of the table—the ewe-lamb of this great, good-humored, talkative giant—his wife! She was as refined and gentle in her manners as he was coarse and ignorant. How astonishingly ill-assorted!

After dinner we traveled several miles under the shade of overarching trees. It was a calm, pleasant evening, and night brought us to the house of a kind Methodist friend, where my husband had often found a resting-place while traveling the Lexington Circuit, ten years before. We were received with great kindness, and I was an object of special attention, the good lady almost smothering me with kisses. She was the sister of brother Cooper, of Lexington. Sleep was a stranger to my eyelids during that night,—I was thinking of the next day, which would terminate our journey, when my weary feet, no longer drifting about in search of solid footing, would find a permanent, life-long resting-place. Our ten days' lonely journey had made us both feel that each would strengthen the other in the performance of life's serious duties, and that our pleasures would be doubled by like sentiments and unity of purpose; yet our natural dispositions were dissimilar in many respects. I was laughter-loving, and at times cheerful, almost to levity; he always grave,—yet there was no gloom in that gravity. Inherently of a lofty and generous nature, his face haunted with earnest thought, he seemed eminently fitted to check the too great exuberance of my own spirits.

Chapter XXIV.

THE morning star was shining in a cloudless sky of deepest azure when, after partaking of a hastily prepared breakfast, we bade adieu to our hospitable entertainers and were on our way to Shelbyville, expecting to arrive there late in the afternoon, as the weather was fine and the roads in an excellent condition. A heavy dew, touched by the frost, stood glistening on every blade of grass, and the mist, gradually vanishing as the sun rose higher, presented, as we moved onwards, a shifting scenery of beautiful landscapes, that would have enraptured the eye of a Claude Lorraine.

The wild grape, winding its pliant vine among, and clinging tenaciously to, the branches, flung leafy garlands from stem to stem, while the grapes hung in large purple clusters, tempting the hand of the traveler.

Towards noon we ascended a gentle acclivity, from whence, at the distance of a mile, we saw Shelbyville, situated on a broken ridge, embowered in foliage, washed on every side except the west by a creek, which at that time was a deep stream appropriately called "Clear Creek." Just as we emerged from the covered bridge we met my husband's youngest brother on horseback, who had come out to escort us to the house of a married brother, where many friends awaited us.

The Annual Conference, with its mighty mustering of the tribe of Levi, was in session. My husband, now a member of this body, was cordially greeted by the preachers, many of whom were old friends. It was a time of unmingled pleasure and happiness.

In the afternoon, a drive of two miles brought us to our father's farm, our home, until we could prepare for house-keeping in the Spring. Quite a bevy of relatives and friends were gathered there also. We were met at the gate by "father," a venerable-looking man, his head white with the snows of seventy Winters, but with a complexion as hale, a step as firm and elastic, as if in the meridian of life. He wore the costume of '76. Bright shoe-buckles, highly-polished shoes, long stockings, knee breeches with silver buckles, a long buff waistcoat, round coat and straight collar, brought up the memory of olden times. His benevolent countenance, smiling all over, and a cordial kiss, won my heart immediately. Then came "mother," whose equally affectionate reception made me love her at once, and that love never grew cold by a more intimate acquaintance. The simplicity of her dress was in perfect keeping with her husband's costume, attractive, yet without any attempt to imitate modern style. A plain gown of dark "stuff," a neat linen inside handkerchief, whose square collar of snowy whiteness relieved the dark dress, a handsome black shawl, pinned over so as to meet in front, and a bobinet cap, the plaited border trimmed with narrow thread-lace edging. A little in the background, and modestly awaiting our approach, was Aunt Nancy, my husband's maiden and maternal aunt, of whose exalted piety I had heard so much. She was tall and dignified, with a thin, pale face, and evidently past the age of sixty. A singular adherence to the Methodist costume of forty years before rendered her appearance attractive, a style which must have had the effect to conceal much of her beauty in youth, but suited exactly her present age; and, as it never could have been at any time fashionable, had the advantage of never looking old-fashioned. I had often heard Mr. Tevis speak of her fervent but unostentatious zeal in serving God, and how, at the early age of seventeen, when it was no small sacrifice in a worldly point of view to become a Methodist, she and one of her sisters, divesting themselves of every weight that might impede their progress in a religious life, setting their slaves free, as required, had resolutely attached themselves to the then despised people called Methodists. The sister married a local preacher, but Aunt Nancy, declining many eligible offers, remained single. She did not think it wrong to marry, but felt that she could serve God better as she was. Like Anna, the prophetess, she did serve him from her youth upwards, and worshiped in the temple with fasting and prayer. Open in word and deed, with an uncompromising directness and singleness of purpose, it would have been as easy to turn the sun from off its course as this noble Christian woman from the path of duty. These three, with Cousin Ruth, formed the household. The last mentioned, though forty years old, was an unsophisticated child in character, thought, and feeling. She, too, was ready with her welcome for "John's wife." Being deaf and partially dumb, she seemed surprised to see so many tears shed upon the occasion that she had anticipated joyously.

Aunt and Uncle Sherman were there; also two other cousins, Matilda and Harriet Crow, both of whom became so dear to me by a more intimate acquaintance that I can not forbear introducing them to my reader. They were among the sweetest personifications of that pure and

undefiled religion which our Savior "went about to teach."
Both were attired quaintly in garments of the same color,
and with that Quaker simplicity remarkable for closeness
and quietness, with an entire absence of pretension which
veils, but does not conceal, the most refined elegance,
setting off, with exquisite taste, the finest forms. Both
wore simple caps of snowy whiteness, but too transparent
to hide the silver threads which time was busily weaving
among the glossy brown hair of their youthful days.
Cousin Matilda, upon whose quiet brow the passing waves
of fifty years had scarce left a wrinkle, had an air of dignity mingled with peculiar sweetness. Her face, uncom-
monly fair, was lighted up by a pair of sparkling gray
eyes, yet corresponding with the gentle manner which
often awakened an enthusiasm, rendered more charming
by the impulse of her quick, ardent spirit. Her countenance, when in repose, reminded one of an alabaster vase,
not displaying the graceful designs on its surface until
lighted from within; so, when excited by feeling, and
during the flood-tide of emotion, aspects unseen and unknown before were revealed in great beauty. Cousin
Harriet's passionless face, across which no worldly shadow
ever flitted, was rendered inexpressibly touching by the
holy light which ever dwelt in her deep, thoughtful eyes.
She looked and acted as one who felt the "littleness" of
time and the vastness of eternity. The sweet tones of
her voice vibrate even now through the chambers of
memory as I dwell upon her excellences. I have watched
her in the performance of her missions of love and mercy
as, with a nursing tenderness, she soothed the sick and
suffering, settled the snowy pillow for the aching head,
handed the cup of cool water and whispered words of
comfort, and, when in the stillness of the solem midnight

hour, with noiseless step she flitted by me, clothed in pure white, I have thought "of such is the kingdom of heaven." The allurements of the world had been counted and resigned by this angelic woman, and a dove-like peace had settled on her soul. A pleading eloquence in her very looks fondly urged those whose hearts were full of sublunary bliss to seek a better portion.

The two sisters were seldom separated, and spent much of their time at father's during the five months of my stay there. Frequently, when listening to their soft voices singing in low, pleasant tones the touching hymns of Charles Wesley, I was transported for the moment to the very verge of heaven. More than thirty years have elapsed. I have passed through many vicissitudes, but neither life's storms nor its calms have banished from my heart those pleasant memories. These two well-beloved cousins, whose mutual lives were so closely bound together, stand out in full relief among others of that family-group in the beautiful picture—

> "It is in the twilight hour,
> The time when memory lingers
>   Across life's dreary track,
> When the past floats up before us,
>   And the lost comes stealing back,"

that I sit in the family room, father on the right, his white hair gleaming like a crown of glory; mother sitting at her work-table, her genial face gladdening all within the sphere of its influence; the sisters, with their needle-work; Aunt Nancy knitting, and Cousin Ruth, with her solemn eyes, showing that though the ear offered to her no medium of communication, the soul, in some mysterious way, held intercourse with the outer world.

Cousin Ruth was one of those remarkable illustrations of the benevolence of our Heavenly Father in compen-

sating for the loss of one sense by the increased suscep-
tibility of cultivation in others. To our eyes she seemed
but a drop falling away from the ocean of existence,
unperceived and disregarded by the great mass. "Little
and unknown" as she was, however, the great God loved,
and, in his rich provision, had not forgotten her. She
had learned to talk when a child, before she lost her
hearing, which occurred, suddenly, when about five or
six years of age, and without any known cause except
standing under the dripping eaves of a house whence the
cold rain fell, drop by drop, upon her head. She heard
well and talked sweetly in the early morning on one well
remembered April day; at night she was entirely deaf;
and as she never recovered her hearing, soon lost the
power of communicating by words. Her enunciation
became less and less distinct, until finally she ceased
trying to express herself except in monosyllables; but
her voiceless language, so mysterious to strangers, was
perfectly understood by the family. She acquired by
practice a variety of intelligible gestures, and it was
interesting to watch her in her long conversations with
mother who understood her best of all. She possessed
the power of hearing sound through a good conducting
medium, and delighted to put a wooden pencil between
her teeth, one end resting upon the sound-board of a
piano. In this way she heard the harmonious sounds
distinctly. There were no institutions for the deaf and
dumb in our country when she was a child; but so carefully had she been trained by her excellent aunt, that she
possessed not only ordinary intelligence, but quick perceptions and the greatest sense of propriety. The simple
loveliness of temper and disposition in this child of
nature made her a general favorite. I doubt if any one

ever looked into her wide open, serious eyes without feeling that they were the windows of a thinking soul. I have seen her sit for hours quietly knitting, without appearing to notice any thing around her; yet, if an article was lost in the house and she could not indicate where it was, no one sought for it afterwards. Often when Aunt Nancy or mother was silently searching around the room through drawers, closet, or cupboard, Cousin Ruth, without raising her eyes, would point over her shoulder to a particular spot, and there the missing article was found. She had the power of discriminating in cases where speech, hearing, and reason failed in others. I sometimes fancied she could read my very thoughts; truly there was something mysterious, if not supernatural, floating around her. Industrious, affectionate, happy, and kind, she neither vexed others nor fretted herself; and, when the time came for her to die, she manifested to those around her that she was happy in the prospect of going to heaven where, she had been so often told, speech and hearing would be restored to her.

During the sitting of this Conference I first became acquainted with Rev. H. H. (now Bishop) Kavanaugh, then about twenty-two years of age. Just recovering from a long illness, his fragile form, marble complexion, and small white hands gave him a feminine delicacy of appearance, that seemed to render him an unfit subject for the itinerancy; the rough encounters and constant exposure of which, in those days, would startle the young preachers of the present generation into immediate location; but this young brother, unhesitating and ingenuous in spirit, freely sacrificed all personal considerations for the high honor of Jehovah's service. My first introduction to this good brother was when, a few days after

our arrival at father's, my husband placed a bundle of
flannel in my hands, saying, "Julia, can't you make a
couple of shirts for a young preacher who has been very
ill?" I only hope they gave him as much comfort as the
making gave me pleasure.

Mr. Kavanaugh's earliest efforts showed that he possessed the very important talent of preaching the Gospel
fluently and acceptably; yet, as I have recently heard,
he was at one time, in the early part of his ministry, so
discouraged at seeing no fruits resulting from his labors,
that he thought he had mistaken his calling, and determined to withdraw from the ministry. One night after
preaching he retired weary and dispirited, surrounded by a
gloom which enervated his spirit and relaxed the steadfast
temper of his soul. The result of this severe trial of his
faith, and under which our young brother had well nigh
sunk, proves that the best of men are but imperfect
judges of the wisdom of a gracious, unerring Providence;
and it was, in the end, divinely overruled with more than
common benefits to himself and the Church, and made
the interesting means of introducing him to new displays
of the eternal goodness, resulting, as it did, in a more
intimate and hallowed communion with his God.

During the night referred to, he dreamed that he was
casting a net for fish in troubled waters; after some
unsuccessful efforts, he caught two—one a beautiful,
large, white perch, the other a little brown fish with no
comeliness. He had scarce secured his treasures when
he awoke, deeply impressed with the idea that, like
Elijah in the wilderness, he had failed to see clearly the
ways of Providence. His eyes, anointed with a divine
unction, were now opened, and he resolved to "stand
still and see the salvation of God."

At the close of his next sermon, thinking of his dream, he walked down from the pulpit, "opened the doors of the Church," and forthwith stepped forward a large, fine-looking woman. "Well," thought he, "here is my white perch." Standing behind her at a modest distance, was a humble looking person, weeping bitterly, but not offering to join the Church; he stepped forward and said, not doubting that this was his brown fish, "Do you wish to join the Church?" "Oh, yes," said she, "if I may be received;" and, sobbing with deep emotion, she raised her eyes to his face and gave him her hand.

After this revelation our young preacher never again faltered. Long years of usefulness have demonstrated that he was called of God, and that great and glorious Being, whose honor he has always so zealously asserted, has caused him to be highly esteemed among men. "Him that honoreth me I will honor," saith the blessed Redeemer.

The whole life of this excellent man has been the reflection of an unclouded mind and of a conscience void of offense. Married to one of the best of women—"a mother in Israel," he long enjoyed the highest earthly happiness in her companionship, both serving God with singleness of heart. They were *real* helpmates to each other; and, though subject to many vicissitudes and bereavements, yet these did but ripen virtues for their appropriate sphere in heaven.

No very striking events mark the history of these two followers of the cross,—another proof of that well-established fact that the most meager annals belong to those epochs which have been the richest in virtue and happiness. When the companion with whom he had so long taken sweet counsel left him for a better world, and his last earthly hope had fled, it was beautiful to see how, like Ezekiel when bereft by one stroke of the light of his eyes, he bowed to the command of God, and with deep resignation bore the terrible affliction. Then did the light of his divine religion shine inward and dispel the gloom in which unassisted man would have sunk in despair.

An early formed habit of journalizing rescues from dreary forgetfulness incidents and personal remembrances which give beauty and reality to the past, and keep fresh in the memory the lessons of life's varied discipline. A diary is the soul of days gone by, returning to us invested with a spiritual presence; a voice that touches the sealed fountains of the past, and opens a stream of living water to purify thought and sanctify feeling.

Between the years 1830 and 1850 the Kentucky Conference could boast of many ministers of striking individuality and energy of character, preachers of righteousness. Dr. Bascom was one whose intrinsic worth was not, perhaps, very well known to the public, wide-spread as was his fame. And I may here be indulged in a sketch of this accomplished gentleman and exemplary Christian, the long-tried personal friend of my husband and myself.

It is too much the fashion of modern times to refer to Cicero and Demosthenes as the only models of eloquence worthy of imitation. While we respect the past, we need not bury ourselves in it. The fanatical admirers of antiquity might find now, in the noonday of Christianity, examples far more luminous and worthy of emulation than could have been found in the palmiest days of Greece and Rome.

The clarion voice of young Bascom was heard in the western wilds when he was but a smooth-faced boy of sixteen. He was, beyond question, the most fluent and brilliant speaker of his time. Henry Clay pronounced him the greatest of living orators, though there were at that period many distinguished public speakers both in Europe and America. His style was peculiar to himself and inimitable, and we can gain but an imperfect idea of the grandeur and magnificence of his sermons by reading them. In print they are but the cold, marble representation, without the living, breathing soul. His language was rich, elegant, and perspicuous; his imagery often bold, and always just. He seemed to possess an inexhaustible fund of grand, forcible, and majestic words, and a memory as surprising as his fluency. His elocution was correct, manly, and graceful, with the added charm of a strong musical voice. He used but few gestures, and these few were marked by a noble simplicity. But, after all, the irresistible influence of his sermons was due to the power of Gospel truth skillfully applied and enforced by "heaven-enkindled love." He spoke not as one seeking applause, but as deeply concerned for the eternal interests of his hearers. The unbounded admiration which his eloquence excited never seemed to move him from his dignified self-possession. The earnestness of his labors left him no time for fashionable small-talk or idle ceremony; yet he was genial and agreeable. I never heard him laugh aloud; but when his face was lighted up with a smile it shone all the brighter because of its usual sedate seriousness. His lofty bearing and commanding presence were not the result of artificial acquirements, but the choicest gifts of lavish Nature. He was too proud to be vain, but was rigid in his exactions of outward respect. While preaching, if his congregation failed in their accustomed attention, a shadow crept across his brow, observable even through the sunlight of his eloquent face.

Dr. Bascom had difficulties to encounter in his early manhood which nothing but his own irrepressible energy, aided by the grace of God in his heart, enabled him to overcome. He knew how to profit by the lessons of wisdom taught in the school of adversity—a school which it would seem is indispensable to the training of great men. The pampered and delicate children of easy fortune are often enervated in the bloom of life, and lulled to inglorious repose upon the downy lap of prosperity.

In contemplating the life of this extraordinary man we are amazed at the variety and multiplicity of his labors. In the establishment and well-being of Augusta College, Kentucky, he exerted a controlling influence. Though too poor himself to bestow upon it any money, he subsidized other kindred spirits, unlocked their hoards and hearts, and endowed it with his own labors. His intellectual qualifications and his moral greatness shone not only here, but while he served as President of Transylvania University. In this wider field of usefulness he gained the respect and admiration of the community as well as the enthusiastic love of those under his care.

Dr. Bascom was devotedly attached to Methodism, and clung to the Church of his choice even when, as was more than once the case, while in the zenith of his fame, temptation was placed before him in the shape of large salaries by wealthier denominations. His body was literally a "living sacrifice" to God and duty. He completed his self-immolation in mid-life, yet, philosophically speaking, his death at fifty-five was not premature. His work was done, his life had been crowded with thought and action. He died a bishop in the Church in full possession of the confidence and love of the people whom he had served so well and faithfully. His character admirably fitted him to manage the affairs of the Church and preside over its conferences.

John Newland Maffit was another of those bright stars in the ecclesiastical firmament of America which shone contemporary with Dr. Bascom.

More remarkable vicissitudes than those of Mr. Maffit have rarely signalized so brief a career in any age or country. His whole life was one brave struggle with adverse circumstances. No man ever secured warmer friends nor provoked more unrelenting enemies. Without the advantages of early education, without fortune or friends, he acquired by persevering industry an attractive eloquence which drew thousands of listeners, at the same time when Bascom and Summerfield were electrifying not only the religious communities of the land, but causing a prodigious stir in the outside world.

With fewer of the externals of piety than usually manifest themselves in the clerical character, fashionable in his attire, polished in his manners, and with a fondness for excitement, he was denounced by many as wearing the livery of an ambassador of the meek and lowly Savior, while utterly destitute of living faith and godliness. On the other hand, there were others living in close communion with him, sharing his sympathies and familiar with those inner traits of mind and character so frequently concealed from the world, who asserted his unblemished piety, his devoted observance of all the private duties of a Christian minister, and who triumphantly appealed to the fruits of his ministry as evidence of his sincerity; and of the aid and sanction he was constantly receiving from heaven.

Few men were capable of producing a more profound sensation in a congregation. Small of stature, but strikingly elegant in his personal appearance, his soft and melodious intonations, faultless gesticulations, and rounded periods, his glowing language and lofty imagination, and, more than all, his prompt adaptation to the circumstances of his auditory, seemed to attract all tastes and furnish materials for the conversation of the week following the delivery of a discourse. Those who censured him in the drawing-room and on the street, and were continually calling in question his piety, listened enraptured to his words, forgetting the man in the fascination of the orator. Always persuasive, never denunciatory, he charmed and soothed the heart with Æolian melody, rather than stirred its depths with the massive strains of martial music. And yet there were occasions when he seemed to evince a perfect contempt for the tropes of rhetoric and the graces of poetry. On such occasions he was plain, practical, evangelical.

I heard him for the first time in our dear little old Methodist church in Shelbyville. It had been announced that Mr. Maffit would fill the Sunday pulpit, and long before the hour of morning service every seat and every square inch of the aisles was occupied. At last he arrived, and, tripping lightly up the pulpit stairway, stood before the almost breathless and expectant audience. The hymn was meekly and impressively read, and sung with thrilling emotion by the whole congregation. Prayer followed, and the preacher, opening the Bible, prefaced the reading of the text by pronouncing slowly and gently, and with great solemnity, "the Word of God." A deep interest

pervaded the assembly.   Many an obdurate heart was
softened, many a veteran of the cross felt his hopes revived and his zeal rekindled by the anointing tones of
that searching, eloquent sermon.   It was long, but when
the last sentence died upon the ear no expression of
fatigue was visible upon the countenances of the attentive audience, and the preacher's voice rang out silvery
to the last.

The life of Maffit appears to have been far from
infertile in incident; the incidents, however, are uncon-
nected and, perversely enough, often obscure and misrep-
resented.   It would be singularly interesting to trace the
personal history of this wayward genius; but, seemingly,
no soul was magnet to his—there was none with whom
he could mingle sympathies.   Too erratic to be fettered
by ordinary conventionalities, he would never submit to
the regulations of a conference, and was but an offshoot
from the Methodist Church.

We can not withhold from one the sun of whose life,
though culminating so brilliantly, was obscured at its
setting by clouds of calumny and abuse, the merit to
which he is justly entitled, and which, at least, should be
recorded with his faults.   The heart is known only to
God; and the unerring decisions of the last day will,
doubtless, reverse more than one earthly verdict, which
seemed based upon conclusive evidence.

I was never an enthusiastic admirer of Mr. Maffit.
There was, at times, much in his demeanor to occasion
distrust of his fitness for the high and holy office of the
ministry; much in his mode of conducting public services which savored of a love of the praise of men, rather
than of a desire to please God and save souls; and yet
there is always room for charity in our estimation of

character. How do the frequent misconstruction and perversions of the acts of men prove the fallibility of human judgment. I was sufficiently well acquainted with this "much-enduring man," to be assured that he was slandered—yea, persecuted even unto death. He literally died of a broken heart. If guilty of half the crimes charged against him, John Newland Maffit deserves the execration of his race and the most condign penalties of a hereafter; but if innocent, as we believe he was, he was certainly a martyr, and has already received a martyr's reward.

Exuberant hopefulness irradiated for a time the clouds which lay dark in the western horizon of his life, and sustained him under the most trying circumstances; but pursued with unrelenting severity by foul-mouthed slander, envy, and hatred; humbled, prostrated, and crushed, he descended, while yet in the Summer of his life, to a sorrowful grave, thus ending the sad evening of a stormy life. No monumental stone marks his resting-place; yet the Savior knoweth his own, and he judgeth not as man judgeth. May we not hope to find him coming with his fellow-laborers, bringing his sheaves with him to the great "Harvest Home?"

Chapter XXV.

I HAD been so long a desolate bird on the wide waste of life's unstable waters that when with folded wings I rested in the family homestead, I felt like the dove sheltered in the ark. My dear little room was near the roof of the house.

It was cold enough for fires. Winter was creeping on, and a ruddy blaze on the hearthstone filled the cozy apartment with warmth and gladness; and when I sought rest my head pressed a lavender-scented pillow of unrivaled whiteness. Our mother had brought from her own Maryland home the habits of thrift and industry that characterized that estimable people. Table and towel linen, and, indeed, all the household linen so abundant with them, was of domestic manufacture. No idle hands were there, and yet no bustle. Quietness and regularity pervaded every department. They arose, breakfasted, dined, supped, and went to bed at exactly the same hour the whole year round; clock-work was never more regular. Spinning and twisting and reeling, together with the swift-flying shuttle, did daily duty in the right time and season. Plenty reigned in the parlor, and there was abundance in the kitchen. What a blessing to a family is a good housekeeper! I tried to take notes, but all in vain,—I was born to fill a different sphere. Teaching was my vocation, and I have always found it easier to take care of girls than a house.

The Conference closed, and my husband was stationed

in Louisville, somewhat disappointed that he was not placed in Shelbyville, where I must locate. I shed a few natural tears, but love's simple magic swept the gathering shadows from my brow, and I heartily co-operated in every arrangement to promote the good of the Church. He commenced his ministerial duties in Louisville immediately, living at home and going to his appointment the latter part of every week, circulating among his flock, filling the pulpit twice on the Sabbath, and generally remaining on Monday to attend to his pastoral duties.

The Fourth Street Methodist Church was the only one at that time in Louisville. The membership was numerous, and a large congregation always in attendance; but the minister had an arduous task to perform because of the discord among the members, arising from the turbulence of some of the floating material. "The ship of Zion" had been rocked by storms, and, at one time, was nigh overwhelmed by the surging billows; but was saved, as Bishop M'Kendree afterwards observed, by the weekly prayer-meetings of the pious female members, whose noble and constant devotion formed an era in the life of Louisville Methodism; and I can not help saying, just here, that I truly believe it was owing much to my husband's efforts that the anchor was finally fixed "within the veil." He stood in the breach, stemming the adverse torrent, bravely combating all the unfavorable circumstances surrounding the struggling Church, and met opposition

"Like an unmoved rock,
Not shaken, but made firmer by the shock."

Before the year closed many were added to the Church, peace dwelt in the tents of Israel, and there was unity among the brethren. One, added to the flock during this memorable year, became the firm and unalterable friend of the pastor. He had been a dissipated man (I have heard him tell the story), and "loved to look upon the wine when it was red." His pious and excellent wife ceased not to be present when opportunity offered at the sanctuary of God. He would attend her to the door, but would not enter. Once, at length, he did so. Smitten by conviction, he found peace only in a Savior's love. He cast away the intoxicating cup, and joined himself to the people of God. His house ever offered a quiet nook for the itinerant Levite. He died full of years. The world misses him; and the name of ˋColeman Daniel is emblazoned among the archives of the beloved city with which he was almost coeval, and by which he can never be forgotten.

The first Winter I spent in Kentucky was mild and genial, the grass did not lose its verdure, there was neither ice nor snow, and the ground was scarcely frozen at any time more than an inch in depth; indeed, I do not remember a Winter when we had snow enough for regular sleighing, or ice thick enough to put up, until the year 1835.

It was on the 28th of December that God gave to us our first-born, a son whom we called Benjamin Pendleton, after my father and my husband's brother. I need not say that this was the child of many prayers, and that he was dedicated to Him who bestowed the gift, with thankful hearts.

How pure the rill that flows from the unsealed fountain of parental love! My cup of happiness was filled with nectar, and I sipped the sparkling bubbles with a trembling joy, lest, haply, they might vanish too soon, or I become intoxicated with the delicious draught.

At that time I can truly say our life floated a banner of beauty,—a warm, purple tinge, like sunlight on the river. The month of March, 1825, on one of our cherished anniversaries, we commenced housekeeping in Shelbyville. Has not every observer of human nature a feeling, in excess of happiness, that makes him jealous of its ability to last? I had enjoyed so much quiet serenity, such a perfect retreat from care, that I dreaded a change, and felt something like a shadow creeping across my sunshine; and, in the words of a great poet, "I wept to have what I so feared to lose." I can never forget how sad I felt on leaving the pleasant farm-house, with its yard full of locust-trees, which, though the last to don their green glories and the first to scatter them to the winds, are yet desirable, because their pinnate leaves not only afford a soft shade, but suffer the sunlight to filter through, without obstructing the cool breeze on its errand of mercy, fanning the hot cheek and cooling the fevered brow.

Five months of inactivity had cultivated the indolence of my nature, and I slightly shrank from entering again the arena of school-teaching. I was singularly ignorant of every thing connected with housekeeping, and dreaded the ordeal through which I must pass to render me at all efficient. Our first day's wants were anticipated by mother, and baskets, stored with provisions ready for the table, preceded us to our home.

Our house, standing on the brow of a green and goodly hill, in view of a wide open country on the north, presented a scene of great beauty. Slopes and swells of luxuriant green, trees drooping their verdant boughs almost to the ground, lined the banks of the stream that swept around the base of the hill, mingling the grand and

the beautiful into an enchanting whole; and when we
first became the occupants of this, our life-long residence,

> "Flowers were bursting on the tree,
> And earth was full of melody."

Our extended view rested upon cultivated farms and intervening woodlands, over which the cool winds swept,
bearing health and fragrance on their wings. South of
us was the dear, quiet little town, near enough to contribute all its conveniences, and yet so shut out as to
leave us free from the annoyance of public gatherings on
court days.

Cheerfulness is, perhaps, the word that best describes
the appearance of the sunny little village,—clean, airy,
orderly, and comfortable,—amply compensating for whatever want of modern elegance or modish luxury might
be observed. The county-seat of Shelby owed much of
its importance to its district and circuit court sessions
and election days, which brought from time to time an
influx not only of the county people but of strangers.

Several peculiarities have ever characterized this place.
The inhabitants, dwelling in their own houses, among
their own people, and knowing but little of the world
abroad, live too much within doors, and there is, consequently, but little of that social intercourse and interchange of the common courtesies of life that render a
village life so charming; yet they are "not forgetful to
entertain strangers," and are remarkable for their noble
charities, liberal donations, and readiness to help in any
enterprise promoting the general good.

Another feature of this highly favored spot is the
attention paid to public worship. With a population
never exceeding fifteen or sixteen hundred, it has a Baptist, a Methodist, a Presbyterian, and Reformed Church,

all of them filled each Sabbath with a well-dressed and orderly congregation. Not a family in the place, perhaps, that has not its Church-going member or members.

I early came to the conclusion that these same good people had become well to do in the world, or made fortunes, by minding their own business; and experience has taught me that people may be unsocial, and still have hands "open as melting day to the calls of charity;" and though they may not be found upon the corners of the streets, pharisaically blowing their own trumpets, their money is readily found when sought for; and in our community those hearts that have been trained to give by constant appeals to their charity are ever ready to give more.

I do not wish to say too much about Shelbyville; but my readers will pardon me, as it has been so long the home of my heart. Shut out from the busy mart of men, no malarious surroundings to engender disease or foster epidemics, it is decidedly a healthy place. This, combined with its rural beauties, renders it a desirable location for a school. Here Spring wears her greenest garments, and Summer crowns her brow with roses sweeter than the most fragrant exotics. Here Autumn ripens her most luscious fruits, and Winter garners an abundant store of golden apples and other treasures for home consumption; and though he sometimes crowns himself with glittering diamonds, yet his warm and sunny smiles kindle the heart into rapture and dissipate the gloominess of the season.

Our first duty was to erect a family altar, where my husband was to officiate daily when at home, and I, by agreement, whenever he was absent, so that this ordinance might never be omitted, unless providentially. The recollection of many interesting scenes connected with family prayers comes floating over me, like clouds from the horizon of memory, with a shower of emotions and thoughts, to receive whose precious fall my heart opens like a thirsty flower. The time of morning prayers was half an hour before breakfast,—in the evening soon after supper, that the children might not have to sit up too late, nor be permitted to retire before this duty was performed. We made this arrangement in the beginning, and have never found any good reasons to change it; on the contrary, when the time became a fixed fact all difficulties vanished. The regular and punctual performance of these duties, with all the preliminary sobrieties of slow, quiet, and reverential manner, tended to inspire religious sentiment among our pupils.

Mr. Tevis was said to be eloquent in prayer, but this inestimable gift was the result of a devotional spirit. The Bible was his constant companion; this he read and studied daily, and often upon his knees. I have heard him repeatedly say he never read a novel in his life. He eschewed political papers as well; but he was surrounded by religious periodicals and biographies. No one can doubt that the soul, fed with pure nourishment, and growing, undisturbed by sickly fancies, like a tree planted by the River of Waters and fed by the dews of heaven, sends forth its roots into a fertile soil, and lifts up its branches into the sunlight of that better land—the home where it shall find its proper sphere.

From the family altar the soul may go forth on its errand of mercy, its enterprises and missions, and there return to receive its rewards. To me this sacred institution, through long years, through dangers and sorrows, in prosperity and adversity, has been an exhaustless fountain of delight and purifying influences. The sweetest type of heaven is a religious home, and heaven itself the home for which we are all striving. Prayer should begin every day's labor, and stand at the end of every day's journey. This life would, indeed, be cheerless and meaningless did we not discern, across the river that separates it from the life beyond, glimpses of pleasant mansions prepared for us. When God gives us a home it should be to us and our children the fountain and reservoir of our daily life, and family prayer should be made a permanent and indispensable part of our household duties. It is the center where all the sweet affections are brought forth and nurtured,—the spot to which memory clings most fondly, and to which the wanderer returns most gladly.

God pity the poor child who can not associate his youth with an institution so rife with sweet religious reminiscences, whence he drank in life's freshness, and shaped the character he bears!

CHAPTER XXVI.

MONDAY, March 25, 1825, our school opened with eighteen or twenty pupils. We did not expect a larger number because we had taken no pains to advertise in any way, consequently it was not known abroad.

I had four boarders to commence with; Miss D., a tall, slender girl of fifteen, with an open countenance, fine, frank manners, and without much cultivation, but as witty as if she had been fed on Attic salt. Her quick repartees brought her into frequent difficulties, but her unfailing good humor removed them as readily. She was a cheerful companion and an agreeable girl in school. Then there was Miss W., a laughter-loving, country lassie, whose well-molded form, golden hair, blue eyes, and glowing complexion, rendered her one of the sweetest, loveliest girls that ever romped upon the greensward. She seemed born to wear white hats wreathed with flowers, and to bring sunshine and laughter to the play-ground where the fairies dance. Another, Miss L. J., a singularly interesting young person to me, was possessed of those delicate graces which rendered her a model pupil. She was quiet, orderly and serious almost to sadness, with a loving and tender heart that rendered her the friend of the younger pupils, and the aid and counselor of her companions. Considerably advanced in her "teens," she was ever meditating how she might best improve and fit herself for life's duties. Truly a lovely girl; her full soul

> "Rich as the lustrous gems which line
> With ruddy light the Indian mine."

My fourth was Margaret. The degenerate days of "Mags and Maggies" had not then come to pass. Remarkable for her unobtrusiveness, she made an impression upon my mind as being an agreeable and affectionate girl.

I have before said, that one may teach well without being in love with the work, if one has the ability to impart knowledge and a respectable fund of knowledge to impart. I had not yet so learned to love my vocation as not to look forward through long coming years to the time, when I might conscientiously live within the limits of my own domestic circle; but I bravely determined to discharge my duties faithfully and in the fear of God, encountering difficulties that I never could have overcome by my own unaided strength. What an inestimable blessing it is, that our Heavenly Father renders pleasant that course of life marked out by a sense of duty! The most rugged pathways are made smooth, while clouds of incense from our grateful hearts cast their soft shadows around us like blessings from the upper world.

Few of my pupils had been subjected to the wholesome discipline of a well-regulated school,—thus they required to be taught the simplest rudiments of knowledge. Some had been properly instructed, but so irregularly, and by so many different teachers, that I found it necessary to tear down a portion of the superstructure and lay the corner-stone more firmly—preparatory to the cultivation of thorough intellectual habits.

There was not a positively disagreeable girl among

my limited number of boarders, the first year; and my day scholars were docile, and placed so entirely under my control by their sensible parents that I passed many pleasant hours in the school-room,—and the fruits of my efforts in their behalf soon became apparent. Amid all my anxiety for their mental improvement, one object I kept steadily in view—the cultivation of the affections and giving them right views of the claims of God upon their hearts; and I cherish the hope that at the day of final account it may appear that my labor was "not in vain in the Lord."

We were so situated that, unembarrassed by other considerations, I could so lay plans and make arrangements that I felt myself at liberty to give undivided attention to the business of teaching, with the perfect assurance that minor affairs would be promptly and effectively rendered subservient to this our settled vocation. I had spent so much of my life in boarding-schools, taking notes all the time, that I was anxious, while adopting with them the regular routine and the salutary discipline necessary for success, to avoid the many objectionable features.

I determined, in the first place, that my table should be well supplied, though I knew that many, like the rebellious Israelites, would complain of the fare even should they have enough and to spare; because it ever has been and ever will be *"la façon de parler."* My experience then, and nothing has since contradicted it, was that those who lived best at home complained least at school.

One evil I had so much deprecated in other schools I would never submit to; namely, the girls congregating in their rooms, even at intervals between school hours, to romp and gossip. Their bed rooms should be well aired and kept in good order, no matter how plain the furniture. This has been carried out literally. The boarders had free access to their rooms until they abused the privilege by disobedience of orders; after which I adopted a system which has worked well and brought good results. More of this anon.

The externs formed but a little flock for the first few weeks, but soon increased to the number of thirty-five or forty, their ages varying from ten to fifteen—girls were too old for school at sixteen! There had been no female school of any importance in the place previous to our coming, and yet the good people of Shelbyville were not unmindful of the rising generation, sustaining a mixed school of juveniles in the Academy. There was also a "dame school" for little masters and misses that were not old enough to enter the Academy and be regularly instructed.

No lapse of time will ever efface from my memory the recollections connected with my first year's teaching in Shelbyville; and never shall I forget what I endured during the receptions of the first day. How clearly I was scanned, and how thoroughly examined by the newcomers! and then the grave instructions and positive injunctions of mammas and papas, guardians and aunts. The fact was, before the day ended I was wearied into a fit of tears and glad to seek rest in sleep.

I arose the next morning, wearied in advance with the painful drudgery before me, contrasting my anticipated future and the cares upon me with the quiet life I had enjoyed during the last five months in the country; but, naturally buoyant in spirit and of a happy temperament, the clouds soon gave way to sunshine, and in less than a week the wheels moved smoothly on, and again I became accustomed to the shrill voices and rapid motions of children, and gradually took increasing delight in that which at first made my head dizzy. My Wythe Court-house experience with a large and growing school was put into requisition, and I soon took deep interest in the bright and happy faces around me.

Among several little girls, day scholars, whose names were enrolled on my first list, was one whose appearance I remember so well, that I can not help drawing the picture as it then appeared. A tiny girl, scarce ten years old, she had traveled a flowery pathway up to that time, chasing the butterflies of life's morning, and drink-ing the sparkling dew-drops from its flowers. Her laugh-ing eyes looked searchingly into mine, as her mother presented her, and seemed to say, "Please, ma'am, don't be too strict." For many years her light footstep and musical voice rang changes through corridor and hall, and many a pleasing tableau do I recall connected with this dancing fairy whose flying feet scarce prevented the grass from growing under them. I loved her then as a pupil, and since, in blooming maturity, as a friend. Two daughters, in after years, were committed to my care and instruction; so that link after link has been added to the chain of friendship even down to my old age.

This is not an isolated case; many others among the bright young girls of Shelbyville are still remembered as cheerful sunbeams, chasing away the petty vexations of the school-room, and gleaming through the shadowy vista of by-gone days. I have known these through the succeeding eras of maidens, wives, and mothers; and their daughters have occupied the same desks that the mothers did before them. I confess to a lurking partiality for the grand-children who have stepped in one by one, to fill their appropriate niche in my heart; yet I do not think I have ever relaxed my discipline on that account or manifested any favoritism.

My little commonwealth grew so rapidly that I soon found my time fully occupied in teaching, and could look but little to the ways of my household except where the girls were concerned. I was occupied at least seven hours daily in the literary department during the first year; taught drawing and French besides, and gave some music lessons. There were, however, but few pupils in these accomplishments, and I gave my drawing lessons in the school-room, and my music lessons in the intervals between school hours—often rocking the cradle, at the same time, with one foot or holding the baby in my arms.

I have often risen at three o'clock on a Winter morning and sketched enough for the day's occupation. Many little fingers plied the busy needle on gay-bordered samplers, but I eschewed the tall brick houses, the angular figures and stunted trees sometimes decorating this species of needle-work, with the twenty different stitches taught in the olden times. I have now before me a sampler worked by one of my pupils forty years ago; and though the colors are faded, there is a witching sweetness in the memories that cling around its pale flowers, and cause me to turn with strange tenderness to the past.

CHAPTER XXVII.

A FEW months increased my boarders to the full capacity of the house; and, with all my vigilance, I found myself totally unequal to the task of contending with the careless, slovenly habits of eight or ten light-hearted and boisterous girls, without drawing tighter the reins of government; and I appeal to every one who has had the like thorny road to travel if the wish has not been formed again and again that mothers would begin earlier to induct their daughters into habits of neatness and regularity. Think of a number of girls from different families and of different ages, thrown together at a boarding-school, where there must be a certain degree of self-dependence exercised, and of the painful drudgery of being obliged to teach them the most trivial things necessary to the formation of tidy habits! Many a painstaking and affectionate mother, injudiciously, and sometimes from indolence, would rather do herself what it is her duty to teach her young daughter to do; while others shift the responsibility upon a young and inexperienced governess, who proves little better than a nursery-maid so far as these habits are concerned.

During my long career, I have been afflicted with girls who, previous to entering my family, had scarce done more than put on their own shoes and stockings,— much less were they able to decide what dresses they should wear day by day. It gave me an immense amount of trouble to correct these inefficient habits. It is a hard matter to undo, in two or three years, habits acquired in fourteen or fifteen. "A place for every thing, and every thing in its place," is a maxim in every body's mouth, but seldom enforced; from the neglect of which arise those irregularities which afflict most families.

One case now presents itself. A young lady from the Far South, the unhappy owner of twenty-five dresses, was found one morning weeping bitterly, and wringing her hands in the deepest grief. My sympathy was excited towards the poor child so far from home, and I asked, in a soothing voice:

"What is the matter? Have you heard any bad news?"

"Oh, no," said she, her sobs increasing as if her heart would break; "but——"

"But what?"

"I have n't got any thing to put on."

The bed before her was covered with dresses.

"Why, what do you mean, child? Are these not yours?"

"Yes; but one is torn, another has no hooks and eyes, and there are none of them fit to wear. I wish I was at home; mother always told me what dress to put on, and had them kept in order for me."

And then followed a fresh burst of tears.

Children, if not made to wait upon themselves as soon as they are able, will form the items of as untidy a generation as ever trod the floor of a school-room, or moved upon the tapis of society. The teacher must therefore stem the tide, or she will fail to perform her duty to parents and pupils.

I began my reform by excluding the girls from their bed-chambers after they left them in the morning. They made their own beds, swept and dusted their rooms, and put every thing in order before the school hour. As soon as the school-bell rang in the morning, and after the rooms had been inspected by a careful eye, the doors were locked, and the keys placed in the hands of a careful person appointed for that purpose, only giving the girls the privilege, when necessary, of getting the key and returning it as soon as the errand was performed,—thus making them thoughtful as to what they might want during the day. This proved an excellent arrangement. If there were several girls in a room, the duty devolving upon each in turn, of keeping the room in order, made them cautious in throwing articles of clothing about, knowing the penalty would be a demerit mark, a dictionary lesson, or several pages of extra writing.

I grew fonder of teaching as days and months rolled on, and moved steadily onward with my daily duties, courageously encountering difficulties, looking full in the face whatever was before me, and taking most conscientious care that my pupils should never be neglected, nor the duties of to-day left for to-morrow. Consequently, it was not an uncommon thing for night to find me still at my post, too weary even to sigh. Yet I was never gloomy, never desponding; and amid all my perplexities prayer and the Word of God had the living power to stir my heart to its very depths and prevent that stupor and apathy which sometimes settles on the soul. In the darkest hours of doubt and foreboding I rested strongly upon the abiding faith of my beloved husband as a treasure of our common life. Trust flowed into his heart as rivers enter the sea; his soul was like a well-watered garden planted by the river's side.

I watched my flock constantly, and did not, as soon

as school was over, try to lose sight and sound of children, books, slates, and blackboards. My thoughts were ever with them, and I was often content to be in the school room half the day on Saturday. Earnestly desiring to make mine a "home school," I felt the responsibility of a mother, and was accessible to my pupils at all hours of the day, trying never to be weary of them, however tiresome they might be, while I could assist, teach, or comfort them. The only difference between being with them in school and out of it was that I exchanged long lessons for long stories, and pleasant conversations; and sometimes exhortation and reproof ended in watching over and assisting them in their amusements. Thus, though they murmured at my strictness, the awkward and boisterous profited by reprimand, and the untidy and slovenly never rebelled against my authority. Many a blotted exercise was tossed into the fire; many a smuggled novel, when found in the corner of a desk, was made an auto-da-fe, to the terror of evil doers and the edification of the younger girls.

I do not think I was ever what might be called cross or ill-natured; nor did I search out faults as with a lighted candle, for the express purpose of scolding; yet I was often provoked by some indication of latent disorder—a stray handkerchief, an odd glove, or an old shoe peeping out from its hiding-place, indicating the propriety of a general search through desks and rooms, to find what was out of place, and bring under my eye all contraband articles.

It has been a continued effort on my part to break up that code of morals so prevalent in schools and academies by which every species of evasion and cunning is allowable to hoodwink and deceive teachers. I have endeavored to accomplish this, in the first place, by giving the girls no more leisure than was good for them, cultivating a spirit of candor, placing confidence in those who deserved it, and making such "keepers of their brothers," but by no means spies or tale-bearers. Such a course, judiciously carried out, will not utterly fail of the desired effect.

There is nothing more painful to me than to hear men and women boast of the scrapes and practical jokes of their school-days, concealing lies and dishonesty under the name of harmless fun. Such a course of conduct at school lays the foundation of an unstable, unreliable character in after life; and, if viewed through the crystal medium of truth, is calculated to make one shudder at the possible consequences of bad habits early formed. These "innocent pleasures!" "harmless sports!" often fatally lead inconsiderate young persons astray. Whenever my watchful eye has detected, or the vigilance of my assistants discovered, any irregularity, it has been promptly and efficiently put down. The rules by which the family and school have always been governed are few and simple, and have needed no printed cards to enforce them. They were positive, but not severe.

I have cautiously avoided that disagreeable and obnoxious proclivity so often observed in teachers and parents, favoritism, rigidly eschewing all undue partiality. The fact was well understood throughout the household that our laws were not cobwebs, made to entangle the weak, but through which the strong might break with impunity. The moral and religious discipline exercised has been generally attended with the happiest results. We have tried to make the pupils feel that their interests were our interests. There is nothing so fatal as party spirit in a juvenile community,—one common bond must exist. Teachers and scholars should never stand in the attitude of belligerents; and from the time a pupil entered the institution she became one of us.

Pocket-money has never been left at the disposal of the pupils, but immediately placed to the credit of the parents and guardians; neither have they been allowed to make bills on their own responsibility, but all their wants being referred to me, our accounts, presented half-yearly, included every expenditure. No indulgence within the limits of prudence has been denied them, while every thing necessary to promote their comfort and facilitate their improvement was supplied. This has obviated all fictitious distinctions formed upon an undue amount of "spending money" on the one side, and a meagre allowance on the other, and the harmony and good-will of the whole has been promoted. A strict adherence to this wholesome regulation has worked wonders in producing a contented spirit,—the wisdom of which has been proved by years of experience.

Every girl, except the very young, has been required to keep her wardrobe in order; and I have found the Southern girls, though supposed to be thriftless and self-indulgent, well acquainted with the use of the needle, and quite willing to use it in plain sewing; many of them, accustomed to have a servant for each finger and toe, readily and cheerfully falling into our way of helping themselves, rejoicing, as it were, in their emancipation from the conventionalities so rife in Slave States. True, it was hard at first to pick up their own skirts, hang up their own bonnets, and fold up their own shawls; but they very soon learned to dispense with "Phœbe" and "Quashy," and cheerfully submitted to the pains and penalties that marked the road to the desired attainment of those useful habits which must be practiced in after life.

On the contrary, I have known some from the Free States, whose mothers were models in their housekeeping arrangements, the very atmosphere in which the young plants had lived being infected with fastidious neatness, who, when transplanted to a boarding-school, were proverbially careless and slovenly. Mamma was too neat to endure the failures of the daughter's early efforts, and preferred doing to the trouble of giving line upon line and precept upon precept.

Alas, how much have I suffered from this omission, and the necessity of trying to fill up the gaps left by good and otherwise painstaking mothers!

My amplification upon this subject will be readily pardoned as this work is intended partly as a guide-book for young and inexperienced teachers. I recollect how anxiously I sought instruction upon such subjects, and was enlightened only after a long and somewhat painful experience, and I do not wish my experience to die with me.

In this connection I have often lamented neglect with regard to the early formation of character upon the immutable basis of truth. This should begin at the first dawn of reason. We are taught in the Bible that the enemy of souls is never idle; and if we do not cultivate the virgin soil Satan will do it for us. Power is possessed by the early guardians of the human soul to grow the good seed of truth while the soil is still wet with the dew of heavenly grace, in virtue of the sacrificial death of Christ. "Time enough yet," is a fatal delusion.

Our first session passed off pleasantly, and, though principally composed of raw material, we managed by persevering industry to weave a tissue of considerable strength and beauty for our examination in July, when the exhibited attainments of the pupils, by a thorough sifting of the classes, proved to a curious and inquisitive audience that our method of teaching was well adapted to draw forth even the most latent capacity, and elicit some sparks from the cold steel of the dullest brain.

The finale of that examination was beautiful,—every body was charmed, and none more so than the children, going home for the holidays with gratified fathers and mothers, delighted to be free from school restraints for a season, that they might frolic in the woods and play "hide-and-go-seek" amid the tangled shade and sunshine. The grass and the flowers and the trees were never so full of beauty to them, as if in reward for their long confinement.

Chapter XXVIII.

OUR vacation was spent in making improvements preparatory to the next session. September came, and, though Summer had gathered up her gorgeous robes and like a dream of beauty glided away, her warm smiles yet lingered, heralding the approach of an Indian Summer. I knew from the many applications that our school would be full, but had not anticipated a crowded opening. In less than a week the school-room was filled almost to overflowing—not a niche unoccupied—and we had as many boarders as we could accommodate.

The scenes and events connected with this year were so many and so varied, that much of interest has escaped my memory. Among my new pupils was a gentle, timid girl from the far South. This only and beloved daughter of a tender father had been reared like a hot-house plant, and when she reached the age of fourteen, her father wisely determined to send her to Kentucky, his own native State, that the cool breath of a Wintery sky might strengthen her constitution and bring out the roses on her cheeks.

A gentle, drooping creature, she blushed on being looked at, and dreaded to be spoken to, reminding one of the shrinking mimosa. Large, luminous eyes, a profusion of soft brown hair, and a sweet, flitting smile which came out like sunlight over her pale brow and fair face, when pleased or excited, rendered her exceedingly attractive. She had been always feeble; probably in consequence of too much nursing, and her father asked permission to send a servant maid to wait upon her at school. This was declined upon the plea, that, if in sufficiently good health to be at school, with proper attention on our part, she would need no such assistance. She must learn self-dependence by being kindly and gradually urged onward.

The first week was full of trials to the little exotic, but they were nobly overcome by her perseverance. To make up her bed was her first trial; in this she succeeded only after an hour's continued effort, taking several resting spells. She soon found use for her hands and feet as well as her mind. It was scarcely ever necessary to chide her, she was so gentle, and there was something with this gentleness, of purity and dignity that clung to her like a garment—insuring respect as well as love; and with it all, a natural taste for elegance and refinement. The grandmother of this young lady lived within a few miles of Shelbyville, and being provided with a beautiful little carriage and two ponies by her indulgent father, the arrangement was made that she should go every Friday evening to spend Saturday and Sunday with her aged relative. This afforded ample opportunity for country air and exercise, so that this delicate and fragile girl, before many weeks had passed, began to bloom with a freshness and beauty almost marvelous. As the elements of health breathed roses on her cheeks, and "touched her soul to finer issues," the golden rays of intellect fell upon the mind and ripened its expanding faculties.

Mr. Tevis, though as much as ever devoted to his sacred calling, found time to give his personal attention to some classes, attending also to the general business of

the establishment; indeed, he was so completely iden-
tified with the institution as to embody his firm and
unyielding views of right and wrong with it; and it was
my highest aspiration to co-operate with him, in striving
to render our school acceptable in the sight of God. We
desired that the examples given and the precepts taught
therein should be a practical comment upon the truth of
Divine Revelation, and determined from the outset that
while the mind should be cultivated, and the manners of
our pupils rendered easy and graceful, dancing should
never be taught within its walls; and that those placed
under our charge should never attend dancing parties—
nor, indeed, parties of any kind during the session.

Music in its sweetest and most elevated character
was cultivated, and no real accomplishment neglected,
feeling it to be a fact, that nothing better can be done for
a bright girl next to forming her religious principles, than
to open her vision to the loveliness with which God has
been pleased to fill creation, and make fact of what the
the poet says,—

> "To her there is a story in every breeze
> And a picture in every wave."

Cultivating a taste for the fine arts is part of a liberal
education, and throws an atmosphere of refinement around
well-instructed minds, that favors all beautiful growth
of thought.

One Monday morning our little Southern girl failed to
return; this was unusual, but it was a dreary day, and
we thought it possible she might be detained on that
account. The afternoon came, and the sun shone pleasantly; still she did not make her appearance. Just
before school closed it was whispered in my ear, "Mrs.
—— has a dancing party this evening, and Miss L. is

there to attend it." I felt very anxious and troubled, scarce knowing what to do. She well knew she was violating one of the most positive regulations of the family. Should it be passed by unnoticed? Immediately after supper I communicated it to Mr. Tevis. He picked up his hat without a moment's hesitation, saying,

"I will go for her." Mrs. B.'s home was only about a hundred yards distant.

"Stop a moment," said I, "wait until she returns to-morrow morning; perhaps she can give some good excuse."

"I think it best to attend to it now," he replied.

I waited his return with intense anxiety, knowing well what would be the consequence if she did not return with him; and I loved her too well to be willing to part with her under such circumstances.

Scarce half an hour had elapsed when my husband's well-known footstep was heard. I met him at the door just in time to catch a glimpse of Miss L.'s slight figure as she passed quickly by me and ran hastily up stairs.

"She has returned, tell me all about it," said I.

Mr. Tevis replied, "I called for Miss L., and was admitted into a room where Mrs. ———— was superin-tending the last touch of her cousin's toilet before she should enter the ball-room. Declining an offered seat I told Miss L. I had come to take her home.."

"She can not go, sir; she is engaged to spend the evening with me."

"We do not permit our boarders to attend dancing parties, madam."

"She is only your boarder from Monday morning until Friday evening," replied the lady.

"This is Monday evening," said Mr. Tevis.

"True, but she came here without going to your house this morning, and you have no right to take her home with you under the circumstances."

"I differ with you, madam, and insist upon Miss L.'s returning with me immediately or not returning at all to my house."

The timid girl stood motionless in the middle of the floor, her downcast eyes filled with tears. Turning to her, Mr. Tevis said,

"Miss L., will you go with me, and remain under our guidance and protection where your father placed you, or will you stay here, and take the consequences?"

"I will go with you, Mr. Tevis," she said, springing forward and seizing his arm, as if afraid to hesitate; and, hastily snatching up her sun-bonnet she pulled it over her face as if to exclude every surrounding object, and walked out, regardless of the angry gesticulations of her disappointed relative. Not a word was spoken on their way home; it was the triumph of right principle and I was satisfied. My heart yearned over the gentle girl, and I could not sleep without seeing her. Going up into her room I found her with her face hidden in the bedclothes, sobbing as if her heart would break. I tried to soothe her by expressions of approbation for her decision; and though she uttered no word in reply, I felt that my kindness had the desired effect, and left her to sleep away her sorrows. The next morning she was down bright and early, deeply engrossed with her books. Not the slightest allusion was made to the past, but I noticed the drooping eyelid, and saw how the soft color came and went upon her cheek, and her evident embarrassment mingled with shyness whenever Mr. Tevis spoke to her, though in his tone and manner there was no remembrancer.

This affair made a great deal of talk in our little town, and stirred up the dancing element amazingly. My brother-in-law, thoroughly a man of the world, but truly interested in our prosperity, expressed his fears that this arbitrary measure would blight our prospects.

"Brother John, you will ruin your school; people will not submit to such dictation."

"They must, if they place their children under our care. I shall never compromise with the world, nor seek favor but from God, to whom I have committed my soul's best interest, and with whom I am also willing to trust my temporal prosperity."

We lost no pupils, and the event proved that the confidence of parents and guardians was more firmly established than ever. We had no further trouble, and Miss L. continued one of the most tractable, studious, and affectionate of our pupils during the three years she remained with us. She came to us a frail and delicate blossom, she went home with a constitution so firmly established that she outlived three husbands, was the mother of a family of children, and died only four years ago.

I would repeat here that I do most heartily condemn dancing; its associations and its influence upon the general system of society being pernicious in the extreme. Dulling the sense of moral feeling, it establishes the reign of false appearances, lowers the standard of true taste, and drives from its circle those by whose virtues or by whose talents that circle might be adorned. How often do we see young persons, whose independent spirit would make them shrink from the hurtful influence of the hollow pretensions and empty parade of the world's low pleasures, and those captivating and dangerous lures

which beset the pathway of the young, wanting in that
mental vigor supported by moral and religious rectitude,
which would secure the firmness to resist hurtful allurements. Yet parents should studiously avoid that
cold severity in which young minds find an excuse for
artful conduct. Let the young also remember that a
crooked policy, even under the most trying circumstances, always brings a thousand nameless terrors, calculated to destroy all peace of mind.

I have before remarked that one of the greatest afflic-
tions in a commonwealth of young girls who have not
been accustomed to look after their own wearing apparel
is their reckless abandon with regard to such matters;
and nothing tends more to encourage slovenly habits
than too extensive a wardrobe. Give a school-girl just
enough, and she will learn to dress with more taste, and
display more ingenuity in keeping her clothes in order,
bringing into exercise that constant industry which will
teach her to make her toilet quickly and give her a
womanly tact which could scarcely be acquired under
other circumstances. A contrary course multiplies our
Flora M'Flimseys to a frightful extent, reminding one of
the sailor who said "he never could do any thing with
his rope if it was too long, but if it was too short he
could splice it."

Young girls are apt to be charmed with "braided
hair, or gold, or pearls, or costly array," and to conclude
that they are respectable and admired in proportion as
they are fine; but I know by experience that the touch
of velvets and the gloss of silks, together with flowers
and feathers, have but little virtue to reconcile them to
close application, or school duties generally.

For the benefit of inexperienced matrons in large

schools, where pupils of various ages and acquirements
are mingled, I would suggest a plan that I have found to
work exceedingly well; namely, selecting for the younger
pupils what are called in English institutions "school
mothers," who shall take particular supervision of the
pupils placed under their care, assisting them in their
lessons, keeping their wearing apparel in order, and, in
fact, helping them to acquire good habits, referring to a
superior when necessary. I have known many dear little
girls, that would have been otherwise lost amid the
bustle of a large school, thrive rapidly under this double
training. Thus, while every body concedes the fact that
a boarding-school is not the most suitable place for a
little girl, yet such direct and individual attention is an
excellent means of forming the character, cultivating the
manners, developing the affections, and nourishing much
that is lovely and of good report in many an orphan
deprived of parental care when most needed.

But, after all, no one can so well form the character
as a judicious and religious mother, who has the best
right to a permanent place in her daughter's heart, and
who can throw around her the necessary restrictions, ·
without exposing her to the hurtful influences of unsuitable associations. The mother can best prevent the development of that unlovely trait of character which leads
her to complain of those whom she should respect, and
who really deserve her gratitude. Yet we often find in
a well-regulated school more vigilance exercised in the ·
inculcation of moral principle than in the far better opportunities of home. Children are not taught early
enough to ask, "What is truth?" and made to know that
"lying lips are an abomination unto the Lord."

Many incidents occurring in my own school have

impressed and deepened these reflections. Let me give a case in point.

"Come, Mary, the bell rang more than five minutes ago. Get up, or you'll be punished for disobeying the rules," exclaimed Jane, as she seized the cover under which the indolent girl had buried herself.

"Let me alone," cried Mary, angrily; "I shall sleep as long as I choose. But, look; now I am up"—and she jumped out upon the floor. "See, girls, I'm regularly up!"

They looked around, when, deliberately betaking herself to bed, she prepared for a second nap.

"Do you call that getting up?"

"To be sure I do; did n't I get up?"

"Suppose you should be asked if you arose when the bell rang, should you say yes?"

"Yes; why not? I certainly did get up. Nothing is said in the rules about lying down again."

"Well, that is a funny way of keeping the rules," said a little blue-eyed listener, who was putting on her shoes and stockings. "That's keeping the rules, and not keeping them either. Well, I should follow your example if I were not almost dressed."

"It's a downright breaking of the rules," interposed Jane, "and nothing else."

"It does seem so," said the little girl, who was under Jane's charge, and whose notions of right and wrong were not so clear as they should be; "and yet she did get up."

"She obeys the letter," said the other, "but breaks the spirit of the law. The rule says we shall rise and dress when the bell rings, and attend to our morning duties."

"Nonsense!" cried the sluggard, vexed in spite of herself at the serious manner in which her delinquency was regarded. "Who can be so particular as all that? What harm is there in sleeping when we want to? I am not afraid of your preaching."

"No," said Jane; "but you ought to be afraid of doing wrong."

This was sowing seed by the wayside, and some of it fell upon good ground; for the little, earnest listener referred to received the truth, and it nestled in her heart like the dewdrop in the flower-cup.

An hour passed. The prayer-bell rang; and poor Mary, whose uneasy conscience permitted her to sleep but lightly, sprang up, and in great trepidation tried to dress in time; but her utmost efforts only enabled her to creep stealthily into the chapel and slide down on her knees, where, instead of praying, she was doubtless thinking how she could excuse her late appearance; and when called on she pleaded in excuse "a very bad headache," thus adding lying to disobedience. One sin always opens the way for another, and true it is, "*Ce n'est que 'le premier pas qui conte.*"

Children of warm imagination are apt to view things through a deceptive medium. Turning away from the homely garb of truth, and trusting to their own unformed judgments, they launch out upon the perilous sea of exaggeration, without rudder or compass. Laughed at, flattered, and even admired by the silly and inconsiderate, they sail for a while smoothly onward, rejecting the warnings, the admonitions, and the communicated experience of those who have observantly performed the voyage of life, until wrecked amid the storm and tempest of their own delusions.

There is but one way to secure that true elevation of character, which is, neither to "lie nor be associated with liars." Children's minds should be so rooted and grounded in the conviction of the truth of Divine Revelation that nothing earthly shall be able to shake their faith in the awful declaration, "Whosoever loveth and maketh a lie" shall have no right to the tree of life, nor shall they "enter in through the gates into the city."

The all-pervading influence of my husband's consistent piety was felt in every department of our household. We tried from the beginning to make the Sabbath a means of securing more religious instruction than under ordinary circumstances. The Fourth Commandment was carefully enforced, as far as possible, upon all under our control. My good husband literally found the Sabbath "a delight," and not only by precept, but by example so eminently beautiful, taught others, "If thou turn away thy foot from the Sabbath, from doing thy pleasure on my holy day, then shalt thou delight thyself in the Lord," etc.

Regarding the Sabbath-school as the nursery of the Church, we considered it a duty and privilege to promote its advancement. Every body belonging to the family and school, unless providentially hindered, was found there in place and in good time. I have often thought, as I listened to the Sabbath-school children singing, that I would rather hear such a chorus of young voices than the most accomplished "prima donna" that ever dazzled and entranced the world. How sweetly does their singing float around the heart and fill the soul with joy! Nature has given to the human voice, when bursting in simple harmony from the spotless hearts of children, an irresistible power over our sympathies. "No ear so dull, no heart so cold," but must feel that nothing on earth is so thrilling as the musical tones with which they pour out their unchained spirits.

I have superintended and taught during the Sunday-school hour for many years, but I can truly say, I do not remember ever to have spent an irksome moment there. They have been practically, as well as poetically, rosy hours—hours that have gone to heaven to bear a good report, I trust, for my own soul as well as the souls of my pupils.

Every body attended Church at eleven o'clock, and this was a fact so well understood, that few and feeble were the attempts made to evade it. We had children from families of all denominations, yet I was never sectarian enough to wish to proselyte from other Churches into my own; but my boarders attended the Methodist Church, that they might be generally, as well as particularly, under my supervision. Some were permitted, occasionally, to attend the Churches in which they were brought up or to which they belonged, under proper surveillance.

Having myself been accustomed to attend Church twice on the Sabbath, I felt the necessity of substituting something that would employ the girls for an hour in religious exercises in the afternoon, as our second Church service was at night. I formed, therefore, a Bible Class for my boarders, giving to externs the privilege of attending, which many of them gladly embraced. To render the hour pleasant as possible, after passing over one or two chapters selected as topics, the girls were encouraged to relate something from their own experience, or that they had read—incidents, anecdotes, or short poetical recitations, all having a religious bearing.

By this means, many of them acquired a store of religious knowledge which told for good upon their future
lives. This Bible Class has been kept up, without
interruption, during vacation as well as term time, and
generally with the happiest results. No one was ever
excused from the class, but the rest of the afternoon
might be spent as each one chose, with the restriction
of being quiet. Of course, they were never permitted
to study or attend to any of their weekly duties, nor
were they compelled to attend the Church service at
night. The influence of endeavoring to keep this holy
day was felt not only throughout our own establishment
but extended itself to the community.

CHAPTER XXIX.

IN the Fall of 1826 began my acquaintance and friendly intercourse with the family of Mr. Charles Wickliffe. Elizabeth was placed under our care at the age of eleven. There was something in the very appearance of this young girl that instantly awakened my interest. She had no self-confidence, and was so entirely dependent upon those around her, that she clung closely to my side in and out of school. Isolated occupations were irksome to her; she preferred even to study with a bevy of girls around her, and could enjoy no pleasure unless shared with another. Loving, amiable, and obliging, she seemed born "to be the shadow of another soul." I shall never forget her introduction and how she clung to her father as if afraid to let go his hand. There she stood,—her timid face, though beaming with good humor, suffused with blushes,—her voice when she spoke scarcely audible from emotion. When her father left, commending her to my special care, she would have followed him had I not gently restrained her, but in a few days she was thoroughly domesticated. She remained with us several years, spending only her vacations at home. There was a winning simplicity of manner about this lovely girl, that drew me towards her more and more until, when she left school, I felt as if I had parted from one of my own children. Her love for us was life-long, and at her death, which occurred a few years after a happy marriage, she gave the strongest evidence she could, of her continued affection, by asking that her youngest sister should be named for me. She was lovely in her life, admirable in every relation she sustained; possessing that meek and quiet spirit, which, in the sight of God, is above all price. She died, cut off in her "youth and beauty's bloom," leaving a memory embalmed in the hearts of all who knew her, and went to enjoy in full fruition, the blessing pronounced upon the pure in heart.

Mr. Wickliffe's five daughters were principally educated at our school, and certainly women more lovely, more worthy of respect and esteem never blessed American homes, or adorned society; and I proudly recognize them as among my most loved and cherished pupils—the remembrance of whom brings light to my eyes and warmth to my heart.

To this family is due some of the happiest hours of my Kentucky life; and though this is not the place for eulogy, yet a sincere appreciation of these my life-long friends, induces me to say that Mr. Wickliffe's real worth as a private citizen, independent of his public career, for that belongs to history, has been felt and acknowledged by all who have known him. Unlike many of our greatest statesmen, his private life is a model for imitation; unstained as it has ever been, by moral pollution of any kind, and marked by a truthfulness and sincerity resulting from the strong religious reverence investing his soul, Mr. Wickliffe's eminent characteristics have ever been fast fidelity to his friends, and a tenderness which rendered his presence agreeable and cheering in every domestic relation; thus dignifying every position he occupied by his high moral character, and adorning every sphere in which he moved.

Mrs. Wickliffe was connected by marriage with my husband's family, and when I first knew her was in the full bloom of matronly beauty. Her face was rendered singularly attractive by eyes into whose depths one might gaze with the certainty that they were wells of thought and feeling; these, though possessing a gazelle-like softness in repose, in animated conversation sparkled like gems in the heaven of intellect. Her nose was finely formed, and around her delicately chiseled mouth a sweet smile forever lingered; and even when her finely set lips showed strength and decision, benevolence beamed from every lineament of her face. Her conversation was characterized by a delicate and respectful regard for the feelings of others. None, even the most insignificant, ever spent an hour with her in conversation without feeling a degree of importance and self-complacency never felt before. With an exquisite poetical taste, she always kept embalmed in her memory some of the finest selections from the best authors, while the varied and extensive information acquired by reading made her an entertaining companion and a choice friend.

Her figure, of medium height, was full of grace, and every movement a combination of ease and elegance, which is, perhaps, the most distinguished proof of a noble mind; and which we never fail to attribute to the consciousness of good birth and breeding. Mrs. Wickliffe was noted for her unostentatious benevolence and unusual kindness to the poor. "When the ear heard her, then it blessed her; and when the eye saw her, it gave witness to her, because she delivered the poor that cried, and the fatherless, and him that had none to help him. The blessing of him that was ready to perish came upon her, and she caused the widow's heart to sing for joy."

Truly her heart was alive with religious feeling and a constant recognition of Bible truth.

Long years of unchanging friendship, unfettered by the cold formalities of the world, endeared me to Mrs. Wickliffe more than words can express. A constant interchange of affection and feeling kept alive the flame of love upon the heart's consecrated altar; and, thank heaven, it stood the test of years, undimmed by even a passing cloud. But words are both idle and insufficient, and no flourish of sentiment is needed where the heart is concerned. My beloved friend passed over Jordan in December, 1863—"gone like a dream of light and life." Yes, and, as fond memory dwells on the delightful associations of the past, the image of this dear friend comes up warm and glowing. I almost feel the spirit-breath stirring my time-bleached locks—the vision

> "Wears no cold livery of earth,
> But shows the brightness of its birth,
> And links my soul to heaven!"

I too have changed; the world has wrought its chilling task on me; yet friend after friend departing forms one more tie to bind my spirit to its home.

Our first visit abroad was during the vacation of 1826, at the house of a relative, Judge Davidge. It was the season for enjoyment, and we were in the right mood, and in the right place. How keenly we appreciate rest and liberty after long application to business, however pleasant our duties may have been; and how different from the rest, if it may be so termed, that follows the dissipated routine of fashionable idleness.

I have always been remarkable for an elasticity of spirit following a release from close confinement. Our road was through a rich country, and my happy soul invested every green tree, whose expanding branches were flung out upon the air, with a beautiful mystery. Its web of glossy leaves, interwoven with sunshine, was looked upon with a blended feeling of reverence and devotion, as I rejoiced in the perfection of the works of God; and my heart exclaimed, "My Father made them all."

Our hostess was a charming woman in the fullest sense of the word. Though in the maturity of woman-hood, she still had a complexion delicately fair, and a brow as calm and noble as on her bridal day. Health and contentment shone in her well-defined and harmonious features. There was nothing of hurry and bustle in her household arrangements, and no undue excitement no matter how great the number of guests. Her manner was gentle and decided, and I never heard her speak in a loud tone of voice. She practiced in an eminent degree those two duties which run through the Christian life like the warp through the woof—"blessing and trusting."

When religion flourishes in the soul, it knows how to naturalize spiritual things, and how to spiritualize natural things. Mrs. Davidge—and all the country around would indorse what I say—was a rare instance of one who mingled with the world without being of it,—often struggling with domestic cares and perplexities, and courageously meeting sorrow, having before I knew her been deprived by death of more than half her numerous family of children. At one time she buried five in two weeks; but during all this her faith failed not, and she was never known to "charge God foolishly." Living in the world she had stemmed the tide of its ungodliness unsullied by its impurities, and without making shipwreck of her hopes. In the genial atmosphere of her own home she flourished, a model of all that is excellent in woman.

Judge Davidge presented a fine specimen of our Kentucky gentlemen under the old *régime.* He was well known and highly esteemed in his official capacity as circuit judge, under the old Constitution, before the good people of Kentucky had turned upside down our most stable foundations, and left us afloat upon the dangerous sea of excessive liberty. Under the old Constitution a man had time to practice his profession after he learned it, to the edification and benefit of the community; now he scarcely recovers from the excitement of his election and takes his seat in the curule chair before he is ejected by a new-comer.

The general character of the Judge's physiognomy was intelligence, and that perfect self-possession born of a feeling of superiority. A profound metaphysician, his logic and rhetoric were of the true Baconian school. He presided with great dignity on the bench, and never permitted the slightest disrespect to his official character,— governed the jury with unflinching severity, and has been known upon several occasions, when they could not come to a decision in time, to take them all around the circuit with him. He was highly esteemed for true patriotism and statesmanlike qualities. His friendship, once secured, never failed, and in truth, though he lived above commonplace things, was warm, generous, and social. Such friendships did the providence of God lead me to form— friendships which will run parallel with the day of eternity.

I learned useful lessons from Mrs. Davidge with regard to the training of children. She thought me too strict and too watchful over my little boy, and, in fact, too much disposed to find fault with trifles. Experience had taught her that a little wholesome neglect was sometimes beneficial, and that this might be combined with real care and never-ceasing watchfulness. "It does wonders," said she, "in the work of setting human beings on their feet for the life journey." To educate children is to act constantly upon their impressible natures. Education ought to be the object of home—education by example as well as precept. To inculcate truthfulness you must not make them afraid of you. A confiding, trusting child will receive punishment as readily from a kind parent as he will enjoy reward from the same source.

How deep the lessons of a mother's love, the influence of which is felt long, long after the lips that uttered them are sealed in the silence of the tomb! In this family religion was not altogether a Sunday garment—a robe too fine for common wear, put on solemnly once a week as upon state occasions, and gladly laid aside when the occasion was over.

Chapter XXX.

CHILDHOOD! O blessed childhood! though quickly passing away like the falling of a shadow on the floor, we look back fondly upon it, "blossom of being, seen and gone."

Our second child, a lovely little girl, was dying. Even now I can not revert to that day, though nearly forty years have elapsed, without anguish of soul. This lotus-blossom from the shores of the River of Life, destined to bloom for the short space of twenty-two months, exhaling its fragrance throughout our household, had filled my cup of happiness to the very brim.

Little Mary was born Sunday, January 15, 1827, and died on Sunday, November 30, 1828. My husband bore the loss with the humble resignation of a Christian; but he missed the little pattering feet that often followed him to his private devotions, kneeling down close by his side, echoing his sighs as if participating in his fervent prayers,—never growing weary or impatient, no matter how prolonged his stay.

My grief, at first, was almost beyond control. Nothing but the Bible, which I kept almost constantly open before me, or the soothing voice of my husband in prayer, could fit me for my daily duties.

We often talk of our submission to God in the sunshine, and then resist and struggle when the storm arises.

Our Southern pupils from this time began to increase in number; and as the institution became known abroad through the medium of those sent forth from under its care, "epistles to be known and read," there was a gradual influx from the surrounding States. Up to this time, and for some years afterwards, we issued no circulars and published no catalogues, simply advertising the time for the opening and closing of the school in the New York and Western Christian Advocates. When it became generally known that a Protestant school was located in Shelbyville, it shared much of the patronage formerly bestowed upon the Catholic schools of Kentucky, among which Nazareth, situated near Bardstown, was the most conspicuous, and deservedly the most highly appreciated.

Ours was the first Protestant female academy founded in the Mississippi Valley, except that of the Rev. Mr. Fall, situated in Nashville, which antedates it a few years. Mr. Fall afterwards removed to Kentucky, and located near Frankfort, in one of the most enchanting places I ever saw, reminding one of the Happy Valley of Rasselas. Mr. Fall was eminently fitted for his lofty calling, not only as an educated man, but by his aptness for teaching and power of communicating knowledge. The many accomplished and well-educated young ladies from this institution prove his faithful diligence and consequent success as a teacher.

For years we had semi-annual examinations and two vacations,—one in February, the other in August. This was the custom in Kentucky, and we adopted it without reflecting upon its inconvenience. Every vacation we found it necessary to improve and extend our buildings; for each succeeding term the number of boarders was increased. We tried at first to limit our school, but were unsuccessful, there being generally no limit except want of room. I would greatly have preferred no externs, but that could not be, as we were under obligations to the town and vicinity. Much care was exercised in regulating our terms so as to leave an open door for those in moderate circumstances; and we endeavored always to promote a prudent economy in our arrangements, while we left no means untried and spared no expense to promote the highest interests of education. Our ambition was not to accumulate wealth, though we wished remuneration, but to render the school a blessing to the rising generation,—and certainly we have not been altogether disappointed.

Teaching should be considered as a profession, and the loftiest calling except that of preaching the Gospel. To communicate moral and religious truth is the very noblest employment of an intelligent being. Teachers, as well as preachers, should never sigh for that ease which some think so "friendly to life's decline."

During the first ten or fifteen years of my teaching in Shelbyville girls cared much less for personal adornment, and studied with a more hearty good-will, than at any time since; whilst I took the greatest pains possible to cultivate as much taste for dress as was compatible with the highest intellectual improvement. I remember but few girls during the period referred to that gave me much trouble on this score. Those with the most limited wardrobes were the best students, as well as the neatest in dress. A well-cultivated mind scorns tawdry finery, and teaches us the refining truth that cleanliness is next to godliness.

Much annoyance was felt the first few years by invitations through the medium of the post-office to parties and balls—a custom prevalent in all the little towns of Kentucky, but fatal to good scholarship, making fashionable young ladies of children from the ages of ten to fifteen. They were, in fact, the society of the place; married women, no matter how young, were never invited to places of amusement, and a girl of eighteen or twenty was quite *passée*. I tried to change the custom as far as my school was concerned, by returning the billets unopened; this failing of the desired effect, I sent for the managers and expressed in plain terms my wishes and intentions, requesting them, at the same time, not to make another attempt for it would always prove useless. My kind but positive manner had the desired effect; and I would take this opportunity to say, for the benefit of those who preside over female institutions, where there are also male schools and colleges, that a candid, open course pursued towards both boys and girls will generally break up any clandestine communications. This will cultivate a high moral sense of personal responsibility, and, under strict surveillance, give a security not obtained by any other means. Let there be no mystery and as little suspicion as possible.

Our school and family were proverbial for health; no bad colds were taken from sitting up in rooms insufficiently warmed and dawdling about half dressed. Some persons have expressed their surprise that the girls preferred to study together in the school-room, and were more successful in their recitations. Two good reasons may be assigned for this. One, that the teacher is ever at the desk, ready to solve any knotty question and aid the timid inquirer; the other, it prevents interruption from the idle, noisy, and trifling.

Our family habits were regulated according to the strictest notions of Joshua's resolution, "As for me and my house we will serve the Lord." No one could be absent from family prayers without a good excuse. So well practiced was Mr. Tevis's eye that a glance around the chapel enabled him to detect the absence of a single girl. His devotional spirit rendered his manner so impressive as to prevent any tendency to levity during family worship; and, indeed, it mattered not how full of fun and frolic the girls might be, his appearance produced a serious and respectful quietness among them, for all loved and honored him. In his religious character, an ardent and steady zeal for the promotion of the good of the Church predominated, combined with an unswerving faith in those evangelical doctrines which gave special unction and energy to his conversation, to his prayers and to his discourses.

Mr. Tevis was as much a preacher of righteousness at home as abroad, and we had the blessed privilege of knowing that impressions were made from time to time upon the hearts of our pupils, which wrought a happy change in temper and character. Many a careless one, who came into our family thoughtless and indifferent as to her soul's welfare, left either an humble penitent or a true convert to Christianity. Some have gone forth as missionaries of the Cross among their own people, and to bless the world by their pious example. Sunday-schools have been established in the far South ; Churches founded in desolate places have brought many a truant heart to God, and scores have been led to worship their Creator, who had previously burned incense only upon the altar of mammon.

I may, without boasting, glory in the fact that the institution has always been self-sustaining, never having had any endowment nor appropriation from the Methodist Church nor any other source except the well-earned tuition fees. It is but justice to add, however, that we have lived in an enlightened community, and among a people who gladly embraced the opportunity of sustaining such a school by a hearty and liberal patronage.

During the Conference in 1828, held again in Shelby-ville, I became acquainted with several of our senior bishops—M'Kendree, Roberts, and Soule. The first had always been a warm personal friend of my husband, and highly appreciating his services as an itinerant, did not seem to approve his remaining permanently stationed as the superintendent of an Academy. He expressed his fears in his own peculiar, laconic manner, "Act in haste and repent at leisure—and take care of the world, brother;" but he afterwards most heartily coincided with Mr. Tevis and the Conference, that it was right and best for him and the Church—regarding the school as a nursery to the Church.

Bishop M'Kendree's feeble and declining health left Bishop Roberts to preside, and Bishop Soule was merely in attendance. They all came to tea with us one evening, and I was anxious to make a good impression upon these high dignitaries of the Church, especially upon Bishop M'Kendree, the only bachelor among them. He, like Bishop Asbury, had never been willing to acknowledge that a good wife was a good thing, and felt, that though it was right for some to marry, it was better for others to remain in single blessedness.

I determined to bring to bear all my tact in good housekeeping—which, by the by, was very little—in honor of my distinguished guests, and spent so much time in the supervision of my supper-table, displaying to the best advantage a small service of china, cut-glass, and silver that I lost the opportunity of profiting by the rich experience and heavenly conversation of these holy men of God. Imagine my mortification when, seated at the head of the table, heated by over-exertion, my face glowing like a peony, to hear Bishop M'Kendree say, as he declined every offered delicacy, and devoted himself to a corn-cake with a glass of milk and water, privately prepared at his own request, "But one thing is needful, sister." I thought I could see a lurking smile in his mild reproving eye, and the lesson was not lost.

Notwithstanding this *contretemps* I think the Bishop afterwards knew me well enough to believe that I fully sustained the pledge made at the time of my marriage— "never by word or deed to throw any impediment in my husband's way as a preacher of the Gospel;" and that I always felt in my heart what I professed at the beginning, "that I would rather be the wife of a faithful itinerant preacher than to wear a jeweled crown and be dressed in purple and gold." I believed in the promise added to the blessed admonition, "Seek first the kingdom of heaven."

Though I saw Bishop M'Kendree often afterwards— for he never came to Shelbyville without visiting us,—I heard him preach but twice, once at a camp-meeting with "a tented army of pilgrims to eternity" before him. His text was, "Ephraim is joined to his idols, let him alone." He first portrayed the repeated effort made by the Spirit of God to call the sinner to repentance; and in accents softened by the emotions of his own heart, uttered the Scripture admonition, "Turn ye, turn ye, why will ye die!" until he excited the deepest interest in his hearers, touching a chord that vibrated through every heart. Then he drew a life-like picture of the obstinate, worldly-minded man who, steadily refusing all calls to repentance, rejects the allurements of heaven, the flatteries of the world and its deceitful riches rendering his frozen heart impervious to the sunshine that floods the earth and skies so graciously. His doom is sealed, his heart seared. The earth pours its riches in abundance, the rain and the dew nurture his vineyards and crown the year with fatness; plenty reigns in his house, and his barns are bursting forth with the golden harvest; but then comes the awful voice in the stillness of the midnight hour, "Thou fool, this night thy soul shall be required of thee." The effect upon the audience was electrical, and many dated their return to the shepherd and bishop of their souls from that hour. His imagery was beautiful, his illustrations perfect.

Once again, in the old "White Church" of blessed memory, he was illustrating the gradual influx of divine light into the soul. "See," said he, "that window with its half-closed shutters, admitting but few rays of light. Open it a little more, and you will see objects more distinctly; a little more still, and you will not fail to see how indecently the men treat the floor." Every tobacco chewer instantly cast his eyes in that direction; they felt the reproof, and there was no more spitting during that sermon. This apparent step from the sublime to the ridiculous was characteristic of the Bishop.

His success as a preacher was not owing to grace of manner, nor richness of voice, nor fullness of matter; but that indescribable unction obtained by prayer, profound meditation upon divine truths, and a deep conviction of the overwhelming importance of eternal things,— that anointing of the Holy Spirit which no man can counterfeit, and no audience mistake. Inspired with the utmost desire for the salvation of souls, his thoughts kindled into living flames, and his words fell upon the ears of his hearers with irresistible power. His plain, unaffected manners, simplicity of character, singleness of purpose, and the purity of his life made a profound impression upon every community in which he preached. His religion had no mixture of coldness, no exclusiveness, no bigotry. "The Holy Truth walked ever by his side." Independence of thought and action towards men was mingled with the deepest humility and reverence towards God. The frailties of others were regarded with gentleness and pity, but he was a rigid disciplinarian towards himself; and though of a feeble constitution, fasted much, often for a whole day at a time. He believed in St. Paul's admonition —"keep the body under." Upon one occasion, failing to preach in a manner satisfactory to himself, he determined to eat no meat during one weary round of his parochial district, though this kind of nourishment was best suited to his state of health.

He possessed much of that dry wit that sometimes disturbs the quiet equanimity of the most serious. Once overtaken in a lonely ride by an inquisitive countryman, after the usual interchange of wayside courtesies, a monotonous silence ensued, interrupted by the trot, trot, jogtrot of the travelers' horses. At last,

"Where mout yer be goin', mister?" to the Bishop.

"About and about," was the laconic reply.

Another grave pause of painful intensity, and

"Conclude to get home to-night?"

"No."

Another mile through the mud, and our "quidnunc," with inflexible perseverance, tried him again.

"Well, stranger, where do you live?"

"About and about," said the Bishop.

The man's heart failed him, and the mysterious silence continued until their roads separated, when the baffled questioner whipped up his horse and soon lost sight of his companion.

When I recall the image of this holy apostle, the light of heaven seems to shine around me. He was so pure and noble, that when in conducting family prayers he raised his eyes full of devotion from the sacred volume, and lifted his hands, saying, "Let us pray," I felt that the gates of heaven were thrown wide open, and that he had access to a throne of grace through a living faith in the Redeemer, and that we were all in the exalted presence of the angels of mercy.

Bishop Roberts frequently tarried with us as he passed to and fro. Many happy reminiscences of a life-long itinerancy are connected with his visits. His genial, cheerful conversation always amused and interested his hearers. As a pioneer preacher, he was well acquainted with the history of the Methodist Church, from the time it was but a handful in the wilderness—feeble, struggling through poverty and opposition, yet led onward by the pillar of fire by night, and shielded by the friendly cloud from the blaze of persecution by day. He had lived to see her come up through tribulation, "looking forth as the morning, fair as the moon, clear as the sun, and terrible as an army with banners," a blessing to multiplied thousands. He went forth among the aborigines, on the outskirts of civilization, and preached the unsearchable riches of Christ to those dark sons of the forest, perishing for the bread of life. I have often heard him say that the poor heathen when converted were Christians of the noblest stamp; showing that the salvation offered by the Gospel is not the prize of lofty intellect, but of a penitent soul and a lowly mind. The truth, as it is in Jesus, is in one view so profound, that the highest arch-angel's intellect may be lost in the contemplation of its mysterious depths; in another, so simple that the lisping babe at its mother's knee may learn its meaning.

The heart of Bishop Roberts was the seat of all those emotions that sweeten human life, adorn our nature, and diffuse a nameless charm over existence. I was not per-sonally acquainted with his excellent wife, but she was said to be in every way suitable as a companion for this holy man. They had no children; yet the providence of God gave them seventeen or eighteen nephews and nieces to bring up in the fear and admonition of the Lord. Both the Bishop and his wife manifested the exquisite simplic-ity of the essential facts and principles of our holy relig-ion. They were co-laborers in the Lord's vineyard, working for the salvation of souls, "till the busy wheels of life stood still." Sister Roberts outlived the Bishop several years, an honored resident of Greencastle, Indi-ana, where she was tenderly loved and watched over by many devoted friends. Ready and willing hands were always at her service, but she would be chargeable to no one so long as her hands and feet could perform their accustomed offices. Her life was a simple, consecrated one; she served God faithfully all her days, and has gone to that home where day and night divide his work no more.

Among the sacred pictures treasured in the gallery of my heart, I would fain select another, Bishop Soule—a tall, grave-looking man of noble presence, with a steady, determined sort of face, resembling a granite pillar of magnificent proportions. The Bishop had a "touch-me-not" sort of stateliness of manner, yet he was neither stiff nor freezing; and though as uncompromising with the world as St. Paul himself, he had a strong perception of the beautiful, both in nature and in art, which enriched his highly cultivated mind with the brightest jewels of intellect. He might have been a harsh man had he not been a Christian. Emanations from the heart always soften the asperities of the natural character. He was kind, but never familiar; polite and social, but guarded well the dignity of his episcopal office. Christianity, instead of sinking the distinctions of society, elevates and guards them, and employs the most sublime truths to enforce the minutest offices of social life. A rude, uncivil man, of an unsympathizing nature, is not one in whom holy emotions are likely to dwell; and yet there may rest, in the humblest laborer's heart, a spirit that dignifies the coarsest toil, and renders drudgery divine.

Bishop Soule was sometimes abrupt in his candid, laconic speech, but never yielded to anger, and never condescended to be irritable. He did not win friends as rapidly as Bishop Roberts or Bishop M'Kendree, yet those who knew him well, loved and admired him above all others.

CHAPTER XXXI.

I AM well aware that the minute details of a school-room are apt to be tiresome, yet a teacher who has spent a life-time in the vocation need not look abroad for interesting matter. Before the channel of education became deep and broad as it is now, we had much more raw material to work upon from the far distant West and South. Some queer specimens of girls, who had "come up" pretty much of themselves, and who had, from child-hood's happy hours, reveled in idleness and ignorance, were brought to us. Dull, mentally and spiritually, neither sheen of silks nor sparkle of jewels, piled upon and scattered over them by wealthy papas and mammas, could render them other than rough and ungainly—igno-rant of the very first principles of literature. Upon these I was expected to do a variety of polishing, removing, as with a magic wand, the accumulated rust of fifteen or sixteen years; giving a "finishing touch," as they called it, in three or five months.

Just such a Kentucky girl was introduced to me one bright September morning by her mother. "Here, ma'rm, is my daughter; I calculate to send her not more than three months, and I want you to push her just as fast as you can, because you see she are sixteen year old now. She talks grammar proper enough—knows all about geography, and is been a readin', and a writin', and spellin', dear knows how long; so she need n't waste no time in the likes o' that. If she do n't know enough of 'em she can larn 'em at home, and she wants to go in the tip-top class and not be a foolin' away her time."

"I examine my pupils, madam, when they enter school, and place them just where, in my judgment, they will improve the most; we never class a girl according to her age, nor the number of books she has gone through, but in keeping with the real knowledge she possesses."

"That'll do when they've a good while to come to school, but my daughter's old enough to be keepin' company *now*, and I don't want her to be a studyin' all her life. *I* got along mighty well without any education."

"What do you propose to have her learn, madam? Arithmetic."

She interrupted me quickly, "No, no, she ciphers well enough, and, if she don't, her brother can larn her that; she wants to know philosophy, chemistry, and astronomy, and the likes o' that. She might take a spell in writin' compositions and larnin' geometry and what you call algebray—and I want her to keep on a studyin' an' singin,' and the rest o' the time she can take up with studyin' the piany. I don't want her to study no French, nor none of the other dead languages; she talks fast enough without any o' that outlandish gibberish."

You may be sure I dreaded the daughter after these special directions from the mother. I do not think she stayed six weeks with us.

Engaged in a round of occupations that admitted of no leisure hours, with a heart fully devoted to my duties, weeks and months sped rapidly by; and though time did occasionally cast a shadow from his wings when in my busy school-room, all was forgotten beyond its limits.

That was my world, there I gave instruction, and thence I drew lessons of experience which rendered me, from year to year, a more efficient teacher. There I learned to moralize, as the painful conviction forced itself upon me, thus: "How strange it is, and not more strange than true, that so few parents in this Christian land, where the Gospel light is shining with noon-day splendor, lighting up every niche and corner of their habitations, should be so slow to enforce the Bible admonition in reference to the early instructions of children by precept and example." In some families children are regarded as stumbling-blocks, in the way of thrifty mothers—and, in the habitations of the gay, the wealthy, and the fashionable, as soulless pets. I have heard the argument strictly maintained among sensible people, "Oh! do not trouble them with this everlasting teaching, they'll have enough of it when they go to school; let them enjoy life while they are young!" I have known parents, who studiously avoided throwing any impediment in the way of the indulgence of all sorts of selfishness for fear of seeing a frown upon the brow of their children, leaving their minds almost a perfect blank, so far as duty was concerned; or worse, filled with false impressions and precocious wickedness. Children are a study for the most acute mind. In them we find the natural movements of the soul—intense with new life and busy after truth. They are all sensation, and their wakeful senses are ever drinking in from the common sun and air; every sound is taken note of by the ear; every floating shadow and passing form comes and touches the sleeping eye; little circumstances in the material world about them must be the instructors and formers of their characters for life; hence the necessity for that constant watching and teaching the Bible speaks of—making them know and desire what is right, rather than what is agreeable; teaching them so as not to lose the distinction between principle and selfish gratification. All selfishness hardens the heart; but there is no kind which hardens it so effectually as that weak indulgence which permits a child to have its own way, rather than take the trouble to correct, restrain, and punish, if need be.

Many came into our family from year to year who required to be taught the simplest rudiments of religious knowledge, for they were as destitute of any right views of God, and of his claims on their hearts, as if they had been born in the jungles of India, or amid the deserts of Africa. It was our incessant study, and particularly that of my husband, to present the Scriptures in such a manner as to attract their attention and, without fatiguing, interest their minds. All Mr. Tevis's teaching was directed to this one great purpose. History and science, all the daily changes and trials of life, were rendered subservient; and, above all and over all, was continually recognized the hand of God, their Creator, whose eye was ever upon them, observing their conduct, and desirous, above all things, that his erring children should return to him and receive the sweet assurance of his forgiveness through Jesus Christ. The law of God was made the rule of daily life; his Word the standard by which every act, motive, and principle was judged; and his favor and approbation the highest good. When the mind has no employment, the affections are apt to be dormant; when the head is vacant the heart is often cold. Many, when first brought under the restraints of a school, regard it as decided tyranny to require their regular attendance at Church and Sunday-school; and often an imaginary headache, gotten up for the occasion, has kept a girl at home, when her bonnet, cloak, or some other trifling accompaniment was not in keeping with her wishes. They had been accustomed to do what seemed good in their own eyes. Yet, under all these disadvantages, combined with the early neglect of literary culture, I found scores of quick and ready scholars, with retentive memories, and minds ready for the acquisition of religious as well as literary knowledge.

A teacher should never make a requisition that can not be enforced. To threaten a punishment, and then contrive in some indirect way to abate its vigor, destroys its good effect. The most noble character may be marred by a too yielding habit in matters of conscience; a want of moral courage is injurious, not only to ourselves, but to all under our authority. Induct into the mind the solemn fact that martyrdom in the cause of truth and uprightness deserves our envy rather than our pity.

Chapter XXXII.

OUR second son, with his bright, wide-open eyes, by the time he had attained the wise age of four years, became so perfectly acquainted with the topography of his home and its immediate surroundings that there was no *terra incognita*, no mystery in or about the establishment, that he had not solved—save one; and that was a cistern without a pump, and with only a trap-door through which the water might be drawn up. It was near the laundry, and on forbidden ground to children. He had, time and again, watched the old washerwoman drawing water from it, but was never near enough to examine it. His nurse scarcely ever lost sight of him long enough to give him time for exploration; but it so happened, one day, that he slipped quietly away to the forbidden spot, and, finding the old woman's back turned, stepped noiselessly along, and in his haste to peep down plunged in head-foremost. A splash, and then the fall of the trap-door—no scream, nor any other noise; but the old woman knew instinctively that the curious child was in the cistern, which contained about ten feet of water! She raised a cry of terror as she tore off the loose planks and shouted for a ladder. The only one on the place was at the stable, some distance off. A servant-man went for it.

Meantime my mother reached the cistern, caught the child's eye, which was soon fixed steadily upon that dear familiar face with a mute appeal for help. He had sunk once and risen to the surface,—his blue woolen slip and trowsers were strong and not easily saturated with water, and his upper garment, floating, helped to bear him up.

"Keep your hands down, son; paddle, paddle—hands under water—that's a brave boy! Swim, swim! the ducks swim."

Her voice trembled—he was sinking.

"Come, Joe; come quick! Put down the ladder."

In his trepidation he struck the child. Down—down he went; up again instantly, and was caught by the strong arm of the man just as he was about to disappear. In a minute more the drowning child was in the arms of his grandmother, but totally unconscious.

To rub and roll him in warm blankets was the work of a few minutes, and soon he quietly slept, with renewed life and restored sensation.

"Why, Bob," said his grandfather, who was watching his returning consciousness, "what did you do in the cistern?'

"O danfather, I thus fum like a duck," was his reply.

A hearty laugh from the old gentleman was the finale to this disaster.

From that good hour we eschewed cisterns without pumps.

About this time, in the year 1832, a little orphan girl was placed under my care; and she came like a gleam of light across the the shadow of memory to fill in some measure the void in our hearts made by the death of our precious little daughter, though we did not forget "our buried one that calmly rested under the daisies;" and I often felt, even in my happiest hours, an intense yearning for that spirit-land where she had gone in all the freshness of her budding loveliness,—that happy place where all is bright and glorious.

This dear little pet of the household became to me a daughter, and to my children a sister. There was something about the child, left so young to the guardianship of strangers, that awakened sympathy; and she soon became not only an object of interest, but securely nestled in our warmest affections. Her name, too, was Mary—a name that never failed to produce a thrill of tender emotion. Her face was very fair, with soft, ruby lips, and cheeks warm with Summer flushes; but her blue eyes were sad looking—not a painful, but a timid, sadness, that lay like a veil over their brightness. After she began to feel at home among us this vanished, and we found her a merry-hearted, gleesome child, with every motion full of dancing, rippling light. And yet she manifested an uncommon degree of pertinacity in whatever she desired to have or do, her self-will being unusually deep-rooted; but as I had determined from the first to rear her as if she were my own child, and had adopted her from the purest motives of affection, I corrected, reproved, and punished every fault. My disciplinary admonitions, under God's blessing, turned into the proper channel energies that formed a very lovely character.

I realized then that the first great lesson to be taught children is submission and obedience, as introductory to every good in this world and the world to come. A stern sense of duty to my own children made me feel the weighty trust and responsibility in regard to others.

If children be subjected to school discipline at too early an age, and forced to the irksome task of committing to memory what a childish mind can not comprehend, they may become thoroughly disgusted with all books, including even those fairy tales, adventures, and travels which are as much the proper food for little folks

as the higher works of literature are for advanced scholars; and they may never be awakened to the necessity
of fitting themselves for a life of usefulness and the enjoyment of a cultivated mind. If they sleep away their
childhood over unsuitable books, they will sleep away their
youth over the same when the proper time for studying
them has come; and besides, having never had the opportunity nor the encouragement to exhaust the glorious
fields of ·choice juvenile romance, they have still the
ungratified yearnings of children, and will be apt to
plunge indiscriminately into the sea of popular fiction.

Happily, there is now a growing conviction that every
thing should come in its order: first, perception; then,
fancy; next, memory, and, lastly, reason. Let children
be children, not philosophers, and then they will make
men, and not mere walking pedants. Those nursery
tales and juvenile story-books, so congenial to the taste
of pure childish fancy, ought not to be rejected entirely;
for even the fleeting images produced by the jumbling of
"Mother Goose's Melodies" will nourish the imagination,
as well as quicken the perception. The childish eye may
be taught to glance from heaven to earth, and from earth
to heaven, as in fancy it follows "The old woman sweeping the sky," "The cow jumping over the moon," and
"The man into the barberry-bush," before the mind is
sufficiently matured to tax the memory much.

It is the boast of our day that the child is familiar
with the results of a life-time of philosophical investiga-
tion. Every thing is simplified. Astronomy, Chemistry,
Geology, Mental and Moral Science, are all taught in
nice little primers. A conceit of knowledge is thus gen-
erated, where, in fact, the outlines and elements are not
even mastered.

I have had girls of scarce sixteen Summers enter my school, having gone through the whole circle of the sciences, and exhausted every branch of literature, ready to receive the last polish of society, and yet they could not read intelligibly, write a legible hand, nor compose a page grammatically—some could not even spell the commonest words in our language—did not know the four points of the compass, nor could they name the capitals of the States; were deficient in the elementary principles of mathematics, though they had gone through Algebra and Geometry. The excuse for entire deficiency in Arithmetic has generally been, "Oh, I have not had time; my brothers will teach me to cipher when I go home." And yet these same girls had, for years perhaps, been confined in school from six to eight hours a day; at night carrying home a number of scientific works of which they scarce knew the author's name,—thus spending what should have been the merriest, happiest, and most profitable part of their lives in attempting impossibilities, and acquiring a distaste for learning,

The minds of children should not be left unimproved. Much can and must be taught them before they enter the school-room. The judicious system pursued by the ancient Persians showed that they well understood the intimate connection between training and character, though they were heathens, and unacquainted with the injunctions of Divine Revelation upon that subject. They inculcated moral principle almost from the cradle, and enforced gymnastic exercises for the purpose of strengthening the body and preparing it as a suitable habitation for an enlarged and enlightened mind. They had no books, but the open volume of Nature was before them; and practically they were, according to Xenophon, models of virtue and morality, and physically superior to all the surrounding nations until ruined by the effeminate luxury of the Medians.

The Athenians commenced a verbal course of teaching their own language as soon as reason dawned; and thus the whole population of Athens, from the meanest beggar to the most elevated statesman, pronounced and spoke their beautiful vernacular with such correctness that even a market-woman could distinguish a foreigner from a citizen of Athens by his shibboleth, or the peculiar pronunciation of his vowels.

How often do we find parents sending their children to indifferent teachers, where they con over a few lessons in any fashion they may choose, provided they do not disturb the high dignitary who calls them together daily in a heterogeneous mass, to spend hour after hour acquiring idle habits and perverting their best faculties. This is done in some instances to save the trouble of parental instruction, and in others to save expense, which must be incurred in the end by keeping them longer at school. It is not an uncommon thing to find children thus acquiring ruinous intellectual habits, and so utterly gone astray in the simplest elementary principles, that it would take a life-time to undo these perversions; and yet the parents are astonished that their children do not come forth from a "finishing-school" models of elegance, erudition, and accomplishment.

Again, because the education of females was formerly so totally neglected, many are anxious, under the new *régime*, to have them learn every thing without regard to the sphere they are to occupy in life. They would crowd into a few years as much learning as filled the brain of Socrates or Plato, and would have them so excellent in a thousand unnecessary things, as to lead to an entire loss of every thing useful and practical.

Another evil, not less than those alluded to, is the frensy for external accomplishments. Often our best literary institutions are rejected and the most fashionable schools chosen, where girls may be taught to carry off the prize for music or dancing, and to enter and leave a drawing-room gracefully, as if life were to consist of one universal holiday. And, oh, painful to tell, many Christian parents think they can not do justice to their daughters unless they give them an opportunity of acquiring that gracefulness of carriage from a dancing-master, which the pious mother or the religious teacher is not thought capable of imparting. Would any rational Christian suppose that dancing, or learning to shuffle the feet *a la mode*, is requisite for an introduction into heaven—the final destiny hoped for our daughters?

To so great an extent was this infatuation carried a few years ago in one of our largest Western cities, that some, who held their heads as high as wealth and pride could raise them, laid aside all early prejudices and countenanced that equality truly shocking to a sense of propriety, by having their daughters instructed in this so-called graceful and elegant accomplishment by a *negro man*—a lineal descendant of Ham, and once a slave—and this was done in a slave State. Query: Might not one polished enough to educate our sons and daughters for the ball-room be allowed an opportunity of sufficient mental culture to raise him to the standard of a rational Christian?

I would not be supposed to be maintaining a war against all elegant, external accomplishments, for certainly Christianity would be no gainer by rendering her

disciples dull and unattractive. Religion, woman's diadem of beauty, does not forbid the acquisition of that
which is truly agreeable and justly admirable,—awarding
to these, however, their proper place, and esteeming the
art of pleasing just in proportion to its value,—never
suffering it to exclude the higher and more useful attainments. Accomplishments should be cultivated to amuse
leisure, not to engross life. The injudicious practice of
endeavoring to originate talents where they do not exist
by nature can not be too much discouraged. Education
only develops the latent powers of the mind and disci-
plines its native forces; hence the truth of the assertion
that where too much is attempted it has the unhappy
tendency of weakening the powers of the mind by drawing
off its strength into too great a variety of channels; and
I well know that the crowding of a multiplicity of employments into the few years allotted to girls for the
acquirement of a good education rather creates a thirst
for novelty than for knowledge; it is in reality promoting
ignorance. Every body acknowledges the fact that the
human mind is so constituted as to be enabled to attend
to but one thing at a time successfully; and if the day
be cut up into many separate portions it can not profit-
ably be employed. It requires close and constant application for years to secure a sufficient amount of the
current gold of literature, in addition to the regular
foundation training, to prepare a young lady to be useful as well as ornamental in society. No railway has
ever been constructed, no locomotive invented, by which
the student can be saved the labor of thinking or acting
for herself. The burden of application can not be taken
from her shoulders and stowed away in the baggage-car.

With singular inconsistency a girl's educational course

is mapped out to be completed before the age of seventeen or eighteen; and she leaves school at the very time
when she is best prepared for the acquirement of solid
learning, after which, instead of remaining at home three
or four years to obtain a knowledge of those domestic employments which are calculated to keep up a sense
of that mutual dependence which binds fond and loving families together, she dashes into society indiscriminately banishing all such employments as fit woman for
the sphere she must occupy. What becomes of the
time she intended to devote to a more general reading
of history, biography, and travels? When is she to learn
to sew and knit, to brew and bake? all of which are necessary to fit her for a good housekeeper, an excellent
wife, and a mother competent to the task of instructing
her children in early life.

Boys, on the contrary, spend four, five, or six years at
school, learning the sing-song inflections of Latin nouns
and verbs, poring over Greek grammars and construing
Virgil and Homer, after which comes a college course,
and then years devoted to the study of a profession.
This is all right, and nobody complains of their wasting
time in academic halls; whatever else the world does
or leaves undone, it seems a fixed fact that the controlling influence of custom will have it just so; and is this
past remedy?

And here again I may be charged with repeating what
is in every body's mouth, undeniable things known to be
as true as that two and two make four; but my reader
must bear with me, recollecting how much the subject of
education has been handled; remembering, also, that
though there is nothing new under the sun to be said
upon this matter, yet there is a necessity that it should

be repeated and held up to view, to impress the world with the importance of brightening, as much as possible, the destiny of woman; and so thoroughly is woman's elevation interwoven with every fiber of my heart that I wish to leave a testimony in this book to be read by many when my voice shall no longer be heard in the school-room.

We see and lament the defective course pursued in the present age with regard to the cultivation of the heart and the formation of the mind—especially, in our own country, where people are so busily striving to accumulate wealth. True, much has been done, and more said, and much is still being done to remedy this evil. Doubtless we shall eventually succeed, with God's blessing, in "bringing forth the top-stone with shouting."

The progress of human knowledge is slow; and, like the uprising sun, though we may watch it ever so intently, we can not see that it moves; yet, after the lapse of time, we know by comparison that it has progressed. Hence I would admonish my co-laborers in the noble work of teaching not to be discouraged. Having put our hands to the plow we must keep steadily onward, root out early prejudices, and prepare the ground for the reception of that good seed which shall strike downwards and spring up to eternal life. Lessons early imparted and daily interwoven by practice and habit become second nature, and thus perform the office of lawgiver in maturer years.

I would advert to the long-contested question whether private instruction or boarding-schools ought to be preferred. Many wealthy families provide governesses for their daughters, not only because they wish to keep them at home, but with the expectation that they will be more

25

thoroughly educated. I would not presume to dictate, though I may advise, and yet I hardly think it necessary to argue the advantages and disadvantages of private instruction, as few in our own country are able to educate their children at home; nor do I think it desirable. I have it in my power to answer some of the objections made against large schools. It has been frequently said that children are exposed to the danger of having their morals corrupted in a boarding-school by improper associations. This is not the case in a well-regulated and properly disciplined school. In fact, much depends upon the natural disposition of children, or I should rather say upon their previous training and the care bestowed upon them before they leave the parental roof. Children frequently hear and see things *at home* of which they ought to be ignorant during their whole lives. Thus evil becomes incorporated in their nature, and it is not uncommon that, from neglect of proper instruction at home, they become vicious before knowing what vice is. Often breathing nothing but luxury and pleasure, living in almost total indolence, and daily acquiring bad habits, they become disorderly and irregular in their conduct, and carry evil influences along with them into school, instead of receiving them there. On the contrary, in a good school, under the strict supervision of competent teachers these selfish habits and irregularities may be greatly subdued and sometimes eradicated.

The second objection offered by some is, that their advancement is not so rapid, and much more superficial than when a teacher has one or a few to instruct, and each one of these attended to individually. But this has been disproved by the experience of many. I have tried both plans, and am prepared to speak confidently on the

subject. The worth of an institution of learning does
not depend altogether upon the amount of information
which patient teachers may, in a few years, pour into
empty heads; but rather upon the proportions which the
intellectual nature may acquire by the thoroughness of
discipline to which it is subjected, and the bearing of
such an education upon practical life. The chief object
of a collegiate or academical course is *discipline*.

Under private instruction, children are also without
that emulation, which, when properly excited, is one of
the greatest advantages of large schools. This emulation
is wanting where the pupil is not stimulated by being
classed, and has no one with whom she can compare herself; she either becomes dull, languid, and dejected, rusts
in a manner, or else falls into an opposite extreme, grows
conceited, and values her attainments more highly than
she ought. Besides the ardor, which a noble emulation
well managed gives to young minds, such institutions
afford ample room for the exercise of the greatest virtues,
and lead to the most arduous undertakings in the path of
learning. The pupils also form acquaintances and cultivate friendships which often last as long as life itself.
Some of these associations are of the best kind and have
a happy influence on their future destiny.

Another advantage is, that a child profits, not only by
the instruction given to her, but by that imparted to
others. She meets also with such models in her companions as she flatters herself with the hope of one day
equaling, if not excelling. This gives a new impulse to
the powers of mind and heart, and awakens some latent
faculty which might otherwise have remained forever
dormant.

One unfortunate practice, which greatly prevails in

our country, is that of frequently changing schools. It is utterly impossible for a young lady to be any thing like well educated under such circumstances. As well might we expect a rolling stone to gather moss, or a sieve to be filled with water. No matter if each successive school have equal advantages; each has its own peculiar rules, regulations, and prescribed method, and every teacher who possesses any tact in communicating has her own course marked out; hence every change throws the pupil back, like the snail that climbed five feet up the wall in a day and fell back three at night.

Last, but not least, I refer to the importance of teaching girls the religious use of time,—the duty of consecrating to God every talent, every faculty, every possession. They can not be too particularly guarded against idleness and a slovenly habit of wasting time. Let them be accustomed to pass from serious business to animated recreations, and be preserved from those long and torpid intervals between both—that inanimate drowsiness which wears out so great a portion of life in both young and old. Activity is necessary to virtue, and indispensable to happiness.

We are all aware of the influence woman has exercised over the destinies of the world, from Mother Eve down to the present time; and when we consider the variety of mischief which an ill-directed influence has been known to produce, we are led to reflect with the most sanguine hopes upon the beneficial effects to be expected from the same powerful force when exerted in its true direction. It is a fact that the state of civilized soicety depends much upon the prevailing sentiments and habits of woman, and upon the nature and degree of estimation in which she is held. Many readily admit the power of female elegance and refinement upon the manners of men, yet do not always attend to the influence of female principles upon their characters.

Reflections like these should suggest the necessity of neglecting nothing in the formation of morals, mind, or manners, that might tend to purify, strengthen, and adorn the characters of our daughters,—that not only they, but the world into which they are thrown, shall have reason to arise and call them blessed; and that in the great day of general account every Christian parent may be enabled through divine favor to say, with humble confidence, to our Maker and Redeemer, "Behold the daughters thou hast given me." Let us well remember that this is a dignified work in which we are engaged, a high and holy calling,—no less than that of "preserving the Ark of the Lord." Let mothers begin the great work upon the minds of their daughters in infancy, and root out with a strong hand vanity, selfishness, obstinacy, and every other hydra-headed monster, which may show itself in the secret and complicated workings of the human heart.

Young persons should be taught to distrust their own judgment, and never murmur at expostulation. They should be accustomed to expect opposition, and learn to endure it; for this is a lesson which the world will not fail to furnish, and they will practice it the better for having learned it early. A submissive temper and forbearing spirit should be particularly inculcated, which must be practiced, not on the low ground of its being decorous, feminine, pleasing, and calculated to attract human favor, but on the high principle of obedience to Christ, and on the practical ground of laboring after conformity to Him who has said, "Learn of me, for I am meek and lowly in heart," and who has graciously prom-

ised that the reward shall accompany the practice, by
encouragingly adding, "And ye shall find rest for your
souls."

Of all the troubles of education, none are to be compared to that of bringing up a child that lacks sensibility.
Lively and sensitive dispositions are capable of great
wanderings. Passion and presumption lead them on, but
they have great resources, and often return from error.
Instruction is in them a hidden germ, which sometimes,
when experience comes to the assistance of reason, and
when passion is cool, blooms and bears fruit, especially
if the teacher can render them attentive and awaken their
curiosity; whereas you can have little influence upon one
of those passive minds, one whose thoughts are never
where they ought to be. Neither reproof nor correction
can move them; they hear all, but feel nothing.

Indolence renders a child negligent and disgusted with
every thing she does; and the best education runs the
risk of being thrown away if we do not hasten to check
the evil at an early period. Many teachers suppose that
every thing depends on education in forming the mind,
and that nature has nothing to do with it; while the fact
is, there are some dispositions which resemble an ungrateful soil for which culture does but little. These trouble-
some characters should neither be crossed, neglected, nor
ill-regulated in the commencement. Endeavor to discover
if the temper you have to govern be wanting in curiosity,
and if it be insensible to honest emulation. In this case
it will be necessary to stir up all the resources of the soul
to overcome the lethargy. Do not at first press a formal
course of instruction. Take great care not to overcharge
the memory; do not fatigue by restraining rules, but
enforce instruction according to the occasion, by little and

little, as it may be required, and according to the capacity of the mind to be instructed. By patience and perseverance that may be accomplished which might at first seem an impossibility, and the most ungrateful soil may be made to bring forth fruit.

Some of my readers may feel disposed to complain of my repeated comments upon the necessity of the early training of girls. But can we hope to accomplish the end we have in view, to regulate the temporal and spiritual interests of the sex, without keeping this subject constantly before us and showing it up in the strongest light? What is the world but an assemblage of families? and who can regulate these families with a more exact care than women who possess the advantages of a suitable education? No one can describe the influence of a female who, to an excellent heart and a cultivated mind, joins a soul superior to the frowns of fortune or the temptations of the world, and who is calculated for all the duties she owes to God, her neighbor, and herself. Diligent and religious, she is the soul of her family. She is gentle, forbearing, and full of that sweet benevolence which, forgetful of itself, respects the feelings and interests of others.

> "A woman, loveliest of the lovely kind,
> In body perfect, and complete in mind."

If education be a school to fit us for life, and life a school to prepare us for eternity, too much care can not be taken to begin and continue upon that system most likely to effect the desired end. I have frequently reverted to the subject of religious culture, but would, if possible, enforce it more strongly. Many well-meaning persons have deprecated the practice of instilling religious knowledge into the minds of children, under the pretense that it is important to the cause of truth that the mind should be kept free from prepossessions, and that every one should be left to form such opinions on religious subjects as may seem best to his own reason in maturer years; but this is to deny the truth of Christianity, if not effectually to destroy it under the plausible excuse of free agency.

We should be careful, it is true, that the religion we teach should be the religion of the Bible, and not the inventions of human error and superstition; and that what we attempt to infuse into others should be the result of close scrutiny, and not the offerings of credulity and bigotry. There are certain leading and fundamental truths, certain sentiments on the side of Christianity as well as of virtue and benevolence, in favor of which every child ought to be prepossessed. We need not fear that the young mind will have too much light on the subject of what is right and true; and I might add that to keep the mind void of all prepossessions on any or every subject is a vain and impracticable attempt, the very suggestion of which argues ignorance of human nature. We must sow good seed in the heart, or the devil will sow tares, and that so abundantly as to render the soil difficult of cultivation for good. Our Savior has said, "Suffer little children to come unto me;" thus we should begin, continue, and end with Christianity. Shall so much time be spent in the acquisition of physical and intellectual advantages, and none, comparatively speaking, for eternity? Do young ladies, become musicians, linguists, and mathematicians by early study, and shall they become Christians by accident? Oh, fatal mistake! Shall all these accomplishments, which perish in the using, be so assiduously, so systematically taught, and shall the knowledge which is to make them wise unto salvation be picked up at random? Shall that knowledge, which parents are required in the Scriptures to teach their children diligently, commanded to talk of when they sit in their houses and when they walk by the way, when they lie down and when they rise up, be omitted, deferred, or slightly taught, or superseded by things of comparatively little value? Away with such a soul-destroying doctrine from the earth! No; let us have the Bible for our text-book on all occasions; for if that be the purest eloquence which most persuades, and which comes home to the heart with the fullest evidence and the most irresistible force, then no eloquence is so powerful as that of the Bible.

Intelligent Christian teachers will be instructed by the Bible itself how to communicate its truths with life and spirit; while they are musing the fire will burn,—that fire that will preserve them from an insipid, dull, or freezing mode of instruction. It has been falsely asserted that the Bible is too intricate to be presented in its own native form, that it puzzles and bewilders the youthful understanding. In all needful and indispensable points of knowledge the Bible is as clear as the noonday sun. The darkness of Scripture is but a partial darkness, like that of Egypt benighting only the enemies of God, while his children are left in the clear daylight. What then? banish the Bible from our schools? God in mercy forbid! Rather let it be the *vade mecum* of every school-girl. It is the only pure fountain of morality and true religion, and should be our principal reference-book throughout the journey of life. Without this chart and compass, the *ignis fatuus* of worldly learning would lead to inevitable shipwreck.

Woman was first in the transgression, and how lovely

and acceptable in the sight of God that she should be the first to return to him. The most distinguished women the world has ever known have been eminent for their piety. It is piety that brightens every charm, and gives grace and glory to the unfading coronet that crowns the intellectual brow. 'T is true we read of some flashing meteors among heathen women, and in later ages of some who rejected the Bible as their counsel; but they soon disappeared amid the darkness of their own vices, and their names serve only to blot the pages of history. Our hearts sicken to know that such ever existed. In vain may we expect to find good fruits amid the impure exhalations of an unhealthy soil, or suppose that virtue may be produced from a ground that has been exhausted by repeated crops of vice. Some good and pious people, most unfortunately for their children, consider them as possessing a kind of hereditary claim to perfection, and suppose the necessity of culture to be superseded by the parent plant. This is a fatal mistake. Children inherit nothing so much as a propensity to sin,—all else must be taught them. The mines of Golconda were of little worth to the owner without being wrought.

Education—female education! Who will not say, God speed this glorious cause? Yea, with heart and hand, let us unite in promoting its advancement.

Chapter XXXIII.

A s I write, the vision of a Lancastrian school which I attended long, long ago in Georgetown, District of Columbia, rises up before me—one of the most pleasant reminiscences of my life. This excellent system of mutual instruction was introduced into England by the good old Quaker, Joseph Lancaster, in 1803, and thence into the United States about the year 1814. It was a vast improvement upon the old style of forcing wayward children into a proper appreciation of school privileges. I have often wondered why these institutions did not become more popular, and take deeper root in our country, where a rapid and general diffusion of knowledge is so desirable. Our common-school system is, doubtless, a modification of the original plan, and may be an improvement when properly conducted, but my own experience of the rapid progress made in the elementary branches, especially in reading, writing, and arithmetic, the arts by which the sciences are to be acquired, has left a vivid impression on my mind. The general good order, strict discipline, and beautiful arrangement of that school, the judicious appointment of well-qualified teachers, who selected efficient and faithful monitors, brought forth results fully demonstrating the practical value and thoroughness of the instruction given.

The Female Department was a spacious room with lateral aisles, along which were arranged in regular succession a number of semicircular recitation forms. Long rows of desks occupied the center of the room. The classes were seated at these in regular gradation, the younger ones being nearest the teacher's desk, which was upon a raised platform at one end of the room, very much resembling the pulpits of our modern churches. Here our Minerva stood armed with her magic wand, swaying the multitude before her. From six to eight classes, besides the one taught by the principal, were reciting at the same time to monitors with but little noise and no confusion. These in regular routine came once during the day under the examination of the principal. The words, "attention! look!" and "listen!" were never heard except through the silver tones of her little bell. During the time of my sojourn in this school a lovely Quakeress presided—a woman of commanding presence, and a genuine, conscientious teacher of great experience. She was an ornament to her sex, and a model worthy to be known and studied. Her very appearance was so prepossessing that you loved her almost as soon as you looked upon her. She wore the full Quaker costume, with all its minutest proprieties—her beautiful brown hair closely braided on her calm forehead, that snowy Friends' cap, which never loses its form even under a close bonnet, a pure white muslin handkerchief crossed over her bosom in the exactest folds; a dove-colored silk shawl, just large enough to reach to her elbows, pinned on each side. She wore no ornaments of any kind, her handkerchief being confined at the throat by the daintiest of common pins; no little point was overlooked or omitted upon which the propriety of the whole depended; no *something* was added, though a mere nothing in itself or in the eyes of others, that might mar the whole.

Miss Margaret Judge had that decided expression of

countenance that indicated a clear head, strong good sense and great firmness of character. A quiet, self-possessed demeanor, resulting from integrity of purpose that goes at once to the point without circumlocution, amounted almost to severity, was yet tempered by the tenderest and truest of female hearts. I never heard her laugh but her sweet face smiled all over with the illumination of a sanctified soul, and often brightened into an intensity that bespoke an intellect highly cultivated and beautifully refined. We loved her with all the reverence of profound respect, mingled with the devotion of young enthusiastic hearts. I have seen more than three hundred children decorous and quiet under the influence of her mild yet firm government. So habitual was her precision of mind and action, that whatever she did was done by rule. Her motto was, "Whatever is worth doing at all is worth doing well." Though on the verge of forty, she was handsome, with a face as smooth as that of a child, resulting from the quiet tenor of a life spent in the cultivation of the affections and free from the touch of its anxieties. Hers was a sympathetic character, full of energy and glowing with enthusiasm for the beautiful, the true, and the good; eminently adapted to the position she occupied in this admirable school, which aspired to no more than could be well done from the A B C scholar, who formed letters in the clear white sand, until perfectly familiar with these foundation principles, onward through the most rigid course of intellectual training.

The Lancastrian schools occupied neutral ground, and struck bravely for the cardinal principles of a liberal education—exact scholarship in the elementary branches. The rapidity with which the children learned to write and the elegant penmanship of the higher classes were remarkable. I learned to write there so beautifully that a silver pen and pencil, the first I ever saw, was awarded me as a premium, and I have been a ready writer ever since.

No 'ologies were forced upon us in the transition state of the growing mind; none of that hot-house system so greatly to be deprecated, and so fatal to the acquirement of real knowledge. The plain old Quaker, Joseph Lancaster, knew that there must be time for mental as well as physical development. Minds were suffered to expand into their full stature and native proportions. Good and faithful teachers will not try to *grow* minds, but *let* them grow as rapidly as nature will permit. The citizens of Georgetown liberally patronized this school—even the most aristocratic—feeling that not only the improvement of their own children, but the general interests of the whole community were involved in it; they did not reject it, though a free school; and thought it not derogatory to enroll their boys and girls among its numbers. We had monthly examinations, at which time the large folding-doors were thrown open, giving a full view of the Male Department, over which presided a thoroughly well-bred Englishman of dignified manners and profound erudition. Mr. Old was a man who left his impress upon the hearts and minds of his pupils.

What a privilege we girls considered it to visit his school-room on Saturdays, and listen to his description of England's rural scenery, dotted with ancient cathedrals and ruined castles, whose intricate passages went rambling about in such strange fashion, and from whose turrets crept many a thrilling story of the Middle Ages. We helped to stitch his pamphlet copy-books, ruled the

lines and dusted his library; and then came the reward of
our industry from his well-stored memory. I remember
how I used to fancy him a disguised nobleman, and that
by and by would come the *finale* of my own romance,
by his marrying Miss Judge, whom really he seldom saw
and never conversed with except on school matters.

One of the sweetest personifications of girlhood I
ever knew was a sister of Miss Judge, a little maiden
just entering her fourteenth year, and to whom I was
very much attached. Though completely hedged in by
that peculiarity of dress belonging to the sect of her
fathers, and not permitted to vary her garb with every
phase of fashion, she had a certain modified style about
her, chastened always by parental authority, that rendered her appearance very pleasing. Thus Susanna, in
her light dove-colored dress and a bonnet as plain as her
grandmother's in fashion and color, looked really elegant
and attractive. The "dew of youth" was upon her
beautiful face, and her dark hair fell in a mass of glossy
curls almost to her waist when not confined by cap or
bonnet. No wonder that an occasional glance in her
tiny hand-mirror gave rise to the coquettish desire to be
seen and admired. No wonder that she sometimes
made a display when from under her mother's eye,
which raised the admonishing finger of "Sister Margaret." "Take care, Susanna, thee must not cherish
vain thoughts! bind up thy hair, and keep on thy cap;
cast away that pride of heart so unbecoming in a young
maiden!" And, again, "Susanna, I must inform father
if thee will display thy curls, and they will be cut off."

It is a common thing to deride school-girl friendships,
and to compare them to the morning dew; but there are
some that outlive time and circumstances and, like the

last roses of Summer, shed a fragrance over life's dreariest hours. There was a chord in Susanna's heart which vibrated in unison with my own; we sat together on the same form, read together from the same interesting book at play-time; walked arm in arm from school that we might linger over an interesting conversation. Scott's novels were just then being rapidly issued from the press and were exciting an intense interest in the reading world. We were both fond of reading, and were often hid away between school-hours, and so deeply absorbed in one of these historical novels that we caught many a reprimand for being tardy.

Good and religious persons condemned Scott's novels too severely; they certainly have the merit of producing a purer taste among romance readers, and yet danger does lurk among the folded leaves of the best written novels—cultivating, as they do, a taste for fiction rather than fact. Our people read, and read a great deal, and it is a pity that the press should teem with multiplied thousands of trashy books; yet perhaps no other country can present a population of more general intelligence or one better informed. Knowledge is distributed over every community with the undistinguishing profusion of the breath of heaven.

> "Her handmaid Art now all our wilds explores,
> Traces our waves and cultures all our shores."

The sources of this mental cultivation may be found in the munificent public provision for schools, and in the cheapness and multiplication of useful books; yet we have comparatively few men of eminent learning and profound erudition; it takes time, wealth, and leisure to produce such.

Sometime during the year 1830, a little negro girl

was introduced into our family, and became an interesting study to those who watched the development of her mental faculties. She was dwarfish and deformed, but showed a brilliancy of intellect worth remembering, an illustration of the truth that the colored race is capable of improvement. The girl was not more than eight or nine years old, and just high enough to reach the dining table conveniently. Her right shoulder protruded considerably, and as she grew older continued to enlarge more rapidly than any other part of her body. Her head was large but perfectly symmetrical and covered with an abundant quantity of real wool, eyes clear and full of vivacity, nostrils large and sensitive, lips thick; but she articulated more distinctly than white children of her age generally. Of unmixed African descent, she was a real negro, though born in the United States, and showed their usual love of finery by decorating her fingers with rings and making as great a display of colors in her dress as a South Sea Islander. This taste, however, vanished by degrees as her mind was improved, and her opportunities for observation developed a feminine tact for congruity and appropriateness.

Engaged in a round of occupations that admitted of little leisure, I scarcely noticed the rapidity with which our little ebony dwarf learned any and every thing. Her spelling, at first, was entirely phonetic, yet she soon learned to read understandingly, and seemed to drink in knowledge through every surrounding medium. Listening and learning whilst others taught, she acquired the habit of expressing herself in good language and soon learned to write neatly and intelligibly.

After the lapse of a year or two, music was added to her other accomplishments. She played many sweet and

26

touching pieces on the piano, the keys of which she could just conveniently manage when standing, and over which she had the most perfect control, her long, flexible fingers looking as if made for the purpose. Her voice, like that of all the best singers of her race, was plaintive, low, and sweet.

She played altogether by ear, her musical taste being too exquisite and natural to be subjected to the apprenticeship of the instruction book. The ordinary drilling was so entirely distasteful to her that the girls who from time to time tried to teach her to read music gave it up in despair.

She never seemed to make a false note, but struck at once the right chord of the tune she had heard, as if by intuition. The sound of musical instruments in full orchestra made her frantic with joy. After ascertaining this fact, I always gave her an opportunity of attending concerts or musical entertainments of any kind. She brought back every piece at the ends of her fingers. Her soul, like a harp, possessed capabilities for plaintive, joyous, or solemn music; but when her fingers swept the chords of the piano, or touched the guitar, she usually brought forth those wild and plaintive strains so congenial to her race.

Ritta's memory was remarkable for capacity and for tenacity as well. The transparency with which her earliest recollections lay mirrored in her mind rendered it a shifting panorama of amusing pictures. Her woven mysteries reminded one of Scheherizade, her stories were more than a "thousand and one," yet were her wondering and admiring auditors never wearied by tediousness nor palled by monotony. She possessed in an eminent degree that variety which is the spice of life.

Her conversation, even before she had reached her teens, differed so much from that of her fellow servants and the colored people generally, that they found fault with her as being not one of them, though she tried her best not to excite their jealousy; and often after she had grown older and more thoughtful she vainly endeavored to imitate their manner of talking.

She became decidedly religious, a Methodist after the strictest sect, though she never gave up her love of fiction, and her disposition to devour, stealthily, marvelous tales and romances. Yet as her judgment matured, she grew more reticent, and combined with her general reading history and religious biography.

At the age of thirty we desired to send her to Liberia, feeling assured that she would make a competent teacher, and be very useful in that colony. She positively refused to go. "I do not know," said she "how long I shall be able to take care of myself, and I am not willing to become a stranger in a strange land." She sometimes thought she would like to be free, but refused to accept her freedom upon the condition of leaving us.

Her last illness, though lingering and painful, was marked by patient resignation, and by that pure intelligent faith expressed in the words of St. Paul, which brings "peace with God through our Lord Jesus Christ, rejoicing in hope of the glory of God."

The case recorded is by no means an exceptional one. I have known many others, though not so remarkable, that might be adduced to prove the fallacy of the assertion often made, even by intelligent people, that the negro race has no capacity for improvement.

CHAPTER XXXIV.

SCATTERED all along the years intervening between 1829 and 1836 arise some of the sunniest recollections, as well as some of the saddest that mark the changeful pilgrimage of my teacher-life. Pleasant, indeed, it is to review those busy days crowded with reminiscences; some agreeable, some provoking at the time, but mellowed by the lapse of years, are now a source of amusement.

My time-worn and faded school register presents many cherished names. One group I particularly remember as a happy illustration of what school life ought to be. They had joys and pleasures with which the world meddled not; though no book-worms, they studied well, read much, laughed heartily, and never kept their thoughts baled up until they became stale. What they knew they were willing to impart to others, and, like the little busy bee, improved each shining hour for present pleasure as well as for future usefulness.

Jane C., Amanda M'A., Zerilda S., Anna M., Julia B., and my two little pets, if I ever had any, Polly Monroe and Sarah Dubberly, both of whom entered when quite young, and continued with me until their school education was completed. Among them also conspicuously appeared my sister, Arabella, as the bond and mainspring. There were many others, whom time would fail me to mention, mingling in the bright galaxy which spanned the intervening arch, but these were particularly associated together and remained longer at school than was then customary. The dear and cherished picture of this little circle often rises unbidden before my eyes, and I always feel reluctant to part with it. They emulated each other in works of usefulness, and aimed at excellence in the accomplishment of whatever they undertook. Here arises the question, What is genius according to the common acceptation of the term? Nothing but labor and diligence. The principle of industry, properly inculcated, will radiate in all directions, and illuminate difficulties by that light which duty alone can shed.

These mind-expanding girls deemed the attainment of the objects they had in view a sufficient reward for their application. Often when the recitations of the day were over, they might be seen by twos, threes, or fours, in some quiet spot, talking or comparing notes upon their daily acquisitions. With spirits radiant as the Summer sky, they sought no greater happiness than was found in each other's society; and I venture to affirm that the subjects of their conversation never turned into the ordinary channels, "What shall I eat, what shall I drink, and wherewithal shall I be clothed," and any of them would have been as likely to make the contour of her face, or the color of her eyes an excuse for not attending Church, as the cut of her garments, or the shape of her bonnet. Nor did they give their mutual friendship the weakening expression of silly phrases, but the strengthening one of action. Their friendship was not characterized by that violent intimacy sometimes existing in schools.

How beautiful is that moderate and everlasting love which gives warmth without casting forth sparks, flames straight up without crackling, and is neither subject to conflagrations nor eruptions!

The depth and constancy of pure disinterested friendship is characterized by a noble emulation in the path of duty. No drop of envy mingles with the sparkling bubbles sipped from the cup of knowledge; on the contrary, there is a manifest disposition to lend a helping hand to others traveling the same rugged pathway. Such were these girls, they assisted the younger ones, and scattered flowers in the way of the inexperienced, and practiced the precept, "Whatsoever we possess, becomes doubly valuable when we are so happy as to share it with another."

Amanda's practicability and mathematical cleverness, her dignified, quiet, kind, and cheerful manners, combined with a proper thoughtfulness about every thing, gave her a position of considerable importance in school.

The quaint humor of Zerilda, the sweetness of Jane's poetical effusions, whose inspirations were often checked by her faithful, matter-of-fact, but intelligent and truthful friend, Arabella, strengthened the bond which united these three. Arabella was an indefatigable student, and by her large acquaintance with books possessed a fund of ready knowledge which rendered her an entertaining companion.

Zerilda read history *con amore*, and would select by preference "Rollin," or "Josephus; but she loved occasionally to refresh herself from the "Castalian spring." Upon one occasion I saw her at a distance, apparently quite absorbed in a large book open before her.

"What are you doing, Zerilda?"

"Reading a little *Moore* in *Josephus*, Madam," she smilingly replied, exhibiting a minute copy of Moore's poems, with which for a while she had shut out the dry details of Josephus.

The laughter-loving and agreeable Julia was a ready friend, and her very presence had a kindly influence on her companions; like a sunbeam, she was clear and bright. Her presence "bade dull care begone;" grief and melancholy fled before her, and she stirred up the saddest spirits into a pleasing motion.

After leaving school their paths widely diverged,— some blessed the home circle, others shone in society or became faithful teachers of the young; but whenever a happy circumstance has thrown them together their conversation has been sure to turn upon the gay and tender recollections of Science Hill.

So much of the sunshine of this period and so many pleasant little incidents were connected with the two little girls, Polly Monroe and Sarah Dubberly, that I can not pass them without further notice. They entered school about the same time, and were for years classmates and intimate friends, so that the history of the school life of one is interwoven with that of the other. Sarah was the "Benjamin" of her mother's heart, one of the happiest little creatures in the world, and the light and life of the household. Her little head would probably have been quite turned by the flattering attentions she received had she not been blessed with a judicious mother. The world, with a singular inconsistency, always apologizes for an only child, and especially an only daughter, when spoiled by hurtful indulgences; as if it were not so much the more necessary to endow this center of affection, and it may be the sole prop of devoted parents, with every virtue, and all the excellencies that might have been divided among a numerous family. Though enshrined in the widowed mother's heart as the darling of her old age, Sarah was not the object of idolatrous affection. Mrs.

Dubberly was a practical woman, of large experience and good sense. She knew that mere external advantages could not supply the want of loveliness of character. She nurtured her daughter in this belief, and secured prompt obedience to her wishes and instructions. Thus, when Sarah was old enough to have her school duties interfered with by little visitings and holidays, she was sent to a boarding-school. The little girl was full of love and sunshine, cheerful and obliging, but quick, impulsive, and sometimes out of humor, though "anger never rested in her bosom;" and when in fault she was so easily subdued, so ready to apologize, that it was impossible to continue displeased with her.

Her own mother visited her occasionally during term time; but I do not remember a single instance of her having been kept at home, during the seven years she was at school, to the detriment of her regular school duties.

In comparing the past with the present I can not but remember how perfectly satisfied the girls of twenty and thirty years ago were, though accustomed to every indulgence, with the systematic regularity of our home school, and with their plain but wholesome food. How much less they seemed to covet sweetmeats and sugar-plums! True, then, as now, there were found unthinking mothers who kept their children gorged with confectionery, thus rendering them gourmands, and stupefying the intellect.

The paths of Polly Monroe and Sarah Dubberly ran parallel for many years. Polly was the third daughter of Judge Monroe, of Frankfort. Two sisters had preceded her at school. Thus she was no stranger when she came to us! and though but nine years of age she walked as naturally into the school-room as if she knew her place by intuition, and from that moment she continued to be every body's pleasure, and in nobody's way.

Years have rolled by since I first became acquainted with Judge Monroe's family, bound to them by the strongest ties of affection—my life-long friends and patrons. I must linger awhile over the pleasing scenes so intimately connected with them. Widely known as one of the most delightful families to visit, none ever mingled socially or intimately in the family without cherishing a lively and pleasant recollection of all its members.

Mrs. Monroe was a daughter of Governor Adair, and shared largely in the well-known tact and ability of that family to render themselves useful and agreeable. I found in her a kindred spirit, and we visited each other upon terms of the closest intimacy. All of Governor Adair's daughters were charming women—some of them remarkable for their intellectual attainments, and gifted with fine conversational powers. A clear, strong current of good sense, and a sparkling effervescence, were the distinguishing characteristics of these agreeable women.

From Mrs. Adair and Mrs. Monroe I learned some interesting facts connected with the life of Rev. Valentine Cook—a pioneer Methodist preacher who went forth, like Abraham, at the call of God, "not knowing whither he went,"—one of that noble army of self-sacrificing men who could sing, in spirit and in truth,

> "No foot of land do I possess,
> No cottage in this wilderness."

He literally obeyed the Savior's command, setting forth on his itinerancy without money or scrip, yet never lacking. The Lord provided, and he was a welcome guest in any house that he had once visited as a messenger from heaven. He was eminently fitted for the work

of an itinerant in those days,—possessing an iron frame
which could endure any amount of fatigue, a strength
and freshness of mind which nothing seemed to impair,
and entire devotion to his calling. He preached and
prayed as if a live coal from the altar had just touched his
lips; and though he carried all the energies of his soul
and of his gigantic mind into the pulpit he never de-
claimed; and yet there was the earnestness of inspiration
in his tender, manly face, and a self-forgetting enthusiasm
that carried conviction to the hearts of his hearers. He
is described as having distinctly marked and well-formed
features, forehead broad and full, strong gray eyes, expressive of firmness of character, and a very large mouth,
which when open displayed a full set of fine teeth. Thus
his very appearance introduced him favorably to strangers.

His connection with Governor Adair's family, which
ripened into the strongest friendship, arose from the circumstance of his having been employed as a teacher for
his daughters; and such were the benefits reaped by
them from Mr. Cook's intellectual and religious training
that much of their superiority was attributable to these
advantages, and he was ever spoken of with love and
gratitude by the whole family.

An anecdote related to me by Mrs. Monroe shows
how deeply abstracted he was when rapt in religious
contemplation. A revival was going on at Harrodsburg,
a few miles from the Governor's residence, and crowds
were in attendance from all the surrounding country. It
was beautiful Summer weather, and the moon was at her
full. Mrs. Adair said, one morning:

"Bring some of your friends home with you to-
night, Mr. Cook, and give them a quiet rest. We shall
close the front part of the house, but leave the back

door open, so that you can enter without disturbing us."

It was after midnight when the meeting closed. Mr. Cook and two of his friends walked out from town to the residence of Governor Adair. The moon was gliding on her way through masses of fleecy clouds. He left his friends on the front porch, whilst he went around with a view of entering through the back door to admit them. The friends waited and waited. More than half an hour elapsed, when the ladies above heard the deep rich tones of his clear voice ringing out amid the surrounding silence,—

"In a chariot of fire, my soul mounted higher,
And the moon, it was under my feet."

Presently the awakened ducks and the geese and the whole poultry-yard joined in full chorus. A hand lightly touched his shoulder, and a gentle voice said:

"Why, Mr. Cook, have you forgotten the gentlemen you left in the porch?"

"True, true," he exclaimed, recollecting himself, and, walking hastily into the house with Mrs. Adair, he found the gentlemen already admitted and enjoying a laugh at his expense.

Mr. Cook's faith, like that of Moses, seemed all-prevailing; the sanctified light of the Christian religion which shone into his soul cleared up the dark enigmas of life. His daughter was once sick many miles distant from her home. A courier was dispatched for the father, "Come quickly, your daughter is extremely ill." He started within an hour on horseback, accompanied by his wife—the way was long and tedious. A painful silence was observed for many miles, when Mr. C. said, "Wife, let us get down and pray." The horses were

fastened by the wayside while they went a little way off,
and, kneeling down, prayed fervently with many groans
and tears. As they arose to pursue their journey, he
said, "Our daughter will not die, but live—the Lord
has told me so." They went on their way, and having
reached the end of their journey the mother asked, as she
entered the house, "How is Mary?" "She is improving." And it came to pass that she was soon able to
return home with her parents. God made him a useful
and an honorable man. He fed thousands of souls with
the bread of life, and, like his Divine Master, preached
in the wilderness and solitary places of the earth.

Among all the school-girl friendships I remember
none more striking than that of Mary Ann Dickinson
and Anna Monroe. Mary Ann was a quiet, thoughtful
girl, prepossessing in appearance, with a fair face and a
fine forehead. Sympathetic and cheerful, but never boisterous,—sometimes, indeed, her equanimity of temper
annoyed me—she enjoyed success and endured defeat
with the same composure. Anna was quite the reverse.
Each was perfectly independent in character and sentiment, yet strongly attracted to the other upon first
acquaintance. Their fresh, pure, and unsophisticated
souls were soon knit together like those of Jonathan and
David. Anna's ardent nature, her vivacity, and sometimes too great volubility, led her into difficulties, from
which Mary Ann was ever ready to assist in extricating
her. If Anna leaped at the stars and fastened in the
mud, her friend was prepared to help her out. Theirs
was the true, steadfast love of warm hearts, continued
through the years of girlhood onward to maturer life.

> "Two bright spirits blended
> Like sister flowers of one sweet shade."

We were early risers in those days, and the girls were required to be up as early on Saturday and Sunday mornings as on other days of the week. One unfortunate Saturday morning the two friends were missed from their accustomed seats at morning prayers. After breakfast they were called upon to give an account of themselves, properly rebuked, and warned as to the future. As they left the room one was overheard to say, "I expected Mrs. Tevis to punish me; I wish she had, for I was prepared to bear any thing rather than that sad and reproachful look with which she admonished us." "Yes," was the reply, "and I can never be so lazy again." The Sunday morning following was very cold; a cheerful, good fire had been burning all night in my room for the sake of a little nursling in the cradle. The clock in the corner of the room striking four awakened me from a sound sleep, and, opening my eyes, I saw two figures, one on each side of the fire-place, reading silently from a large volume. I rubbed my eyes, thinking I must be still asleep. Not a breath of noise was afloat, and they sat as immovable as statues until I exclaimed, "Who are you, and what do you want?" "It is Mary Ann and Anna. We are reading our Bibles and trying to make up for yesterday—won't you forgive it? and pray do not look sorry at us any more." The fault was fully atoned for.

Among the crowds of young ladies that have been taught music in this institution, I have known but few that kept it up after leaving school, and especially after marriage. Mary Ann Dickinson was one of the few; music continued with her a passion. I have known her to sit down and play on the piano with as much interest after she was the mother of many children as when a blooming school-girl; and even up to the present time, though a grandmother, her music is not neglected, and amid the roar of the bounding billows of the Pacific, in Oregon, where many years ago her home was fixed, almost beyond the boundaries of civilization, the notes of her piano are heard. It was the first piece of furniture unpacked and assigned its place—even before the cooking-stove. How I long for the time to arrive when music shall form an essential part of every American household! Many lackadaisical, sentimental girls waste hours in trying to express their delicate thoughts in poetic numbers, and yet are not willing to cultivate a taste for music either vocal or instrumental. Music is heart-painting; its task is to attune the mind, to arouse the feelings, and to express the play of the sensibilities. I must confess, however, to an utter want of appreciation of the modern and fashionable taste displayed in the execution of long and difficult compositions. I feel like a young friend of mine who asked his cousin to favor him with some music. He endured a long and, perhaps, a finely executed piece, then impulsively exclaimed, "Cousin Mary, do you inflict that upon every body who asks you to play?" That only is music that touches the heart and fills the eye with tears. The wealth of melody and harmony contained in those old Scotch airs and other sweet, touching ballads of the same character, is wonderful. They are ever fresh, ever pleasing for those who have a true soul for music. It is greatly to be regretted that so few of our best performers give them a proper appreciation. Girls may scream Italian songs, and render an uninitiated ear frantic with elaborate instrumental pieces; but, when asked for one of Burns's sweet ballads, unless they happen to be the fashion of the day, will reply, "I do n't sing them, they do n't suit my voice, and they are absolutely out of date." Can music that thrills the soul ever become stale? Should such ever be out of fashion? No, not until feeling and sentiment are out of fashion, and we become mere moving, breathing automatons; yet so seldom do we hear those simple airs, replete with melody, that 'tis really refreshing to find a performer whose appreciation of the beautiful is in harmony with the charming simplicity of nature, rather than the unnatural flights and rich confusion termed music in the fashionable world.

Chapter XXXV.

"TEACH your pupils Natural History," said a learned and distinguished Doctor of Divinity, who presided over a certain college in the West forty years ago; "that's enough for girls. You are in advance of the age; let Chemistry alone."

And is not Chemistry a branch of Natural Science? It certainly is a subject calculated to train both the mind and the hands of young people to habits of industry, regularity, and order; and the necessity of carrying on the different steps of an operation in a systematic, cautious manner, must have a corresponding influence upon persons of the most careless disposition. Chemistry is especially requisite for the successful progress of our inquiries and researches into the nature of those things whence we derive the means of our comfort, our happiness, our luxuries, our health, and even our existence; for in examining the various objects which compose the mineral, vegetable, and animal kingdoms, it is essential.

The Pharmacopœia is but a collection of productive experiments, containing instructions for preparing the chemical substances employed in medicine—thus every intelligent girl, who has well learned the A B C's only of this widely extended science, is furnished with the means of preparing a domestic pharmacopœia which will prevent that quackery so often found in families—leading to danger and sometimes to death. Let the mother understand that the "flowers of sulphur" and "arsenic," though so much resembling each other by candlelight, are widely different in nature and composition, and she will not leave them side by side unlabeled, neither will she be liable to administer a tea-spoonful of deadly poison instead of a gentle alterative.

I think I hazard nothing in asserting that a large proportion of the girls who have studied chemistry under my tuition, even during the brief period of their school career, were sufficiently acquainted with its elementary and practical principles to render it useful to them in after life. Many found it the most delightful of their studies, practically illustrated as it was in our laboratory, and carried away with them a knowledge of poisons and antidotes that could only thus have been obtained. Chemical experiments upon a small scale form an admirable exercise for young students, and girls may acquire from them much valuable information. They have the further beneficial effect of habituating them to careful manipulation. Ignorance is not bliss, in a case where a mistake in the nature of a drug may endanger life. It is wonderful what a vast number of substances used in every-day life are brought within the limits of this science. All the processes of baking, brewing, and most of the culinary arts are chemical operations. We do not need an extensive laboratory to begin with; materials in small quantities are sufficient to enable us to ascertain their properties and reactions on other substances; metals, salts, acids, alkalies, and other commodities of the druggist all yield to productive experiments and give valuable information to the manipulator. In an experimental science, where truth lies within our reach, we should make use of our senses and judge for ourselves. Our business in teaching chemistry to girls is to make

27

them acquainted with what is already known and determined by the experiments of others; and if they pursue
the study with only a moderate degree of zeal, they
must add something daily to their stock of intelligence.
Chemistry ought to be a stated branch of a liberal education in every female school. The variety of unrecorded
facts which continually strike the eye of an industrious
experimenter is indeed surprising; and the science is so
entirely founded upon experiment, that no one can
understand it fully without manipulation. The hearing
of lectures and the reading of books will be of little benefit without this experimental instruction.

It has long been a subject of the deepest interest to
me, and has occupied a considerable portion of my time
as a teacher for more than fifty years. Slow but sure in
its uprising from chaotic darkness, its startling develop-
ments have done much to prove that "man need not die
before his time comes." Unveiling the hidden truths of
the *materia medica*, it has placed in the hands of edu
cated physicians remedial agents by which health is promoted and life prolonged.

I do not mean to convey the idea that synthetic
chemistry will, in its progress, reverse the process of final
dissolution, or reveal an elixir that will render man impervious to disease, or shield him from the dangers
that stand thick around him. No, that power belongs
but to the Creator; and the sublime chemistry of the
Bible alone reveals the process by which the desolation
of a thousand generations shall in a moment be repaired,
and heaven enriched with new forms of beauty, repro-
duced immortal, from the ruins of the tomb.

But is not health a virtue so far as it is in our power
to preserve it? Does not a knowledge of its require-

ments multiply our comforts and extend the sphere of our usefulness? Should we merely satisfy our curiosity by seeing the instrument and watching the fingers that play upon it, knowing nothing ourselves of the mysterious essences that constitute the vital harmony of the whole?

We turn over page after page in the great volume of nature; we search for the hidden glories of the mighty mind, and seek to grapple with its lofty aspirations; we bow down before the gifted impulses of genius, and strive to make progress in every other science, but measureably neglect this keystone in the arch. Chemistry, like astronomy, is replete with wonders. While the latter exhibits nature in the aggregate and stupendous massiveness and magnitude of her empire full of grandeur and sublimity, the former descends to the analysis of her multitudinous organizations, in the minutest particulars, and unfolds to view that secret laboratory where daily, hourly, and even momently, she is engaged in producing her almost magical transformations. Truly, here is great power! It brings up the pearl from its hidden depths and reveals to the daylight and to the rapt gaze of the admirer all its beauties. It bursts the rocky incasement, and lets forth the imprisoned brilliancy of the diamond upon the world. In short, it throws wide open the capacious storehouse of earth, and brings to light and to use all its precious and priceless treasures.

The well-remembered year of 1833 was one of general gloom with us. Every city, village, and neighborhood throughout Kentucky was visited by cholera. The richest portions of the State, and particularly the low lands, were fearfully scourged. Death was upon the highways, and terror in our streets. There was no use fleeing from one place to another. The dark wings of the destroying angel were outspread over the whole country. None knew when the next vial might be poured forth.

When the cholera commenced its fearful ravages on the Ohio, we vainly hoped it would only skirt the river shores, and that we, being thirty miles inland, might escape. It was midsummer, and it seemed difficult to look up at the sky above our heads so bright in its blue serenity, and at our picturesque surroundings, over which swept a breeze seemingly so health-inspiring, and believe that suffering and death could be near us. As soon, however, as the plague began to shake his dusky spear over Louisville, we dismissed our day-school and asked the speedy removal of our boarding pupils. A few only remained, and these from the far South, it being unsafe to travel on the Mississippi River.

The Southern and Western people were at that time inveterate calomel eaters, absolutely thinking it a specific for every disease under the sun; and many a young disciple of Æsculapius started out to seek his fortune, armed with a bottle of calomel, nothing more; this was his panacea.

A case in point will show the Cimmerian darkness which then prevailed in the valley of the Mississippi in reference to the use of this metallic poison. I found one day under an apple-tree, a young girl of seventeen munching the unripe fruit at a fearful rate. I reprimanded her sharply for this imprudence.

"Do you not know the cholera is abroad in the land?"

"Yes, ma'am," she replied, "but I'm not afraid; I have a bottle of calomel in my trunk."

"Where did you get it?"

"I brought it from home, and know exactly how much to take if these apples make me sick."

"What! without the advice of a physician?"

"Yes; I often take it at home for indigestion. Ma never allows any of us to go from home without a small vial of it."

I listened with perfect astonishment, and, as I gazed at her pale face, now flushed with a glow of excitement, I thought of Moore's remark about American ladies, "Roses in a grave-yard." Her coral lips, when parted, displayed a set of decayed teeth. She was really sick the next day in consequence of her cramming, and I administered, not calomel, but salt and water—an effectual remedy for such indigestion.

The deprecated evil paid Shelbyville but a short visit, and though it raged fearfully for a week or ten days, only eleven deaths occurred; and two or three of these were the effects of calomel, not cholera. We lost the youngest and darling of our flock—a lovely little boy twenty-two months old, reduced in a few hours from a sweet, fair-faced child to one having the withered appearance of old age, with the ashy hue peculiar to that blighting plague. On the same night a bright boy of fourteen passed from my brother's household. The latter had recovered from an attack of cholera, but the calomel, administered to him in large quantities, left its deadly impress upon his system, and destroyed all chance of his recovery.

During the time it prevailed among us we were so strictly dieted that the finest fruits and vegetables, which were unusually abundant, perished where they grew, being prohibited articles of food. The days were intensely hot, but we dared not enjoy the cool night breeze, though the bright moonlight was so inviting, for the physician decided that the night air was death.

When Summer had gone, and the atmosphere no longer

hung heavy with the odor of fruits and flowers, and the fresh cool breezes of Autumn swept over our country— hope, like "a sunbeam on a sullen sea," imparted cheerfulness to every heart. The whole community felt a sense of relief, as if a weight had been lifted, and man met his fellow-man with a more cheerful countenance; and those that were left were bound together by stronger ties of affection and friendship. Like mariners who survive a sinking wreck, there were daily congratulations and a constant intercourse, even between those who had hitherto been almost strangers.

The Indian Summer of 1833 is embalmed in my memory as one of great beauty. It lingered longer than usual, crowning the woods with intenser hues, making up a wealth of beauty and of glory, upon which the eye might revel. A dreamy warmth invested every thing with a palpable loveliness. The whole earth seemed transfigured by the soft amber drapery of that charming season. The clouds, as they came floating toward the horizon, appeared through the hazy atmosphere as if woven of fluttering gauze spangled with silver and gold. This lasted until the middle of November.

Our Fall term had opened prosperously, and, amidst the busy hum of school-life, we were forgetting the sorrowful past, over which the remorseless waves of time would soon have closed completely, had not the dark shadow of death again fallen upon our threshold. In the latter part of November, after a week's illness, my beloved mother was taken from us—taken to that glorious and happy home toward which her footsteps had been tending for so many years. Though a ripe Christian, and presenting a beautiful example of the self-educating power of a good life, she was not weary of life, but ready to give it up when asked for, having learned that there is no absolute rest except in submission to the will of God.

The sunlight of affection shone softly upon her declining years, and her last days were among the most quiet and peaceful of her life. How wonderful and beautiful that calmness and resignation appointed to the Christian believer in the hour of dissolution! It is an easy thing to look upon the King of Terrors at a distance, but quite another to face him in the sharp conflict of death. How impressive a lesson, and what a privilege to see a follower of the blessed Redeemer sinking into the cold river without a shudder, as he catches, through the rifted clouds, the refracted beam of a Savior's love! So died this dear mother, and yet it was hard to give her up. Her vacant chair could never be filled; nearly the whole journey of my life had been made by her side. The past buries in oblivion all things else, before it effaces those lessons imprinted upon our minds, ere we had passed the rose-entwined boundaries of childhood.

I remember my mother as a young, handsome woman, before time had bleached her raven hair, or left a wrinkle on her brow; before sorrow had dimmed the brilliancy of those clear and truthful eyes, than which I thought there could not be such another pair in the wide world. Her finely molded arm and exquisite hand were never-ceasing objects of admiration. From her I learned to love the Bible and its precious truths. She aimed to inspire all her children with a love of truth and a hatred of vice, and never placed an example before them, that they might not imitate.

How often now do I, in dreams, visit my early home among the mountains of Virginia, and wander in fancy among those enchanting scenes, the form of my mother hovering around me like an angel of mercy! Oh, those dead and bygone years! With what a yearning does my heart call them back! What pleading arms do I stretch out to them, so full are they of all that is dearest and brightest—so hard is it to let them go!

Home, the consolation and anchor of the world-wearied soul,—and what is home without a mother? I loved my mother, and for no consideration would I, while she lived, have dashed her cup with one drop of sorrow; yet when she had gone I would have given worlds to call her back, that I might fall at her feet and ask pardon for all omissions, and renew my efforts to made her happy and comfortable. I have learned to think of her now as at rest. Oh, if we could always thus remember our buried ones— think of their white robes and tuneful harps, of the spirit-wreaths that crown their shadowless brows—of the hands that bore the cross, now lifted up before the great white throne—think how the feet that faltered along a rough and darkened path now tread the streets of that Golden City where they have no need of the sun, nor of the moon, for the Lord is the light thereof,—we should rejoice that they are there, our beautiful and blessed dead! And in the hereafter, when the sun of our own life goes down behind the mountains of eternity we shall join them in that land of the living; and when the sea of death is passed it matters not how mournfully its billows once dashed upon the shores of time.

Chapter XXXVI.

I HAVE but little faith in itinerant teachers and lecturers who profess to impart a knowledge of the sciences in a set number of lessons, and have rarely ever patronized such. It is insufferable pedantry, if not positive ignorance to propose teaching Grammar by charts alone. Astronomy by magic-lantern exhibitions, or to pretend to impart a sufficient knowledge of any modern language in two weeks' reading. The eye may open and the panorama pass before it, but the impression vanishes. The picture must be touched and retouched until deeply engraven upon the mind.

A few exceptions I have known, however, where permanent good was derived from these meteoric lights. I have a pleasing remembrance of a Mr. Mulky, who lectured many years ago, upon the subject of Orthoepy, in Shelbyville. From early childhood I had been drilled into a correct pronunciation of the English language, besides having associated much in after life with the best speakers and writers. I treated Mr. Mulky, at first, with great coolness; but after having conversed with him freely upon the subject, and examined his unfolded plan, I found there was yet room for improvement. My constant practice through life has been "to listen and to learn." Solomon deigned to receive instruction from a bee, and none of us are Solomons.

I was also well acquainted with Professor Bronson, decidedly the best elocutionist I ever knew. His reading,

I might well say dramatic impersonation, was so characteristic, so artistically complete and telling. Then, too, his voice was so flexible, its intonation so perfect, that he charmed his auditors into enthusiastic admiration. When he lectured, it was like listening to fine music—every note, syllable, and word carried its full force. His style was beautiful, and enriched with gems of wisdom selected from the treasured stores of his extensive reading. Mr. Bronson was an earnest, aspiring, industrious man, his eminence in his profession being the result of untiring energy. He possessed the power of giving graceful utterance to his emotions, and thus produced in others the sensations that thrilled his own bosom with ecstasy. Full of the poetry of life and thought, ardent and impulsive, he became morally powerful and intellectually eminent; but his enthusiatic devotion to the science of Elocution, upon which he wrote, lectured, and talked, sometimes led him beyond plain matter of fact.

It is about as difficult to make a man unlearn his errors as his knowledge. Mal-information is more hopeless than non-information; for error is always more busy than ignorance. The latter is a blank sheet on which we may write; but the former is a scribbled one, from which we must first erase. Ignorance is contented to stand still, with her back to the truth; but Error is more presumptuous, and proceeds in the same direction. Ignorance has no light, but Error follows a false one. The consequence is that Error, when she retraces her steps, has farther to go before she can arrive at the truth than Ignorance. Hence the difficulty of attempting to teach children to spell, pronounce, or read correctly, unless you begin with the Alphabet. Now, our Alphabet has only twenty-six characters to represent thirty-six sounds.

Until this deficiency is supplied, children ought to be thoroughly taught to utter the different sounds of the vowels as if each had its written name.

I think both Mr. Mulky and Mr. Bronson were men of peculiar tact, taste, and ability; but they never received the patronage they deserved. Error and prejudice in favor of the "old ways" operated against them. But the drafts which true genius draws upon the public, although they may not be honored as soon as they are due, are sure to be paid with compound interest in the end.

"O girls," exclaimed a rosy-cheeked little gypsy, running against a knot of her companions, who stood in the yard trying to get a peep at the new-comer, "our new music-teacher has come. She is as tall as a grenadier, but does not look as if she ever drank a pot of beer. There, now! don't I remember Mother Goose,— though Mrs. Tevis says I never recollect any thing?"

"Capital news," said one. "Does she look good-humored? I hope she is more agreeable than that cross old bear, Mr. S. If she is not I'll give up music, or feign sickness, to get rid of my lessons."

"Nonsense!" chimed in another; "you'll do no such thing. However, she looks well, notwithstanding the reflection of this cold, gray, February sky."

"Stop," said a third; "don't let us pass judgment until we know something about her."

The supper-bell rang, and the youthful gossips, mingling with their companions, followed their dignified teachers into the dining-room. Miss D. sat at my right hand, all the time fluttered and uncomfortable, as if fully aware of the glances slyly directed towards her from every part of the table. She was actually running the gauntlet, and they were taking notes.

As soon as the girls were released from the table they congregated in the school-room to comment upon the interesting stranger, glad of any little excitement to break the monotony of boarding-school life. All talked at once; there were no listeners.

As I was entering the school-room shortly after, for the purpose of inviting a few of the older pupils into the parlor, I noticed an unusual excitement among the girls, and paused a moment unperceived at the half-open door. They were gathered in clusters, conversing with animated gestures upon the all-absorbing topic of the new teacher.

"I hope I shall like her," said a bright-eyed little girl. "I love music dearly, and I would rather take lessons from a nice young lady than a cross old man."

"I don't intend to try to like her," chimed in a fair-looking girl, as she pushed back the silky braids of light hair from her alabaster brow. I declare this humdrum school life is insupportable. I am tired to death of strict rules and watchful teachers. I want a breeze."

"You may do as you please," said one of my good girls; "but, mind what I tell you, the rules here, in regard to respectful obedience, are like the laws of the Medes and Persians."

"Humph! what do I care for the rules? I shall take no more trouble than I please. I am sick of music, any how; and all teachers are hateful."

"Hush!" cried another; "make the best of it. My motto is, Be good, be industrious, and write Wisdom on the wings of time."

I selected a few of the best performers among the older pupils, returned to the parlor, and introduced them to Miss D., who entered into a free and easy conversation with them. I noticed how eagerly they listened, and was charmed with the simple modesty of their replies.

Miss D. was certainly a prepossessing woman. Her face, in repose, wore a sad, sweet expression, and her fine dark eyes were radiant with feeling and intelligence. Presently she invited one of the girls to the piano, who sang and played several pieces, and then resigned her place to one of the best performers in the school. She executed one or two of her most brilliant solos. Then some duets followed, and the girls crowded around, begging Miss D. to favor them with some music in return. She declined, evincing at the same time a painful embarrassment which brought a deep blush upon her face. I should not perhaps have noticed this, as blushes had been the livery of the evening, had not Miss D. immediately requested permission to retire, on the plea of fatigue.

It was late at night, the stars had long been keeping watch in the quiet skies, and yet the light still shone from the window of Miss D.'s room. Fearing she might be sick, I stepped across the way, and, in passing the window, caught a glimpse of her. She was in a kneeling posture, with several pieces of music spread out before her on the carpet. Her hands were clasped closely against her heart as if to quiet its throbbings. Her half-raised face wore a pale, quiet, resigned look of intense suffering. I gently tapped at the door; springing to her feet, she admitted me, but covered with confusion, burst into tears.

"What is the matter, my dear Miss D., are you sick?"

"Yes, heart-sick," she replied. "I have undertaken what I can not accomplish. I can not teach instrumental music in your school. But," she continued, while her tears fell thick and fast, "do not think me an impostor. I am innocent of any intention to deceive. Seeing your advertisement for an assistant music-teacher, and, having been for several years a teacher of vocal music, with some practical knowledge of the piano, I was persuaded by my injudicious, and, I might well say, ignorant, friends to apply for the situation. 'With your theoretical knowledge,' said they, 'you are capable of giving lessons on the piano, and may do so without presumption in the far West, where there are so few fine musicians, and the pupils in their best schools are but beginners.' You may well imagine my astonishment at the performance of the young ladies in the parlor this evening; my mortification is inexpressible. I am not fit for the place. What shall I do?"

A fresh burst of tears relieved her overcharged heart, and we were both silent for some minutes. I resolved upon my course at once, charmed into sympathy by her candid acknowledgment. I seated myself by her side, and we entered into as confidential a conversation as if we had never been strangers. Believing from her own account of her success as a teacher of vocal music that it would be well to retain her, I proposed that she should take charge of a singing-class, and devote a portion of her time also to teaching in the primary department. We had a large number of children in our school at that time, and I had long desired to have singing introduced as a regular branch of their education. The proposition was gratefully accepted.

Miss D. proved to be an amiable, interesting woman, of refined manners and cultivated tastes. Often during the hours of recess the older girls might be seen flocking around her, asking assistance in learning their new songs, or seeking advice in some projected amusement. She made herself so agreeable, that even the girls who at first determined not to like her became her fast friends; while she was almost worshiped by her little pupils, whom she made as happy as the birds in their Summer bowers. A new impulse was given to their mirth, and their gleeful songs resounded through the play-ground. Thus what commenced in sorrow with her ended in joy. Her stay at Science Hill was an episode of sunshine and singing. I am somewhat of the opinion held by the good old German teacher who set his boys to singing when they were perverse and cross, as, he said, "to drive the devil out."

In the course of my long experience as a teacher, I have seen so many painful results of the neglect of early instruction, that I shall not be blamed for reverting to it again. One fact is worth a thousand fictions. In appointing woman as a helpmate, the Creator marked her destiny; and, to fit her for the task, mercifully infused into her soul deep attachment for home, and that constancy in affection which rarely decays till her heart is cold in death; and it is a well-established fact, that where opportunities are afforded, and motives for exertion presented, the female mind possesses sufficient soundness and power to rise above the superficial, the showy, and the frivolous. It is worse than weak, it is wicked, in those who have the charge of these immortal souls during the state of their pupilage to let them grow up with no higher aim than to heighten and set off their personal attractions by external adornment.

Firmness in the discharge of a conscientious duty is often of great importance, and it should be the study of our lives to stand erect even among those "who care for none of these things;" knowing that truth only can administer to our happiness and reflect a permanent radiance upon the heart.

I faithfully promised, when we first commenced housekeeping, that I would conduct worship at the family altar when my husband was absent, unless some other person were present who could officiate. This was always a trial; but never once did I neglect or evade the duty. The path was plain, and I realized the blessed promise, "As thy day so shall thy strength be."

Once we had in school a fragrant little human blossom which had been suffered to waste its sweetness "on the desert air" in one of the wildest and rudest portions of our State. Until she entered her teens she had been in a mixed school of chubby-cheeked, freckled-faced, romping children, where she had learned to read, but not to understand. Her pious Methodist mother, though one of the gentlest of human beings, "comely and delicate," refined in manners and agreeable in conversation, was entirely uneducated. The father was a rough, good-natured *Bruin*, with mind as uncouth as his manners, looking for all the world as if brought up on "hog and hominy." Profane to a proverb, yet respecting his religious wife, he left his only daughter entirely to her direction. This daughter was literally the keystone in the arch of the mother's existence. She was early taught to love God, and keep his commandments; and when old enough to leave home, the mother brought her to our school with a request that we would finish what she had begun. The child was delighted with the Sabbath-school, and enjoyed the privilege of attending Church every Sunday. At home she had heard preaching not oftener than once a month.

The first time her father came to visit her, he seemed

exceedingly embarrassed, and scarce knew how to conduct himself; but the caresses of his daughter, and the
welcome he received, soon reassured him.   He was invited to tarry with us.   Mr. Tevis was not at home, and
my asking a blessing at supper appeared to confound
him.   He spoke but little, and hardly raised his eyes
during the meal.   Half an hour after the bell rang again.

"What's that bell for?"

"Prayers," replied the daughter.

Well," said he, "you can stay and chat with me until
it is over."

"No, papa, we must go in; every body attends family prayers, no matter who is here."

"Well, go ahead; I suppose I must follow."

He walked in and took a seat near the door, listened
attentively to the reading of the Scriptures, and appeared
deeply interested during the whole service, reverently
bowing down with the rest.   It was touching to behold
him kneeling there among,

> "Fair young heads,
> With all their clustering locks untouched by care."

When rising from his knees, he caught the hand of his
little daughter, who, with a blush on her bright face and
an expression of love in her clear, eloquent eyes, followed
him into the parlor.

"Well," said he, drawing a long breath, "that's the
first time I ever was on my knees in my life, and
wouldn't ha' been then, hadn't a woman prayed."

He told a friend afterwards that he would not have
been so much scared before an army of men as he was
in that prayer-room full of young girls; "and," he
added, as a shade of sadness stole over his rough face,
"I shall never forget it."

28

D URING the Summer of 1834 my health and strength rapidly declined, and I was scarcely able to pass through the ordeal of the closing exercises of the school in July. My physician advised a change of scene and entire release from care. We left home the first week in August, intending to visit Harrodsburg Springs; traveled slowly in a private conveyance—Mr. Tevis and myself, with a child six months old and a nurse. The first day's journey ended in Frankfort. Here we met an intelligent physician, who, after having made himself acquainted with my case, pronounced it bronchitis, which, if not speedily arrested, would terminate in consumption. This was a new idea, although my voice had been reduced almost to a whisper, and it was with difficulty I swallowed food enough to keep me alive. I do not know whether his opinion troubled me much, as I felt satisfied the Lord would let me live till my work was done, and I could trust him for the time whether it were days, months, or years. I knew also that my recuperative powers were very great.

Early the next morning we continued our journey towards Lexington, as our physician had earnestly recommended "Blue Lick" instead of "Harrodsburg." Sick and languid as I was, having had a poor, thin sort of sleep, in which I did not entirely lose consciousness, there still dwelt within me that well-spring of healthy vitality, which always responded to the cheerful influence of a fine morning. The advancing day was lovely. The air from over the hills breathed the fragrance of new-mown grass, and we were sheltered from the heat of the sun by the dense foliage of overhanging trees. Nature wore her coronation robes, trailing their radiance in our pathway. Soft Summer clouds were sailing in the blue sky above like white-winged vessels freighted with pearls for some impoverished land. At noon we rested and lunched by the side of a clear spring, under the branches of a sugar maple, which hung its grateful shadows over the green turf. Early in the afternoon we reached Lexington, and here met some pleasant friends, who spent the evening with us.

We left the next morning at a very early hour, in order to avoid the heat of the day and reach the end of our journey before night. During the forenoon we traveled through "a land flowing with milk and honey." The scenery was a continued panorama of blue-grass meadows with tangled wilds of verdure. That delicious day is embalmed in my recollection as a "joy forever."

When we reached the little bridge flung across the Licking River, we paused for a short time to take a view of the surrounding country. On the left, beyond the river, was the rocky ridge, its bold front cutting sharply against the sky, upon which was fought the battle of "Blue Licks," August 19, 1782—the bloodiest and most disastrous in the annals of savage warfare except Braddock's defeat. A deep ravine on each side of this ridge, thickly entangled with bushes, enabled the Indians to lie in ambush and watch in silence the coming enemy. Quietly they waited until the Kentucky troops had reached the top of the ridge, which was perfectly bare except a few dwarfish cedars, and a multitude of rocks spread over the surface, rendering it still more desolate in appearance.

One may well imagine the feelings of our brave men when, having reached the summit without hearing a sound or seeing a foe, the terrific war-cry of the savages rang out upon the air. They were soon completely surrounded by a force far outnumbering their own. No alternative remained but to cut their way through, which was done with a bravery and desperation worthy the palmiest days of Sparta. The Indians contested every foot of ground, and compelled them occasionally to stand at bay. The slaughter was greatest in a large cedar grove near the river bank. That grove is now set in blue grass, and affords a delightful retreat for visitors during the heat of the day. Finally, our men dashed tumultuously into the stream, the Indians in hot pursuit, mingling with the whites in one rolling, irregular mass. Some of the fugitives, plunging into the thickets, escaped by a circuitous route to Bryant's station, twenty miles distant. Others found a passage above the ford by swimming. Many who could not swim, were overtaken and killed at the edge of the water. A few finely mounted horsemen crossed the river in safety, and firing upon the Indians saved those friends still struggling in the stream. The result of this terrible battle shrouded the new settlements of Kentucky in mourning.

I was struck with the insignificance of Licking River, whose sluggish waters flowed sleepily onward, swaying the masses of weeds just beneath the surface. The river banks were overgrown with reeds and willows, and the dull, gurgling sound of the water added a deeper gloom to the surrounding solitude. After crossing the bridge, a drive of about two hundred yards brought us to the boarding-house, which, at that period, did not present a very inviting aspect. There was a lawn shaded by tall evergreens, with here and there a venerable old tree. These have long since been removed, and extensive and beautiful improvements have taken their place. The Blue Lick was not a fashionable watering-place, but the resort principally of invalids, with the few who were seeking quiet and retirement from the busy haunts of men.

My first night was a rest indeed, and I did not awake in the morning until the sun was flooding my chamber with its silent arousal. Half a glass of wine and a piece of bread constituted my first breakfast there. Having, in vain, endeavored to drink the water when deprived of its sparkling effervescence, I was obliged to walk to the spring, which I could not accomplish the first day without assistance, though the distance was short. There I found health-seeking invalids drinking and resting alternately and watching the new-comers in their laughable efforts to swallow the distasteful water. Some caught the sparkling bubbles of gas as they streamed up to the surface, and swallowed cup after cup, looking, for all the world, as I fancy Socrates did when he drank the hemlock, doubting whether it would really introduce him into Elysian fields or not. I drank sparingly, but at short intervals. My appetite gradually increased, as my health improved, and in less than a week I was able to take my meals at the "*table d' hote*," and stroll over the grounds without assistance.

The spot, at that time, was as solitary and romantic as an oasis in the desert, though situated on the renowned Maysville turnpike, not then finished, yet it was the great thoroughfare of the State. The spring flows apparently from an exhaustless source, and, like the wells of Solomon, it is ever brimming. Bubbles of gas are constantly chasing each other to the surface, and spreading over it like gleaming sun-jewels. Sulphuretted hydrogen, carbonic acid, common salt, sulphate of magnesia, and soda are the principal elements. For many years it is well known that this water has been an important article of commerce. Thousands of barrels are annually exported, enriching the owners independently of the profits derived from visitors.

At an early day it was a place of great importance, as it was chiefly here that the first settlers procured their supplies of salt. In January, 1778, Boone was encamped in the vicinity with about thirty others making salt for the different stations. This cane-covered land was the Indian hunter's paradise. Numerous herds of buffalo, elk, and deer roamed over the hills and through the valleys of the Licking.

One day, when Boone was out hunting alone, he encountered more than a hundred Indians. He instantly fled, but being over fifty years of age, could not outstrip the young warriors in pursuit, and was taken prisoner. According to their custom he was treated kindly until his fate was determined. They led him back to his encampment. Here the whole party of whites surrendered upon condition of being spared and well treated. The savages faithfully observed this promise. How differently have the civilized whites acted! Timidity was an unpardonable blemish in the character of a Kentucky huntsman, and so, indeed, was mercy toward an Indian.

It was an established rule among the early settlers never to suffer an Indian aggression to go unpunished, but to retaliate a hundred fold; and sometimes when no resistance was offered, their villages were reduced to ashes, their corn cut up, and their whole country laid waste with unsparing severity. No quarter was given, no prisoners taken—every thing within the reach of the avenger was completely destroyed. The brutal ferocity of the whites on some occasions might call a blush to the cheek of a savage.

The first day of February, 1835, we left home with the intention of visiting some of the Eastern cities. Our party consisted of Mr. Tevis, myself, my sister Arabella, and Eliza Ann Wilson, a lovely young girl, who had been one of my pupils, and was just about to step upon the tapis of society. Our trip to Louisville was charming. The morning was spring-like, the birds singing in the leafless trees, and the little streams winding through meadows, which had worn their green garments all Winter. There was loveliness on the earth and in the air, and all nature smiled a welcome for the coming Spring.

Before we reached Louisville, however (we traveled in slow coaches then), we felt an ominous keenness in the air, which compelled us to wrap our mantles close about us. The next morning we took passage on a small, but comfortable, steamer for Pittsburg. The cold continued to increase, and by the time we reached Cincinnati ice began to appear in the river, and we began to apprehend that we had mistaken the season; however, we were not discouraged. We had quite a reunion of friends and acquaintances on board, and among them merchants from Shelbyville going for their Spring goods. Our little town boasted at that time of not less than fifteen dry-goods stores, which were principally supplied from the Eastern markets.

We frequently met in the ladies' cabin, and each tried to make to-day agreeable, heedless of to-morrow. On the afternoon of the first day out from Cincinnati, it was discovered, to the horror and amazement of every body on board, that we had barely escaped being blown up. What a scene ensued! Every body talked; nobody listened; the ladies screamed, although the danger was over, and the captain swore at a terrible rate.

A careless deck hand had left a piece of candle, not more than an inch long, stuck on the corner of a pine box in the hold of the vessel. The mate fortunately entered the hold in time to extinguish the just kindling box, which was a large and heavy one containing kegs of powder. Upon inquiry, it was found that the contraband article had been smuggled on board. After diligent search the culprit was found and dragged into the cabin, half dead with fear. The captain could scarcely be prevented from pitching the man overboard, though the poor fellow solemnly declared that he had taken charge of the box at the solicitation of a friend, without knowing its contents. The passengers pleaded for him, and, while arguing the matter, a flat-bottomed boat was seen coming down the river, and the difficulty was settled by putting the man and his box on the boat to float back to Cincinnati.

During the excitement, in which every body seemed to join, I was amused watching the imperturbable gravity of an old German, who sat smoking his pipe until the drama was over.

"Well den," said he [I had taken a seat near him], "here is von great fuss for notin' at all."

"Why," said I, "we were in great danger of being blown up."

"Vy, vat you care for dat? dat's notin'. I vas been blown up vonce, and, ven all vas over, I finds myself sittin' on a tree, notin' lost but my shmok-bipe and mine hat." Then he grunted and smoked away more vigorously than ever.

"Was nobody hurt?" said I.

"Oh, yas, some legs, some arms vas gone, and many folks vas kilt." And he smoked again without the slightest evidence of concern for maimed humanity or darkened homes.

"Well," said I, "I wonder you ever came upon a steamboat again."

He uttered a guttural laugh, and said, as he shrugged his shoulders, "Dere is no help for it. Ve must travel; if de steamboat blows up, den it *must* blow up, and if ve gets kilt, den ve travels no more."

Never in my life did I meet with a more thorough "I care for nobody, no not I, nobody cares for me."

Each succeeding day brought an increase of cold, thickened the ice, and thus we moved but slowly onward. To add to our discomfort, provisions were growing scarce. The captain had expected to supply himself, as usual, by stopping at different landings, or purchasing from the riverside market-people, who always brought fresh butter, eggs, and fowls to supply boats as they passed along. The ice-incrusted shores prevented our landing, and finally we were reduced to one meal a day, of crackers, tea, and rice. The wood was giving out, the fires in the furnaces could not be kept up, and it was feared the river would soon be blocked up with our "phantom ship" in the midst of it.

Meantime we were cutting our way slowly through the accumulating ice, striving to reach Guyandotte, the nearest place where we could hope to find relief. In the midst of these depressions, with the apprehension of some greater calamity, every body was good-humored and amiable. One evening while walking the guards rapidly for exercise, we heard a stentorian voice on the lower deck addressing an apparently listening audience. Curiosity drew many of the cabin passengers below, and there stood a tall, double-fisted fellow, mounted on a rostrum, swaying his arms like a Fourth of July orator, and holding forth in something like the following:

"Fellow-travelers,—I exhort you to courage and submission to your lot. I know you are a miserable set of sinners, and so is your humble servant; and as we must fast we ought to pray also. Don't let his Satanic majesty have dominion over you any longer. Awake from the sleep into which the old Sarpent has lulled you and clear away the mists from your bleared eyes. Now don't be down-hearted. I should be ashamed if any of my brave companions couldn't face hunger as well as cold— and as for the tea, crackers, and rice, don't let's be niggardly about them, give to the weaker sex the last morsel on board. Three cheers for the ladies! God bless them!" The cheers came with a hearty good will. "And now in conclusion, friends and fellow-sufferers, I would whisper a word in your ears," and, lowering his voice, "I am afraid we have a Jonas on board, sent, perhaps, to preach to some great Nineveh (Cincinnati, it may be), but, instead of going, has hid himself among us poor sailors. Now if the worst comes to the worst, we will pitch him—not into the sea—but into the ice." Thus did these hungry but jolly and good-natured fellows while away their unemployed and uncomfortable time.

Night came on soon after, a moonless night. Jagged

and heavy masses of clouds, broken occasionally so as to let a single star peer through upon the darkness below, were swept swiftly over the sky by a howling north wind. We went supperless to bed, to sleep or to await, with what fortitude we might, the coming day. Contrary to our expectations the wind died away during the night, and before sunrise the men had cut and cleared away the ice around the vessel; their efforts being aided afterwards by the heat of the sun, we were enabled to move onward, though the cold was intense. Some of the gentlemen, becoming impatient at our detention, left the boat and walked across to the Virginia shore, and thence onward seven or eight miles, until they reached a station-house, whence they journeyed on by stage, leaving their baggage on the boat to be forwarded.

I never shall forget that cold Friday afternoon when the remainder of us reached Guyandotte. This town is situated on a bluff. The steamboat could not reach the shore, and we walked across the ice. The wind swept around the sides of the surrounding hills with the force of a hurricane. But we were amply rewarded when we reached the hotel. Blazing log fires, warm, comfortable rooms, and downy beds awaited us. We were first ushered into a cheerful dining-room, and, being closely drawn together by common misfortunes, we formed but one party, about twenty in number. A supper of delicious, well-cooked venison, rich coffee, and hot buckwheat cakes in abundance, satisfied our appetites, and rendered us a cheerful company of way-worn travelers. A night of balmy sleep restored our tired natures and buried the memory of our discomforts.

The next day we marshaled our forces, and found each member of the party disposed to contribute to the

comfort of the others during our sojourn at Mr. Wright's.
Captain William Winlock, a merchant and good Methodist brother from Shelbyville, was the Orpheus of our company. His soul was full of music, and he played exquisitely on the violin. So chaste and beautiful were his selections that even the most conscientious could not object to the instrument; on the contrary, its tone thrilled in harmony with all that was elevating, noble, and devout, quieting the restless pulse of care and beguiling the tired spirit into rest.

My husband was too faithful a follower of John Wesley to remain idle. He prayed wherever he could, and went out every day, freezing cold as it was, to hunt up the Methodists in the neighborhood. Once I went with him, three miles in the country, to spend the day with as primitive a Methodist family as might have been found in the days of Whitefield and the Wesleys. The sky was overcast, and the clouds were burdened with a wealth of snow, that soon began to fall so thick and fast as nearly to blind us, and we quite lost our way. The only alternative was to give the reins to the horse; and, after a few windings and turnings, he took us safely to the place, an old-fashioned, substantially built farm-house, with a long porch in front, and a little room cut off at one end. This had been the homestead for many generations. We were met on the threshold by a dignified old man, dressed in homespun, and his matronly wife, neatly attired in a dark worsted gown. She was followed by her daughter, a lovely young woman, all greeting us heartily, and ushering us into the best room. A blazing fire burned in the wide-open fireplace. The hearthstone was white and polished; a carpet of domestic manufacture covered the floor; heavy, high-backed chairs of mahogany were arranged around the room, and in the chimney-corners were large, cozy arm-chairs. An antique looking-glass, with a mahogany frame, hung at an angle of ten degrees, according to the fashion of the times; and a tall, old-fashioned clock completed the furniture of a room genteel enough for any body. Sofas, marble mantels, and folding doors were not considered indispensably necessary, by these simple-hearted people to render the house tenantable; yet they were rich in this world's goods, and distributed liberally to the poor. The wayfaring man and the stranger found a welcome at their hospitable board. Their sons and daughters had been educated intellectually as well as religiously, and had gone forth into the world to be blessings to society.

What a delightful home, thought I, as I looked around and felt the glowing warmth of the clear, snapping wood-fire, with its huge logs looking as if they might never be consumed.

My own busy life rose up before me, and I almost envied this "retreat from care, which never must be mine." I fell quite in love with the family, and affectionately venerated the two old people; such power there is in established piety.

An enthusiast in antiquities, I strive to lay under contribution all the well-stricken in years within my reach, and deem it the performance of a grateful duty to society to rescue from oblivion the long gone and forgotten anecdotes and curious facts connected with the early settlement of my country. Many circumstances, not of sufficient importance to be admitted into history, may find their proper place in biography. They will amuse our children; and, indeed, there is much of which the younger part of the present generation is wholly ignorant. These things, trifles as they may at first appear, are worth preserving; all who remember the olden times will do well to contribute their mite. Unfortunately, the prevailing spirit of the age is to make all things new; and the generation which, by personal knowledge or by tradition, possesses the power of telling things just as they were is fast passing away.

These dear old people contributed much to our entertainment by their reminiscences of the first settlers in Western Virginia, entering into the minutiæ of their customs and habits, far more illustrative of their character than great events. They were rich in traditions handed down through a line of ancestry extending back to Captain John Smith.

It was near nine o'clock at night when we left this hospitable family, and we enjoyed the drive back exceedingly. The full moon was looking down from a clear sky, sprinkling with silvery showers rock, tree, and shrub, and clothing in mysterious loveliness the yet untrodden snow. A guide accompanied us until within sight of the town.

A week had passed, and we were still at Guyandotte, watching the ice as it floated down the river; yet we were spending our time neither in a sad nor useless manner. The Sabbath was near at hand, and it was decided that we should have religious service in the school-house. There was no church in this little town set on a hill; but they did not suffer the watch-fires of religion to be extinguished, nor put their candle under a bushel, but gladly embraced every opportunity of hearing the Gospel preached. The appointment was published abroad during the week, but the weather was so intensely cold that the congregation was small—the guests from the hotel and a few towns-people; yet the preacher needed not a large audience to call forth his soul in behalf of sinners. His conscience held him with a grasp of iron to unceasing labor in the vineyard of the Lord, and a sense of duty awakened an enthusiasm that enabled him to preach with as much earnestness to one as to many. The closing appeal was forcible and eloquent; and no doubt some felt the influence of deep and irrepressible feeling in the preacher, and dated convictions from that hour that told not only upon their future lives, but upon their eternal destiny. Who knows?

Ten days elapsed before the joyful news was announced that the captain thought we could proceed on our trip with but slight impediment from the ice. Many who landed with us at Guyandotte had found an opportunity of going through Virginia by stage, so that our party was considerably reduced in number.

One bright morning we bade adieu to Mr. and Mrs. Wright, not without regret. They had contributed so much to our comfort and happiness during our sojourn in their model hotel that, though we met them as strangers, we left them as friends. We were soon comfortably situated on the brave little steamer, congratulating each other on the prospect of a speedy termination of our journey. But we had proceeded only a few miles up the river, when such a quantity of floating ice came crushing and crowding around us, and so impeded our progress, that it was late in the afternoon before we reached Gallipolis,—we could proceed no farther. The river was completely blocked across, and we had to walk on the ice to reach the shore.

Surely, never did any little town present so gloomy an appearance. The miserable little tavern that received us

was crowded with all sorts of travelers, presenting no
evidence of comfort within or around it. For the first
.time I felt discouraged and homesick, and declared I
would go no farther, and would take no part in the consultation as to what was to be done next. It was finally
concluded that if a conveyance could be found we would
cross the country to Chillicothe, whence we might proceed on our route by stage-coach over the great National Road as far as Wheeling, and thence through
Pennsylvania.

After an hour's search an old coach was found, belonging to the mail contractor, once used as a passenger-
coach, but now, as the road was little traveled, and the
country sparsely settled, the mail was carried on horseback. The mail-carrier undertook to drive the coach for
a consideration. The landlord was asked if he could
furnish some straw or hay to put in the bottom of the
coach, which was leaky, and hardly road-worthy.

"Hay! no, indeed," said he; "and straw are skercer
still."

So onward we moved, but so slowly that I was satisfied the driver was a cautious man. We had proceeded
about half a dozen miles when we reached a declivity in
the road made slippery by the snow and ice, and the
passengers were requested to turn out,—the gentlemen
being informed, meantime, that they must hold up the
coach on one side to keep it from turning over.

"Can't the ladies stay in?" said the four gentlemen,
as they tumbled themselves out.

"To be sure they must," said Mr. Tevis, "for it is
impossible for them to walk down this hill."

"They be liken to have their necks broke if they do,"
coolly replied the driver.

The ladies were all out before the sentence was finished. The night was dark, but the dimly burning lanterns aided us in finding the way, though we were slipping, sliding, and trembling at every few steps. One queer fellow, who had at first positively declared he would not get out, as he had paid for his passage and the driver was responsible for his safety, was rolling and turning summersaults all the way down the hill, to the infinite amusement of the whole company.

After the perilous descent was accomplished the driver picked up his passengers, and moved on again at the rate of two miles an hour till midnight.

At last we came to a dwelling standing quite alone—a large, rambling log-cabin. Through the unchinked walls and open door issued an inviting light, which made us insist upon getting out to warm. By this time our discontented passenger, who had refused to get out, and had been left behind in the snow, made his appearance, and we all entered the cabin without ceremony as there was no door at which to knock. The fire was replenished from a brush-heap in the corner, and around this we all gathered, chatting merrily over our misfortunes—not as yet having seen any sign of an inhabitant.

Presently the gentlemen began to talk politics, and Jackson's Administration was alternately abused and lauded. The United States Bank, the Maysville Turnpike, and the President's vetoes were the all-absorbing topics. One gentleman declared that Jackson was worthy of being elevated to the standard of General Washington. Just then, to our extreme amazement, a loud voice from the remotest corner of the room cried out:

"Yes; I'll tell you where he ought to be elevated—on a *gallus* high as Haman's."

Then a weird-looking figure, whose elf locks seemed electrified by the cold, walked slowly up to us. Some of the company rose to their feet.

"Keep your seats, ladies and gentlemen"—we were all sitting on the floor—"you are heartily welcome to warm by my fire. Sorry I ain't got nothin' to treat you with—not a drap of liquor in the house. I'd ax you to eat a bite, only my wife and children's asleep, and we ain't got nothin' cooked."

Involuntarily I turned to the corner whence he sprang, and there saw a mound of dirty bedclothes, under which they were all probably snugged away.

> "Living in a house without any door,
> With an unlaid hearth and an unfinished floor,"

and discussing the affairs of a nation! Could he read? Doubtful. But he was *twenty-one*, could vote, and was one of "the people."

We resumed our journey, the darkness of the night relieved only by our lanterns dimly burning. The road becoming rougher and the country wilder, the horses were fatigued, and stumbled dreadfully, being scarcely able to drag us along. No dwelling-houses were to be seen. We were so cold and restless that sleep was a stranger to our eyelids, and the night seemed interminable.

But "time and the hour passed." Morning broke, and before eight o'clock we reached the breakfast station. It seemed that they had received information of our coming, for breakfast was ready, and we were quite ready for it. The fat landlady, with a face as blooming as a cabbage-rose, and full of bustling insignificance showed us into the dining-room. Fried ham and eggs, hot coffee and smoking potatoes, milk, honey, molasses, and pies, with a dish of pork and beans in the center, presented a repast which I thought good enough for a king.

Attached to our party was a merchant from one of the county towns of Kentucky, who thought himself quite fine, with his dingy shirt-ruffles sticking out fully an eighth of a yard, his glittering breast-pin, monstrous seal-ring, and flashy gold watch-chain. Patronizingly surveying the landlady, he said, in the blandest tone, after drinking his first cup of coffee:

"Madam, where are the milk?"

"There it are, sir," said she, pointing to a stone pitcher with her fat finger.

A suppressed titter from the girls was silenced by a look from Mr. Tevis, but their gravity was again upset by:

"Miss, them are molasses, if you please. Is them home-made, Ma'am?"

"Yes, sir; and I can ricommend them as being sweeter and better than any of yer furrin 'lasses; clearer, sure, than any of yer Muscavaders."

This was too much for the girls, and their efforts to suppress their merriment forced them to leave the table with but half-satisfied appetites.

As there was no prospect of the cold's abating, we hired from the landlady several blankets, to be returned by the stage-driver. At noon we stopped at a house on the roadside, if haply we might procure something to eat—not having been wise enough to bring with us a lunch. It was a dreary-looking place, not a living being to be seen, though the driver assured us it was inhabited. The door was opened by a little boy about ten years of age. Two or three children were parching corn in a skillet placed on the hearth, in which they were so much interested that they did not raise their eyes to look at us. The boy was sprightly, and showed not the least timidity.

"Can't you give us something to eat, my son?"

"We ain't got any thing for ourselves," said he, "but this parched corn."

"Where are your father and mother?"

"Daddy's gone to Jackson, and mammy's gone to mill."

There was not a particle of furniture in the room except a few old chairs, two or three stools, and a stout deal table, upon which stood a barrel with a convenient stop-cock.

"What's in that barrel? Cider?"

"No, that's prime old whisky. We sells tavern here. Want a dram?"

Suiting the action to the words he seized a tin-cup and was about to draw the liquor. "Stop! stop!" said Mr. Tevis, "we do not want any, and you must never drink it yourself." The gentleman gave a few small pieces of silver to the children, and after being well warmed we left.

Just as twilight was deepening into darkness, we reached the town of Jackson, and were driven up to the door of the tavern kept by our driver, who was also stage contractor and mail carrier—a thrifty man, who turned every thing to his own advantage, and who would do any thing within the bounds of honesty "for a consideration." We all rushed into the reception-room, and were soon comfortably seated around the hottest fire I ever saw. We left the frigid zone out of doors, but found midsummer in the house. Logs of wood were heaped up nearly to the arch of the fire-place—the interstices filled with great lumps of coal.

Mr. Tevis had traveled through that region as an itinerant preacher long years before, and as he understood there was to be preaching in the Methodist Church, a quarterly-meeting being in progress, immediately after supper he went to Church, and there met many of his old friends, and, at their earnest request, preached for them. They urged him to remain several days in this cozy little town, which, to our great regret, he was obliged to decline doing.

The night spent in Jackson was one to be remembered. When introduced into our sleeping apartment I was amazed to find no covering on the bed. The naked tick presented itself to my eyes without the slight relief of even a calico spread.

"What!" said I, "do you intend for us to sleep without a cover?"

"Oh, no," replied the attendant, and raising up the corner of the bed-tick, showed beneath it thick, warm blankets, white and unsullied as newly fallen snow.

The feather-bed was the outside covering. This little woman had come from the "Father-land." That night was one of dreamless rest.

Early the next morning we were *en route* for Chillicothe—a merry coach full of rested travelers, not a sour-visaged dyspeptic among us. We had learned one lesson never to be forgotten—in all conceivable circumstances it is good policy physically, morally, and religiously to be cheerful; yea, merry, in the sense that Solomon uses the word, "A merry heart doeth good like medicine." Discontent gains nothing for soul or body. Cheerfulness is in keeping with the true spirit of Christianity.

We hailed with delight the first glimpse of Chillicothe which we reached before sunset. Sliding over the frozen streets, we were put down at the excellent hotel of Mr. Medeira. We were not sorry to learn, upon inquiry, that every seat in the stage was engaged as far as Wheeling for days to come, and that we should thus have time for rest and recreation.

Chillicothe is beautifully situated, and makes a pleasing impression upon strangers. We were there under what might be considered unfavorable circumstances. The trees stretched forth their leafless arms towards a murky sky—icy Winter had scattered all their Summer glories, not a leaf or a bud to be seen. Yet there were pretty buildings, neatly inclosed yards, clean streets regularly laid out, and, best of all, the spirit of kindness reigned pre-eminent among the citizens. Our excellent host and hostess, ever on "hospitable thoughts intent," made every thing subservient to the comfort of their guests.

After a few days we were again on our way, not rejoicing but with fear and trembling, lest we should have our necks broken. The weather was so bitterly cold the stage-drivers were as savage and as surly as polar bears. Poor fellows, I could not help pitying them, though they were so awfully wicked. For many, many years I had not heard an oath, and these men swore so constantly and so horribly, that I was actually afraid of them, and felt that it was almost wrong for us to travel under such guidance. Meantime we moved on rapidly day and night, always finding some tolerable refreshments at the post-houses, until we reached Wheeling, where we rested and slept in a bed for the first time after leaving Chillicothe.

We had rather a pleasant trip through Pennsylvania, and reached Philadelphia after an absence of three weeks from home. The cordiality of our reception by friends and relatives, and the luxury of feeling that we had no more difficulties to encounter, fully compensated for what we had endured. Strangers have often complained of a certain reserve and formality in the Philadelphians, which I failed to discover, either during this or subsequent visits. On the contrary, I think the permanently settled inhabitants of the city possess, in an eminent degree, the qualities essential to friendship and genuine politeness.

It is a great mistake to suppose that hospitality consists in giving sumptuous feasts. In the dress, manners, habits, accomplishments, and learning of these people— indeed, in every sphere and department of life, public and private, was seen the pervading, beautiful, and honest simplicity which characterizes the "Friends." And, certainly, the spirit and principles inculcated by William Penn were eminently calculated to diffuse harmony and order, to systematize society, and to promote tranquillity. I have been in Philadelphia frequently, but have never lost the agreeable impressions first received.

The spirit of its illustrious founder is visible in all the institutions of this noble city. Homes for the destitute, house of refuge for the outcast, hospitals for the sick, and benevolent societies in every direction proclaim the golden rule of brotherly love. Charming parks and open squares refresh the heart and delight the eye in various parts of the city. These are free to all classes. Here the weary foot may rest and the sorrowing soul forget, for a while, the heat and hurry of existence. Here, in Summer, the song birds hold their jubilee, and the fragrance of flowers floats on every breeze. Here, amid the laughter of gay and happy children, which comes like sweet music to the listening heart, persons may be seen sitting quietly under the shade trees, reading or watching the shifting scenes of loveliness by which they are surrounded. I have often wished that our beloved city of Louisville were so blessed with breathing lungs for her many and heart-burdened population.

The days flew by as on the wings of the wind—each full of interest, instruction, and enjoyment. Teachers should travel occasionally, brush off the dust of the school-room, and see something beyond the precincts of its limited sphere. Rational, sensible travel corrects false impressions, enlarges our views, and increases our knowledge. The mind needs relaxation after months of constant exertion. The bow must be unbent now and then, or it will snap asunder. Many selfishly seek recreation without having earned it—these seldom find it equal to their expectations.

Chapter XXXVIII.

IN the garland of love and memory woven about this period, is a flower of surpassing loveliness. So natural and without disguise was the character of Susan W. Henning—so child-like her innocence, and so sweet her timidity, allied to a tone of pervading cheerfulness, that the girls sought her companionship.

> "Her speech and gesture, form and grace,
>   Showed she was born of gentle race."

Yet every thought of practiced effect or haughty pretension was foreign to her nature. Possessed of natural talent and that pure good sense which originates in fine feeling, she was, from her first entrance into school, a perfect type of girlish loveliness. Obedience to rules, accuracy and clearness of recitation, the correct style of her written thoughts, combined with a propriety of demeanor which no ill example could overcome, rendered her a model pupil. Her countenance wore a beautiful expression, and in her clear, truthful eyes was mirrored an elevated soul.

She was married young to one every way worthy of such a prize. Edward Hobbs won, even in his early manhood, the respect and esteem of all who knew him; a character which has not only been maintained, but has brightened and widened into an earnest goodness that renders him an acknowledged benefactor.

For many years we kept up the custom of crowning a "Rose Queen" in May, and enjoying a holiday in the woods. Happily for the girls, I greeted the return of the festal day with a gladness almost equal to theirs, for I retained enough of the freshness of youth in my heart to enable me to participate with zest in the joys of childhood.

"Once upon a time," after a long severe Winter, followed by a Spring of unusual beauty, it was determined to celebrate the day with great rejoicings. The girls were wild with delight at the prospect of a whole day's release from slates, books, and blackboards—a charming episode in the drudgery of their every-day life. Ah, happy children! to whom every glimpse of nature is beautiful, and every blade of grass a marvel! Give them ever so small a bit of green meadow checkered with sunshine and shade upon which to revel among buttercups and daisies, and "little they'll reck" how the world goes on.

There was but little opportunity for canvassing or intrigue in the election of Queen. Fanny Henning was chosen by acclamation as best fitted to grace the regal authority. Fanny possessed a mind and a character as transparent as a clear brook. Her ingenuous face, her self-forgetting and amiable bearing towards her companions made her the loved and cherished of them all. She also held a distinguished place in the estimation of her teachers for superior excellence, dutiful affection, and modest deportment. Thus it was universally conceded that "Fair-handed Spring" might well resign to Fanny her sovereignty for one day over the brilliant treasures of garden, glade, and forest, awakened into life and brightened into beauty by her magic wand.

The rosy hours followed each other in quick succession until within a few days of the anticipated time,

when lo! the "queen elect" broke out with measles.
The whole school was filled with dismay, bitter tears of
disappointment were shed by some; others predicted
that she would be well enough to go through the ceremony. Fanny, uniting in their hopeful aspirations, prepared her coronation speech and rehearsed it to perfection, for, though confined to her room, she was not
really ill. On the eve of the appointed day, however,
the doctor pronounced her too feeble to endure the
fatigue. What was to be done? The trophies of many
loyal hearts were ready to be laid at the feet of the
queen. Spirit hands seemed dispensing blessings, and
guardian angels extending their wings over these healthful, happy girls as they diligently wrought sparkling
wreaths and arranged beautiful bouquets.

The banners were prepared, the white dresses were
trimmed with evergreen. The Seasons, the maids of
honor, and all the officials were in waiting, but "*Hamlet*
could not be left out of the play. One modest little girl,
after listening in silence to the suggestions of the others,
raised her eyes to my face and said hesitatingly:

"Can't Emma Maxwell be queen in Fanny's place?"

"Oh, no!" said another; "she could not possibly
learn the speech in time."

"No, indeed!" exclaimed several voices at once, "that
would be impossible; but she might read it."

"Yes, yes! let her read it; the queen's speeches are
read in Parliament!"

"Will you accept the proposition?" said I, turning
to Emma.

"I think I can learn it," she replied, "and will try if
you wish it."

The coronation was to take place the next morning at

ten o'clock. A previous rehearsal would be impossible; but what Emma proudly determined to do was generally accomplished.

The evening star looked out bright and clear in the blue deep, thrilling the hearts of these young girls with the prospect of a pleasant morrow.

Most of them were stirring before sunrise. "Is it clear?" "Are we going?" And from every room issued the sound of cheerful voices; and then such shouts, such hurrying and bathing and dressing as was seldom known before.

Ten o'clock came, and the yard, where the temporary throne was erected, was soon filled with spectators and invited guests, mingling with the children and participating in their pleasure. The proxy queen bore her blushing honors meekly, going through all the coronation ceremonies with a charming dignity. She stood Calypso-like among her train of attendants in full view of the audience who listened in breathless silence to her address. I watched her closely; she seemed to plant her feet firmly, as if to still the beatings of her heart; no gesture except a gentle motion of the right arm as she swayed her scepter majestically around, her eyes steadily fixed upon some object beyond, with which she seemed completely absorbed. Not a word was misplaced, not a sentence omitted, of a speech long enough for a Parliamentary harangue. No one prompted, nor did she once turn her eyes towards the scroll she held in her left-hand. Enthusiastic and excessive were the rejoicings of her juvenile auditors.

Fanny witnessed the whole ceremony through a convenient window which framed for her a living picture of ineffable beauty, and on this clear day, with only a few white Spring clouds floating over the bluest of skies, it was a sight of earth that makes one understand heaven.

The Seasons followed in quick succession, proffering homage to the queen; then came the "rosy Hours" with their sweet-toned voices, and the ceremony was completed by a few words from "Fashion and Modesty," the latter gently pushing the former aside, and casting a veil over the burning blushes of the queen. The address being finished, queen and attendants walked in procession to a grove that skirted the town, where beauty filled the eye, and singing birds warbled sweet music. When tired of play, a more substantial entertainment was provided. Group after group spread the white cloth on the soft green turf, and surrounded the plentiful repast, gratefully acknowledging the Hand that supplies our wants from day to day. He who called our attention to the "lilies of the field," stamps a warrant of sacredness upon our rejoicings, in all that he has made.

There was something very remarkable in the quickness and facility with which Emma Maxwell memorized the queen's speech. She was a girl of more than ordinary vivacity, of a highly imaginative, impressionable nature, and seemed to have the gift of bewitching all who knew her. She occupied a commanding position in her class as a good reciter, but I had not hitherto noticed any great facility in memorizing. I called her the next day, and asked her to recite the piece to me alone. She stared rather vacantly at me, and said:

"I can not remember a sentence of it."

"What! when you repeated it with so much facility yesterday! Explain yourself."

"I do not know how it is," she replied, "that though I can learn with the utmost precision, mechanically, whatever I choose, in a short time, yet under such circumstances my memory has not the power of retention. If my train of repetition had been interrupted for one moment yesterday, I should have failed utterly."

"What were you looking at so intently the whole time?"

"I was looking at certain objects about the yard and house, in connection with which I had studied the speech the evening before."

"Yes; but you certainly can repeat some portion of it to me?"

"Not one sentence connectedly; it has all passed from my mind like a shadow on the wall."

Yet she was a girl of good judgment, read much, talked well, and possessed in an eminent degree the indispensable requisite of a good memory — power of attention.

The unfolding drama of my school life introduces another May Queen of more than ordinary interest as connected with so many pleasant remembrances, a gem in my heart's casket, that still gleams with a steady luster. Margaret Thorpe bore for many years an intimate relation to Science Hill, first as a pupil, then as a teacher, — her never-tiring mind going on from strength to strength until she stood firmly on the platform, a successful teacher. If I may claim credit for the results reached in the education of this estimable person, I flatter myself that I should have in that fact an enduring monument of the value of my efforts.

Mary Hamilton bore the sobriquet of "Lexington," her place of residence, to distinguish her from another of the same name. Her name is embalmed among the most pleasant memories of Science Hill. Her cheerful smile and cordial "Good-morning," the introduction to her well-learned lesson, rendered her particularly agreeable in the class-room,—a sweet young girl, gentle and timid as a fawn, her dove-like eyes half-veiled by silken lashes, with the form of a sylph and the foot of a fairy, yet possessing firmness of purpose and energy of mind, combined with perfect self-reliance. She was neat, good, and industrious, and I do not remember that it was ever necessary to chide, reprove, or punish her while a member of our school.

"How sweet the recollection of such girls," forming precious bouquets, redolent with "rosemary for remembrance and pansies for thought," in which the purity of the lily is combined with the softest bloom of the rose! 'T is like the perfume of sweet violets, floating around the senses in a dream of beauty.

Many a region of still life is illustrated with unostentatious goodness. The great virtues do not blaze forth to the admiration of the public eye,—they often pass away, altogether unknown and unacknowledged beyond their own neighborhood till some stray gold-dust floats down before the eye, and guides it to a mine of moral wealth and worth.

Chapter XXXIX.

When I first commenced teaching, want of experience, and a great desire to be faithful in the performance of my duties, made me confine my pupils too many hours to the dull routine of books. Neither did I spare myself; my mind wanted discipline, and thus its work was never done. I could not dismiss my cares and annoyances when I dismissed my school. Not only my daily thoughts, but my nightly dreams, were of the school-room and the peculiar emergencies of my position. Exhaustion, weariness, and anxiety, combined with that constant vigilance necessarily emanating from the central authority to the continually extending circumference of a large school, more than once brought me to the verge of the grave.

The academical year of 1839 closed without any definite prospect of reopening the school; if ever, again under my superintendence. Just here let me give the result of my experience, in the sure conviction that six hours daily devoted to the work of teaching and controlling a school is quite as much as either teacher or pupil can bear without detriment to bodily health and that general intellectual progress which is the end and aim of instruction; and even this could not be borne without that change of employment which sometimes takes the place of recreation.

My conscientiousness permitted too little relaxation, and the school up to this period was, as a friend expressed it, a "perfect flint-mill." Under the gloomy prospect just referred to our first catalogue was published,—a diminutive pamphlet of six pages, closing with a few remarks, and promising that in due time the opening of the next term should be made known to the public.

Traveling had benefited me under like circumstances. Physicians and friends decided that I must go and leave all perplexing cares behind me. My longing heart turned towards the mountains of Virginia, and thither we went. My health improved daily after reaching those elevated regions around which floats an atmosphere pure as ether, and youth and strength seemed "renewed like the eagles." I drank in new life from every surrounding. The old-fashioned coach was filled with cheerful, happy passengers, and as we wended our way leisurely onward over lofty mountains, "with their silent shades and arbors darkly wreathed," a fountain of enjoyment was unsealed, whence flowed an exhilarating current, sparkling as nectar. The soul is like a harp, with capabilities for plaintive, joyous, or solemn music; and when beauty, with its train, sweeps over it, it murmurs a response, chanting, like the choristers of old, praises to Him who fashioned the heavens with their glory and the earth with its beauty.

After a few weeks of travel and delightful sojourning among friends and relatives, we were home again, with renewed health and strength. "The Lord had been with us and kept us by the way," and with grateful hearts we earnestly prayed that henceforth our united lives might be a continued hymn of praise to our Heavenly Father.

Again the school opened under prosperous circumstances, and, having been successful in securing able and competent teachers, my own cares were lessened, and obstacles vanished like the airy fabric of a dream.

A well-established institution of learning, with an unblemished reputation, and extensively known, can never die if God's blessing rest upon it. Languish it may occasionally,—ephemeral schools may spring up with a mushroom growth, only to perish after the lapse of a few years. A good school must be permanent, and will be sustained in spite of the fickleness of popular favor; but the great fault with many teachers is want of patience with the order of nature,—they can not wait for the changes. Time is requisite for the accomplishment of any great work, and many failures are attributable to that feverish impatience which characterizes some worthy enterprise. Much is due, under Providence, in the success of this school, to the unwearied perseverance of both teachers and pupils. Multitudes are only half educated for want of patience and perseverance to pursue a course, the chief difficulties of which they have already overcome. Patience under great discouragements is an attribute of exalted characters, and one of the essential conditions of success in all the chief pursuits in life.

I have learned to know, by long experience, that "it is the twig, the tender shoot, which is bent, and not the full-grown tree," and I have also learned another fact, which seems in our "fast age" unknown or unrecognized by many, and that is that in four years a complete college course, embracing all the sciences and many of the languages, can not possibly be accomplished. Scholars, who at the age of "sweet sixteen" are deficient in spelling, deficient in the pronunciation of their own language, and incapable of writing a letter grammatically, and without being able to bound the United States or to name the principal cities in the Union! Think you such, or even those more advanced in an English course, could acquire even in a dozen years what is professed to be taught in many of our most distinguished female colleges in a four years' course? that which would fit them for statesmen, doctors, lawyers, or any other position in public life? The absurdity is palpable.

Thus I have never proposed a full collegiate course for my pupils, and I glory in the old-fashioned name of "Academy," which I think includes a full requisition of all that is necessary to make an elegant, cultivated, refined woman for society, and fit her for the higher duties of home life,—like Cornelia, displaying her jewels around the fireside, and fitting them not only for the outer world of to-day, but to send rays of light through ages to come.

When will we learn this truth, that *women* should be the best economists of time and best fitted to dispense those blessings of home life which are given to us through them by our Heavenly Father? Some blessings are bestowed upon us in clusters like the fruits of the vine; but time, the golden elixir of life, is poured upon us drop by drop, minute by minute, one is gone before another is bestowed.

In the administration of an institution so large as ours promised to be from the beginning of 1840, so varied in its departments of learning and arduous and unremitting in its duties, it was found necessary to make some changes and improvements for its future success. This was promptly attended to and its onward course was marked by uninterrupted prosperity. A thousand recollections crowd upon my mind as memory retraces the scenes of my pathway dating from the re-opening of my school in 1840, so that I am bewildered as to choice. My work would be too voluminous, and time would fail me.

My cares and sorrows, troubles and perplexities are forgotten as I gaze on the number of interesting young girls passing in review. Some have gone home after having finished their work on earth, leaving the assurance of a blessed immortality, "where their works do follow them;" others still live to show the good effects of a well-cultivated mind, and to preside with wisdom and dignity in well-ordered homes, and to show forth by their example how beautifully a moral and religious education affects the soul. It is a well-known fact that true piety and virtue shine with double luster when the intellectual faculties are well cultivated.

While many a lovely vision has passed away, and many a sacred record shines but in the moonlight of memory; yet few, very few of the pictures in the gallery of my school life have been obliterated, and often now, in the twilight of life's evening, the magic touch of some connecting link brings up before me form after form, with the intensity of a life-like presence. O beautiful memory! How delightful to build our recollections upon some basis of reality—a lovely face, an interesting scene, a beautiful country, a local habitation! How the events of life and its thrilling scenes vibrate through our very being! We look back upon the well-remembered family group with its rays of golden sunshine lighting up the happy faces; we see, too, before us here and there, dim and silent places always shaded with darker hues to us— where sorrowful remembrance weeps forevermore, and from whence arises a resurrection light which mingles with the full blaze of an eternal day.

The constitution of every good school is an absolute monarchy, but under the control of moral principle which must be the guiding power, as far as possible, in the government of its subjects. The more tenderly the feelings of the young are handled the more sensitive they will become; the mildest reproof given to a timid girl in the hearing of her companions, is often a punishment greater than she can bear. Rough treatment is calculated to harden and stupefy some who might be saved by a different course. A public exposure may so destroy the sensitiveness as to render the subject of such treatment impervious to admonition or reproof.

The superiority of a teacher does not consist in making her pupils fear and tremble, but rather in securing their own self-respect and making them feel that the end of good government is to promote their comfort and improvement. An effectual way to insure the good will of pupils is to keep them interested in their studies. No drones should ever be tolerated. Idleness at any period of life is dangerous to virtue, but more to be dreaded in youth than at any other season; therefore, never let a school-girl have time to count the flies on the wall of her study-room or gaze at surrounding objects. Keep the mental powers active and awake, and never allow them to be without a sufficient sphere of operation within the limits of their capacity, else they will become headstrong, fickle, vain, self-sufficient, averse to consideration, intent upon the present moment, regardless of the future, forgetful of the past, and fit subjects for temptation.

Some teachers in striving to impress their pupils with their own infallibility by professing to know every thing, lose that confidence which they are striving to secure. Let children know that it is not universal acquisition, but a well-balanced mind and fixed principles of action and systematic habits that distinctly mark the boundary between knowledge and ignorance.

A well-organized and well-governed school greatly diminishes the trouble of teaching. Cheerfulness, order, industry, and propriety of conduct are essential to the highest interests of the school. No disorder of books or desks, no leaving seats without liberty, no communications either by whispering or otherwise, except by express permission of the presiding teacher, should be the inviolable law of the study-room.

I have said there must be but one supreme controlling head in every school, thus preventing jealousy among teachers and insubordination among pupils. But in a large school, where there are several teachers, each should be the supreme ruler in his or her department; there should be no appeal to the principal except for consultation. A meeting of the teachers is desirable now and then to compare notes. A perfect unanimity should exist; one single jarring string destroys the harmony and clogs the onward progress of the pupils.

Children love to work, and nothing charms them more than to be made to feel their importance. I have often endeared a young girl to me by asking her assistance, and many an idle one have I made industrious by finding her something to do for others, when she was unwilling to work for herself. A personal attachment of the warmest kind may thus be awakened between teacher and pupil. We must be careful, however, while asking the assistance of some and showing an honest gratification for the assistance rendered, not to awaken the jealousy of others. I have seen the happiest results attending judicious measures of this kind. The time is well spent, even if the regular course of study be interrupted, when we can induce our pupils to act in concert with us, and make them feel how much pleasanter it is to co-operate than to thwart and oppose; yet whenever reproof or correction is necessary, the teacher must be a throned monarch; look on the favorable side as far as is consistent with duty, but be ever ready with an efficient hand to arrest evil.

I have had very many excellent assistant teachers of both sexes, superior in tact and successful in their vocation, yet I do not hesitate to give it as my decided opinion that women are the best, the most patient, and the most successful teachers save, perhaps, in the higher and more abstruse sciences, which belong to the learned professions. They are certainly better fitted to govern a female school.

Several are now passing in review before me, each possessing those excellent qualities and high credentials that fitted her for the lot assigned her by Providence—a model of patient industry and untiring interest in her vocation. One I must detain as an example of all a teacher should be; she rises in queenly dignity, pre-eminently successful in her vocation, upon which she entered in the morning of life. Thoroughly educated and intelligent, she rapidly acquired those qualifications that fitted her peculiarly for this delicate and elevated position, which she continued to occupy. Like the Roman emperor she considered a day lost in which some good was not done or acquired. Her personal appearance prepossessing in the highest degree, with a voice low and sweet, yet clear and distinct; manners dignified and reserved, though never cold nor repellent, she impressed favorably upon first sight, and never failed to insure esteem and confidence upon more intimate acquaintance.

A magical reformation was produced by her connection with our school, particularly in the department where she presided, system and order followed her footsteps as naturally as flowers rise up under the elastic tread of Spring. I have never known this lady teacher to use harsh language or reproachful epithets. She proceeds cautiously and tenderly, but with an air of uncompromising authority and power. When reproof is necessary and forbearance no longer a virtue, her tone and manner become those of a judge—decisive, not persuasive.

Faithful teachers will never be satisfied simply to hear recitations, to keep the order of the classes, and to impress the contents of text-books. These are parts of their vocation, but with a solemn sense of the worth of immortal souls they will strive to provide their pupils with moral and religious, as well as intellectual, work-habits, principles, and affections that make life beautiful and death a messenger of peace.

If it be true that memory is but little more than fixed attention, the faculty of attention should be cultivated from the dawn of reason as the key to knowledge. Children should be taught that it is morally wrong to forget what they are expected to remember. It is inexcusable in a student to utter the phrase, "I have forgotten," without sorrow and a fixed resolution to prevent its recurrence if possible.

Great care will be taken by a good teacher to cultivate the powers of expression and correct pronunciation. A bungling, unintelligible answer should never be received. Under no circumstances ought we to accept the common excuse, "I know, but can not tell," for if any one knows he can tell it—and tell it just as well as he knows it. An instructor who has the tact to awaken interest and inspire a class with enthusiasm by a lively and interesting style of teaching is a blessing to the school-room. If wanting in the ability to do this, he is mistaken in his calling and should seek another occupation.

Prompting should be considered as a punishable offense. In the first place it prevents that moral courage and independence which gives a pupil self-respect; it encourages idleness and, worse than all, the habit of deception. Recitations should always be mingled with explanations. I never could confine myself to a text-book, and, with my advanced pupils, have been in the constant habit of reading selections from standard authors, ancient and modern.

Next to reading and orthography comes a clear and beautiful penmanship—graceful and easy to be read. Too much attention can not be given to these. My own handwriting is remarkably distinct, clear, and smooth even at the age of sixty-eight. This is due, not only to early and constant attention, but to the fact of having been obliged to copy much for others. I was the amanuensis of my father from the age of twelve to twenty.

What is the best method of teaching the art of composition? This question has frequently been asked, and many have expressed the decided opinion that it is best not to attempt the carrying out of any particular rules, leaving circumstances to direct. This is equivalent to letting it alone altogether.

After trying various methods suggested by my own experience, I long ago settled upon the plan of requiring original specimens from the hands of even the youngest writers, no matter how simple in form and expression. Do not *look* for faults to correct. Little inaccuracies, at first, must be passed over; this gives confidence to young composers. Encourage them to tell the first things they can remember, to relate whatever made an impression on the mind when young. Pass over all that you may with propriety. Do not criticise their feeble efforts before the class, where all compositions must be read by the composer, or you will check the free growth of thought and the increased power of expression. Such indulgence takes away all excuse from even the least informed. The most timid girl may be prevailed upon to write some little anecdote of her own life, and that which at first seems so unconquerable and difficult becomes a source of interest and amusement. After these compositions have been read before the class, correct them privately with the writer, pointing out the false orthography, ungrammatical expressions, and other errors. I have been surprised at the increased facility acquired by this judicious management.

Chapter XL.

MANY a bright young face rises before me connected with these happy, busy days; now and then one calls for something more than a passing glance.

A fair-faced child with a profusion of rich, auburn hair, than whom none has made a deeper impression upon my heart, came to me from Clarke County, the land of my birth. School life was rendered pleasant to this little lassie by the cultivation of kind affections toward her school-mates and respectful obedience to her teachers. With a step light and springy, a ready disposition to oblige and always merry-hearted, she soon became a prime favorite.

When Amanda first entered school, she was particularly pleased with her own performance on the piano, and never lost an opportunity of displaying her acquirements. Her laughter-loving companions, infinitely amused at her childish vanity, would frequently smuggle her away into a retired music-room, and, while she played, would loudly applaud. This continued to delight the little girl immensely, until she discovered, upon one occasion, that they were amusing themselves at her expense. She darted off, and no persuasions could ever again prevail upon her to play for them, and indeed it made her reluctant for a long time to touch the piano at all.

Among her most pleasing and attractive qualities was her power of lively description. Possessing a wonderful memory, she never forgot persons, places, or things.

Thus her mind was stored with pleasing incidents and amusing anecdotes, rendering her an agreeable companion at home and abroad.

Why is it that many "would-be favorites" are slow to learn that pleasant looks, affectionate words, and obliging deeds, not only render them lovely but beloved? These characteristics, with their quiet, but infallible tracings, make the unfading pictures in life's book of beauty, which diffuse over the whole countenance a coloring of inexpressible loveliness, and, even in extreme old age, are the last remembrances that time effaces from the mind.

Mere personal attractions are nothing compared with that soul-beauty beaming forth even in childhood, like the flashing rays of the uncut diamond. I learned to love this little maiden very dearly. Often when wearied with the bustling perplexities of school she was the privileged one who glided into my room, and, with her smiling face and gentle, prattling voice, soothed the throbbings of my restless heart.

This child of brilliant promise did not disappoint the hopes of teacher and friends. She grew up an elegant woman, as remarkable for wit and refinement of manners as for her Christian graces—bearing no obscure handwriting on lip or brow.

Children may be denominated creatures of imitation, and upon this instinctive faculty more depends in the formation of habits and character throughout the whole course of life than upon almost any other. Conscience must be enlightened and settled on proper authority; it must be corrected and strengthened, and rendered quite unbending to every influence and temptation from the association of company, passion, or interest.

Young imaginations are so easily wrought upon, that not only pernicious books and unhealthy literature should be carefully eschewed, but the associations promptly and constantly attended to. The good or bad influences to which girls may be subjected tell for weal or woe upon their future. Of all the unnumbered mercies of Providence, none are greater, or more affecting in the recollection, than those which I received ere yet a light from above shone into my heart. In the peculiar gift of companionship I was often preserved from imprudence by the warning admonition of a judicious friend. Minervas are sometimes found among school-girls, and we should be assiduously anxious, as well to secure their healthy companionship, as to prevent those intimacies which selfishly ignore but the favored one—maintaining like the Jewish rabbi, "if there are but two wise persons in the world, my son and I are the two."

Suffer two silly, indiscreet girls to become intimate, and they will be icebergs to the rest of the school. They must sit side by side in the study room, in juxtaposition at the table, go arm in arm to Church, linger far behind the rest in walking, showing in every thing an exclusiveness that becomes exceedingly offensive to others. Finally, an explosion takes place, and a multitude of others are set on fire by the revelation of sarcastic remarks, aside communications, and betrayals of confidence.

The opposite of this is found in the noble friendships of the large-hearted, who can love each other dearly and still be just to others. True as the needle to the pole, each may be the cynosure of the other, and yet shed an ever-beaming light upon all who come within the circle of her perpetual revolutions. The united aims of two such may be to promote the interest and happiness of others without impairing their inexpressible tenderness and devotion to each other.

There is nothing like school life—nothing that could take the place of its reminiscences. Other memories may fade, these brighten with the lapse of time, and even to the latest hour of life, amid the fondest scenes of recollection a classmate's is still the most eloquent face to be casually encountered. Where do we find so great a variety presented as in the shifting panorama of its everyday life? The amiable and the peevish, the thoughtful and the reckless; the tender, so ready to receive impressions that scarcely a sound falls unheeded; and the obdurate, over whose conscience every admonition glides like raindrops from polished steel; and again, trusting, susceptible spirits of whom a teacher loves to think as having been drawn out and beautifully developed under the myriad-handed genius of industry.

Now softly gliding into view comes Barbara Thruston, with her quiet face, and "stature small but firmly knit." There was a serenity and composure of manner not common in young girls which gave the impression of dignity, and rendered her prepossessing upon first acquaintance. A more intimate knowledge of her character showed that the neat little casket contained a gem that would amply repay the educator's care.

There seemed a slight dash of haughtiness in the curve of her closed lips—a look of quiet decision and fixedness of purpose that made me fear there might be some trouble in bending her will to the strictness of our regulations. But this was only imaginary; she was reticent from sheer timidity, and though possessing firmness of purpose and strength of character, she never for a moment lost her serene repose of manner nor departed from that quiet demeanor which so well became her. Under the drooping lids of the young girl, there were soul-lit eyes sparkling with good humor, of which there was a rich store hid beneath the surface and appearing on all proper occasions; while an earnest desire for knowledge led her to love school, conform to its regulations, and respect her teachers.

Many pleasant recollections are connected with Louisville, from whence I received much of my early patronage. There are households in that city where cultivated taste, united with the more vigorous facilities of the understanding, governs and controls the family, and where now is found a presiding genius who once formed a part of the family circle of their school.

Five daughters of our much esteemed and life-long friends, Mr. and Mrs. Samuel K. Richardson, were among my pupils. Four of them yet live, presiding over homes where the stranger and the friend can repose with delight; one has gone to her celestial home, to reap the reward of a useful life. The oldest, and first that came to us, was lovely and beloved, and always exerted a happy influence over her companions.

. She is now a grandmother, and has beautifully fulfilled all the requisitions of a noble woman. Time has touched her so lightly as to leave only the graceful traces of maturer womanhood.

Among the many friends and patrons of Science Hill Mr. David Thornton occupies a prominent place. This excellent man was a fountain head of social and religious life in the community in which he dwelt. Just in all his actions, faithful in all his words, he pursued the even tenor of his course, and, dying in the triumphs of a victorious faith, he left behind him the remembrance of his

virtues and bequeathed to his children the inheritance of
of an unstained name.

Our well-beloved pupil, Hontas Thornton, his daughter,
yet lives to exemplify the fact that a moral and religious
training brightens the intellectual faculties and fits us for
a higher state of existence. She was always cheerful,
but never boisterous, and her sparking wit never degen-
erated into asperity. She knew that human happiness is
founded upon wisdom and virtue, and by these she
seemed to be guided in all her aspirations. But "time
would fail to me to tell of Gideon and of Barak and of
Samson and of Jephthah, of David also and Samuel and
of the prophets."

As I do not pretend to write a regular, connected
history, I shall certainly not challenge criticism by introducing link after link of the family circle, as well as so
many marked and characteristic illustrations of young
persons figuring at different intervals as pupils in my
school.

My only living daughter, and the last but one of seven
children, was in truth a great joy to the family circle.
Cherished by a host of tender relatives, she learned even
in babyhood to feel her importance. I prayed most
earnestly that she might be permitted to live and "walk
as an angel by my side" through life's journey. And
though I trembled lest the cup of my earthly joy might
overflow, I felt a sweet assurance that He who inspired
the wish would grant the request. Submitting all to the
divine will, I did not ask for riches, nor grandeur, nor
beauty, nor fame, nor worldly position for this dear child,
but I asked of the Lord that she might be good and
useful in this world, and hereafter dwell with the saints
in glory.

I began early to weave the net of education of fibers as fine as the gossamer, which were in time to become stronger than tempered steel, praying all the while that the light of a true Christian faith should irradiate her intellectual attainments, giving them a brighter luster.

This newly opened page of life I contemplated with a pleasure that caused a flood-tide of affection to be poured upon the little girl, and filled my mind with a repose in the enjoyment of the present that shut out all fears for the future. She was impulsive. The simplicity and ingenuousness of her emotions were manifested in her expressive features with such transparency that her thoughts were known even before she was conscious of their existence. She was a happy child, enjoying the present and never speculating upon the future, living on from hour to hour amid the sweet surroundings of home life like a bird or a blossom, unconscious that darker days might ever come.

I thought I could discover intellect in her glance— what mother does not?—even in early childhood. Her large, wide-open eyes brightened at every fresh object, and her desire to learn was exhibited in a curiosity to *know* and to *understand*. Her questions were always answered, and the warm and rapid thoughts of her soul were nurtured into life under the ardent solicitude and affectionate care of her instructors. An only daughter is generally the synonym for spoiled child. To prevent this she was under the strictest domestic control, and grew up under the same discipline as her school-fellows, being neither rocked in the cradle of indulgence nor fed on lilies.

A constant effort was made to rear her in the nurture and admonition of the Lord. Belle had from childhood

31

a ready flow of language, and knew, as if by instinct, where to place the emphasis in her pathetic harangues for peace and pardon, after having violated, even with Solomon's injunctions before her eyes, any of those early taught habits of order, neatness, and obedience.

My Heavenly Father, in his goodness, still spares her—a comfort to my declining years.

Chapter XLI.

Days and months have slipped by almost imperceptibly since I closed the preceding chapter, intending to finish my book with a concluding summary. I had not thought to defer it so long, but time passes quickly with us as we approach the evening of life. I remember when it was different. Had I been told the first twenty years of my life would seem the longest portion of it I should have doubted; but now, when the evening comes, and the day's work is nearly over, it seems but a short space since I entered upon its duties and its responsibilities.

January 8, 1870. Just fifty years ago I began my career as a teacher, and have continued with but little interruption,—no rest from duties save in the vacations.

When the light of the sun grows dim upon my fading eyes, when the fountains of life are low, when the frosts of age descend upon my feeble frame, then through the halls of memory, like the "still, sweet strains of music far away," will come tender recollections of the happy throngs that have hearkened to my instructions. The grateful remembrance of those for whom I have patiently and zealously toiled casts a halo of light over life's decline, soothes the infirmities of age and kindles upon the altar of my heart a purer love for the human race. Each pupil, whom by advice or encouragement I prompted to nobler aims or urged to higher attainments, is a gem in my casket of more worth than the treasures of the deep blue sea.

Twilight is deepening gradually about me; no evil bodings disturb the tranquillity of my closing days. My heart throws off link after link of this world's bondage, and the soul, losing its sternness and the keen excitements of a busy life, is becoming subdued as a child's.

I can not forget my early dreamings and youth's cherished associations; they still come thronging back like sad angels, and my spirit reaches yearningly after the good and true whom I knew long ago. But I think more of the unseen world towards which I am so rapidly borne, and of the mysteries of eternity.

Long years of toil and care have not weakened my interest in the advancement of science and the budding growth of mind. I have watched the dawning intellect, and rejoiced in the prospective usefulness, of thousands. I wish to impress as deeply as possible the result of my observations and experience upon those who will follow me.

Teaching, when pursued with a strong conviction of the value of the immortal soul, becomes a high and holy work. The good begun on earth, the seed sown in its few fleeting years, will yield fruit divine in heaven. "They that sow in tears shall reap in joy,"—and come up before the eternal throne rejoicing, bringing their sheaves with them.

Notwithstanding the apparent monotony of a teacher's life, it is made up of varied and shifting scenes. A thousand nameless cares and perplexities sweep over us at times, quenching like a flood every ray of hope. Wearied with the more than thread-bare round of duties, and with the captious and incorrigible conduct of juvenile delinquents, discouraged by the indifference or ingratitude of parents, we almost despair of accomplishing any good;

and sometimes, weighed down by anxiety, exhausted by labor or depressed by indisposition, we would gladly fly from the school-room, never again to enter its confines. But this is the result of that occasional *ennui* to which the most devoted and eminent teachers are subject.

These dark clouds of discouragement will presently be chased away by the sunlight of promise and joy, and leave us under an open sky of cheerfulness and serenity that "lets in blue banner-gleams of heaven."

With a proper arrangement of duties and recreations a healthy tone of body and mind may be maintained, and the teacher live to possess and enjoy the fruits of his labor. The intervals of relaxation are enjoyed by him with a zest greater than is known in other conditions of life. When he goes forth from his dusty desks and perplexing problems, the very trees seem to lift their verdant crowns and bend in salutation to him, and the flowers send sweet invisible messages to greet his delighted senses. The whole garb of nature seems dyed afresh in emerald tints, and the balmy gale breathes into his sinews new strength. There is a precious reward for him in the pure, untainted affection bestowed upon him by ingenuous hearts, unpracticed in the deceptive arts of maturer years. His young pupils come to greet him each morning with light hearts and bounding steps; the little grievances and asperities of yesterday's births are lost in the oblivion of the night's repose, and they come with faces radiant with kind regard and good intentions. The faithful instructor feels that he bears no unimportant part in the grand drama of human affairs. He is training the immortal mind, and even in some degree influencing the eternal destinies of the soul.

The standard of scholarship for girls is undoubtedly

much higher in this country to-day than it was fifty
years ago; and teachers of experience and more extended
information are needed for their training. Hence he who
aspires to be successful in this vocation must be up and
doing, not content to sit by the roadside an uninterested
spectator while the grand procession moves on; he must
fall into the line and march. He must keep up with
new books and new systems. The mind of a teacher
must be a fountain, not a reservoir of knowledge,—the
pure stream must gush from the overflowing depths of
his own being, not be drawn up with rope and bucket
from the moss-grown wells of antiquity alone. His own
spirit must be breathed into the worn text-book, and its
hidden characters made to glow with new meaning.

It can not be too forcibly impressed upon the mind
of a teacher, in his efforts for success, that the duty of
habitually and systematically caring for the health of
pupils should be rigidly fulfilled. When the hours allotted to the duties of the school-room are over the seasons
set apart for recreation should not be infringed upon.
The urgent necessity for physical exercise and mental
relaxation must be apparent to all.

There is nothing in the life of a teacher, when thus
properly regulated, that needs be prejudicial to health
or longevity.

I have referred to a time when, owing to the constant
self-imposed strain upon mind and body, my health so
utterly failed that I was compelled to pause in a career
hitherto happily successful, and use every available
means for my restoration. After that a part of every
vacation was invariably spent in seeking recreation,—
sojourning sometimes amid mountain scenery, sometimes
upon the sea-shore, or at some quiet watering-place,

among cheerful friends and agreeable surroundings. When I left home I left all care behind me, and sought only enjoyment. The result was, renewed energy and health.

Science Hill is now the center of my thoughts and the subject of my daily prayers. Many a pure joy has blossomed here. For more than fifty years I have lived and worked in this spot hallowed by a thousand tenderest associations.

For its advertising the institution has depended to a great extent upon the friendly interest of its pupils, having but seldom published in the newspapers. The living stream grows wider as it flows onward, and in not a few instances we find in its catalogues three successive generations of the same name and blood.

The internal economy of the school is not unlike that of a well-ordered college.

Our school has grown up, like a tree, by slow and gradual increase. The wise and patient system of financial economy pursued under the direction of my husband gradually increased our prosperity, and gave ample opportunity of supplying all the helps requisite· for our success.

The enthusiastic regard and reverence which our pupils entertained for Mr. Tevis is the highest encomium which could be paid him. They feared him, but not half so much as they loved him; they knew that he was their friend—great-hearted and true.

It would seem that his manifold labors as a minister of the Gospel were enough to exhaust the energies of any ordinary man. But in the midst of these he gave much of his time to teaching, besides attending closely to the business affairs of the school. Whatever his hand

found to do he did, never deferring till to-morrow what
should be done to-day.   He found time to pray with the
sick and dying and to attend to the wants of the poor
always.   The Bible was his guide in this respect as in
all others.

During his life there went forth more than two
thousand who had knelt under the hallowed influence
of his prayers and treasured up his words seasoned by
divine grace—for he was taught of God.   Many of these
yet live and come often to revisit the place where once
they listened with reverential attention to the teachings
of its patron saint.   They gather like children about an
old home—

> "Returning from life's weariness, tumult, and pain,
> Rejoiced in their hearts to be school-girls again."

Their kindly visits make many a green spot in the
Wintery scenery of my life.

On the 25th of March, 1875, we celebrated the fiftieth
anniversary of the founding of Science Hill Female
Academy.   I subjoin a letter published in the *Western
Christian Advocate*, as also a communication from a cor-
respondent of the Shelby *Sentinel*, as sufficiently descriptive of the occasion,—

A TEACHER'S SEMI-CENTENNIAL.

[Western Christian Advocate.]

The Semi-centennial of Science Hill Academy was celebrated
at Shelbyville, Kentucky, March 25, 1875. Mrs. Julia A. Tevis,
founder of this far-famed school, and its principal for fifty years,
opened her house on that day to welcome her old pupils, who,
going out from their school-life, have been scattered over more than
half the States of the Union, and number over three thousand
persons. Some three hundred came, representing every class from
1825 until now. Of those present at the opening of the school, fifty
years ago, but four are now living, two were present—Mrs. Agnes
Ross and Mrs. Martha Redding. Many grandchildren of the first

pupils are now in the school, and some of the third generation are already graduated. It was a scene of rare interest to behold the woman of more than threescore years, with daughter and granddaughter, coming to greet the noble woman who had taught them all. Hundreds of congratulatory letters and telegrams were received from those who could not be present in person. An old lady of Wytheville, Virginia, seventy years of age, writes like the school-girl of half a century ago: "I know Miss Julia Ann would like to have me present on the 25th, for I was one of her very first pupils in the little school of fifty-five years ago."

At twelve o'clock the parlors were thrown open, and seated upon a dais Mrs. Julia A. Tevis, the venerable founder and principal of the school, received the congratulations of her former pupils. Thronging memories and deep emotions stirred her inmost heart at the sight of the old familiar faces, making the tax upon her physical strength severe, yet she looked as well, and bore up as strongly as at any of her annual class-days of later years. Five years beyond the allotted threescore and ten, she was permitted still to be actively engaged in teaching, looking back upon fifty-five years of eminent success as a teacher, fifty of which were spent in this school, without an intermission of a single term.

At one o'clock the spacious dining-hall was thrown open. Rich viands of every description were arranged with the most exquisite taste; upon several tables fruits and flowers vied with each other in lending charm to the scene. To Mrs. Dr. Tevis all honor is due, who, as presiding genius of the feast, made us both glad and sorry, as we proved our full appreciation of her superior taste and knowledge in this department.

After dinner the guests repaired to the Chapel. Mrs. Tevis occupied a seat upon the rostrum, with Bishop Foster and Bishop Kavanaugh on either side. Over the rostrum were hung large portraits of Mr. and Mrs. Tevis, and above them, in evergreen, the inscription, "With joy we greet you." Bishop Kavanaugh opened the exercises with prayer. Music, vocal and instrumental, was rendered by the pupils of to-day. After a short address by Mr. Beckham, of Shelbyville, Bishop Foster spoke for twenty minutes. In concluding, he addressed Mrs. Tevis, presenting her with an elegant gold medal, a token of love from her children. It was a scene not to be forgotten.

Mrs. Tevis addressed the audience in a voice which, for that occasion, seemed to gather its power of twenty years ago. She said, "My emotional feelings, combined with my exhausted strength prevent me from taking each and every one of you by the hand,

and bidding you farewell; but I take you all to my heart. My life-work was not of my choosing. I followed it from a sense of duty until I learned to love it. All has been done with an eye to God's glory, and whatever of good has been accomplished has been of the Lord."

Mrs. Speed, daughter of Mrs. Tevis, read, with fine effect, "Sir Marmaduke's Toast to his Mother," after which Dr. Speed read a beautiful and original poem, upon the same subject. The closing exercises, which occupied an hour and a half, and which seemed all too brief, passed off delightfully, and reluctantly the guests prepared for departure. The reunion was a grand success. All were "girls again." Snow-crowned seventy and sweet sixteen mingled their voices in merry reminiscences of the past and joyous expectation of the future, all uniting with one accord in loving homage and admiration of her who for more than half a century has devoted herself to the advancement and ennobling of woman. The day was one of unclouded sunshine.   J. D. W.

MEMORIES OF SCIENCE HILL.

[Special Correspondence Shelby Sentinel.]

The morning of March 25th dawned bright and beautiful; and how vividly it brought to mind a bright September day, thirty years ago, when I was led a trembling little child, into the presence of her, whose invitation brought us to celebrate the fiftieth anniversary of Science Hill.

Old memories, how thickly they crowded upon us! We forgot, for awhile, the world, its joys and sorrows, reviewed the scenes of other days, and wandered hand in hand with companions of childhood's happy hours. Then, the world with all its bright allurements was as yet a vision to us; ever joyous and free, we danced to the music of our own glad hearts, and gathered the blossoms of wisdom and love that were strewn o'er our pathway by gentle hands and loving voices.

The shadows and sunshine that have since so fitfully chased each other have each left some impress upon our hearts, some remembrance of the joys and hopes that may come to us no more, but serve to guide our wandering footsteps by the lessons they have taught.

There were many familiar faces; some who started with us; some who left us when we were children, but alas! how many absent.

But amid all the changes—while each one present like myself missed some dear particular friend—our teacher still remains, with the same gentle dignity and pleasant smile we so well remember. Year after year I sat beneath her counsel and heard her admonitions; how her heart seemed to yearn over us before the commencement exercises which scattered "our class" so far and wide.

> Commencement! yes, of duties,
>   Of the many braided strands
> That is only kept from tangle
>   By the skill of woman's hands—
> Of waiting days and watching,
>   Of long unanswered prayers;
> Beginning of life in earnest,
>   With its thousand joys and cares.

Among the treasures of memory, the following lines from her own pen, written just before I left her, have been particularly cherished.

"I dare not omit the opportunity of whispering through this silent medium, advice—*advice* which you shall in coming life perchance look upon, and, in so doing, remember one who always loved you, and most heartily desires your welfare, and who would fain shield you from those storms of sorrow incident to human life— but as that can not be, let me in loving earnestness admonish you to place your standard of moral excellence as high as the Scriptures direct. Take the Word of God for your counsel, and seek earnestly to keep the witness of the Holy Spirit as a testimony of your acceptance—and its enlightening assurance that you are striving to please God. Live, as it were, in sight of Calvary—at the foot of the Cross, and though you may find thorns enough in life's pathway, yet there are sometimes lilies and roses to be gathered in its highways and hedges. The eye of your Heavenly Father will be ever on you for good if you are faithful to your duty, and the loving Savior will never leave nor forsake thee! Be grateful for the blessings you do enjoy, and have enjoyed, and hopefully, prayerfully trust for what is yet to come."

The *thorns* have been many and hard to bear, but the *lilies* and *roses* have blossomed all along the way, and I trust her counsel for higher aid has never been forgotten, and now that many years have passed, I would come again as a little child to bring this tribute of a grateful heart thankful for all her tender ministries—for words of love and gentleness and truth, for longings after a higher and purer womanhood, and above all, for the example of a life whose influence can never be measured, and whose reward can only be meted by the Hand from whom all blessings flow.

As the noonday of her life has been made bright by Heaven's smiling approbation, may many years and blessings be added to her old age, and the evening of her life be crowned with the loving kindness of a gracious Providence?

January 26, 1861, at the age of sixty-nine, my husband was permitted to rest forever from his labors! "He giveth his beloved sleep."

"God moves in a mysterious way."

How difficult is it to recognize in the death of a cherished son just entering upon life's duties with noble purposes—the idol of home, the pride of the social circle, holding all hearts by a magic chain—the loving hand of a kind Father! Ah! when Rachel weeps for her children, who shall comfort her desolate heart? His name was interwoven with the interests and affections of all hearts in the little world of Shelbyville. All knew and loved "John Tevis," all hearts were clouded when he, the young and strong, was laid low.

Who shall say it is easy to utter the submissive, "Thy will be done"—easy to drink the bitter cup proffered to the lips? yet the souls chastened by that mighty hand do find consolation. This dear young man "had, from a child, known the Holy Scriptures," which, as I believe, "made him wise unto salvation, through faith in Christ Jesus." He was conscientious, truthful, simple-hearted, and high in purpose. He loved God and "opened his hand wide to his brother" distressed. He seemed to know intuitively when he met the needy, that they were objects for his help and ready sympathy.

This fair young life was cut off from the earth in its flushing grace and beauty, just two weeks before his father. He escaped the chastenings of the weary three-score years and ten allotted as the pilgrimage of many.

"As for man, his days are as grass." "But the mercy of the Lord is from everlasting to everlasting, upon them that fear him."

"Stricken, smitten, and afflicted," now, we shall know hereafter why we were called to "pass under the rod." My son "sleeps well," and I shall one day see him arrayed in the glorious image of the dear risen Christ. Amen! So let it be!

Thus sorrowful bereavements have swept away many of my heart's brightest jewels. One by one my early friends have dropped into the grave, and the outer world is changed around me; but the heart does not grow old while its life-blood beats in loving sympathy with those who are left still clinging to the household tree. As one object is removed, the severed tendril takes hold upon another. Strange fondness of the human heart, that makes us covet length of days for the sake of those we love!

My life seems fast slipping away, but its purposes are being accomplished by that good and gracious Providence which has guided me all along the journey. I regard length of days a blessing, and desire to live for the sake of those who are left on earth; indulging always the glorious anticipation of a reunion with the departed ones, which anticipation gives to this life all its unity, peace, and hope.

FINIS.